INDOMITUS

INDOMITUS

GAV THORPE

BLACK LIBRARY

A BLACK LIBRARY PUBLICATION

First published in Great Britain in 2020 by
Black Library,
Games Workshop Ltd.,
Nottingham, NG7 2WS, UK.

10 9 8 7 6 5 4 3 2 1

Produced by Games Workshop in Nottingham.
Cover illustration by Paul Dainton.

A CIP record for this book is available from the British Library.

ISBN 13: 978-1-78999-128-4

See Black Library on the internet at

blacklibrary.com

Find out more about Games Workshop
and the world of Warhammer 40,000 at

games-workshop.com

Printed and bound in China.

For more than a hundred centuries the Emperor has sat immobile on the
Golden Throne of Earth. He is the Master of Mankind. By the might of
His inexhaustible armies a million worlds stand against the dark.

Yet, He is a rotting carcass, the Carrion Lord of the Imperium held in
life by marvels from the Dark Age of Technology and the thousand souls
sacrificed each day so that His may continue to burn.

To be a man in such times is to be one amongst untold billions. It is to
live in the cruellest and most bloody regime imaginable. It is to suffer an
eternity of carnage and slaughter. It is to have cries of anguish and sorrow
drowned by the thirsting laughter of dark gods.

This is a dark and terrible era where you will find little comfort or hope.
Forget the power of technology and science. Forget the promise of progress
and advancement. Forget any notion of common humanity or compassion.

There is no peace amongst the stars, for in the grim darkness of the far future,
there is only war.

PART I

'Their holds filled and courage rude,
They left the Sol for distant stars.
With fears stilled and joyous mood,
Not knowing of their future scars.
So light a flame and send a prayer,
For the souls of the Cursed Fleet.'

– 'The Lament of Quintus',
an Imperial Navy shanty.

CHAPTER ONE

'They shall be pure of heart and strong of body, untainted by doubt and unsullied by self-aggrandisement.' Praxamedes had spoken without thought, the words of the Codex Astartes coming to him unbidden and reaching his tongue before he could stop them.

'Is that censure of a senior officer, Lieutenant Praxamedes?' asked Aeschelus as he looked away from the command bridge's main viewing display. The Ultramarines captain paced across the strategium of the *Ithraca's Vengeance*, heading to where his second-in-command stood alongside the task force's other lieutenant, Nemetus.

The polished blue of their armour danced with the amber-and-red glow of console lights, smudged by a bright plasma gleam shining from the tactical videolith that dominated the wall of the large command chamber. Tac-slaved servitors wired to terminals and augur banks grunted and chattered their dataflows to azure-robed overseers, who in turn compiled reports for their Space Marine officers. Behind them, Shipmaster Oryk Oloris, in heavy trousers that were tucked into knee-high boots and a crisp white shirt beneath his Ultramarines uniform tunic, prowled the deck with a watchful eye.

Praxamedes instantly regretted his momentary lapse.

'As a scholar of the lord primarch's teachings, you would know that the Codex Astartes has much to say on respect for the chain of command.' Aeschelus came alongside his two officers and half-turned back towards the main screen. He opened his hand towards the screen, indicating the starship that drifted across the spray of stars, plumes of blue and white plasma ejecting haphazardly from a ruptured reactor. 'Our preliminary surveyor reports indicate that we have disabled their weapons grid. The threat is minimal.'

'My words, brother-captain, were in reference to Nemetus' overly keen desire to lead the boarding,' Praxamedes told his superior. 'There are still enemy vessels in the vicinity.'

'Two destroyers,' scoffed Nemetus. 'Too fast a prey to hunt on our own. As soon as we give chase, they will disappear into the asteroids and gas clouds on the boundary of the third orbital sphere. Would you follow them into that, knowing that they could turn on us under the cover of our overwhelmed scanners?'

'That was not my suggestion, brother-lieutenant,' said Praxamedes, frowning. It was an occasional fault of Nemetus to protest against an ill-thought strategy that had not, in fact, been raised, perhaps purely to show that he had considered and discarded such action himself. 'Our primary objective is destruction of the enemy. Boarding brings unnecessary risk, at a time when the battle groups of Fleet Quintus must conserve their strength.'

'That is a Hellbringer-class cruiser,' added Nemetus. 'Nobody has built one for eight thousand years. It is a piece of archeotech in its own right.'

'The lord primarch would also favour heavily any intelligence we might glean from its cogitator banks,' said Aeschelus. 'We are at the forefront of the crusade, encountering foes fresh to the battle. This is a raider, an assault ship built for planetary attack. Perhaps this ship comes from beyond the Cicatrix Maledictum and could shed light on what is occurring in the Imperium Nihilus lost beyond the warp rifts.'

This time, Praxamedes was wise enough to hold his tongue, wishing the whole conversation would be forgotten. Aeschelus noticed his lieutenant's reticence and continued.

'You urge caution with a depleted resource, which is laudable, but I would not spend the lives of the lord primarch's warriors needlessly.' Aeschelus allowed his voice to travel a little further, carrying to other members of the command crew across the strategium. It was typical of Aeschelus' fine touch of command that he would turn potential remonstration into a moment to inspire others. It was a knack that Praxamedes sorely lacked, nor had any idea how to acquire despite his efforts.

'For near a decade, as ship-board chronometers reckon it, we have fought hard in the crusade of the lord primarch. At the outset there was treachery and catastrophe, losses suffered before the fleet had even left Terra. Our own task force lost its noble group master to the plague purges. Those here, and that came before, knew that there would be no easy victories, that a galaxy broken asunder by the witchery of our enemies would be an unwelcoming battlezone. Yet even the most pessimistic among us would not have countenanced the uncountable labours and obstacles that Fleet Quintus has found in its path.

'Every victory has been hard-fought and we have met with more reverses than those in other fleets. Each foe must be overcome in turn – every opportunity to rise from the shadows of past setbacks must be seized. Before us lies a prize, won by our own endeavour, that may lift the fortunes of not just the *Ithraca's Vengeance* or Battle Group Faustus, but perhaps bring heart to all of Crusade Fleet Quintus that our extraordinary travails have been to purpose.'

'A prize that is even now trying to slip from our fingers,' growled Nemetus, nodding towards the videolith. 'See how they crawl towards the stellar flotsam, seeking sanctuary in its midst. We must seize the moment, brother-captain.'

'And I stand ready to lead the attack, as always,' said Praxamedes. 'As the longest serving lieutenant it would be my honour to do so.'

'I have no doubt that you would be determined and diligent in the execution of the attack, Praxamedes, but I think this operation is more suited to the temperament of Nemetus.' The captain turned his full attention to the second lieutenant. 'Assemble your boarding force swiftly. Take control of the enemy strategium and extract what you can from the cogitators.'

'You'll need charges, to scuttle the ship when you are done,' said Praxamedes.

'There will be no need for that,' said Nemetus. 'It looks as though their reactors are already descending towards critical state. A few hours from now there will be nothing left but plasma.'

'All the more reason to fly swift and fight with narrow purpose,' said Aeschelus.

'If we're set on the mission, I'll review the augur data and calculate the approach vectors that will bring you most swiftly to your objective, brother.' Praxamedes lifted a fist to his chest to salute the departing officer.

Nemetus returned the gesture of respect with a nod. 'For the primarch and the Emperor.'

When the lieutenant had exited the strategium, Praxamedes turned to move towards the augur terminals. Aeschelus stopped him with a hand on his shoulder. He spoke quietly.

'I know that you think I undervalue you, Prax. I will give you battle command soon, I give you my word. It's just…'

'Nemetus is the more dynamic of us?'

'Restless,' Aeschelus replied. 'Nemetus excels in direct action. In all truth, would you have him providing overview for the expedition while you were leading the squads? Is that truly the best use of his and your aptitudes?'

Praxamedes said nothing. He had spoken out too much already and did not wish to push his superior's patience any further. In truth, he felt it was Aeschelus, in longing to prove his worth in the eyes of the primarch, that felt undervalued. Like many in the latest cohort of recruits pushed to the leading edges of the crusade, Aeschelus had not been in the fleet when those early disasters had occurred. He had not witnessed how the hope and excitement of the crusade's potential had withered in a matter of months.

Perhaps that was a good thing. Praxamedes had enough self-awareness to admit, to himself if no other, that those early experiences had given him a more pessimistic outlook than his new commander. The captain hoped Nemetus would bring glory to the *Ithraca's Vengeance* with some daring act, and Praxamedes was well aware of his own deficiencies in that regard. He was neither charismatic nor blessed with startling initiative. He was diligent and capable, and those were qualities that perhaps Battle Group Faustus needed right now when another serious setback might break the morale of the whole Fleet Quintus.

But Aeschelus was not interested in such thoughts and so Praxamedes kept them to himself.

'As you will it, brother-captain,' he said simply.

* * *

Aeschelus gave a nod of dismissal to set Praxamedes about his task, yet as the lieutenant moved away the captain felt the admonition in his formality. His second-in-command doubtless meant well but the last thing the command needed at the moment was negativity. There were finally reports of good news from the other battle groups, and while Faustus still laboured hard against warp storms and a ceaseless swarm of small but diverting traitor attacks, Aeschelus was determined that he would make a breakthrough soon.

Praxamedes tended to think in tactical terms, lacking the longer view of the strategic that had been inculcated into Aeschelus as part of his rapid training to the rank of captain. He and others like him had been despatched to the cutting edge of the Indomitus Crusade to bring some renewed urgency, particularly across Crusade Fleet Quintus.

Fresh blood, fresh energy.

Those had been the words of the lord primarch. Not heard in person, as Lord Guilliman was far from Terra leading the crusade when Aeschelus had been sent to his command. It wasn't like the days when Praxamedes and the first torchbearer fleets had been sent out. No fanfare, no primarch. Just reinforcements and a renewed will to press into the darkness.

One day, perhaps soon, Aeschelus would have the honour. One day he would stand before the lord primarch in victory, recognised for an effort that changed the fortunes of the fleet.

The captain broke from his reverie to find Oloris standing close by, a dataslate in hand. The shipmaster raised a fist to his forehead.

'Latest fleet dispositions, captain.' The unaugmented human presented the dataslate and withdrew a step, brushing a wisp of blond hair from his pale face.

'Anything of note?' asked Aeschelus, knowing that Oloris could be trusted to review the information relevant to their current course of action.

'We received word that *Sword of Justice* and the *Vaputatian* both broke warp to rendezvous with the support fleet.'

'That leaves nobody on our starward flank. A little early for refit.' Aeschelus scrolled through the report but Oloris provided the answer first.

'They each had an unexpected encounter with a battleship-class enemy. They were able to break away but not before taking heavy damage.'

Aeschelus found the entry and accessed the engagement report. 'No identifier. Possible traitor flagship. Heavy lance arrays outranged our ships.'

'And us, captain,' said Oloris. He hesitated, cleared his throat and continued, 'Lieutenant Praxamedes wishes to know if we are proceeding with the boarding action.'

Aeschelus looked up. The lieutenant was at the augur console, ostensibly engaged in his preparations, though his enhanced hearing was more than capable of picking up the conversation between captain and shipmaster. It was protocol for any matters concerning the running of the vessel to come through the shipmaster, but it seemed peculiar on this occasion that Praxamedes had not delivered his question directly. It was likely that he was being more circumspect after his uncharacteristically outspoken moment.

'You have concerns, Prax?' the captain said, hoping informality would assure his subordinate that he was not in any way being censured. 'You think there is a danger presented by this rogue battleship?'

'It is a possibility, captain,' said Praxamedes, turning from his work. 'The engagement with the *Sword of Justice* took place within the last two days, only four hundred and fifty thousand miles from our current position. What if it's the Desolator?'

'I am surprised you put stock in such tales, lieutenant,' said Aeschelus. He snorted, shaking his head. 'The Desolator? Rumour and hearsay. The grumblings of reluctant Imperial Navy officers.'

'You think there is no truth to the reports, captain?' Praxamedes approached, darting a look towards Oloris that betrayed their conspiracy. 'Seven vessels lost or driven off in the last thirty days, all within this sub-sector.'

'There is no phantom enemy battleship striking with the speed of a frigate and disappearing.' Aeschelus raised a finger to forestall Oloris as the shipmaster opened his mouth to speak. 'And it certainly is not *The Ninth Eye*, that identification was based on the tiniest fragment of augur return and vox-scatter. Battle Group Command insist that there is no Alpha Legion presence in this whole sector. You want me to ignore the prize we have won based on the chattering of Navy officers?'

'I wished to clarify our intent, captain,' Praxamedes said stiffly. 'Your will is clear.'

'It is,' growled Aeschelus, now irritated by the lieutenant's intervention. 'Ready your calculations for Lieutenant Nemetus as quickly as possible.'

Aeschelus turned his eyes back to the drifting ship on the main display. This equivocation and rumour-mongering was just one of the many symptoms of the fleet's morale problems. He should not fault Praxamedes for falling prey to the same deficiencies as others caught up in the long tale of misfortune, but it was starting to affect his judgement. Despite his earlier words to the lieutenant, this kind of irrational behaviour, coupled with overfamiliarity to the non-Space Marine crew, made Aeschelus wonder if Praxamedes really was suited to any kind of battle command.

With the order for the boarding action given, the tone aboard the *Ithraca's Vengeance* changed from one of pensive watchfulness to energetic activity. The crews of the gun decks remained alert, sensor stations poring over the broken flank of the heavy cruiser, seeking any sign of sudden life from their foe. From the command bridge came firing solutions, pinpointing breaches in the enemy's armoured skin, selected to prepare the way for the incoming attack. In the flight bays the roar of plasma engines joined the thud of armoured boots, filling each launch deck with the noise of pending war. Red-clad tech-priests croaked and burbled sermons of the Machine-God to bless their charges before launch, lower adepts of the Cult of Mars anointing the gunships' weapons and targeting arrays with unguents while nano-laced censer smoke drifted into idling intakes to cleanse engine feeds.

Squad by squad, the boarding parties assembled at the mustering deck between the two flanking launch halls. Nemetus paced the concourse at the hall's centre, passing a critical eye over the thirty Space Marines as they came to attention. From the ship's complement he had selected three squads of Intercessors, the backbone of the new Primaris formations. Standing to attention, weapons presented, an unmoving line of Ultramarines blue, they awaited the order to break rank and move to board the gunships.

Unsullied by self-aggrandisement.

The words of Praxamedes lingered in the thoughts of Nemetus while he readied himself for the battle ahead. Whether intended for Aeschelus or Nemetus, that softly spoken line from the Codex Astartes had carried the same vehemence as a shouted outburst from any other. Praxamedes was calm to the point of coolness and guarded in everything he said. To have spoken as he did was almost without precedent.

Helmet under his arm, Nemetus walked along the ranks, inspecting every warrior. Each was impeccably turned out, a credit to themselves and the dedication of the armourium. Sergeant Villina lifted fist to chest as Nemetus reached the front of the formation once more.

'Most excellent, brother-sergeant, fit for a parade before the lord primarch himself!'

'And ready for more than just a parade, brother-lieutenant,' added the veteran sergeant.

'I am sure of it, Villina. It is my honour to lead them again.'

The Codex *Preparatory Statements on the Nature of the Adeptus Astartes* continued, and it was from the following words of the lord primarch that Nemetus took inspiration.

They will be bright stars on the firmament of battle, Angels of Death whose shining wings bring swift annihilation to the enemies of man.

A bright star in the firmament of battle.

Bright stars were in short supply of late, with the Imperium beset by all foes, both ancient and modern. A relative latecomer to the Indomitus Crusade, Nemetus had learned from afar of its great reconquest whilst undergoing his transformation and training. He knew the power of the stories that returned from the exploits of humanity's finest warriors. He had heard temple bells ringing the triumphs of the lord commander, listened to the cheers from hundreds of thousands of throats as great victories were read from the balcony-pulpits. As a Primaris Marine, he was to be the new exemplar of everything the Adeptus Astartes represented.

And yet the words of Praxamedes still bit deep.

Unsettled, he passed an expert eye over the next warriors – a squad of Eradicators, their melta rifles at the ready. They would be the breaching team once the expedition reached the enemy strategium. Nemetus' gaze moved between them and the Intercessors, noting that most of their wargear was freshly issued.

Many of Aeschelus' command had been sent as reinforcements to Fleet Quintus, as had he and Nemetus; only a few were longer-serving, having departed Terra at the crusade's outset. Praxamedes was among those that had seen the earliest fighting, the most terrible wars and dogged campaigns. A member of Fleet Quintus since its inception, he had risen from the ranks while Nemetus and Aeschelus, and no few others, had been trained to their officer roles. Such had been the early casualties among the Space Marines – a force that lived by the creed of leading from the front – that deaths among the first Primaris officers had eliminated almost half the Adeptus Astartes leadership of Fleet Quintus within three years. Battlefield promotions and brevet ranks were good as a stop-gap, but as a longer term solution Nemetus and others had been command-trained from the outset of their inductions.

Was Praxamedes' slight genuinely aimed at Aeschelus, a subtle admonition for a superior who had been promoted ahead of him?

That was an unkindness to Praxamedes, Nemetus decided. The very moments before battle were not the best time to weigh up the motivations of his brother-officers, and Nemetus had nothing but respect for his fellow lieutenant. Praxamedes had simply been urging his usual circumspect approach, nothing more.

Nemetus turned his attention to the remaining members of his expedition. A little apart from the Intercessors stood ten Incursors, two combat squads of dedicated close assault specialists under Sergeant Dorium and Sergeant Lato. Clad in armour incorporating the most sophisticated internal auspex systems, they would pave the way for the main force, their bolt carbines ideally suited to the closer confines of the enemy starship. It had been just days since they had last seen action, and their wargear told a different story to that of the Intercessors. Here and there the lieutenant spied bare ceramite over some recently suffered damage, and the paint of their livery was much scratched.

'Is that blood?' Nemetus demanded, directing an accusing finger towards the gauntlet of Brother Sennecus.

The Incursor lifted his hand and inspected it. He flexed the red-stained armoured digits.

'Yes, lieutenant,' Sennecus replied. 'I ripped out the heart of a secessionist in our last engagement. The red mark is a trophy of our victory, brother-lieutenant.'

'Yes, I have heard of this "battle paint", brother.' Nemetus took a step closer and was about to deliver his chastisement when a voice cut across the muster hall.

'A fitting memorial to a traitor,' rasped Judiciar Admonius.

Armoured all in back, the Judiciar cut a sinister figure. At his waist hung a great hourglass, filled with dark sand: his tempormortis. Each grain came from the debris of Callosi station, a renegade installation atomised in the first engagement of Battle Group Faustus. Admonius' zealotry in that action had seen him recruited to the position of Judiciar, on the pathway to becoming a Chaplain.

The dedication that had drawn Admonius to the Reclusiam's ranks had increased with his acceptance, as if he were afraid that his status as novice would count against him. Nemetus knew better than to gainsay the Judiciar and instead raised a fist in salute.

'You are joining the boarding force, Brother-Judiciar?'

'Of course. It is my duty to prosecute the war against the traitors with every fervour. Did you think I would pass on this opportunity?'

Recognising the rhetoric in the question, Nemetus returned his attention to the warriors under his command.

'Brothers.' He took a breath, trying to ignore the nagging thoughts that came to him.

Self-aggrandisement.

Was he guilty of that crime?

'Brothers,' he began again, taking inspiration from his own mood. 'Some of you have raised your weapons beside me in battles before this day. Many of you have not, and indeed this is the first encounter with the foe since your preparatory missions. It matters not. We are all Adeptus Astartes. We are all sons of Lord Guilliman. We are all servants of the Emperor.'

He could not resist a glance towards Judiciar Admonius before he continued.

'It is not for ourselves that we fight, though we owe our brothers our commitment. We were created to spearhead a war far greater than any single warrior. Our foes seem without limit, but we will find it. We shall slay as many as needed, until the galaxy is secured once more for the dominion of humanity.'

He took another breath, settling into himself, finding direction from his own words.

'Remember that every blow you strike, every bolt you fire, is directed towards that single duty. Know also that at our backs stands the whole of the Imperium, its will bent to the reconquest of lost realms, the succour of enslaved worlds and the destruction of the dark enemy that has brought this wrath upon them. You are the implementation of that will. You are the Emperor's strength given form. Fight well and you shall not die, for your names shall live on ever after in glory!'

As his triumphant shout reverberated across the hall, Nemetus signalled the embarkation to begin. He felt Admonius beside him and turned his gaze on the Chaplain-in-Waiting.

'A fine speech,' said the Judiciar. 'Now let your deeds echo your words.'

CHAPTER TWO

While he waited for the augur attendants to collate their latest servitor reports, Praxamedes considered Aeschelus' apparent determination to board the enemy vessel no matter the risks. Taken at face value, the captain's rebuke was perfectly in order. The battle group had not officially recognised the presence of an enemy battleship in the system. It was only off-channel intelligence that argued the case.

It was the dismissal of the source that nagged at Praxamedes. Imperial Navy officers were not warriors of the Adeptus Astartes, but they were also brave, capable men and women. Prone to superstition? Yes, but also with an instinct for their ships and environs gathered over many years of service. The informality of the intelligence was also its strength. Navy personnel gossiped, but there was always a kernel of truth in every story.

Experience told Praxamedes not to dismiss the rumour of *The Ninth Eye* as easily as his captain.

He raised a hand and signalled for the deck officer in charge of the augurs, Lerok Catriolis. The young woman stepped smartly to attention at his side.

'I want ranging scans of the dust clouds and orbital debris, at three-minute intervals.'

'The debris field stretches for twenty thousand miles, lieutenant. Which part do you wish to scan?'

'All of it,' Praxamedes replied sharply. He moderated his tone. 'Power down our aft arrays to minimal passive coverage. There is no enemy behind us for fifty thousand miles. Divert the power to boost the active arrays and widen the search beams.'

'Yes, lieutenant. Are we looking for anything in particular?' Lerok kept her eyes fixed on the Space Marine, face impassive. 'So that we can calibrate the surveyors more tightly, lieutenant.'

Praxamedes fought the urge to turn his gaze to the captain, who he could see in the periphery of his vision checking the weapon banks. Praxamedes was tasked with oversight of the ongoing mission, and it could easily be argued that taking the precaution of monitoring the nearest celestial cover was well within scope of that station.

Aeschelus might not see it quite so clearly. It was not a direct contradiction of his orders, but it did seem against the spirit of the captain's intent. Praxamedes did not relish the thought of testing his commander's faith further, but his sense of duty was stronger than his fears of personal or disciplinary consequence.

'Plasma signature, void disturbance.' He uttered the words quietly, as though the issuing of them from his lips was a fresh conspiracy.

'Understood, lieutenant,' she replied with another crisp salute. Her gaze lingered on Praxamedes a few seconds longer. 'I shall personally oversee the array and report directly to you.'

It was an odd thing to say, so it took a few moments before Praxamedes realised that she was offering to keep the captain and shipmaster ignorant of her new orders for the time being. Her implied consent to the conspiracy brought back Praxamedes' nascent guilt, but he ignored it again.

'Thank you, Lerok. There is no need to distract the captain at this time.'

She nodded and turned away, their pact finalised.

Praxamedes tore the scribe-copy of the collated augur data from its slot and gave it a cursory glance. As expected, all that could be found were the after-flares of the battle with the enemy ship and the flight tails of its fleeing escorts.

'Void is clear, captain,' Praxamedes called across the bridge.

Aeschelus turned, striding back to his position in front of the main display. 'Very good, brother-lieutenant. Flight paths are locked in?'

'Yes, brother-captain.' Praxamedes crossed to the display controls and overlaid the tactical grid onto the live feed. Dotted lines of three gunship routes cut across the intervening space, splitting up to present no single target for anti-assault craft turrets, coming together at the last few miles for a final run on the starboard side of the target, just aft of the control bridge. 'Embarkation complete. Boarding parties are ready for launch.'

'Gunnery crews stand to!'

Aeschelus' shout was picked up by the strategium systems and transmitted across the whole ship. He could have voxed the orders to the individual stations but public address allowed everyone on board to follow the progress of the operation.

'Open launch bays!'

A schematic of the *Ithraca's Vengeance* changed state at the bottom of the screen. Weapons batteries cycled through orange to green as they came on line, the magazine halls following suit a few seconds later. In contrast, the starboard and port launch decks turned amber as hull integrity was relinquished, the bay openings held by energy screens only.

'Commence preparatory bombardment!'

The schematic lit up again, bright flares of energy as the cannons opened fire, even as the rumble of their discharge shook through the deck. Trails of plasma and fire sparked across the dark void to smash into the upper decks of the target vessel. Debris scattered like leaves in a wind, lit by bright moments of destruction.

'Launch boarding parties!'

Against the backdrop of fury unleashed by the weapons of the *Ithraca's Vengeance*, three gunships powered across the void. They were almost insignificant against the bulk of the strike cruiser and its target. The spark of their engines was lost in the blaze of weapon batteries and bombardment cannon, their blue hulls lit by the flare of impacts, detonations flashing in the reflection from armourglass windows.

Through the canopy of the lead gunship's command deck, Nemetus watched the firepower display with a grim smile. He tracked the course of shells ripping aftwards along the closest weapon decks of the foe, turning thick armour to ragged shreds of ceramite and pulverised plasteel. The rhythm of rapid gun deck impacts was punctuated by the larger, slower hits of the cruiser's dorsal cannon, each building-sized shell obliterating a buttressed gun housing or tearing away a length of decking.

There was no return fire.

Perhaps Praxamedes was right. The *Ithraca's Vengeance* could turn the enemy ship into a rubble cloud and not a single Space Marine would risk his life in the achievement of victory.

Bright stars in the firmament of battle...

It was not for the safe life that Space Marines were created from the best of humanity. It was their duty to die in battle, to give their lives and ultimately their deaths in service of the Emperor. Often the better victory was harder won.

Nemetus turned his attention to the scrolling pathway painted in light across the interior of the canopy – an azure thread laid down by Praxamedes' computations that the gunship's machine-spirit followed towards their target. An icon briefly flashed bright in the display.

'Three miles from target point,' the pilot announced.

The fire of the *Ithraca's Vengeance* crept along the length of the enemy ship as the cruiser's guns tracked the progress of the gunships towards their landing zone. Like fire consuming parchment, the line of detonation blossoms worked its way towards the cathedral-like rise of the command superstructure. Increasing the magnification of his helm, Nemetus looked along the line of approach towards their goal. There was a victualling platform about half a mile from the main bridge, exposed to the void by a series of earlier hits. A landing dock, ideal for the gunships, giving direct access to the main arterial corridors that would take the force to the strategium.

Perfect.

Too perfect?

There was no reason to second-guess Praxamedes' plan. By all doctrine laid down in the Codex Astartes, the ingress mission was a balanced combination of support firepower, speed and location. On any account, Praxamedes had surpassed a mission commander's needs. Even so, Nemetus found himself accessing the artificial eyes of the gunship, more powerful than the lenses in his helm, augmented by medium-range augur feeds.

The target site was a mess of broken ship and fluctuating energy readings. The gaping hole in the side of the upper deck was consistent with the impact of a bombardment cannon hit, the point defence turrets around the locale devoid of power.

It was too easy, too neat.

Literally too neat, Nemetus realised as he panned the scryers back across the breached loading dock. Both doors had sheared away, leaving the entirety of the inner deck in view. The massive hinges that had held the portal in place had all come away, leaving a rectangular hole about sixty yards across and twenty high. Not a single hinge had stayed attached to the ship.

Another signal flashed momentarily through his vision. 'Two miles to target,' the pilot announced. Nemetus felt the slightest push against his secure harness as the gunship started to decelerate to combat speed for the final approach.

Half a mile. Close enough to the bridge to be tempting, far enough to give room for a defence force to hold ground.

The lieutenant signalled the cruiser.

'Ship command, have we identified the target vessel?' Fingers working the scrollball of the augur controls, Nemetus flicked the view to a section of hull closer to the strategium.

'*Negative, assault command.*' Shipmaster Oloris' reply was staccato with interference from the bombardment. '*No registry information found corresponding to the target vessel.*'

'Understood, ship command. Assault command out.'

Whose ship was it? There were no obvious fleet or traitor markings.

While scanning for any tell-tale signs of who or what was aboard, Nemetus found something else. A darker patch, a shadow behind the spread of the command bridge as it jutted either side of the dorsal armoured ridge. Nemetus increased magnification further, losing sight of the shadow for a few seconds before locating it again.

Another breach. A hole no more than ten yards across, almost within bolter range of the strategium itself.

It would be a difficult landing. Too tight for a gunship to enter, they'd have to void-jump the last few yards, right under the gaze of the defenders. But if Nemetus' growing suspicions were right, the victualling dock would be even less welcoming.

'One mile to target. Starting attack approach,' signalled the pilot.

A last rage of gunfire slammed into the target area, the brightness of the detonation momentarily turning the auto-senses of Nemetus' armour to dull monochrome as they compensated. Then nothing. Darkness returned, the flight of the gunships taking them into the line of fire from the cruiser.

At approach speed, a mile would take less than thirty seconds to cover.

A lot could happen in thirty seconds. Half a minute could be the difference between victory and defeat. Battles far larger than the one about to begin could turn in a heartbeat – or at the ending of a heartbeat.

'I have control,' Nemetus announced, dropping out of the gunship's augur systems. He grabbed the guidance column in both hands. With a shrill whine of protest, the machine-spirit disengaged its influence and he started to turn the craft along the flank of the enemy ship. 'New target vector. Follow me in.'

A red warning rune flashed across the videolith, snaring Aeschelus' attention for a few seconds before Praxamedes' call cut through the chatter of the strategium.

'Boarding group is off trajectory, captain!'

That much was already obvious, as a dotted red line diverged from the established flight path of the gunships, breaking slightly towards the prow of the target vessel. A cluster of orange glows around the projected landing point warned of a concentration of energy signatures. Praxamedes was already aware of the issue and was on the general vox before Aeschelus could speak.

'Assault command, your flight will take you into range of enemy defence turrets.'

'Acknowledged, ship command,' came the reply from Nemetus.

Three more seconds passed with no further comment from the lieutenant. Aeschelus and Praxamedes looked at each other, surprised by the silence.

'Make your report, assault command,' barked the captain. 'What in the primarch's name are you doing, Nemetus?'

'It is a trap, company command.' Nemetus' communication came in clipped bursts. *'Too obvious. Too easy. A false flank.'*

It was not unreasonable to think that the enemy were aware of their parlous situation and expecting a boarding attack rather than a bombardment execution. If that was the case there would be anomalous energy readings around the original target point.

'Augur control, display the directed surveyor data from the attack zone,' Aeschelus announced, his gaze roaming the command deck until it fell upon Lerok. The surveyor officer seemed startled by the request.

'Sorry, captain, there is no directed surveyor data.'

'The oversight's mine, brother-captain,' Praxamedes said quickly, stepping in front of her. 'I followed boarding protocol, but it didn't occur to me to order a direct scan. To do so would have compromised our ship-wide augur sweep to locate a boarding point or brought a significant delay to the action. It was made clear that speed was the greatest priority in launching the assault.'

Aeschelus frowned but could not fault the lieutenant's answer. There was something curious about his behaviour, and the reaction of Lerok, but now was not the time to ponder it.

'Assessment?' he demanded, looking at Praxamedes.

'Lieutenant Nemetus is assault command. He's best placed to judge the matter and I accept his premise.'

'*Glad to hear that, brother-lieutenant,*' came Nemetus' voice over the vox.

His tone was flippant but the situation was far from casual, aggravating Aeschelus' sense of unease. Initiative was well and good to a point, but a well-ordered and prepared battle plan was the underpinning of far more victories than individual acts.

'Can we re-plot firing solutions to assist?' Aeschelus asked.

'Not unless the assault group breaks away and then commences a fresh approach,' replied Praxamedes.

'*Negative, company command,*' added Nemetus. '*If we take too long the enemy will just relocate their defence. If we strike now, we shall turn the ruse against the foe and catch them out of position.*'

'Accepted, assault command,' said Aeschelus. 'What do you require?'

'*Nothing, company command, everything is in hand. We are twenty seconds from target.*'

Aeschelus stared at the videolith but there was nothing he could do from the strategium that would make any palpable difference to the mission. Not for the first time he wished he was aboard the gunship instead of Nemetus, but that was not his primary role. Orders from the lord primarch to the new Primaris cohort had been to risk less and learn more – the loss of experience for Fleet Quintus had been almost as damaging as the lost warriors.

'Assault command, proceed as you see fit. For the Emperor!'

'For the Emperor!' Nemetus signed off, deactivating the strategic vox. He switched the channel to company address, speaking directly to every Space Marine across the strike force. 'The enemy have sought to entrap us by our own doctrine, but it is time for some improvisation. Assault priorities have been changed. I will lead the landing with squads Temerity and Audacity, while support Intercessor squads will move up behind us and give covering fire if needed.'

At that moment an alarm wailed, warning of an enemy lock-on. No more than a second later, bright red flares of energy spat from one of the target ship's secondary turrets, zipping past the incoming gunship.

'Evasive manoeuvres, lieutenant?' suggested the pilot, reminding Nemetus that he had taken command of the controls.

'You fly, brother. Take us in straight and fast,' he replied, lifting his hands away from the guidance systems. 'Suppressive fire on defence turrets.'

The gunners of the assault craft opened fire immediately, streams of bolts and heavier ordnance streaking out from wing and fuselage weapons, raking across the exterior of the ship ahead. More incoming fire erupted as the defence turrets found their range, rockets and spirit-guided missiles launching in blossoms of fire.

'Sequential landing,' Nemetus continued. 'Support fire from other two gunships during disembarkation. Then withdraw to safe distance until we eliminate the defence turrets.'

'What about extraction?' the pilot of Gunship Secundus asked across the vox.

'Once we have seized the strategium we shall have control of their systems and you can come in. Speed, everyone. Speed and shock will win this day.'

'Ten seconds, brother-lieutenant,' his pilot warned.

'Ready for void-jump, my lead,' the lieutenant announced to the complement in the main compartment of the gunship.

Just as he was standing up, a clang against the canopy above Nemetus presaged a sudden hissing. Ominous creaking followed for several seconds as a crack spread across the fractured armourglass. With a howl of escaping air, the broken canopy gave way, pieces of shattered pane hurled out into the vacuum.

Inside his sealed armour, Nemetus was unharmed, and he punched the open rune to release the door between the cockpit and carriage chamber. The parchment tails of his purity seals fluttered as a fresh gust washed past him.

The Intercessors and Incursors were already on their feet, fifteen of them, filling the space with their bulk. Behind him, below the cockpit, the assault door levered open, revealing a glimpse of cold void before the gunship swung into the attack run, bright lasers and the flare of explosive shells almost obliterating Nemetus' view of the dark ship beyond. The lieutenant's visor display flickered as his auto-senses filtered out the brightness, bringing the ragged edge of the hole that was their destination into sharper focus.

'Kill with honour,' declared Admonius. He raised his tempormortis, the black sands starting to run through the neck of the crystal bulbs. 'Kill for the Emperor.' With his free hand he pushed on his helmet, assuming his vow of battle-silence. As a Judiciar, it was his role to inspire with acts not words, proving his worth as a Chaplain. He lifted the long, square-tipped executioner's relic blade and turned towards the open assault ramp, indicating for Nemetus to proceed.

Nemetus retrieved his cruciform storm shield from where it was stowed. Purple-red energy flowed across its surface as he activated the field generator within. The ten warriors of Temerity and Audacity drew their chainswords, the rev of their motors felt as a slight tremor through the decking. Readying their heavy pistols, the Assault Intercessors fell in behind Nemetus as he made his way towards the open ramp.

His visor rangefinder read seventy-four yards.

A sudden flurry of missiles streaked past the gunship from behind – the covering fire of their companions. Even as the warheads spread into bright clouds of silent fire ahead, Nemetus thrust himself forward from the open mouth of the gunship, pulling free his plasma pistol, storm shield held before him.

CHAPTER THREE

'Assault is underway, captain.'

Praxamedes received an acknowledgement from his superior and returned his attention to the augur console.

Assault is underway. Three words, cold and detached. Nothing to speak of the clamour and anarchy, the split-second decisions between life and death, the blaze of fire and snarl of weapons ending lives. Praxamedes was a veteran by the standards of the Indomitus Crusade and had seen the enemy up close and from afar, and despite Aeschelus' words about his temperament, he was a capable ground commander.

By all rights, if the captain was not leading the mission Praxamedes should.

He knew that his duty was not measured by acts of bravery. The lord primarch was renowned not just for his superior physical abilities but also his strategic and political prowess. The mind was as much a weapon as the boltgun, so the Codex Astartes taught. If Praxamedes so desired to be part of the fighting, was it because he was actually guilty of the self-aggrandisement of which he accused Nemetus? Was his own desire for glory the reason he felt slighted by his role aboard the strategium?

'Lieutenant, should we recalibrate the sensor banks to scan the new battlezone?'

The deck officer's question caught Praxamedes unawares and he spent several seconds looking at Lerok before he could respond.

'No. Once he has established his perimeter, Lieutenant Nemetus will despatch his Incursors. Their suit auspexes are more accurate and responsive than anything we could use at this range. Anything to report from the debris cloud?'

'Nothing new, lieutenant. Background radiation and the plasma plumes of the enemy escorts.' Lerok shrugged. 'Nothing else but rocks, dust and gas.'

Nothing else.

Praxamedes dismissed Lerok but could not stop himself from bringing up the latest augur sweep on a terminal screen. As he scrolled through the data, he activated the command vox and listened in on Nemetus' progress.

Speed. Speed was deadlier than any weapon, a surer guard against defeat than any armour.

Not just physical speed, though the Space Marines under Nemetus' command fought with lightning-quick reflexes as they cut down the disorganised gaggle of traitor crew that tried to hold the passage against their arrival. Not simply speed of thought. Nemetus and his warriors assessed the changing situation more effectively than any cogitator, prioritising targets and snapping off shots with ruthless efficiency. It was these things combined with a speed of purpose. The simple shock of their assault and the unrelenting determination with which they applied themselves to its completion made the Ultramarines irresistible. There was never a moment of hesitation nor a backward step.

The haze of an integrity field shimmered across the opening, enough to retain atmosphere but no obstacle to the incoming Space Marines. The storm shield snarled arcs of lightning as it passed through, but that was all. Within a second of his foot finding purchase on the lip of the broken decking, Nemetus opened fire, his plasma pistol incinerating the head and torso of the first defender. In the azure flash of its firing and detonation he gauged the strength of the force facing him, and the mettle of its individuals.

They were dressed in tunics, much like adepts of the Imperium, though they bore no symbols of allegiance nor any unifying colour. A mixture of men and women, from adolescents to middle age. The one he had targeted on instinct had been a man who, had he lived on Terra, might have seen twenty years. They were shod in boots and some wore heavy work gloves. In the instant of brightness as they recoiled from the blinding flash of plasma, Nemetus counted pistols and basic rifles, a few lasguns among their armaments and a handful of shotguns.

Militia, better equipped than many a planetary defence force Nemetus had seen, but little threat to the Space Marines. Most likely conscripts from invaded worlds, or indentured workers seized in piratical raids on other vessels, or perhaps some had been born into their roles, generations raised aboard the enemy cruiser.

The flare of bolts whipped past him from behind, their propellant highlighting faces that showed fear but also determination – soon replaced with pain and shock as the bolts hit home.

He pounded forward, Audacity and Temerity at each shoulder, the passageway wide enough for six Space Marines abreast. Shooting again, he turned another traitor to vaporised flesh while bolts from his companions ripped away limbs, opened torsos and pulverised skulls. Closer, he saw that the foe were not all entirely human. A hint of feathers, the suggestion of scales and lumpen features marring pale-skinned faces. Digits with extra joints gripped weapons, tails flicked beneath tunics.

Mutants.

'Purge the unclean!' Nemetus roared, holstering his pistol to draw his sword in the last few paces before contact.

'Purge!' his brothers yelled in answer, their words almost lost in the growl of wakened chainswords and bolt detonations.

The two assault squads hit the clump of mutant foes like the teeth of one of their chainswords, not faltering for a heartbeat as they plunged into a bloody mess of swinging blades and point-blank fire. A shotgun boomed next to Nemetus, his storm shield flaring in response. He drove the shield forward, its impact hurling his attacker into the wall, bones pulverised. Continuing without pause into the gap he had made, he swung his sword at the next, its gleaming edge slicing a woman with snake eyes from gut to throat. Those not lacerated by the chainswords of the Intercessors were trampled underfoot, skulls crushed and bodies pulped by the mass of the warriors charging through them.

'Let none live,' snapped the lieutenant. *'Morta extremis.'*

A few survived to turn and run, but not for more than a few paces before a fresh hail of bolt pistol rounds caught them.

'Secure ahead,' barked Nemetus, stopping in his tracks. The following Space Marines parted and slowed, striding with weapons readied to the end of the passageway ahead, suit lamps cutting the darkness. Admonius joined him, head turning left and right as he checked the broken mutant remains for signs of heretic life.

Looking back, Nemetus watched the second gunship swinging into view, hull sparking with the last few defence turret shots. A jumble of body parts and corpses cooled in the thermal glow of his auto-senses, their lifeblood left as orange patches flung across bulkheads and ceiling.

'Junction secure,' voxed Talluin from ahead, sergeant of Temerity.

Fourteen seconds.

Nemetus activated the long-range vox. 'Ship command, this is assault command.' He took a breath, fighting back the rush of battle that had swept through him as he had slain. 'We are aboard.'

Instigating a full retrieval from the augur archives, Praxamedes waited while the surveyor servitors did their work, grunting to each other as mechanically activated fingers tapped at the key arrays before them. Blurts of binaric cant broke their mumbling, staccato streams of information understandable only to the adepts of the Machine-God and their brain-neutered creations.

He told himself he was being thorough rather than paranoid. A small anomaly in the plasma readings could mean anything. Perhaps one of the fleeing escorts had suffered some kind of reactor surge? Or damage from the asteroid field? Or simply mismanaged their engines? All were eminently sensible explanations for the spike in plasma output that had occurred a few minutes after the traitors had reached the cover of the debris cloud.

But it could have been the signature of a larger vessel powering up. A brief engine flare that would set it gliding through the augur-defying cosmic chaff.

Praxamedes resisted the urge to confide his concerns with the deck officer. There was no need for Lerok to be distracted by his almost base-less suspicions.

Baseless? At what point did experience turn his instincts into reasonable suspicion?

There was also a deeper question that Praxamedes was trying to avoid. If he brought the matter to the attention of his captain, what did he expect Aeschelus to do? A cursory look towards the videolith icons showed that Nemetus' force was now fully established on the target vessel. The vox-chatter suggested that resistance was light – his gambit to circumvent possible entrapment at the original target site seemed to be paying off.

Reflecting on Nemetus' course of action brought a stab of awareness to Praxamedes. Should he have seen what his fellow lieutenant had noticed? The original landing zone was ideal in all respects, so did that mean it was false? It seemed highly unlikely that in the course of battle the enemy would have had the wit and means to fake a strike on the ladening hold doors on the off-chance that they would be boarded. The sequence of events to bring such a plan to fruition were dubious at best, and closer to nonsensical.

Praxamedes found his thoughts racing, his cognition boosted by combat-enhancers even though he was not in direct conflict. While it allowed him to analyse the incoming data with the speed of a metric-ulating engine, without focus the overstimulation threatened to create patterns that did not exist.

'Deck officer, attend please,' said Praxamedes, realising that he needed an outlet for his turbulent contemplations. By voicing them to Lerok it would force him to be more sedate in his analysis.

'Yes, lieutenant?' Lerok glanced at the terminal screen. 'You're re-running the augur returns from the battle?'

'I am, but that's not what I want to talk about. Bear with me while I indulge in a hypothetical.'

'Yes, lieutenant.'

'Assumption – the enemy created a deliberately inviting landing site for our boarding party.' Praxamedes moved to another console and brought up the schematic of the enemy ship. An armoured finger high-lighted the original target area. 'Conclusion – the enemy believed that it would allow them to control the route of the boarding attack.'

'That was Lieutenant Nemetus' thought,' said Lerok. 'To set an ambush.'

Praxamedes stifled a chastising retort, partly because he did not want to risk drawing the attention of the captain and partly because he had known Lerok for several years and her opinion was to be respected, even if given without invitation.

'Please don't interrupt.'

'My apologies, lieutenant.'

'Apology accepted.' Praxamedes examined the ship schematic again. 'Assumption – the enemy accepted that a boarding action was inevitable. Conclusion – at some point during the void battle the enemy captain conceded defeat and set about minimising the threat of boarding.'

He noticed that Lerok was struggling not to speak, actually holding her breath to prevent herself intervening.

'Is that wrong?' Praxamedes asked.

'Why would their captain believe that we would board rather than simply bombard them until destroyed? A very unlikely gamble.'

'Except that the early damage to their reactor put them swiftly at a disadvantage.' Praxamedes moved back through the sensor readings of the other ship as though rewinding time itself. About four minutes into the engagement there was a flare from the reactor decks and an almost instantaneous power loss across many of the ship's systems. 'Widespread power failure left them unable to manoeuvre or fire effectively. No longer a threat, at that moment the odds in favour of a boarding attack increased significantly. Conclusion – the captain would prefer to defend against boarding than bombardment.'

Lerok thought for a few seconds, hands on hips, and shrugged. 'That would seem logical.'

'I sense hesitancy in your manner.'

'Logical but not sensible, lieutenant. I don't know all the forces in motion during a boarding action, but there must have been several different ways to ready for the boarding assault. To set up a lure to channel the attackers into a pre-determined point of assault seems overly complex. Why indulge in a very specific subterfuge?'

Praxamedes considered this as the dominant servitor groaned that the retrospective analysis was ready for inspection.

Why indeed?

* * *

The boarding attack was an uncompromising machine of war, cutting through all opposition without pause. At the forefront went the Incursors, their enhanced suit sensors gifting them awareness like mythic seers of old. Walls were no barrier to their auspex-lenses, so that waiting foes could be circumnavigated or caught unawares, and enemy flanking forces found themselves cut off by pinpoint counter-attacks directed by the Incursor sergeants.

In their wake, the Intercessors advanced in tandem, assault squads moving forwards under the cover fire of their companions, before holding newly won ground against counter-attacks while their bolt rifle-wielding battle-brothers closed up. Nemetus joined Temerity while Audacity was bolstered by the presence of Judiciar Admonius.

The Chaplain-in-Waiting was a relentless warrior, cleaving apart his enemies with broad sweeps of his greatsword. While many of the Reclusiam would exhort the battle-brothers with battle-cries and recitations from the Chapter teachings, the Judiciar inspired by presence alone, a silent slayer of the impure. Yet it was not only the Judiciar's efforts that were bolstered by his enforced silence. Knowing that Admonius' eye was upon him pushed Nemetus to greater efforts, conscious that any laxity would be noted and remarked upon later. More than any verbal remonstration, the simple thought of disappointing the great warrior, the merest hint of shameful reluctance, set a fire of battle inside the lieutenant.

It was hard to prove himself worthy of the Judiciar's praise against the chaff that clogged their path to the strategium. Scattered and surprised, the traitor crew came at the Space Marines in piecemeal fashion, easily overwhelmed. In the closer confines of hallways and chambers the superior weapons, armour and speed of the Space Marines was uncompromising.

Even when the force breached into the arterial corridor that ran along the main dorsal structure, they met little organised resistance. Everything was bathed in a ruddy gloom, lit by high lanterns with panes the colour of blood. Clouds of steam and gas issued from broken vents and split pipes, perhaps a sign of a losing battle against the ship's antiquity. Blue-armoured warriors strode through the swirling vapours and shadows, bolts streaking from their weapons to slay mutants lurking behind buttresses and in archways.

'Press on! *Invicta dominus bellicosa!* Show no mercy!'

The war-shouts and oaths of his battle-brothers echoed among the bolt detonations and snarl of chainswords. The enemy crew held their ground and fired in the face of the merciless Ultramarines attack. Their dedication would have been laudable had it not been directed to such ill purpose. Their cries of devotion to the Dark Powers were a twisted echo of the Chapter oaths his brothers bellowed as they cut them down with bolt and blade. It reminded Nemetus of the Chapter serfs that supported the Adeptus Astartes – unaugmented humans that were nevertheless almost as fanatical in their determination as the Ultramarines themselves.

The retort of weapons rang back from high vaults, the ceiling lost to normal sight. Yet there was another sound there, a soft creaking and susurrate breaths. When Nemetus looked up he saw odd shapes clustered in the plasteel braces and arching supports.

'Enemy above!' He opened fire even as he issued the warning, the plasma bolt of his pistol streaking into the body of a bat-winged creature even as it unfurled its pinions.

The air erupted with screeching cries as the beasts dropped, leathery wings gliding rather than flapping, serrated beaks clacking. A cloud at least a hundred strong fell as one, lit through by the streak of the Ultramarines' salvo of bolts, ravaged bodies tumbling amidst the mass, blood drops falling as crimson rain.

The flock swooped low, razor claws and snapping beaks scratching and clattering against uncaring ceramite. Nemetus' shield flared as he smashed aside a diving apparition, giving himself time to swap pistol for blade. Yet in the second it took him to ready his sword, the swarm had moved on, swirling around the Intercessors behind him.

Suddenly aware that his force was being turned by the threat in their midst, Nemetus called to the companions around him to ready themselves. Though the beast assault was an ideal prelude to a counter-attack, the mutant crew did not venture from their hiding places but continued to snipe with poor marksmanship.

Inhuman screeching and the buzz of chainswords sounded from the mists. Blade held high, its gleam lighting his dark armour, Admonius led Audacity in a charge, hacking and sweeping at the winged creatures as they clung and clawed at the battle-brothers.

'Push on,' Nemetus told Tenacity, thrusting his sword towards the waiting mutants. 'Our brothers keep our backs.'

His shield sparking from autogun bullets, Nemetus led the way, the enemy's shells and las-bolts converging and intensifying as he advanced with determined strides along the broad passage. A few rounds zipped past his defence to career harmlessly from his warplate, while the snap of bolt propellant sounded around him, the streak of his battle-brothers' fire like a guiding light, bright sparks that intermittently shattered the darkness ahead.

The mutants held their ground and died where they stood. Their steadfast refusal to withdraw was perhaps strategically unsound, but spoke of a zealotry that was rare to see in the ranks of traitors. Selfishness was a trait that led one to the Dark Powers, but the crew of the enemy vessel seemed not only willing to die for their uncaring masters but perhaps wished for it. Coming upon them with blazing sword, he was happy to make martyrs of them all. None would remember their sacrifice.

As he hewed down a canine-faced woman, Nemetus signalled for the squad to halt, before they became separated from their supporting squad of Intercessors. The fight against the flying beasts had broken down into a few scattered skirmishes, the bulk of the Intercessors now reformed and directing fire once more at the pockets of crew arrayed along the passageway and on gantries and mezzanines above.

Within forty-five seconds of the aerial attack starting, all but a handful of Space Marines were again advancing with purpose.

Relocating the landing zone had taken the enemy completely unawares, it seemed. To Nemetus' mind it appeared that the foe had been so intent upon their lure and ambuscade that they were unable to react with any coherence to the real axis of attack. Crew, both mutant and untainted, scrambled to the defence as best they could, but there was no coordinated effort to draw the Space Marines into a more protracted engagement that would slow or halt their momentum until reinforcements arrived.

'*Strategium access located, assault command,*' reported Sergeant Lato. '*Minimal resistance expected. Scattered opposition.*'

'Acknowledged, brother-sergeant.'

Nemetus drove the tip of his blade through the flak armour of a gangling mutant with three eyes, noting with disgust the yellowy fluid that sprayed forth in place of blood. He took the creature's head off with a backhanded sweep and batted aside the falling body with his shield to fall upon the next foe.

'We have noticed a distinct lack of enemy command figures, brother-lieutenant. No officers encountered, as far as we can tell. No Traitor Astartes higher echelon.'

Gunfire rattled against the lieutenant from his left. He turned to locate the enemy but one of the brothers from Temerity had already found them, a bolt from his pistol turning the traitor's upper body to a splayed mess of blood and fractured bone. The mutant slumped sideways, auto-pistol falling from its grasp.

'Strategium is sealed,' added Sergeant Dorium. 'It is possible they have all taken sanctuary inside. However, enemy crew still appear determined and in good morale despite lack of direct leadership.'

Nemetus considered the situation for a moment. He did not know if the lack of officers signified anything or was symptomatic of the displacement of forces for the unsuccessful ambush strategy. He had reached the next point of decision: to make for the strategium at all speed with every squad, or a more measured attack with a rearguard. Despite being wrong-footed by Nemetus' attack plan, the enemies that he assumed had been waiting around the logistics bay would be redeploying. Four minutes had passed since the first breach, but within four more these corridors could be swarming not with dozens of foes but hundreds, possibly thousands. In such circumstances, the strategium could easily become a mausoleum if he was not prepared.

On the other hand, they were there to seize data, not the whole ship. The longer the Ultramarines remained, the more embroiled in extended combat they would become. If he was to maximise the advantages gained by the shock landing, he had to act decisively.

'All squads, continue rapid advance. Eradicators, move to the fore of the assault and prepare for breaching action.'

Whichever way Praxamedes examined the evidence, he could find nothing to support Nemetus' proposition that the breach in the ladening bay was engineered. At the stage of the battle at which the damage occurred, the only motive would have been to invite a boarding action to forestall destruction by ranged firepower. Even then it was an extraordinary leap of logic, or intuition, by the enemy commander. It was a gamble, but a very precise kind of gamble when weighed up against many other strategies, as Lerok had suggested.

'Lieutenant!'

The deck officer approached Praxamedes with a dataslate in hand, clearly agitated. Praxamedes glanced at Aeschelus to see if he had reacted to her overly strident call. The captain was engrossed in the ongoing assault, working with the telemetristika and her servitors to represent the progress of Nemetus' boarding action on the main videolith. The lieutenant turned his attention to the simulation playing out on loop across the dataslate screen.

He saw an outline of the enemy ship threaded through with dotted grey lines, which moved and pulsed along with an advancing time-stamp. Thicker blots correlated with the reactors, engines and gun decks, and he realised he was looking at a representation of the augur data taken of the energy grid of the enemy ship. Areas thinned and thickened as power was diverted to and then used by weapon batteries and void shield generators.

Most of the lines faded out, leaving the limping, defenceless vessel that now floated in the void just a few thousand miles away.

'Comprehensive, but I don't see what's so urgent.' He attempted to hand the slate back to Lerok, but she did not take it.

'Pay closer attention to the timestamps, lieutenant. I checked with the gunnery files and our surveyor readings. Their void shields fell at four minutes and seven seconds from our first firing. Captain Aeschelus directed fire at the aft sections five seconds later and a targeting solution was laid in at five minutes and seventeen seconds.'

Praxamedes chafed at her unconscious rebuke but let it pass. Her agitated state and momentary loss of decorum suggested she had cause for such insistence. He checked the slate again.

'That seems consistent,' he said, reviewing the advancing timestamp in slower increments. 'Five minutes and thirty seconds into the engagement, the main reactor is hit and its power output goes offline.'

'Yes, but given the delay between the firing order being issued and the time for our munitions to travel what was then fifteen thousand miles, the reactors went offline *before* our shells even hit.'

'Augur data also has a delay. This is within a margin of error.'

'*If* the very first impacts somehow went straight through their armour and hit the reactor immediately.'

'That would be the luckiest shot I've ever seen,' admitted Praxamedes, viewing the timed loop again. He was so caught up in the nature of the revelation that it took him several seconds before he realised its significance. 'The enemy deliberately shut down the reactors?' He looked at Lerok. 'Damage limitation? It may have saved the ship. Had the reactor been fully operational when breached–'

'It's faked!' blurted Lerok. She jabbed at the dataslate in Praxamedes' hands, her finger bringing up a closer schematic of the reactor decks. A plume of heat – presumably plasma – shot upwards from the breached ship.

Or so it had seemed. Now, in the slower time-reel, Praxamedes saw the sequence more clearly. The conduits were being shut down as the *Ithraca's Vengeance* opened fire, and excess plasma was vented to the void. Not a safety measure, but a deliberate act to recreate the appearance of a reactor breach.

'If this was faked, that means the whole ruse with the loading gates was part of a bigger plan,' said Lerok. 'That's what I can't work out. Is it worth the risk of being blown to the abyss and back just to lure aboard a few squads of Space Marines?'

'Captain!' Praxamedes turned away from her, filled with sudden misgiving, and then turned back as thoughts collided with each other and formed a daunting theory. 'Full augur scan of the plasma trails in the debris field, Officer Catriolis. If the whole engagement has been staged, we have to assume that the location is equally pre-determined.'

'What is it, Praxamedes?' Aeschelus demanded. 'Nemetus is about to breach the enemy strategium. This is a critical moment.'

'We have to pull them out, brother-captain,' announced Praxamedes, discarding his usual caution. 'This entire engagement is an elaborate trap.'

CHAPTER FOUR

With the heat of recently discharged melta rifles warping the air in front of them, the Eradicators moved up towards the armoured gateway that barred entry to the main strategium. Intercessors were stationed at important entry points around the position, ready to hold against any counter-attack. The two squads of Incursors were further afield, their scouting role now changed to one of roving picket to bring early warning of enemy dispositions.

'Remember that we need to claim the cogitation banks intact,' Nemetus told his warriors as he backed away from the portal. 'No collateral damage. Mark every target before firing.'

'Understood, brother-lieutenant,' replied their sergeant as the squad came to a halt facing the gate. 'On your command.'

'Audacity, with me on breach.' Movement behind Nemetus drew his eye to Judiciar Admonius, who hefted his executioner's relic blade in meaningful fashion. 'Honoured to fight at your side, brother.'

He took a moment to assure himself that all was in order. It had been one of the most straightforward encounters he had known – though his frontline experience was limited. Even now the enemy showed little sign of making a concerted effort to stop them accessing the command bridge. Whatever officer corps or Traitor Astartes had commanded the vessel earlier, there was no sign of them now. It was entirely possible that they had fled while the *Ithraca's Vengeance* had closed in. A small gunship or saviour boat could easily evade detection at range, using the energy signature and bulk of the ship itself to mask its exit.

That was an issue for later. Even so, the ease of the boarding started to nag at Nemetus the same way the open ladening bay had pricked his suspicions. When their trap had failed, had the enemy instigated some other subterfuge that he could not discern?

Admonius stepped forward, head tilted to one side. Nemetus could sense the Judiciar's impatience.

'Awaiting your command, brother-lieutenant,' said the sergeant of the Eradicators.

A chrono-check showed Nemetus that five seconds had passed since the Eradicators had taken up position. Not long in objective turns, but a significant hesitation to a Space Marine.

'Dorium, Lato, situation report,' he said, signalling to the Incursor sergeants. This was another moment of commitment. Once they were in the strategium the Ultramarines' position would be locked down. He could imagine Praxamedes monitoring the boarding action from the bridge, likely considering how he would have conducted the operation differently. Nemetus was not going to leave any room for accusations of casualness or unpreparedness. Praxamedes would see he could be diligent as well as resourceful.

'*Detecting large movement, assault command,*' reported Lato, who was covering the starboard approaches. '*Motion data and thermal registers increasing rapidly.*'

'*Also significant increase in activity to port side,*' added Dorium. '*Only in the last few seconds. I think this is the counter-attack, brother-lieutenant.*'

'*I concur. Massed movement, enemy numbering hundreds. No powered armour signatures detected. What are your orders, assault command?*'

Nemetus felt the gaze of Admonius on him, and the more distant scrutiny of Aeschelus and Praxamedes.

Breach or withdraw?

'Incursor squads, collapsing rearguard to our position. Intercessor tactical, operational freedom. Move forward to support Incursors' withdrawal and then assume perimeter defence.'

Nemetus readied his shield and plasma pistol, looking at the Eradicators. 'Breach!'

The whine of melta rifles became a screaming hiss of flash-vaporised molecules. The outer layer of the strategium portal exploded outwards in a billow of vapour that sparkled from the field of Nemetus' storm shield and coated the armour of his companions in a molecule-thick layer of glistening metal. The noise of the meltas was drowned out by the shriek of distorted plasteel and titanium as the door bubbled. The pressure imbalance between the strategium atmosphere and the super-heated air in the accessway caused an explosive rupture, the last sheen of metal splaying out from the command bridge, droplets of molten plasteel flying like bullets through the hot air.

Nemetus plunged forward, his armour moaning alarms, dotting his visor display with amber and red as he pushed himself through the radiation cloud that the portal had become. The residue of melta energy fogged his auto-senses for half a second, clearing with scatters of grey static to reveal the interior of the strategium.

He took in the broad sweep of the command platform and dozens of waiting enemies for just a second before warning notes sounded again, even as his eyeline swept to the muzzle of a missile launcher.

Bringing up his storm shield, he stepped to the right as fire filled the tube and the projectile sped from its housing. The missile hit his shield close to the top, the detonation strong enough to break the arm of a lesser fighter. Even with his enhanced strength, Nemetus couldn't stop the shield tipping back, slamming into the grille of his helm mask. The blow staggered him, fogging his vision as blue blurs flowed into view from behind him, his battle-brothers advancing into a welter of enemy fire.

It was hard to follow what Praxamedes was saying whilst trying to keep abreast of what was happening aboard the target vessel. Aeschelus' second-in-command talked about plasma flows and surveyor readings, but the captain was not sure there was anything coherent; at the same time the boarding force had breached into the enemy strategium and from the overlapping vox-traffic it seemed Nemetus might be wounded or dead.

'Stop!' Aeschelus held up a hand to interrupt Praxamedes. He complied immediately while the captain switched to the command channel on the vox. 'Assault command, this is company command. Respond and report.'

The vox hissed for several heartbeats, each passing second raising Aeschelus' concern.

'This is assault command. Enemy are well-prepared in the strategium.' Nemetus seemed out of breath. *'Engagement complicated by need to preserve environment. Confident of success.'*

The link cut off and Aeschelus knew better than to distract the lieutenant any further. He turned his gaze back to his other subordinate.

'It occurs to me that you are telling your story backwards, Prax,' said the captain, letting calm resonate from every syllable. It was not like Praxamedes to be so flustered. 'I trust your observations and calculations are correct. I do not need the theory. Just report the practical conclusions.'

The lieutenant nodded, took a moment and then directed the captain's attention to a display among the augur consoles. It showed a time-frozen picture of the engagement with the enemy ships, their courses and exchanges marked out with lines and sigils, nearly five minutes of conflict captured in a single image.

'The entire engagement has been constructed as a lure, brother-captain,' explained Praxamedes. 'If you recall, we found the enemy battle group thanks to a strange lensing effect of their energy signature. We thought it might have been debris from an earlier battle but did not question it further. I believe it was a deliberate signal. During our approach there was ample opportunity for the enemy to take one of two other courses of action. They could have withdrawn earlier into the stellar debris or they could have closed formation and engaged us directly.'

'The speed of our response took them unawares?'

'I don't think so, brother-captain. At no point in the engagement did the escorts attempt to close with the *Ithraca's Vengeance* nor open fire. There's no evidence that they were even armed vessels, we just assumed they were because of their signatures.'

'False destroyers?' said Aeschelus. 'Meant to deter attack, I suppose. But it did not work.'

'No, they are messengers, brother-captain. Like the escorts, I believe the cruiser is also little more than a shell, with virtually no crew. Looking again at the readings, there's about twenty per cent of the normal life signs for a ship that size. Often that means that the vessel has been infested with warp-denizens, but other than some mutants, Lieutenant Nemetus has met no evidence of the warp-born. Time-lapse conclusively shows that the reactor shutdown and the loss of the ladening bay doors were almost concurrent. They were an elaborate pretence with a two-fold purpose. Firstly, to encourage us to a boarding action. Secondly, to do so through a known route of attack which the much-diminished crew could guard. Nemetus wrong-footed their defence.'

Although he was not sure where the lieutenant was leading him, Aeschelus could understand the logic so far. He looked back at the main display. The fight for the strategium was ongoing.

'I fail to see the cause for alarm,' he told Praxamedes. 'As you say, Nemetus has nullified the enemy ruse with his insight. He will have control of the enemy command bridge within minutes. That reduced crew have been very slow to respond.'

'Why, brother-captain?' said Praxamedes. 'If we assume they were assembled ready to spring the original ambush, what has delayed them from moving forward to engage the new line of attack?'

'I have a feeling you have a theory, Prax.'

'The entire purpose of the ruse has not been to eliminate the board-ing party. By striking for the strategium they are now separated from their exits. It is a literal trap, holding them inside the bridge.'

'A position which they can effectively hold against a far more numer-ous foe. With targeted bombardment and gunship strikes, we could easily provide support for them.' Aeschelus again halted Praxamedes with a hand as another thought occurred. 'Is that the plan? To lure us in closer and then power up the weapons decks from the perfectly func-tioning reactor?'

'With gunnery control in our hands, it would be a fairly ineffective attack, brother-captain.'

'True. So what is the point of keeping our warriors on board?'

'To ensnare the *Ithraca's Vengeance*. What can't we do while our board-ers are away? What would happen if we came under attack?'

'I see,' said Aeschelus. 'You think this is all in place to act like a tether. With our warriors aboard, we cannot move too far away or they will be attacked, and we cannot bring them back while under fire. This is about the Desolator, yes? You have concocted this whole theory on the assumption that there is a battleship out there hunting Imperial vessels.'

'If you'd allow me–'

'No, Praxamedes, *you* will listen to *me*.'

Aeschelus stalled his comments, countering his rising anger. It was ill-discipline on the part of his lieutenant, but overly emotional behaviour would not resolve the situation. With another look at the ongoing assault, Aeschelus assured himself that Nemetus was making good progress even if his other lieutenant was not.

'You are proceeding from the assumption that the Desolator exists, then creating an interpretation of the facts to fit that view. That is not the way of the lord primarch and the teachings you know so well.' Aeschelus could feel frustration emanating from Praxamedes, but his second-in-command had gone too far this time. 'You knew I would not approve of this, so have engaged in this operation without my knowledge. If your history did not present against it, I would think that a gross act of insubordination. I know there is no malice in your intent, only...'

Aeschelus let his gaze move to Officer Catriolis, who was trying to attract the attention of Praxamedes.

'Your part in this episode is not to be unremarked, Lerok.'

'Of course, captain. Whatever consequences you deem fit I shall accept.' She turned and thrust a finger towards one of the augur console screens. 'Our scans of the stellar debris are detecting a massive spike in energy output.'

'The escorts returning?' said Praxamedes.

Aeschelus looked past his brother Primaris Marine and saw the increasing signature of multiple plasma reactors. Three of them. Not separate ships; they were too close together.

One massive vessel.

Engagement complicated by need to preserve environment. Confident of success.

Nemetus had not lied to his superior in his assessment, but had perhaps over-simplified. As a fresh eruption of fire from the enemy skulking around the strategium crashed into the Ultramarines, he wondered whether his optimism had been undue. He drew his blade, shaking the last of his dizziness from his senses as he crossed the main floor of the strategium with the Assault Intercessors around him.

'Fists and blades, brothers,' he called to his companions, seeing Judiciar Admonius racing past, sword swinging out to behead a green-faced mutant using an upturned portable hololith as a barricade. 'Crush them at close quarters.'

The strategium was larger than that of the *Ithraca's Vengeance*, spread across three levels like an amphitheatre. The main doors opened into the middle level, and the bulk of the enemy fired down from the horseshoe-shaped deck above, creating a crossfire, with bullets, shotgun shells and las-bolts also spraying forth from the defenders holding out beneath the broad main display and the bank of cogitators and projectors in front of it. Nemetus aimed left and right with his plasma pistol, looking for a target, but the glimpses of the enemies that appeared in his targeting display were too close to the strategium metriculating engines. Even a partial hit risked incinerating vital databanks.

Nemetus holstered his plasma pistol and started forward again. Enemy fire smacked into his backpack from the upper floor as he pushed on.

'Audacity, vertical assault!' the lieutenant snapped, pulling his sword to gesture towards the upper level while he continued forward into the heart of the enemy fire from below.

The Primaris Marines broke into two combat squads, each heading for the spiral staircases that flanked the upper deck. Trusting them to make short work of the firers above, Nemetus pressed on with Tenacity and Admonius. The Eradicators came after them, melta rifles slung, combat knives drawn. From behind them came the occasional snap of a well-placed bolter round as a few of the Intercessors picked off targets of opportunity. Had the strategium not been the prize itself, Nemetus would have had both squads shred and melt everything in sight, but that was not an option.

Heedless of the enemy's guns, Judiciar Admonius vaulted over the rail that separated the main deck from the display sub-level, crushing a mutant beneath his bulk as he landed. Nemetus followed slightly less spectacularly, descending the rampway with three long strides, shield held up to ward away the weakening enemy fusillade. Chainswords shrieking, the assault squad split between the two officers, some jumping directly into the fray while the rest pounded after the lieutenant.

'Mark your targets, no collateral damage!' Nemetus barked again as Admonius' long blade barely missed a bundle of cabling that hung like an Ascension Day garland between two terminals. He kept his words generic, not wanting to rebuke the Judiciar directly. 'Watch your back-swings and follow-through.'

Like vermin bolting from the exterminator, handfuls of mutants and untainted crew scurried away from the arrival of the Space Marines, some fleeing towards the recesses behind the display, others throwing themselves between cogitator banks and under hololith tables.

'Assault command, enemy massed attack now one hundred yards from perimeter line,' warned Sergeant Dorium from outside the strategium.

'Hard defence, give no ground,' Nemetus replied. 'Estimate strength.'

'Fifteen hundred, increasing, brother-lieutenant.'

How long to interface with the strategic cogitators? How much longer to inload their contents into the datatraps they had brought with them? Ten minutes? An hour?

'Understood. Hold fast.' Time was of the essence. Nemetus slowed and then stopped, holding out his shield to signal his closest warriors to halt as well. He turned and looked up, pleased to see the purge of the upper balcony was progressing quickly. 'Judiciar Admonius and companions will continue the cleanse down here. Ready data terminals for transfer.'

He pulled away the bulky datatrap maglocked to his thigh and set it on the casing of the closest cogitator. He found the data port without problem and joined it to the trap with a snake of cable from the top of the storage device. The handful of Intercessors with him did the same at other consoles.

'Whatever the drawbacks of the Machine Cult's dogma, at least they have not changed their terminal connections in eight thousand years!' laughed Brother Heraclon.

A flurry of sparks erupted from the terminal next to Nemetus, unleashed by a pair of mutants that had crept back through the maze of power conduits and data cables strung between the main display and the control terminals. He turned without thought, catching the next volley on his shield, a few bullets glancing from the pauldron of his armour. Two bolt rifles barked from the doorway and a second later the twisted features of each traitor disappeared in a bloody detonation, their decapitated bodies slumping to the metal deck.

The rev of chainswords was sporadic from above as the Assault Intercessors of Audacity hunted down the last few of the enemy. Nemetus returned to the datatrap and flipped open the case of the runepad and small status screen in its side. It whirred softly as he activated the transfer, recognising scattered pieces of navigational data as it flowed from the cogitators to the storage machine.

There had been no sound of combat for several seconds and he waited for the confirmed clear, ready to broadcast to the *Ithraca's Vengeance* that the strategium was under control. Before he could do so, the command vox chimed in his helm.

'Assault command, this is ship command.'

As he recognised the voice of Praxamedes rather than Shipmaster Oloris, Nemetus' body reacted as though threatened – his pulse suddenly increasing again, providing a shot of energy that coursed along his nerves and blood vessels.

'This is assault command. Enemy strategium seized, data transfer underway.'

'Abort the operation, assault command. Return for gunship extraction immediately.'

The order came like a blow, and it was several seconds before Nemetus could reply.

'Negative, ship command. Negative. We are in complete control of the objective zone and data transfer is ongoing.' He needed something more precise and glanced at the progress monitor of the datatrap. 'Ten minutes, brother, and we will have scoured their databanks clean.'

'You don't have ten minutes, brother. A traitor battleship is breaking from the stellar debris field. Its lances will be in range within seven minutes. You have to extract now.'

His hearts were now a hammer, throat tightening as the substance of Praxamedes' warning settled. Even so, Nemetus' first instinct was to argue. He could not give up on victory just yet.

'Surely you can gain us three more minutes, brother.'

'Plus extraction time. What is your exit status, assault command?'

Nemetus considered the question and was forced to admit that seven minutes was barely enough time to get to a suitable extraction point even if the enemy were not in the way.

'Compromised, ship command. Orders received and understood.'

'I have a plan, brother, but you may not like it,' said Praxamedes.

* * *

When battle commenced, there was normally a sense of focused energy that came upon the strategium of the *Ithraca's Vengeance* and its occupants. Not a controlled chaos, because that implied there was ever anything out of the control of the shipmaster, first lieutenant or captain. It was a sudden tension and efficiency, with every Space Marine, deck officer, tech-priest and servitor forming an individual component of a greater whole. Every part operated independently, yet totally interlocked with the others, from fire control to navigation to propulsion to surveyor command. What needed to be done was done. If a decision needed to be made, it was channelled to the appropriate one of the three due authorities, and the results of that consultation carried back down to those that would execute the orders.

There was no room for doubt, or misunderstanding, or error.

Certainly there was never anything like panic, not even among the human crew who were still biochemically capable of such a reaction. Discipline overruled any instinct to allow fear to dictate poor decision-making. There was a chain of command and a process to guide every decision, with Captain Aeschelus himself as the sole arbiter and executor of free will.

So it was that Praxamedes tried hard to confine himself to the roles directly under his command as not-panic enveloped the strategium. The captain reeled off orders faster than was usual, his words hastened by a sense of urgency not normally seen. This had the effect of creating an unmannerly bustle about the control stations, with deck officers proceeding with unsavoury haste, occasionally getting in each other's way, having to shout to one another for reports, energy transfers and other functions that should have happened seamlessly and without prompting.

At the augur read-outs, the lieutenant monitored the target vessel for any sign that it was powering weapons or shields, while simultaneously viewing another screen that charted the energy distortions in the asteroid field. The plasma readings had been verified, the telemetry triple-checked and his entire terrible theory proven correct.

He really wished he had not been right.

The traitor battleship had given up all attempt at disguising its whereabouts, its commander confident that the Ultramarines vessel had been utterly ensnared in the ambush. Pulsing low-energy navigational shields shunted aside debris and gas, creating a bow wave of stellar detritus that marked its accelerating passage through the cloud.

The distinctive signature of the laser conversion engines of the lance batteries supported the reports of the vessel's primary armament. Bigger than the Ultramarines vessel, itself three miles long, the attacking battleship was also a specialist ship-hunter. Though not especially powerful, the secondary batteries would still be capable enough to overload the void shields of a cruiser-class target with one or two full salvoes. Unprotected, the prey would be cut open by accurate lance fire; shield generators, engines, environment control all pinpointed by ancient scanners and firing metriculators more powerful than anything aboard the *Ithraca's Vengeance*.

In contrast, the Ultramarines warship was dedicated to boarding attack and orbital support. It could hold its own in a fight with a similar-sized enemy or two but lacked the range of a true ship-of-the-line. Flight bays took up more room than gun batteries, and with the gunships launched and a good proportion of the fighting complement on the enemy lure, the *Ithraca's Vengeance* had little with which to strike at long range.

'It is a convoluted plan, risky, with a low chance of success,' remarked Lerok. 'Damned sneaky, though. You must have your own share of cunning to have worked it out, lieutenant.'

'On the contrary, the risk is slight,' Praxamedes replied. Speaking helped distract his thoughts from the motor-function tasks he had to complete. If he had to think about his fingers moving across the runepads they felt slow and clumsy. 'Assuming that if our enemies in this sector had the resources to fully crew two destroyers and a grand cruiser they would do so, giving them a skeleton complement and acting as bait is the most efficient use of what would otherwise be empty materiel.'

With the trap sprung, there was no need to dedicate a complete sensor array to monitoring the gas and dust cloud. Praxamedes powered it down, rerouting the energy back to firepower targeting matrices.

'It's also not through any personal insight that I uncovered the subterfuge. In fact, it was Lieutenant Nemetus' instincts that were the first clue that all was not well. His insight was correct but his conclusions were not bold enough. I've unpicked the enemy plan only through diligent observation of the facts, in retrospect.' He looked at the range to the incoming battleship and checked the chronometer. 'Though too late, possibly.'

Moving to the neighbouring terminal, Praxamedes inspected the recalibration of the telemetric array. He trusted Lerok would have carried out the calculations impeccably but it was his responsibility, and therefore his duty, to confirm them.

'The true masterstroke was in using the escorts,' he continued, stabbing a finger onto the target lock rune. 'Any kind of vox or narrowpoint transmission might be detected. Similarly, any kind of scanning wave from the hiding battleship had the potential to betray its presence. The escorts were like our outriders, the simple fact of their arrival in the dust cloud a pre-arranged signal that the bait had been taken. And two of them means that, should one get caught out by unlikely long-range fire or assault action, another would still survive to bring the message. Every angle covered.'

'You admire them?' Lerok seemed shocked by the possibility. 'It is a coward's way to wage war.'

'It is a pragmatist's strategy,' countered Praxamedes. 'If we can escape the consequences of our oversight, we can take heart that the enemy is not nearly as strong in this sector as we feared. Resorting to such measures indicates not that the enemy are *unwilling* to engage in traditional battle, but are *unable*.'

Praxamedes turned to the propulsion officer. 'Ahead one quarter, bring us to within six miles of the target ship.'

The deck officer signalled his compliance and turned to the controls, his command answered by the grunting of half-dead servitors.

'Captain, shall I take gunnery control?' Praxamedes asked.

'No, I will do it,' Aeschelus answered. 'You make sure that our targeting is right on the mark.'

'Yes, brother-captain.' Praxamedes knew his superior's exhortation was purely reflexive, not an expression of any doubt in the lieutenant's calculations.

'In position, lieutenant!' The officer at the navigational banks turned to the weapons control station. 'Range ten thousand yards from target.'

'Main bombardment cannon ready,' reported Shipmaster Oloris, who had taken over direct command of the gunnery terminal. He in turn looked to Praxamedes. 'Ready to fire.'

'Understood, shipmaster.' Praxamedes activated the command vox. 'Assault command, gunship command, are you in position?'

The pilots signalled their acknowledgements before Nemetus' voice broke through the static of the communications link.

'Ready when you are, ship command.' There was resignation in his voice. *'Target area is clear.'*

'Captain, all stations and commands report ready.'

Aeschelus received the report with a nod, one hand massaging the fist of the other. The following few seconds felt like a lot more, until the captain raised a finger and signalled to the shipmaster.

'Bombardment cannon, open fire on designated target.'

CHAPTER FIVE

The physical attributes of the Adeptus Astartes made them formidable warriors. Their size, speed, weapons and armour made each of them a fighter capable of taking on the worst that xenos and heretics could bring to battle. Psychodoctrination made them fearless. Training and deep learning had turned every Primaris Marine into a tactical expert, able to take up a leadership position should a sergeant fall. Their vox-network, auspexes and other armour systems gave them unparalleled coordination among the soldiers of the Emperor, both between individuals and squads, and all the way up to entire companies of warplate-clad transhumans.

All of this combined to give Nemetus and his Ultramarines the most important quality: absolute trust. If a battle-brother said he would guard a junction, he knew that Space Marine would guard the junction until dead or relieved, no matter what happened. If a gunship pilot asserted that he would be at the extraction point in precisely ninety-four seconds, then Nemetus would know that the pilot would be there if it was possible.

It also meant that when Praxamedes had told him that he had identified a weakness in the dorsal hull of the cruiser, and could crack it open with a single bombardment cannon shot no more than forty yards from Nemetus' current position…

Even so, it was some effort to concentrate on the ongoing firefight that embroiled the halls and corridors on the deck three levels above the strategium. The thought of the broad gun atop the spine of the *Ithraca's Vengeance* turning to bear upon a cracked slab of ferrocrete not far above his head was an image Nemetus could not wholly push away as he slashed his blade through the padded jerkin and chest of a young traitor crewman.

'*Enemy forces incoming from aft,*' warned Dorium. '*Six or seven hundred life signs. Two hundred yards.*'

Nemetus did not need an auspex to picture the situation, his mental image updated to bring in a fresh tide of humans and mutants. He used his shield to slam aside another foe, skull crushed as it flopped to the floor.

'Acknowledged, brother-sergeant. Complete final withdrawal to defensive perimeter.'

A green flash of light bounced from his pauldron and the lieutenant turned, confronting a grey-haired woman with a laspistol held in both hands. She shrieked something in a language he didn't understand, eyes filled with hate. He caught the next flurry of las-blasts on his shield a moment before a bolt from one of his companions punctured the woman's chest and then exploded, cutting her almost in half.

It was without a doubt a very desperate plan, but the alternatives were even less appealing. Only the timely warning from the cruiser had allowed the Ultramarines to break away from the immediate vicinity of the strategium. The sudden massed wave attack of the crew that followed would have pinned them down within a few dozen yards of the command bridge, far from any launch bay or even maintenance portal.

The mutants who hurled themselves along the corridors and hauled themselves up the empty conveyor shafts possessed a frantic demeanour. Nemetus returned to his earlier diagnosis of martyrdom – they were not only prepared to die, they seemed to embrace it. That they likely had lived terrible, maligned lives was coupled with some offer of a far greater reward, an offer of a post-mortem paradise in exchange for their deaths. Release from living misery coupled with eternal indulgence.

With the corridor cleansed of enemies, Nemetus joined the perimeter, his heavy tread crushing bodies underfoot while he swapped blade for plasma pistol. No longer concerned about the effect of collateral damage, he fired steadily, plasma blasts turning bulkheads into detonations of molten plasteel every bit as deadly as a grenade. Where the enemy came into the open, they were easy targets, turned to ash and body parts. Within a dozen heartbeats, he stopped firing, the warning runes on his pistol's plasma chamber gleaming amber with use.

Such was the enemy's zealotry that they were heedless of the concentrated, measured fire of the Ultramarines. Bolt-round after bolt-round unerringly found its mark, heaping corpses in stairwells and doorways so that the mutants clambered over and pushed through their own dead to get at the Emperor's warriors.

'Keep firing. Sustained volley,' Nemetus told his brothers. 'Any bolt left unfired is a bolt wasted.'

Admonius led a counter-charge to the left, aided by the Assault Intercessors. A black point to a spear tip of blue, the Judiciar cleaved into the foe with deadly sweeps of his sword. He fought in silence still, but the battle-brothers that followed gave vent to their battle-ardour, defiant of the cries and screeches of the traitors.

'Heretis mortalis profanum!'

'Slay the impure!'

'I am Guilliman's blade!'

Many of the mutants were unarmed as they appeared, stooping to pick up clubs, blades and guns from the cadavers of their companions, prising them from dead grips or fishing them from pools of cooling blood. No small number simply charged the Space Marines without armaments, a few perhaps thinking their curled horns or bony protuberances might be effective weapons.

They were wrong. Not sharp spine nor fangs were any threat to the ceramite-clad giants. Bolts, blades and fists made short work of the deranged enemy.

Even so, the enemy were not seeking to kill the Space Marines, simply to delay them. The flicker of bolt shells and flash of heavier weaponry created a strobing effect in the dim light of the upper deck. Every half-second seemed to paint a different tableau of disfigured faces, twisted bodies and inhuman appendages clawing at the floor and walls. Determined to give their lives to trap the Space Marines aboard the ship, the traitorous humans and mutants would bury the Ultramarines in corpses and let the incoming battleship annihilate them at will.

The command vox hissed into life with Praxamedes' voice.

'Assault command, gunship command, are you in position?'

The gunship pilots all signalled readiness while Nemetus made a last check of his complement's positioning.

'Ready when you are, ship command.' Though the withdrawal was tactically sound, a necessity in fact, the feeling of defeat weighed heavily on the lieutenant. 'Target area is clear.'

He switched to the battle channel to speak to his warriors.

'Extraction operation in progress. Check mag-locks and boots. Stand by.'

Nemetus followed his own command, assuring himself that his power armour was magnetically attached to the metal deck underfoot. A few seconds of sporadic bolter and melta fire passed.

An explosion above shook the corridors, the shockwave of the bombardment shell's impact throwing splinters and pieces of broken support beam from the ceiling. Cracks as wide as Nemetus' finger zig-zagged through the ceramite, while the ship's damage alarms wailed into life and the lights flickered before cutting out altogether. Dust billowed along the passageway, stirred by a still-functioning filtration fan somewhere behind the lieutenant, coating his armour and that of his companions with glistening grey.

'Breach the doors!'

His voxed order carried to the Eradicators stationed by a sealed security bulkhead about thirty yards up the main corridor. In the darkness, the lieutenant's auto-senses picked up the surge of melta radiation and sudden explosion of heat from the bulwark. In seconds, the yard-thick metal had evaporated, the last slivers blown outwards by decompression to reveal a haze of starlight.

The internal atmosphere became an evacuating gale, carrying corpses and live foes alike, their misshapen bodies slamming against walls and warriors. Nemetus ducked a large mutant with tusk-like teeth, turning his head to see it vanish through the ragged opening along with scores of others. When the rage of air and cadavers finished, a few corpses skidding to the deck around the opening and the passage beyond, Nemetus saw the bright spark of plasma engines against the darkness of the void.

'Gunships incoming. Extraction by squad!' Nemetus stepped back, his steps heavy as his boots pulled his feet down towards the deck.

The sergeants led their subordinates through the broken bulkhead, the first squads met by the ramp of a descending gunship. Nemetus checked his chronometer. Three minutes until the enemy battleship was in range.

'Faster! We have to be aboard in two minutes.' He started down the corridor as the first gunship lifted away, its compartment full. Void-frozen flesh crunched underfoot as he strode over the bodies of the mutants, his gaze occasionally meeting the frozen glare of a heretic. He waited a few seconds, assuring himself that everyone under his command would board before he did. Admonius waited ahead, also opting to be aboard the last gunship. It was the way of the Ultramarines. First to attack, last to withdraw.

A few of the battle-brothers had sustained injuries by sheer weight of fire, but none requiring anything but the most basic aid. All were capable of getting back to the gunships without assistance. In any other situation it would have been an unqualified success, mission one hundred per cent achieved with zero casualties.

Too good to be true, it had turned out.

Instead he experienced a moment of grudging admiration for not only the deviousness of the enemy plan but also for the unflinching hate that had powered it.

He moved towards the jagged opening again. They had to be aboard the *Ithraca's Vengeance* in two minutes or the traitors' martyrdom would be rewarded.

'Master Oloris, status on embarkation?'

Aeschelus asked the question softly, with just a tilt of the head towards the shipmaster at the monitoring station. It was moments like these for which the captain had been created. Not just trained, but moulded from frail human flesh and thoughts into a warrior capable of leading a force of the Adeptus Astartes.

He felt tense. It was counter-productive to suppress all reaction to conflict. His thoughts proceeded without too much biochemical impediment, aided by neuroboosters from his armour. He could see Praxamedes restless at the augury position, probably desiring to oversee the shipmaster's duty. It was to be expected from a Space Marine who had risen through the company from its inception; his first instinct was to personally involve himself, whereas Aeschelus had been inculcated with the need for a certain amount of strategic distance.

Even so, the several seconds it took for Oloris to reply felt much longer.

'All three gunships are returning, captain. First embarkation to commence in twenty seconds.'

Aeschelus did not need to ask how long until the battleship was within weapons range. The countdown was superimposed into a corner of the chrono-display of the videolith, and the captain was subconsciously monitoring it with every second that ticked past.

Sixty-two seconds.

Sixty-one seconds.

'Detecting plasma surge in the enemy vessel, brother-captain. They're powering up their batteries and lances.'

'Void shield generators operational and nominal,' added the deck officer assigned to the defence grid station.

The captain accepted these reports without comment, his attention focusing on the schematic that showed the relative positions of the two warships and the crippled vessel. He let them swallow his thoughts for a short while, the noises of the strategium, the movement in the periphery of his vision fading to nothing. The chronometer crept down and the distance-to-target estimate receded with it.

'First gunship is in the bay, captain,' came Oloris' report.

'Acknowledged, shipmaster.'

To pick up the incoming gunships, Aeschelus had dropped down on the orbital plane by three miles, which had fractionally increased their flight time but placed the lure-ship between the *Ithraca's Vengeance* and the incoming traitor battleship. Not just range but an unobstructed firing solution were needed before the enemy could open fire.

'Augur control, what is the status of the cruiser's reactor?' He looked at Praxamedes. 'Any sign of their weapons powering up?'

'None, brother-captain. I think that whatever system they used to crash-vent the reactor to simulate the breach needs time to reset. All power output on the target vessel is minimal.'

Forty-three seconds.

Forty-two seconds.

It was possible that, with some close manoeuvring and patience, the *Ithraca's Vengeance* could stay in the sensor shadow of the cruiser for some time, repositioning to keep its bulk between the Ultramarines ship and the Despoiler-class vessel that was now hunting them. The enemy commander might even be frustrated into closing the range, giving the Space Marines a chance to break from cover and dare the guns with a hit-and-run attack.

Of course, if that covering ship suddenly restored power to its weapon bays it would be at point-blank range, and certainly powerful enough to overload the Ultramarines' shields. Time did not appear to be on Aeschelus' side.

'Second gunship touching down, captain.'

Aeschelus stepped forward to his command panel and activated the vox-link.

'Assault command, what was the status of your data extraction?'

'Barely ten per cent complete, brother-captain.' Nemetus' breathing seemed slightly laboured, but it might have just been the link. *'It would be a miracle if there was anything much of use in what we managed to upload.'*

'Understood, assault command.'

Twenty-eight seconds.

It was not just the relinquishing of the prize that rankled, though that would be enough to vex any commander. It was the manner of the trap and the ignominy of its conclusion. Aeschelus gritted his teeth, looking again at the schematic, trying to figure out the best way to launch a potential counter-attack. If they closed the distance at full speed, accelerating from the moment the bay doors were shut – damn it, before the doors shut – it would take...

Aeschelus snorted.

Too long.

A few thousand yards closer, maybe they would weather the incoming fire. Maybe they would get close enough to re-launch the assault on a new target, but there was no reason to assume the battleship was as under-crewed as the lure vessel and escorts had been.

He had mentally started preparing the report to the Battle Group Command.

The commander of the Ithraca's Vengeance *is pleased to report a most advantageous and decisive engagement. If it would please Group Command to forward the attached intelligence direct to Fleet Command and the lord primarch.*

What a different missive he would have to compose.

'All gunships aboard. Closing doors, captain.'

If Aeschelus could have reached inside himself and torn out his hearts to offer as payment to make the situation different, he would have done so. The sense of failure burned in his chest like acid, and he desperately wanted to issue an order to attack. Better to strike and fall than to run without retort.

'Engines to full power,' he ordered.

Battle Group Faustus Command regrets to inform the lord commander of a disastrous engagement.

There was no glory in dying without cause. Better to face failure than flee its consequence, and survive to set it right in the future.

'Orders, captain?' Praxamedes' question prompted Aeschelus to look at the chronometer.

Eight seconds.

'Helm, full speed, directly away from the enemy.' The words were like hot nails in his mouth but he managed to say them without anger, not wishing to corrupt the crew with a moment of unnecessary emotion. It was only the taste of his pride.

'Get us out of here.'

PART II

'Across the void to traitors' nest,
They matched their arms 'gainst Death's harsh claw.
Overjoyed to pass the test,
And eager for the righteous war.
So light a flame and send a prayer,
For the souls of the Cursed Fleet.'

– 'The Lament of Quintus',
an Imperial Navy shanty.

CHAPTER ONE

'Everything is proceeding exactly as my cousin requests.' Overlord Simut turned back to the shimmering apparition of Emissary Tholotep. The Silent King's messenger was rendered in blue light atop the black disc of the hierolith, a metallic skeleton figure draped in robes of office and golden chains, much like Simut himself. 'I find this constant inquest unnecessary, Tholotep.'

Simut strode across the command-mastaba of his tomb ship to stand before the dais on which his throne had been installed. The chamber was a large semi-circular structure, its flat wall set before the throne, covered with images translated from the ship's many sophisticated sensors. At this moment in time, they displayed a shifting view of the planet below, the stars, the accompanying tomb fleet and the immense resonator-ships descending to the planet, their jet-black charge a shard of darkness against the pale grey of the world's surface.

The hieroliths, seven in all, were arranged before this wall, a line of three in front of four. Tholotep's ghost appeared on the central disc of the first row, full-size and bright despite the cosmic distance that separated him from Simut. Behind the throne, the curved wall was set within a tracery of mind-circuits, angling around twenty-one sarcophagi alcoves. Lit from below by the energy of the tomb ship, each alcove but for the central niche held one of the overlord's lychguard. Immobile for the time being, they stood as silent sentries, half with warscythes held across their chests, the other half stood to attention with phase-swords bared and shields upon their arms. At the centre waited the broad form of Archimedion Phetos, the royal warden. The overlord's lieutenant bore a large double-barrelled gauss weapon, its energy chambers reflecting the jade light of the surrounding hall.

The throne itself was set upon a dais almost as tall as Simut, reached only by a narrow set of steps at the front. It was a golden chair inlaid with crystal lines that linked the occupant to the energy trove of the tomb ship, the conduits flowing from its base in complex patterns across the dais and the floor of the mastaba-chamber. The back of the chair flared outwards like the wings of a great bird, the lines of the feathers glowing with the same thought-light as that which glowed from the walls. Simut's warblade was set into a clawed holder beside the throne, as tall as the overlord, its long cutting edge dormant for the moment. On the other side of the great chair a frame held a suit of torso exo-armour, the sculpted plates nestling over shoulders and spine, gauss cables hanging free ready to power the overlord's weapons.

'King Szarekh demands that his plan be enacted as he wills it, and it is my responsibility to ensure his commands are followed precisely,' the emissary replied. The image of Tholotep thrust an accusing finger towards Simut, its tip gleaming in the azure light of the astral projector. 'You are thirty-two dekas behind schedule, Simut. Your tardiness will not be tolerated much longer.'

'Tardiness?' Simut's artificially modulated voice rose in pitch. 'I have conquered barbarians and filth in the name of the Silent King, while others have planted resonator pylons on empty worlds, devoid of all glory to the Szarekh dynasty. If I have proceeded more slowly it is because I have walked the harder road.'

'You have certainly made hard work of the task assigned to you.'

'Choose sweeter words when you address me, Tholotep. You would do well to remember that I am royalty, of the line of Szarekh himself.' Wisps of energy flared from the overlord, whipping around him as a visible sign of his displeasure, his eyes gleaming with the same jade power. 'I am Overlord Simut, Stormhawk Commander of the Winter Stars, Ruler of Anthothekis and Akapris.'

'Your posturing will not save you from the displeasure of the Silent King.' Tholotep's sneer could be heard in his tone, though the mouth of his abstract-fashioned death mask did not move. 'Your claims to apparent bio-kinship are irrelevant and your worlds are ill-regarded.'

'Nevertheless, I am overlord and you are but a herald. Your rudeness to me is a slight against the blood of the Silent King.'

'Listen well, Overlord Simut, so that the will of King Szarekh is plain. Any more delays and you will be replaced. The Contra-Empyric Matrix must expand on schedule. No more excuses.'

The image blinked out of existence before Simut could respond, leaving the overlord coiled within his own energy-forms, brooding and angry. He stalked up the steps to his throne and sat down, fingers forming into fists and then unclenching. Around him the mastaba-chamber flickered with agitated energy, fronds of power lapping from the circuit lines, the display wall shimmering with ripples of rogue power.

Behind Simut, one of the alcoves flared into life, bringing its occupant to full wakefulness. Stepping down with a metallic tread, the warden advanced around the dais and stopped before the overlord, lowering to one knee at the foot of the steps. He offered his weapon, laying the gauss cannon upon the lowest step.

'I await your command, Blade of Szarekh, Sunlord of the Dynasty, Rising Light of the Stars of Heloki,' the royal warden intoned, eyes briefly dimming as a sign of subservience while his cortical field connected to the will of Simut.

'Arise, Phetos.' Simut gestured with a metal claw. The royal warden retrieved his weapon and stood. 'Summon the plasmancer. I would know why we have not yet completed the installation of the trans-empyric resonator.'

Simut could have easily accessed the communications conduits directly, but it would be unseemly to perform such a menial task. He felt the brief surge of power flowing into Phetos as the warden directed the energies of the *Barge of the Stormhawk*, sending an invisible beam of tachyons across the vacuum to the plasmancer, Ah-hotep.

While he waited for his subject to attend, the overlord focused the sensor wall on the world below. He turned the attention of his tomb ship on a city on the largest continent, where the cryptektonik survey had determined the pylon needed to stand for maximum effect. Was it coincidence that the most populous habitation on the human world was also the same location, or a sign that unknowingly the ignorant mortals had gathered at the nodal spot, drawn to its empyric footprint as some creatures blindly follow magnetic fields or pheromone trails? With the eyes of his starship Overlord Simut scrutinised and studied, fascinated and disgusted in equal measure by the transient creatures that had swarmed and multiplied across the stars.

As she drifted through the alien city, Ah-hotep felt herself moving through the liminal zone of the matrix. The soul-deadening throb of the resonator and Simut's necrolith-infused warriors lay like a shroud on the buildings, a dead calm that felt like cooling ice on the plasmancer's inorganic senses. It was a sensation of complete and utter stillness, devoid of the slightest turbulent thought or emotion. The stasis faded as she and her bodyguard of Szarekh dynasty warriors advanced on the last zone of resistance. Around them, the conurbation's inhabitants wandered listlessly, sometimes frowning in dismay at the metallic skeletons and wraith-like plasmancer, but such was the extent of their reaction. Most barely registered the necrons at all. They slumped at the roadside or stood staring up at the black needle of the resonator high above, gaze drawn to the pylon that dominated their thoughts and suppressed their souls.

Sometimes the necron warriors had to thrust aside wandering humans, who would stagger away and either sit down or somehow totter a few steps before retaining their balance, coming to an unconscious equilibrium once more. Others would briefly flinch at the skull-faced phalanx, shuffling out of their path in a half-daze. Their mouths fell agape as they watched the column of animated soldiers marching past, strides in perfect unison, the clash of their tread rebounding from glass-faced spires and walls decorated with large ceramic tiles, the light of gauss energy dancing emerald gleams from every reflective surface.

It seemed like an age since Ah-hotep had given her physical environs anything more than a cursory acceptance. She took a moment to study the painted tiles, wondering who the people displayed on the glossy murals were, their hands held up to a bird figure at the summit of the wall. It seemed so inconsequential. In time, nothing would remain of the city except its constituent particles, engulfed by the great void and scattered on the stellar winds. Matter was impermanent; only energy endured.

The thought was prompted by a nagging emptiness in the heart of her floating construct-body. Sustained by incorporeal power, Ah-hotep first and foremost saw the universe as interconnected energies. She could sense the electrical power still coursing along cables beneath the street, and the waves of electromagnetism pulsing around the planet. Each human was a flicker of bioelectrical activity; the heat of slow breath-puffs of lambent radiation.

She turned her attention to one of the aliens, a short male that lingered by the corner of an alley, one shoulder against the wall, a hand half-lifted as though to point at the apparitions marching past. She could see its make-up down to the cellular level, the tiny bonds that kept it held together, so easily parted by the gauss effect of necron weapons. They formed blood vessels that became pulsing rivers of heat and vitality, feeding the organs and the powerful muscles.

Ah-hotep tried to remember flesh, the feel of it clothing a soul. No more. Now she was intellect in a manufactured body. She no longer walked as she would have done in physical life but was kept afloat by the same energies she craved. A chain of artificial vertebrae hung from her torso in mockery of what once was, her shoulders and back splayed with canoptek vaporators that shone with green power as they absorbed the nascent power fields around her.

She lowered her staff of office towards the slouching human, using its gauss coils to extend her own biotek field. Green light lanced from the tip and struck the human, lapping at the particle bonds like a beast at a waterhole, stripping down each layer of its form one molecule at a time.

There was no satisfaction to be had from such a tiny morsel. Ah-hotep could drain the whole city of its energy and still she would want more. She watched the human disintegrate, becoming dust on the breeze and then nothing.

Ahead, the unsuppressed minds of the humans defending the citadel were a far greater noise, a buzz of emerging static on the edge of her awareness. She could feel the throb of the great reactors that kept the defensive screens functioning and powered the weapons that had started to rain down rudimentary chemical-powered projectiles onto the army of Simut. Their energy weapons spat crudely condensed light beams, woefully inefficient yet powerful enough to shatter the living metal bodies of the necrons.

Here and nowhere else, the effects of the Contra-Empyric Matrix were being held back. It was not entirely unexpected that the crux point of the world's astromantic field would prove the most resistant to the soul-deadening overnull, but it was inconvenient. Already several hundred of Simut's warriors had been force-ported back to the tomb ships for reconstruction. The screens themselves oscillated at an astromantic frequency, simulating a breach into the neversea. They swallowed the particle beams and gauss rays of the attackers and prevented translocation to within their effect, so Ah-hotep had brought herself down to the planet to personally denude the enemy citadel of its power.

She liked the sonascape, a calming mix of ambient waves emanating from unattended machinery in the distance. She did not hear as she had done so when mortal, but her highly attuned biotek field could pick up the vibrations of the slightest sound, so that the beating hearts of the nearby humans created a background thrum that danced across every surface. A more aggressive turbulence emanated from the citadel at the settlement's centre, where stabs of generator power and the thud of weaponry created ripples of disturbance through the sonascape.

The enemy fortification was a grandiose structure at the centre of the city, rising above the buildings that surrounded it. Through the shimmer of the screens, Ah-hotep saw banked storeys of battlements and buttresses, broken by cannon turrets and embrasures. The double-headed eagle device of the Imperial humans was carved in relief on many walls and above the great gateways at ground level. That they even dared call their scattered colonies an empire was an affront to the necrons. It had no more claim on a galaxy than the microscopic organisms of a sea could claim to rule the waves. In time the dominion of the necrons would be restored and the child races either exploited properly or exterminated.

The route to the main barbican was littered with corpses as proof of the defenders' reluctance to succumb, though only for a short distance outside the influence of the citadel's astromantic footprint. The humans had learnt early on that if they strayed too far from their defensive line, they succumbed wholly to the overnull's debilitating shadow. This was the weakness of the defence, which Simut had so far failed to exploit. He had despatched his great war engines and elite phalanxes to overwhelm the citadel with a single grandiose attack. This had played directly into the strength of the enemy, giving them valuable targets to destroy at distance.

Ah-hotep had another plan: overcome with attrition. Three thousand of Simut's warriors marched with her along three intersecting routes, and would come upon the foe in such numbers that they would physically breach the defensive screens. Once within, Ah-hotep would draw out the energy of the defenders and hunt down the astromancers whose powers kept the overnull at bay. Once the thought-strong were slain, the resonator would fog the minds of the survivors, leaving them unable to defend themselves as the plasmancer shut down their weapons and defences. Her army would occupy the citadel and the placement of the resonator could be completed.

The guns of the fortress opened fire again in response to the approach of the necron legion. Explosions ripped swathes through the advancing artificial warriors, scattering living metal amid blossoms of intense heat expansion. Where these detonations occurred nearby, Ah-hotep let free her energetic spirit, syphoning away the volatile reactions to channel the power back into the fractured bodies of Simut's warriors. The process was harder than if she led her own troops but the overlord, ever jealous or suspicious of those around him, had forbidden the mobilisation of the phalanxes aboard Ah-hotep's thrallship.

Bolts of star-stuff rained down, turning warriors to molten pools that Ah-hotep spun into renewed bodies with a simple extension of will. Around her the warriors could not die, sustained not only by their own superlative construction but also the energy-wielding abilities of the plasmancer. An emerald ghost-aura danced about her and the nearest echelons, swathing the advancing skeletal soldiers.

Elsewhere the weapons took a greater toll, but it mattered not to the plasmancer. The warriors that were struck down did not perish, but were transmitted back to their tomb ship for reconstitution. Any momentary discomfort they experienced was negligible and acceptable. Their form-deaths absorbed a good proportion of the humans' defensive strength, distracting them from the threat posed by the plasmancer.

Ah-hotep was almost within range of the first shield generator when she felt a tingle in the core of her cortical essence. It was contact from the tomb ship in orbit, but she ignored it. Summoning her biotek field, she started to extend her influence towards the human power source, the first fronds of her touch tasting its crude but enticing voltage.

The communication whisper became more insistent.

Ah-hotep paused and flexed a cortical array to align herself with the incoming signal. She sent a dismissive rebuttal and returned her attention to the citadel.

An instant later a paralysing spasm wracked her body as the overlord's summon-missive scattered through her engrams. Ah-hotep had just enough time to whip her extended essence back into the shell of her artificial body before the summons took effect. Displacement seared through her living metal frame, turning it from matter to energy and back again, translocating her presence to the command hub of Simut's warship. The experience lasted an instant but its after-effects were unpleasant, her senses spinning as she attempted to rectify the massive gravitational displacement that skewed her essence like a mortal suffering vertigo.

Lightwaves flooded into Ah-hotep's single facial lens, bringing her the image of Overlord Simut. He was sat on the command throne, a loop of cortical cabling snaking over his shoulder and into a socket on the side of his chest, interfacing directly with the tomb ship. His expression was a mask, as always, but his cortical aura transmitted annoyance every bit as vehemently as the deepest scowl. Wisps of emerald power flickered along his vestments and leapt to the armour and blade that flanked the army commander. Phetos stood at the bottom of the dais.

'That was... unnecessary,' Ah-hotep said, cutting back the remarks she wanted to share, seeing instantly that Simut was in no mood for disobedience.

His power was limited – the plasmancer had been assigned to the matrix force by order of Szarekh himself and was backed by the shadowy authority of the technomandrites. Within an acceptable margin of error, she was certain that Simut could not have her disintegrated. Even so, he was even more unpleasant when vexed.

'I was enacting your will, overlord, even as you reached out to me.'

'Your excuses are inconsequential, plasmancer. King Szarekh demands results and so do I.'

'The last vestiges of enemy resistance were about to be overcome, overlord.' Ah-hotep thought better of trying to blame Simut for the earlier delays. 'Your preparatory attacks perfectly seeded the field for my phalanxes to harvest.'

'*My* phalanxes, plasmancer.' Simut settled back in the throne, his aura dimming, apparently mollified by Ah-hotep's flattery. 'Your efforts are unnecessary, however. Once the resonator is in place the humans will be rendered harmless. It is only a matter of time.'

'My lord, that has served us well in the past but I do not think the strategy will work here.' Ah-hotep was not sure where to begin describing how irresponsible it was to attempt to bring in the resonator before the enemy was fully subjugated. 'If you would allow me–'

'Witness our next victory in the making,' commanded Simut, one hand gesturing towards the image wall, flecks of power crackling along the arm.

The display was an affectation, of course, emulating the physical senses Simut and Ah-hotep had once possessed. It was not needed; the data represented on the screens could be processed as pure cortical input. Wasteful. Extravagant, in fact, and that was the point. Even so, Ah-hotep had to concede there was something both majestic and comforting about seeing the fleet arrayed above the human world, the glint of ships in the local starlight, the great dark thrust of the resonator being moved into position for final descent to the surface.

A small portion of the screen showed the battle raging around the citadel. Without the plasmancer to break the energy defences, the necron phalanxes were being whittled down by barrages of fire, unable to gain a foothold within the precinct of the defensive structure.

'The mortals' resistance to the overnull is irritating but a passing obstacle,' declared Simut.

'The organisation of this world appears to be different to the previous inhabited planets, my lord.' Ah-hotep allowed her cortical essence to combine briefly with the tomb ship, increasing the size of the citadel image. 'They have concentrated military, civil and astromantic power in this one place. Had the resonator site been elsewhere, the threat would be negligible. Unfortunately, they have positioned their greatest defence almost exactly atop the point we must exploit.'

'And that shall be their undoing. Watch.'

The fleet display magnified, closing in on the resonator. The black-stone shard hung between two gantry-like suspensor vessels, its surface dull but for the reflected light of the local star. The massive obelisk's surface was not flat but carefully faceted, cut through with a tracery of necron astromantic circuitry. More precisely, anti-astromantic circuits, which diffused the power of the neversea.

'The human astromancers are collected in the target area,' said Ah-hotep, watching the resonator-ships accelerate effortlessly into lower orbit. 'We must assume that other defences...'

A brilliant flash of white brightened on the sub-display of the human fortress.

CHAPTER TWO

A stunning combination of shock and horror crackled through Simut. The spear of energy from the planet's surface appeared in the main display, diffracting slightly through the atmosphere so that a rainbow of colour struck the blackstone resonator. The defence laser was not powerful enough to harm the astromantic device but the beam deflected from the hard surface and sheared through one of the support ships.

The two neatly severed pieces of starship disconnected from the resonator and fell into the gravity well with balletic grace. The other vessel halted its inertialess engine immediately, but too late. Already the resonator was spinning into a decaying orbital ring. Within moments it was skimming the upper surface, flares of heat roiling along its sharp edges. Panicked demands pulsed through the tomb ship's cortical field from other vessels, calling for emergency protocols to be enacted. For a few precious moments, Simut was overwhelmed, unable to correlate what was happening on the display with his vision of victory.

He eventually responded, affirming the rescue protocols, diverting processor authority to several lesser officers stationed through the fleet. A squadron of ships darted forward, gravity flails latching onto the departing resonator. The tomb ship sensed the pulse of hyperspatial engines digging deep for traction in the undersphere. Pulsed commands and responses flared between the four necron warships. The exchange resolved into comprehensible language inside Simut's cortical interface.

Barque, Star of Natarun-4: *Gravitic clutch increasing. Powering stabilisers to rear.*

Barque, Star of Natarun-2: *Insufficient dimensional grapple. Recalibrating.*

Barque, Star of Natarun-1 [prime]: *Balance required, stabilising efforts. Stop squabbling.*

Barque, Star of Natarun-3: *Secondary dimensional phase engaged. Motive traction enabled.*

Barque, Star of Natarun-1 [prime]: *All power to gravitic traction. Pull, you fools, pull harder.*

Barque, Star of Natarun-2: *Gravitic slippage critical, atmospheric interaction inevitable.*

As both a falling spark and a stream of telemetry, Simut watched the attack barque burn up in the world's atmosphere. As living metal shed in waves of silver lightning, a last flash of data soared along the cortical field and back to the tomb ship. The barque's engrammatic presence settled into the resurrection core, awaiting the cryptek protocols to re-fashion its physical form.

The other ships managed to slow the descent of the blackstone resonator, aiding the lifter vessel with bursts of their gravitic impellers.

'Fortunately it seems that the human's defensive cannon is still recharging,' reported Ah-hotep.

Simut was sure he detected some smugness from his subordinate, as if this wasn't her failure too. In fact, had she pressed home the earlier attack the entire situation would have been avoided.

'Your presence is no longer required,' said the overlord. 'The resistance to our plans will be eliminated.'

'If you permit–'

'I will not permit you the opportunity to fail me again, plasmancer,' snapped Simut. Green flares of energy pulsed across his body to spiral along the tomb ship umbilical. 'I have been left no choice but to replace you with the Skorpekh Lord Zozar.'

A pulse of genuine dismay slipped across their cortical field connection.

'The Silent King has ordered that we preserve the lower lifeforms where possible, my lord,' protested Ah-hotep. 'They may prove useful later, as potential vessels for biotransference or an indentured workforce.'

Disdain flowed through Simut, discharging itself as jade energy streamers.

'You dare invoke the name of my cousin to intimidate me?' The words of Tholotep cycled through the overlord's memories, goading him. 'I think that perhaps the flesh-memory is too strong within you. You harbour a residual sentiment for these lower beings.'

'Not at all!' The plasmancer floated higher, vertebrae-tail twitching with anger. 'I...' Ah-hotep's protests died away amid a stutter of cortical static.

'You would do what, plasmancer? Take my command from me? Usurp my rule for your own? I do not forget how you inveigled yourself into this endeavour. Do not outstay your usefulness.'

The plasmancer drifted back and forth a few times before descending to the floor of the chamber, her essence purring with placating outputs.

'Grant me one more chance to seize the citadel without destroying the humans entirely.'

Simut would allow her no more opportunity for distracting manipulation.

'I have made my determination – my will shall now be enacted!' Simut rose from the throne and flung a hand out towards Ah-hotep. The jade beam that lanced from his palm carried the dismissal protocols. The instant they touched her cortical pattern the protocols activated the plasmancer's translocation field. A final stab of desperation from Ah-hotep faded as her body became a green mist and then disappeared, leaving a momentary afterglow in the airless command-mastaba.

It was perhaps a spiteful act, Simut conceded, but the plasmancer needed to be reminded of her position now and then. He was losing patience with her incompetence and passive insubordination.

'Phetos, begin the canoptek reanimation process for Zozar and his legion.'

The royal warden turned to his lord, a wave of revulsion playing across the cortical field.

'I am protocol-driven to request confirmation of that command, Celestial Lord of the Seven Stars,' intoned Phetos. 'I caution against waking the destroyers. Once reanimation has begun the end result is unpredictable. Extended exposure to the skorpekh legion increases the risk of engram degradation of all high echelon nobility.'

'Do it,' said Simut, focusing his attention on the citadel below. On the wall display it grew in size, obliterating all other images, an artificial mount surrounded by crackling energy and blossoms of fire. 'Tell Zozar to kill them all.'

The royal warden's eyes fixed on his master as the imperative was instilled across the cortical bonds.

'He will need no such encouragement, my lord.'

Not since her reawakening had Ah-hotep been so sharply conscious of the emptiness of her tomb ship. Vassal to the command protocols of Simut, its stasis chambers remained dormant, only her presence reflecting back to her from the control matrix.

Alone.

Simut's words bit deep, but not because of their truth. She cared nothing for the transient mortals of the world below. The energy they possessed was of passing interest but their existence was of no concern.

But to speak of the flesh...

The curse they all shared and yet most pretended was a gift. The biotransference to their artificial forms was hailed as an epoch of greatness, and not the vilest trick of the star gods. Yet they all yearned for their mortality once more, in many different ways. Eternity was too high a price to pay for dominion, and many of her fellow nobles had not been able to pay it. Ah-hotep's own lusting after energy was perhaps a surrogate desire. Fulfilment was always beyond her but she craved the acquisition of the energy all the same. Like a flighty, mortal thing after all.

She floated along the empty corridors, lit only by the ghost ambience of her cortical field. She could translocate to anywhere on the ship but that cursed physicality hung upon her as heavy as chains. If one no longer cared for form, what was left but predetermined engrams moving along a nebulous cortical spiral matrix? Mortality had a long legacy and the necrons had not escaped its hold though their bodies had survived for an incomprehensible span of the universe.

Ah-hotep drifted, passing the great soldier dorms where five thousand of her warriors awaited the command to activate. A command she could not issue. Everywhere she sensed the hierolock of Szarekh's dynasty, slaved to the will of Simut.

Her anger – a physical, hot-blooded thing that her wraith-body could no longer fully encapsulate – soared at the thought of the incompetent overlord. The humiliation of pandering to a noble who had in life been vain and stupid, and in afterlife was losing such scant faculties. The Silent King wielded his dynasty with unflinching despotism over those bound to his will in afterlife, their fates sworn to his protocols by inescapable cortical bonds. Hierarchy was absolute, the upper echelon a new elite equal to the nobility that had occupied it at the height of the necrontyr empire.

Her movement brought her into the inner chambers, surrounded by her elite guardians, as useless as inert hunks of rock or bags of flesh that had lost the spark of animus. A legion to command, wasting on the altar of paranoia and jealousy.

But there was one vault open, the door wards deactivated, the portal stone disembodied. Ah-hotep passed within, the seals flaring with power in recognition of her presence, burning briefly in hierograms unknown to any within the Szarekh dynasty.

It was no secret that she was a servant of the enigmatic technomandrites. It was, in truth, her relationship to the arch-engineers of the necrons that had brought her to the gaze of King Szarekh. Courting their favour and seeing her potential, the Silent King had readily agreed to her presence within the matrix expeditions. She wondered if it was simply poor fortune or a degree of cunning circumspection that had seen her placed within the tomb fleet of Simut. Had Szarekh deliberately kept her from the main effort? There was no reason to believe the king harboured any suspicions. If so, he was not the sort to indulge potential traitors, even if they came with the seal of the technomandrites. Simpler to believe that Ah-hotep had been placed with Simut because the king knew his cousin was incompetent.

If only Szarekh had seen fit to give her full access to the command protocols.

Instead she had nothing. She accessed the technomandrite dimensional wave transmitter and processed a fresh missive. There was little of note to report and as always she received no reply, not even an acknowledgement that her signal had been picked up.

Resigned to a future of irrelevancy, she closed the dimensional transmitter and relocated back to the command chamber. On arrival she powered the ship's long-range sensors, ready to observe the distasteful spectacle about to be unleashed.

The wan light of the red sun caught in the pupils of her eyes, trapped there for the longest time. Zozar marvelled at the beauty, letting the sight seep into his every fibre as though he could make the sensation last for eternity.

Cleophatia's happiness was infectious. It lifted his spirit even in these uncertain times. She made it easier to ignore the tumours that riddled her body, drew his mind away from the polyps that punctuated his. There was no sickness in her gaze.

They stood like that for a long time it seemed, together on the slope of the Evermount overlooking the capital. The ruddy light washed over the pyramidal buildings of the city below, catching like laser on capstones, dancing from one vertex to the next as a living thing, a monochrome zephyr that streamed along abandoned streets. All was quiet now. The rioters had no more strength, the rebels had been cowed, the disenfranchised infected no longer possessed the strength for upheaval.

Zozar had wanted no part of it. What was the point of wasting the last of one's life in despair? The end came all the same, and Cleophatia had taught him that it was better to embrace what life there was than to spill it meagrely through one's fingers in bitterness and hostility.

A tug at his tunic brought Zozar's attention down to his daughters, Azella and Isoris. The twins looked up at him, so pure, free of the sun-curse.

'Will it hurt, Father?' asked Isoris. 'The biotransference?'

'It will free us from pain, my dear,' answered Cleophatia while Zozar still contemplated the answer.

He realised that the truth did not matter. His daughter was only seeking assurance, which their mother was so quick to provide. Zozar wished he had that easy emotion, to feel the situation rather than think about it. But then it was the complexity of his intellect that Cleophatia said she loved, drawn to and celebrating their differences, of course. And her warmth passed to him so that sometimes, just sometimes, his engineer-brain was set free from the shackles of logic and just floated on moments of joy. Moments like this one.

'Will it hurt though, Father?' said Azella, the one never quite satisfied by her mother's answers. She was more like him, though possessed of a far more forgiving disposition. 'You helped build it, you should know.'

He looked up at the Evermount and the Great Machine that had been erected at its summit. It was true that he had devised some of its angled walls and projecting antennae, stretching like hands towards the rising sun, but of its real workings he knew little.

'I think it will tickle,' he said, prodding both daughters to elicit squeals of shock and joy. Cleophatia's look of happiness intensified and Zozar's heart throbbed with pride, knowing he had done well in her eyes.

As nobility, albeit of low rank, they would be among the first to enter the biotransference halls. Zozar took his daughters' hands and led them up the marbled pathway, while other families gathered ahead at the gates. He realised he was trembling with excitement and they could sense it too. So close to the end of the pain. Zozar could scarce believe that he had played a small part in the creation of their salvation.

He was torn from his reverie by a strange sensation, like grit in his hands. He rubbed his fingers together, realising he no longer held onto his children. It felt like sand falling from his palms.

Zozar looked down at the two girls. Each was falling apart, slowly disintegrating into dull, ruddy crystals. Flesh became dust, slipping away from a shining metal skeleton beneath.

He looked at his own hands, the gnarled, cancer-ridden digits falling on the breeze too. The sensation crept up his arm, freezing for a moment, leaving a chilled numbness in its wake.

Cleophatia gasped in horror.

He turned his eyes upon his beloved but she looked back not with eyes of love and warmth but the cold red stare of optical lenses.

All three had become animated statues, embodiments of death that he had laboured hard to escape. The Great Machine was meant to free them from the burdens of the flesh, but not like this.

His own body melted away, leaving unfeeling living metal.

Zozar's consciousness found movement, still traumatised by the dreams. The scream inside him stopped before vocalisation. It took a few moments to orientate himself out of the dream state, pushing the terrible vision away.

With comprehension came awareness of his physicality inside the stasis chamber. A tripodal body, skeletal beneath plates of armour. Multiple arms, each beweaponed with gun or blade, pulsing with hatred-turned-energy. The skorpekh lord felt no flesh nor organ, and deep within the construct of his form throbbed an emptiness where his half-remembered soul should have been.

The last tattered vestiges of his loved ones fluttered from thought and the emptiness inside swelled with a different strength. Rage. A rage powered by a loss magnified through the lens of aeons. Rage fuelled by a guilt only known to one that had doomed his love by his own hand.

Rage and hate flowed, crackling across metal bones. All living things would perish in the inferno of his anger. All was ruin and all would be rendered unto ruin for all time.

His despair needed venting or it would consume him.

Zozar the Destroyer had woken.

CHAPTER THREE

The Destroyers created an empty zone in the heart of the stasis decks, like a wound in Simut's extended cortical field. To prevent any potential spread of the Destroyer malaise that made them such unrepentant slaughterers, they were isolated from the rest of the cryptek network. Simut did not care to think what pseudo-emotions thrashed about beyond the boundary zone between his consciousness and that of Zozar and his followers.

A dedicated swarm of canoptek constructs attended to the wakening ceremonies. They too were sequestered from the main body of Simut's minions and would accompany the Destroyer legion down to the surface. Only through several layers of secure canoptek nodes did the data flow of the process reach the overlord, passing through triple-redundant decontamination protocols and a final check by Phetos' subsystems.

When all was prepared Simut received the burst-signal from Zozar, demanding he be released from the final quarantine bonds.

'Power up the translocation arrays!' announced Simut, taking his place upon his throne after some time spent inspecting the display screens. The command pulsed through Phetos and into the tomb ship's computational banks. Dimensional grips sank into the subspaces between the spheres, drawing on a limitless supply of power. Deep within the interior levels of the immense vessel pyramidal transformers stirred into action, turning raw power created by the drift between dimensions into energy that thrummed along the circuits of the mastaba, bathing the lord and his royal warden in its jade glow.

The Destroyer tombs crackled with unleashed power, false lightning leaping from chamber to chamber, coursing along corridors to spear from one canoptek attendant to the next. Within moments the whole zone was awash with molecular distortion as the boundaries of space-time collapsed under the will of Simut.

This was what it meant to be a lord of the necrons. He rejoiced in the feeling of control, the very atoms of existence to be pulled apart and reshaped by his will. Simut paused for the tiniest instant, overcome with the sensation of omnipotence. Once his people had worshipped the star gods, but they had enslaved the deceitful C'tan and stolen that power. Thanks to Szarekh and his dynasty, now it was theirs to command. *They* had become the gods!

+RELEASE ME NOW. LET THE PURGE OF THE LIVING BEGIN.+

Even through banks of defensive rubrics the demand of Zozar was a flash of heat coursing into Simut's cortical field. Made suddenly aware of his momentary delusional lapse into megalomania, the lord was overcome with horror. Such was the route to the mind-death that stalked many of the greatest of the necrons. It was potentially the last abandonment of the search for the flesh-gift they all sought to regain. Embarrassed, though no others had witnessed his moment of weakness for he'd disengaged from direct contact with Phetos, Simut activated the translocational array.

Zozar and his legion became a cloud of particulate matter and information. Carrier waves that ran along the fault lines between dimensions flashed down to the surface of the world to reassemble their datastreams into cogent artefacts, the translocation near-instantaneous.

Nearly instant, but not quite. As beings that now regularly part-existed in the quantum world, even the tiniest fraction of time could be spun out to feel like an eternity. Simut despised translocation and chose to descend physically to his conquered worlds rather than suffer the ignominy – and risk – of atomic dispersal and rebonding. He did not fully understand the process and could never shake the suspicion that the entity that was created at the other end of the carrier wave would not really be him. How could everything that made him Simut, Stormhawk Commander of the Winter Stars, Grand Ruler of Anthothekis and Akapris, survive the translocational journey?

'Translocation is complete, Eagle of the Void, Master of the Unending Stars,' intoned Phetos. He approached the screenwall, head tilting to one side. 'The slaughter has begun.'

There was a slight undercurrent of protest in the words and cortical demeanour of the royal warden. Though his personality protocols ensured he was absolutely loyal to Szarekh, and through that loyalty connected to Simut, there were sub-protocols that gave him leave to critique and advise where needed. Simut had suppressed those reasoning loops as much as he could but it was impossible to eradicate them entirely. Why anyone would want a minion second-guessing their commands was a mystery to him, but apparently some of his fellow nobles did not have his infallible intellect to rely upon.

'There is a problem, Phetos?'

Simut leaned forward, magnifying the image of the wall as he did so. He saw smoke already rising from several buildings close to the centre of the human settlement. Zozar's Destroyer-tainted warriors had begun their attack without delay. Zozar led the march, his weapons spitting bolts of gauss fire, his tripodal guard following close behind. Other warriors had transformed themselves into floating monstrosities, eschewing motive limbs altogether. Gauss rifles and cannons crackled disintegrating jade beams through the shuffling mass of the human population, flaying their atoms apart as the beams passed from one target to the next in a near-continuous assault. Behind the most altered members of Zozar's cabal came a phalanx of slaved skeletal warriors, driven by the same urge to slay as their master but dispossessed of the individual sense of self that drove other Destroyers to modify their bodies away from the necron norm. They split into squads, empowered by the skorpekh lord's imperative to slay, and roamed at will through the streets and buildings killing everything they encountered.

'The Destroyers are slaying the general populace, my lord.'

'It was impossible to translocate Zozar within the energy fields and astromantic bubble of the citadel,' replied Simut. 'Some collateral damage was inevitable.'

'The loss of lower life is no cause of regret, my lord. While King Szarekh has ordered that the lower beings are preserved where that does not place unnecessary delay on the expedition, they are plentiful. My concern is that Zozar's legion seems to be moving *away* from the citadel, not towards it.'

Simut saw that this was the case and wondered how he had not realised immediately. Phetos must have distracted him. The general trail of destruction ran perpendicular to the required axis of attack, at best, and in places the Destroyers were getting further and further from their objective.

'I want a secure communications link with Zozar now!'

He continued to watch while Phetos parted the dimensions to create a nil-space connection between the tomb ship and Zozar's cortical field. The bigger weapons of the fortress were firing on the Destroyers, but with little effect. Their living metal bodies and the unifying presence of Zozar made them highly resistant to even the heaviest armaments of the humans. Even those that were struck directly only suffered temporary incapacitation. Canoptek attendants moved from casualty to casualty, rebinding shattered bodies, slewing together fragments of living metal to reconstitute the fallen.

The other humans were starting to react in a vague, herd-like way, responding to the threat on a base level that even the overnull effect could not eradicate, driven by unsuppressed chemical interactions in their brain stems. Most reacted too slowly to evade the strobing gauss beams, but as a mass the populace was moving outwards from the site of the attack, like a slow but inexorable ripple from a rock dropped in a pool.

+THE SLAUGHTER HAS COMMENCED. NO SURVIVORS. ALL SENTIENCE WILL BE EXTERMINATED.+

'No!' Simut slammed a hand down on the arm of his throne, the gesture turned into a pulse of rebuke across the communications link. 'You will attack the citadel! Adjust your assault tangent, you slaughter-brained fool!'

+ALL MUST BE DESTROYED. ZOZAR IS THE DESTROYER.+

'Attack citations transmitted, my lord,' the royal warden reported as a pulse of data flowed across the link. 'Zozar, the enemy within the fortress cannot escape you but they will try to fight you. They must be destroyed. All resistance must be quelled.'

+RESISTANCE MUST BE QUELLED. THE FORTRESS MUST BE PURGED OF LIFE.+

'Yes,' crowed Simut. 'Destroy the defenders of the citadel. All of them!'

+IT SHALL BE DONE.+

Guided by the renewed will of the lord, the Destroyers changed direction immediately, pulling back from their attacks to focus on the shield-swathed fortification. Squads of warriors and teams of Destroyers returned to the vicinity of Zozar, accompanied by their floating and scurrying canoptek allies.

'See, they are ready now,' said Simut, looking at Phetos. 'By my will the citadel shall fall.'

'Masterful, my lord,' replied the royal warden. 'Your victory is assured.'

When the energy screens fell, the citadel was doomed. Towering above his feeble opponents, Zozar led the final charge into the heart of the humans' armoured nest. His slaved warriors advanced around the base of the fortress, cutting off all escape from the gates, while anti-gravitic Destroyers rose along the walls to intercept any craft attempting to leave.

The corridors within were lit by erratic electrical circuits, flickering from the interrupted energy flow. The blast of laser and flash of chemical weapons discharge strafed brightly across Zozar's senses, every glimmer bringing a momentary flicker of remembrance. He saw her face in reflective surfaces, lit by the plasma hail of his foes. He even saw it on their distended, unworthy bodies, their disgusting features twisted to her beautiful looks.

It was all false. It all had to be destroyed to preserve the memory etched into his engrammatic matrix. That was truth. All else was lies, an affront to her purity.

He fired pulses of condensed energy into their flesh, turning bonded molecules to flares of radiation and spreading matter. His energy-edged blade split apart their organic components without resistance, cell shock spreading like a virus from the wound site to evaporate their bodies. Phased to a different dimensional resonance than that occupied by their physical bodies, even those humans that bore a semblance of armour had no defence against the lethal sweeps.

Lifeblood painted the walls in splashes of vivid dissipating heat but there was no pleasure to be taken from the carnage, no artistry in the killing. There was only the rage, no joy. When all was slain, when the memory was safe at last, there would be peace. Until then there would be no relent, and Zozar would be the scourge of all sentient life.

His Destroyers were an extension of his hate. Each had been touched by his grief and found a loss of their own, a seed of anger from which his will could spring unfettered into their thoughts. Their worlds had orbited stars millions of times since they had lost their loved ones, since they had been shamed, since they had been fooled by the promises of the star gods and their own nobles. An eternity to their former selves, rendered a deathless sleep by the artifice of the soul-theft.

Emptiness. Emptiness ruled. Not to be filled by the designs and desires of the ghoulish flesh-wearers, nor ignored by the transcendent post-life canoptek engine-folk. What was lost could never be regained. It was not flesh and blood, to be put on like a fresh robe. The sanctity of being, the soul that had carried their lives and their meaning, had been taken away. Only nothingness held refuge, but there could be no oblivion while life still remained.

A highly energetic pulse caught Zozar on the arm. The star-heat briefly glistened across artificial bones, melting the limb.

He turned, focused the ire of his cannon on the human wielding the armament. Ultrasenses detected the magnetic and radiative pulses coming from the gun's harnessing chamber. Rudimentary fields kept ravening energy at bay.

A captured star in miniature.

The reminder set a fresh tide of rage piling up through Zozar's cortical field, flaring from his weapon as a bolt of disintegrating force. The human disappeared, the wall behind seared in a faint outline of their running form.

There was only the most basic strategy to the attack. Defensive walls had become the jaws of the trap, and it was simply a matter of time before annihilation was accomplished. Counter-attacks and stiffer resistance shaped the Destroyers' advance, but they gave no heed to their own preservation except with the thought that total destruction would be delayed by their demise. Those counter-attacks that threatened to stall the slaughter were met and quashed with overwhelming force. The pockets of resistance were surrounded and extinguished.

Zozar had a faint sense that the higher he climbed, the higher the ranks of the foes he would face. Humans often conflated hierarchy with physical position. He no longer cared for such things. Kings and slaves still perpetrated the crime of life in equal measure.

The noticeable consequence was an improvement in the armour and weaponry of those that fell before his attack. Several times he was forced to pause for canoptek assistance, his assumed form suffering increasing amounts of critical damage.

Each delay served only to spur on his rage.

+ALL MUST BE DESTROYED.+

He came upon a broad hall decked with unruly astromantic symbols. Since biotransference, he had possessed no psychic presence, his soul severed by the means with which his consciousness had been biotransferred into the construct of living metal that had sustained him over the aeons. He mourned its loss, though he could not recall what it felt like to have a soul. It was the principle of the theft that had driven him insane.

So it was with purely cold intellect that he surveyed the inscriptions on the domed chamber, following their symbols and spirals towards a faceted crystal lens at the summit of the ceiling. His senses registered a lack of heat in comparison to the rest of the citadel. Light-detecting arrays picked up stray sparks of high-wavelength emissions. Through the anger he reasoned that perhaps a being with a soul might *feel* something about the environment.

When he had first woken, Zozar had spent a considerable amount of time abducting sentients to analyse their psychic make-up. He had questioned them at length about their feelings, delving beyond systemic biochemical responses to expose the very depths of true emotion. It had been the approach of an engineer, to break apart the problem to understand it, in the hopes that it would contain the solution for its own rebuilding.

He had come to one madness-inducing conclusion.

There was no cure for the biotransference. Whatever plans and dreams the likes of Szarekh thought up, Zozar knew that they could no more harness their lost souls than they could grip the vacuum itself.

There was nothing left to grasp.

His distraction ceased, drawing his attention to the hall's two occupants. Humans. Average height, breadth and mass. They were clad in robes from head to foot, scalps hidden beneath cowls. A flash of memory brought back a vision of his wedding day, the arbitrator clad in similar garb, though adorned with more care than the dishevelled examples before him.

The two of them clasped each other, heads turning back and forth as though scanning the room. Magnification exposed the lack of bio-electrical data flowing from their eye sockets.

They were blind.

Zozar also registered soundwaves emanating from the two humans. He activated a translator protocol, curious to see what the humans were saying in their last moments. Perhaps their death-confessions would shed some secret on the nature of souls.

'The death-in-metal has arrived. A mind-infection malaise-soul disperses fully among the populace. There will be no more. This is ending. Only the power-astromancy-soul has kept us alive in this justice-building-protective-enclave-sanctuary. No more. It is ending. There is no saviour. A warning. Protect others. A warning. Protect others. Death-in-metal walks among our people. Our praises herald the strength of the lord-of-heavens-ruler-guide-protector-eagle-of-vengeance.'

Zozar comprehended that this was not just a prayer to their divinity – the Emperor-Being – but also a constructed message. The entire chamber was an astromantic amplifier. A beacon of sorts, perhaps, or a communications device.

He shut off the audio input and flexed his blades, crossing the hall with a few purposeful strides.

All sentience had to perish.

Peace demanded it.

It was strange to Ah-hotep how much failure could masquerade as victory. From the ruins of the human citadel, she watched the blackstone resonator descending to its resting place close to the outer wall. The ground had been razed to a near-mirror finish, foundations laid by canoptek vassal teams so that the immense structure would slot neatly into place. Even deactivated the blackstone was pulling the edges of the overnull further, separating the reality of existence from the unreality of nightmare, as planned by Szarekh. Another star system subjugated to the great plan. The humans were all but mindless now, yet still the butchery of the skorpekh lord and his Destroyers continued. The over-lord seemed unconcerned that his attempts thus far to halt the rampage had been ignored.

Not far away Simut also observed the proceedings, dressed in full battle panoply and accompanied by his lychguard. Phetos was closer to the contact site, providing the overlord with a secondary experience of the occasion. Other such ephemera of status – cryptothralls and canoptek activators – attended in lines, and behind them the ranked might of the Szarekh phalanx under Simut's command. They stood in the rubble of the citadel among the mangled, bloating corpses of the defenders gathering flies and other carrion-scavengers. Overhead crescent-shaped attack craft flew victory flights about the approaching needle of darkness, while higher up in orbit the tomb fleet attended to the moment of the master's conquest.

On the surface it was a celebration, but Ah-hotep knew that the reality was different. Casualties had been far higher than necessary, among the regular legion and the Destroyers. Had Simut not interfered in her campaign the citadel would have fallen with the minimum of effort, but the overlord was utterly unaware of his own incompetence. Zozar's slaughter was an inevitable and entirely pointless consequence of that ineptitude. She wondered if other branches of the expedition were led by similar mediocre talents, and if many more appropriate generals were held back by the Silent King's need to place trusted confidants in positions of power.

It was a weakness to be exploited, that much was certain, but Ah-hotep was not yet sure how. Szarekh's iron control and Simut's ignorant para-noia made taking any military assets impossible. Forced to do what she could with such scraps of authority and materiel the overlord left to her, Ah-hotep was in a poor position to effect any change to their strategy, nor to rise in prominence within the dynastic hierarchy. The very inadequacies of the master to which she had been assigned was preventing her from fulfilling greater potential for her true lords in the technomandrite ranks.

With a soundwave that rumbled through the city, the resonator entered the docking port and made planetfall. Sliding down into the prepared structures, it shed its descender harness, the living metal fall-ing to ribbons of shining sapphire before disintegrating completely.

At the moment its base made contact with the surface of the world, the blackstone shifted state. Where before it had merely been black, an absolute darkness that reflected no light, now it glowed with an anti-light. It seemed to become a hole in reality, though in truth it was the opposite of a gateway; it had become a barrier. Aligned to the astromantic axis of the planet, the resonator reconfigured itself, facets and plates shifting in complex cosmometric patterns to distort the null-field projected into the star system from other nearby resonators. Like a rudimentary navigation device finding a magnetic pole, the resonator adjusted through multidimensional realities to assume a nodal form, both receiving and broadcasting the overnull signal.

An emerald aura encapsulated the towering needle, bathing the ruins and lines of metallic warriors in its green hue. Rings of pulsing energy ascended the tapering structure, accelerating as they reached the tip to become a blazing storm that leapt jaggedly into the heavens.

The resonator seemed to be operating properly on the physical plane. On the psychic front, Ah-hotep had to trust to the expertise of Szarekh's dimensioneers. Like all of the necrons, her soul had been severed from her physical incarnation during the biotransfer process. She literally felt nothing as the physical world and the neversea were shorn from each other by the intrusion of the overnull. The humans, the few of them remaining, would know it, though. In the last vestiges of their soul they would feel the coldness descending, the spark of animus that gave them sentience drifting away to nothing.

'Another world falls to the glory of the Szarekh dynasty!' declared Simut, raising up his battleblade as if he had personally conquered the world.

There was little glory, in truth. Corralling or killing lower beings rendered thoughtless by the overnull barely constituted a war. Not that Ah-hotep cared. Conquerors and kings could define their own achievements, as long as there was a plentiful supply of energy on which to feast afterwards.

While the legion started translocating back to orbit, ready to move on to the next star system to be folded into the overnull, Ah-hotep drifted towards the heart of the citadel, where her senses told her a thermic reactor was still operational. All other considerations fell away – the politics of the dynasty, the great cosmic plan of the Silent King and her own loyalties and ambitions were as nothing when weighed against the desire of finally being able to feed.

CHAPTER FOUR

The atmosphere in the captain's chamber was sombre when Praxamedes passed through the door. Aeschelus was within, alongside Nemetus and the head of the Navigators aboard the *Ithraca's Vengeance*, Antoansal Kosa D'Fidas. The two Space Marines, like Praxamedes, were dressed in their robes – Ultramarines symbol in silver upon the right breast, gilded cuffs and lapels denoting their ranks.

Kosa also wore official vestments, of a far flimsier and brighter material – a pale yellow that was matched by the iris of the eye symbol painted onto her metal headband. The headband broadened over her brow, concealing all of her forehead and, most importantly, the third eye that sat within. Her facial extremities – nostrils, ear lobes, lips – were all pierced with small rings of gold, which made her whole visage gleam in the lumen-light of the long, narrow chamber. Rings, bracelets and chains of the same hung on fingers, wrists and hands, a throwback to the ancient days when status was displayed by shows of wealth realised as hard-to-obtain minerals. Even now gold still held its appeal to those that wanted to flaunt their rank, despite – or perhaps because of – its lack of wider utility.

Though artificially tall, another by-product of her genetically engineered inheritance, Kosa was a stick-thin figure in comparison to the massive bulk of the Primaris Marines. The biceps of the warriors, straining at their sleeves, were almost as broad as her chest. Her neck was long, giving her a slightly birdlike appearance as she shifted her attention from one Space Marine to the next in quick, nervous movements.

She paced rather than sitting on one of the chairs, which were oversized for the benefit of the Space Marines. The Navigator seemed almost childlike among the larger furniture, no doubt feeling out of place and wishing she was still in the isolated pilaster she shared with the other two Navigators assigned to the cruiser.

The room was functionally furnished, a circular table at one end, a cot at the other with a bookshelf containing expanded, annotated volumes of the Codex Astartes and other Chapter cult volumes. There was a small gold-leaf icon of the lord primarch above the metal headboard, its frame burnished bright by recent polishing. Flanking the portrait were several medals, the genuine awards of which facsimiles were painted on the captain's armour – an iron halo, the laurels of command, the campaign badge of the Indomitus Crusade and a gilt-edged blood drop from when he had been injured at Sethemian Tide. Honours that would have graced nearly any commander's dorm, Praxamedes realised. Nothing of particular note.

'We are going too slow,' announced Aeschelus, glaring at the Navigator. 'We have confirmed our latest translation point as system Omega-Four-Seven-Hercules.'

'A dead system. Wilderness space.' Nemetus leaned forward, fists resting on the chamfered metal of the captain's table. 'Nothing to fight.'

'Seven light years short of Clarion-Sigma,' said Praxamedes, mentally picturing the sector map. 'Only barely halfway to our destination after experience-relative seventeen days of travel.'

'And thirty-nine days actual temporal shift,' added Aeschelus.

'You must understand the scale of the task you ask of us,' said Kosa. 'I have told you before that you cannot use travel determinations that were calculated before the coming of the Cicatrix Maledictum. That we have traversed any spatial distance at all is remarkable, given the warp conditions through which we have been travelling.'

'Oh, you want praise instead?' said Aeschelus. 'Perhaps you would like me to despatch honours to the lord commander for your efforts?'

Kosa said nothing but glowered at the captain's suggestion.

'You gave assurances that as your experience with the conditions improved, so too would our jump distances,' said Praxamedes, sitting himself between the captain and Nemetus. 'That seems to have been an error.'

'No, I stand by the promise,' said Kosa. 'We are getting better, but you need to understand what you have been asking of me and my kin. The whole galaxy is in such turmoil that our charts are almost meaningless. Even the light of the Emperor, the holy Astronomican, is sometimes shrouded from us by the intensity of the storms that engulf the Imperium.'

'We are not alone in this experience, and yet other battle groups, other crusade fleets, make speedier passage than us,' said Nemetus.

'You are being too cautious,' said Aeschelus. 'We make little progress because you drop us back from the warp after such small jumps.'

Kosa laughed bitterly, a finger moving to fidget with the rings through the lobe of her left ear. Her yellow eyes regarded each of them for just a moment before settling on a spot somewhere on the wall behind the captain.

'Cautious?' Scorn dripped from the Navigator's tone, unlike anything Praxamedes had heard from her before. 'We travel across the greatest upheaval to the warp that has occurred since... The chronicles of the Navis Nobilite go back far indeed, to the only other time that the Imperium has been so sundered. A product of the vilest sorcery, it was known as the Ruinstorm and it heralded the near-destruction of the Emperor's domains. Not for five hundred generations has it been more perilous to cross the othersea. If you think we are cautious, it is an accusation I am happy to bear, Captain Aeschelus.'

'Caution did not win the Heresy War,' growled the ship's commander. 'Caution will not push back the forces that besiege the Imperium now. Caution will see us stranded and isolated while our enemies close their grip on all that they hope to steal from the Emperor.'

'And still I would not plunge us headlong into the fastest course to save a handful of days, and risk the ship arriving at all.'

'If we are not cautious, we do not have to be reckless,' added Praxamedes. 'There is hopefully some middle ground to be found between our needs and your concerns, Navis Majoris.'

The Navigator took a shuddering breath, hands trembling as she slowly closed them into fists. Her gaze looked to the ceiling for several heartbeats before she could turn her eyes back to the others in the room.

'The longer we remain in the othersea, the less certain we can be of our position and destination. The faster the current we follow, the greater the risk that we will be swept away or miss our translation point. Every manoeuvre is fraught with peril among these roiling ebbs and flows. If we should lose contact with the Beacon of Terra at the wrong juncture it would be disastrous. You ask us to thread a needle in the darkness while tossed and turned by a whirlwind. I cannot warn against it too strongly.'

'But there are faster currents to use?' said Nemetus. 'It is possible to travel further with each jump?'

Kosa said nothing.

'All of us must strive to give our utmost to the crusade,' said Aeschelus. 'None are excused the labour. I am ordering you to make swifter progress, Navigator.'

'An order?' Kosa smoothed the folds of her robe. 'What would you command, captain? How can you stand in judgement of our decisions when you are not capable of seeing what we see? Would you debate the nature of plasma drives with your chief enginseer?'

'I would if I thought there was a deficiency in their operation,' Aeschelus replied calmly. He laid his broad hands on the tabletop, flattening the palms against the metal. 'Your house gains renown and reward for its part in this endeavour. I imagine a censure from the lord commander would dampen the spirits of your kin. To be removed from position would be a grave matter. Perhaps your reputation would never recover.'

'Threats, captain?'

'Your reluctance forces me to say what is normally unspoken. The bonds between your house and the Chapter go back generations, but they are worthless if they do not provide what I need. I do not doubt your loyalty, Navigator, but your desire to stay safe is too much.'

'It is all of our lives we risk,' snapped Kosa. 'Not just those of the Navigators.'

'This is a warship. It exists to push along the boundary between risk and reward. My warriors cannot do our duty unless your Navigators do better. If that cannot be done, I will find a civilian vessel for you at our next dock.'

Praxamedes watched the Navigator closely. He had spent enough time among the unaugmented humans of the command deck that he could recognise the to and fro of emotions playing out in the thoughts of Kosa. She looked at the captain and saw no flinch in his gaze. Her eyes then sought momentary alliance from Praxamedes, but he shared no sign of support for her. The captain was right; progress was too timid for effective action.

Finally, the Navigator's gaze dropped to her hands, held together at her waist.

'As you bid, captain,' she said quietly. 'On our next jump we shall endeavour to push harder to our destination. We shall seek the faster, more turbulent channels and trust to our powers that we will survive them.' Kosa looked up then, steel hardening once more. 'But under protest only. My oaths are to guide this ship safely through the warp, and to offer such prayers to the Master of the Light that will do so. I wish it to be noted in the records that one cannot win a battle if one does not safely reach it.'

'As you wish, Navigator.' Aeschelus stood up. 'I am captain and all responsibility falls to me eventually. This is my will and the records shall make that known.'

The Navigator nodded and departed with quick steps and a sour demeanour.

Aeschelus let out an explosive breath and it was only then that Praxamedes saw how much of an effort of patience it had been for his captain to treat reasonably with Kosa. Since the debacle with the Despoiler-class battleship, he had been looking for a fresh challenge. Ninety-two-days-perceived had passed since withdrawing from that disastrous episode. Ninety-two days of jumping from dead system to dead system seeking an enemy that appeared to have vanished.

'I do not understand what is happening,' said Nemetus, leaning back. 'Our astropaths tell us that this sector was awash with the enemy when we broke away from the main fleet, but now it seems like they have all disappeared.'

'The astropaths are as perturbed by the warp storms as the Navigators,' replied Praxamedes. 'Who knows how long ago some of those broadcasts were sent? Many have been echoing through the rifts and peaks of the warp since the renewed invasions began.'

'There is something else here,' said Aeschelus. 'A sudden cessation of noise and enemy movements. I cannot believe that they have simply turned back, so we must assume they are hiding something, gathering in force. We have been tasked with locating those threats and locate them we will. The Emperor is not short of foes – we will find one soon enough.'

The hiss of the strategium doors drew Praxamedes' attention to the arrival of Captain Aeschelus. It was not yet time for the lieutenant to step down from watch; nearly thirty minutes remained before Aeschelus was due to stand as command officer. Praxamedes said nothing as his superior started a slow circuit of the stations, inspecting each in turn. Some of the deck officers cast glances at the captain, confused by his unexpected perusal.

Here and there, Aeschelus muttered some comment or slight rebuke about a terminal or its officer. Of late he had withdrawn into himself, stern and critical of the smallest error. His presence on the strategium was like the foreshadowing of a storm that never quite broke, a build of tension that never found release. The deck officers were diligent and loyal but Praxamedes could see that the unnecessary scrutiny and stress was beginning to take its toll.

It was true across other areas of the ship too. The captain's mood, restrained as it was, influenced everything aboard *Ithraca's Vengeance*, from the command bridge to the engines to the gun decks and all between. The lack of action that nagged at him was beginning to wear on the battle-brothers too. It was quite extraordinary that they had encountered no opposition since the Despoiler-class ship. No relent from the monotony of each other's company, nor from the roving eye of Aeschelus seeking any small infraction to provide a momentary break from the tedium.

'Brother-captain?' Praxamedes stepped away from the command throne to intercept his superior before he arrived at the vox console. 'Is anything amiss?'

'Nothing,' growled Aeschelus. He looked at Praxamedes with a grimace. 'Other than the obvious.'

'It's quite inexplicable, brother-captain.' The lieutenant stepped back towards the command position and Aeschelus moved with him. 'You can be assured that I'll notify you immediately if there's anything of import.'

'I would rather spend my time here than rotting away in that chamber,' sighed the captain, folding his arms across his barrel chest. 'I heard over the vox that Fedualis is due to make a report, yes?'

'The astropath is on his way. It's probably only routine communications.'

Aeschelus rumbled a non-committal reply in his throat.

'On a positive note, the Navigators are making better speed, brother-captain,' Praxamedes said, feeling the need to fill the grim silence left by his superior. 'They say we are approaching the Alekra System, crossing over into the Hyperio-Prime Sector.'

Aeschelus grunted his acceptance of this comment but offered nothing else. He sat down in the command throne, though he had not officially dismissed Praxamedes from the watch. The lieutenant wondered if he should volunteer this fact and decided against it – though he was not as affected by the inaction as his superior, he was not wholly immune to the lack of duties.

Praxamedes spent such spare time as he had re-reading his copies of the Codex Astartes, assembling his own notations on the text. Between that and weapons drill he tried to keep his mind active. A few times he had run tactical simulations with Nemetus but the other lieutenant always took his losses poorly, complaining that the battle-system orthodoxy did not allow him the full range of options that he would exploit in real combat. He had been quite scathing in his last comments, and though Nemetus had apologised later Praxamedes had decided not to conduct any more exercises with his fellow lieutenant.

The doors opened again and it was with some relief that Praxamedes greeted Astropath Neriem Fedualis. His green robes of office just skimmed the floor, the hood drawn up over his bald, wrinkled scalp. Eyeless sockets, the organs burnt out by the ritual soulbinding to the spirit of the Emperor, regarded the two officers as though seeing normally. He crossed the strategium with short, quick strides.

'Ah, captain, it is good that you are also here. I was going to ask the lieutenant to send for you.' The astropath spoke with a husky voice, as though constantly on the verge of trying to catch his breath. He never showed any other signs of ill health and Praxamedes just assumed it was some congenital or childhood-acquired condition, or another side effect of his psychic tethering.

'You have news of an enemy?' Aeschelus said quickly, standing up. 'A message through the storms?'

'Messages, yes, of foes and friends,' the astropath said, clasping his hands together so that they disappeared into the voluminous cuffs of his robe. 'More precisely, a missive from the grand fleet command and a vision of terrible events.'

Aeschelus rubbed his chin with the back of his hand. 'I suppose you had best share the message from command first,' the captain admitted. 'A call to arms?'

As they spoke, they walked towards the anterium, a smaller chamber that adjoined the strategium on the starboard side. Moving within, the door closed behind them, cutting off the noise of the main bridge.

The chamber was pale grey, lined with secondary vox, control and augur banks, so that the command could operate entirely independent of the main strategium. Praxamedes settled on a high stool beside the gunnery command console, while Aeschelus stood, arms still crossed. The astropath stepped to the far end of the rectangular space and turned, eyeless gaze fixed on the captain.

'This is a direct broadcast from the astropathic channel at Battle Group Command, currently located on the *Dominus Acastai.*'

Fedualis sagged within his robes, head tilting back as his eye sockets started to gleam with golden light, bathing the inside of his hood. His hands fell to his sides, and for a few seconds he swayed, looking as though he might faint.

The golden light strengthened, as did the astropath's posture. Words started leaving his lips, almost inaudible at first. It was a stream of seeming gibberish to Praxamedes, but he knew that in fact the non-sense syllables were identifiers and calibrating terms prefacing the main message.

The astropath's demeanour changed, straightening, his face assuming a more attentive aspect. When he spoke, Fedualis' voice was his own – but as though used by another. His mind was subservient to the content of the psychic broadcast, so that his lips and tongue became those of another many light years away. What was even more remarkable to Praxamedes, when he considered the miracle of astrotelepathy, was the fact that the puppet-master that had sent the broadcast had done so hours or days ago. The consciousness that animated Fedualis' flesh was a detached thought that had ridden the waves of the warp on its own, to be drawn to the mind of the receiving astropath.

'Message direct from Battle Group Commander Reghus Nor. For personal attention of Captain Aeschelus, Ultramarines Chapter, or commanding officer of the *Ithraca's Vengeance*. Current duties are withdrawn. The *Ithraca's Vengeance* is to rendezvous with an incoming Imperial fleet at Duriem Six with all possible speed. Once united, the *Ithraca's Vengeance* will liaise with officers of the fleet, designated command group Dacedus. The captain and crew to attend to all support needs of the incoming fleet until further notice under the auspices of Admiral V'dag. I hereby commend this message to the void, certified faithful, astropath-prime on behalf of Battle Group Commander Reghus Nor.'

Fedualis shuddered as the presence receded, his eye sockets dimming again. Praxamedes shifted his gaze to his brother-captain, who was staring at the astropath with his jaw clenched and brow furrowed.

'Escort and liaison…' The captain hissed the words. 'Commanded by an Imperial Navy admiral.'

'It must be a significant offensive, if it requires a full cruiser's complement to attend,' said Praxamedes.

'Did you not hear what I heard?' Aeschelus shook his head, finding it hard to acknowledge the content of the broadcast. 'Duriem Six is at least a thousand light years behind the main advance. It is a rear echelon station.'

'As most staging ports are, brother-captain,' said Praxamedes, still failing to see the cause for his superior's reaction. 'The arrival of a fresh admiral could be significant.'

'To the Imperial Navy!' snapped Aeschelus. 'We are Ultramarines, fighting for the primarch and the Emperor. You have spent too much time away from the command echelons to recognise a rebuke when you see one.'

This time it was Praxamedes' turn to shake his head, opening his mouth mutely, with no further comment to offer and wishing not to argue with his captain.

'They are taking away my independent command, lieutenant.'

Suddenly it became clear. Praxamedes had spent a year in charge of a fast-response frigate, but otherwise had always been beneath the pinnacle of the ship hierarchy. It hadn't occurred to him that there was a degree of pride to be taken in operating outside the conventional fleet command system. Aeschelus' determination to make a significant contribution to the effort was a way of proving himself worthy of that independence.

'You had another vision?' the lieutenant said, looking at Fedualis to change the subject of conversation. It would give the captain a little more time to absorb the facts of their new assignment.

The astropath had been watching the exchange in silence, strained from the effort of releasing the psychic message. He took a moment before responding, caught out by the question.

'Ah, yes, a fragmentary burst. Almost missed it among the froth and churn around us.' Fedualis fidgeted with his cuffs. 'Disturbing, but inconclusive.'

'Origin?' said Aeschelus.

'The Casparill System, I think. As I say, it's very choppy, not so much a deliberate broadcast as a shared-dream.' The life seemed to drain from his face as he continued, 'It ends abruptly, which is to say it seems highly likely the origin was cut off during transmission.'

'The astropath was killed?' said Praxamedes.

'Astropaths,' corrected Fedualis, swallowing hard. 'Two of them. They soul-linked, in desperation. Strange that it was not the full choir. I can feel both of them, but there is an odd flatness about it. No texture. Like watching a scene reflected on armourglass.'

'But it was a call for help?' said Aeschelus, moving closer, taking notice of the conversation after a few moments of detachment. 'The Casparill System, you said.'

'Thereabouts,' the astropath replied uncertainly. 'And it felt more like a warning. Scared. Terrified, in fact.'

Aeschelus stepped towards the secondary navigation terminal.

'Ninety light years from our last confirmed position, brother-captain,' said Praxamedes, guessing his superior's intent. Aeschelus looked surprised at the volunteered information. Praxamedes smiled briefly. 'I've had quite a bit of time to study the charts of the neighbouring sectors closely...'

'The distortion, captain, does not bode well.' Fedualis stepped up to the small, blank hololith table and placed his hands on the glassy surface. He moved them outwards, as though parting water. 'A reflection, perhaps. Casparill might not be the originating system at all, just where it met some kind of warp lens and bounced in a strange way.'

'I need to hear it,' said Aeschelus.

'There is nothing of substance, captain.' The astropath retreated from the Space Marine, alarmed at the suggestion. 'It could be centuries old.'

'Or days. I want to hear it for myself. Can you do that?'

Fedualis looked as though he might decline but then relented, shoulders sagging. He darted a look of appeal at Praxamedes, eye sockets empty but still full of emotion. The lieutenant had nothing to offer him.

'Very well, captain.'

The ambient temperature in the room dropped, frosting the air directly around the astropath as he tapped into his psychic potential. Praxamedes assumed a pose of watchfulness, acutely aware that they were in the warp. The Geller field was nominal but he had heard too many stories of intrusions and influence leaking through. The lieutenant visualised exactly how he would seize and break the astropath's neck at the first sign of anything going awry.

Fedualis trembled, the tremor in his hands moving to the rest of his body, becoming a spasm that sent his head twitching from side to side, arms jerking outwards. His tongue worked at dark gums, rolling over the stubs of teeth, while his wrinkled throat bobbed with repeated swallowing. Praxamedes sensed the captain looking at him but did not take his eyes off the astropath to return the glance.

With a shriek, Fedualis fell backwards to the tiled deck, heels banging the floor, hands scrabbling at empty air in front of him. His gestures left faint traceries of shadow in their wake, giving the illusion of something else with him, another humanoid figure within his jerking embrace. There was something wholly disturbing about his movements, which even the psychoconditioning of a Space Marine could not wholly expunge. Looking at the faltering, ghastly display, Praxamedes wanted to step in and crush the man's skull, ending it. Resisting that urge, he realised what was so unsettling. The astropath's motions seemed like they were in reverse, like a vid-feed being wound back to its start.

With a gurgling cry, Fedualis flailed to his feet, gasping for air, lips drawn back from his teeth. A voice issued from him, though it seemed not to come from throat or mouth, but out of the air itself. Two voices in fact, not quite speaking in unison, one male and the other female, and yet both somehow also Fedualis'.

'Xenos have arrived. A psychic virus or warp distortion has spread to nearly everyone on the planet. The final attack is beginning; we cannot resist it. Only the astropathic choir has kept the effect at bay, with the guns of the Adeptus Arbites precinct and defence forces to protect us. No more. All but two of us are dead. Nobody is coming. Beware. Guard yourselves. Beware. Guard yourselves. The xenos are stealing our minds, invading without resistance. Praise the God-Emperor that He delivers you from this coming nightmare.'

A fog-like emanation seeped from the astropath while he spoke, forming shapes out of the air. Curls of vapour sketched the idea of two figures around him, clasping one another. In the periphery half-formed blades wove, getting closer. Praxamedes tensed, ready to act should the apparition threaten any physical harm. The claw-swords struck, shredding the fog into streamers that flew about Fedualis, creating a last view of screaming faces whirling around him.

As it dissipated the aura carved one last vision into the air. A chamfered-cheeked skull, utterly inhuman, looming over everything.

The psychic gleam faded and the astropath fell to his knees, wracked by choking sobs.

'Ninety light years to Casparill…' the captain muttered, his gaze fixed on the dishevelled psyker.

'From our last realspace translation,' the lieutenant answered on reflex. He caught on to his superior's intent. 'We have orders from fleet command, brother-captain. If we fail to meet with the Imperial Navy fleet, it could disrupt an entire battle group offensive.'

'You saw that,' Aeschelus waved towards the astropath, 'and you think we should slink away to a rendezvous, Praxamedes?'

'It's not a personal opinion, brother-captain. It's the instruction of the Codex Astartes. We're not under immediate threat and this isn't a credible call. Our orders were clear.'

'Not credible?' Aeschelus helped the astropath to his feet. 'What was that? Play-acting?'

'We don't know if it really was from Casparill, or even if it was a recent event. There's nothing to suggest the xenos threat will be there when we arrive, or if it was ever there. Fedualis, you need to re-broadcast the vision to Battle Group Command. It is up to them to determine a suitable response.'

'You will broadcast to Battle Group Command that the *Ithraca's Vengeance* is responding to an emergent threat in the Casparill System,' said Aeschelus, stepping back from Fedualis. The astropath looked from the captain to Praxamedes and back again.

'You do not understand, captain. It was a warning, not a call for aid. If it was Casparill, there is nothing to be done. I felt the astropaths' despair. They were about to die and knew that their world was doomed.'

'Other worlds may be threatened,' said Aeschelus. 'By the time we send word to command and receive new orders, or a different ship is despatched, another Imperial world may have fallen to the xenos. We are Space Marines! This is why we are on crusade, to push back these dark forces!'

Praxamedes wanted to say that the role of the Adeptus Astartes was far more complex than it had been in previous decades. They were part of a massive offensive, an endeavour involving not just many Chapters but hundreds of Imperial Navy starships and millions of Astra Militarum personnel. The *Ithraca's Vengeance* was not the captain's personal steed, to chase after whatever shadows flickered across the starlight.

He wanted to say that, but knew he could not. Instead, he bowed his acquiescence.

'I'll inform the Navigators of our new destination, brother-captain.'

'Good.' Aeschelus turned away, focused on Fedualis. 'Are you ready to broadcast, astropath?'

Fedualis took in a ragged breath and nodded with resignation. Praxamedes headed towards the strategium and as the doors closed caught the captain's opening words.

'This is Captain Aeschelus of the *Ithraca's Vengeance*. We have been presented with an opportunity to strike–'

The doors grumbled closed behind the lieutenant. He stood for several seconds trying to order his thoughts. It was hard to shake the final image of the astropathic message, the face of death itself looming over the doomed psykers.

Necrons.

CHAPTER FIVE

Aeschelus stood in his arming chamber performing the mental rituals that accompanied the ceremonial donning of his armour. While tech-adepts and servitors busied themselves around him the captain repeated the litanies of the Ultramarines, lips moving soundlessly in time to the words in his mind. Ratchet-drives and bonding drills whined and crunched as plate after plate of armour was attached to the under-harness. With each piece of curved plasteel and ceramite he also layered on a shield within his psyche, unlocking the processes of the psychodoctrination he had undergone during training and enhancement.

The small shipboard chamber was different from the arsenal hall where he had first worn his Primaris armour, but every step – both physical and mental – was replicated exactly. The oily unguents the tech-priests daubed onto the joints of his suit smelled the same, the binaric clicking of prayers to the Machine-God intoned to the same rhythm as the canticles of hate that flowed through Aeschelus' thoughts.

Piece by piece they assembled him, and piece by piece he assumed the full mantle of the Space Marine commander.

He felt a cold touch of nerve-induction connections fitting into the outlets of his black carapace, synching with the subdermal interface that had completed his transition to post-human warrior. His senses and nervous system interlocked with the artificial muscles and auspex arrays of the battle harness. Inhuman organs grown within him responded to elective stimulus, his third lung and secondary heart picking up on the monitoring systems of the powered armour.

Incense burners left pungent-scented ruddy clouds around the captain. The drifting haze of ceremonial fumes reminded him of the psychic fog that had concluded the astropath's vision-sharing.

His armour did not stop at his skin but was buried deep in his soul. He did not fear the battle to come; he desired it. It was not simply the frustrations of the preceding years that had fuelled his thirst for victory, it was encoded into his being from the moment he had begun the accelerated command induction. He *needed* to lead and to know victory. All else seemed a hollow substitution.

Aeschelus had heard the doubts hovering behind the affirmatives of Praxamedes and the eagerness clearly expressed by Nemetus. He did not blame the former for his reticence and could not indulge the latter in his potential for rashness. Neither understood the reality of being the sole authority for the ship and every individual on board. And more than that, neither had been imbued with the overriding imperative to push forward the boundaries of war, to become the incarnation of the crusade ethos.

Praxamedes thought in terms of logistics; Nemetus was always concerned with individual action. The truth was something else: vision. The lord primarch had created the most effective fighting force the galaxy had seen for ten thousand years, but that was not enough for the uncountable dangers that threatened the Emperor's domains. Roboute Guilliman could not lead every fleet, could not command every battle. In Aeschelus had been placed the kernel of the lord primarch's animus, his gene-seed accompanied by his most important principles.

The Codex Astartes was a beginning, not an end. Aeschelus was the embodiment of the lord commander's will, just as he in turn was the embodiment of the Emperor's will.

A will that was shortly to be made manifest.

The captain found that his thoughts had wandered from the established doctrine, but it did not matter. His own mental journey had taken him to a place of inspiration. He longed to repay the debt he owed to the powers that had raised him to this position.

A sudden three-blast alarm cut through his reverie, accompanied by a surge of sickness in his gut that even his modified physiology could not wholly suppress. A nausea he knew well gave him several seconds of discomfort.

Warp jump.

'Emergency warp translation enacted,' blared the servitor warning. 'Realspace transition completed.'

'Strategium officer!' he barked, activating the chamber's vocal pick-up. 'What is happening?'

'Unknown, captain,' replied Nemetus, his voice issuing from a grille in the wall behind Aeschelus. There was a pause of a couple of seconds before the lieutenant continued, 'The Navis Nobilite contingent are requesting your presence at their quarters.'

Aeschelus growled. He was not finished with the armouring ceremony but it felt as though the situation demanded immediate attention.

'Direct the Navigators to attend to me in my arming chamber,' he announced.

There was some delay during which the voxmitter hissed, crackling loudly as it attuned to a new channel.

'Captain, this is Navigator Kosa. An incident has occurred, incapacitating one of my kindred. We cannot leave him. Please, come to the pilaster as soon as you are able.'

Aeschelus held back his first retort. Even through the distortion of the internal vox-system the Navigator's distress was obvious. There was a limitless number of threats the Navigators encountered in the course of their duties. Kosa's vagueness was perturbing in the face of the potential dangers posed by the warp.

'Very well, I will be with you shortly,' Aeschelus replied. 'I want a full explanation on my arrival.'

The servitors and adepts had paused during the conversation, some with pieces of armour still in clawed grips, others with oils at the ready to anoint his warplate. Caught part-armed, his battleplate was not yet fully functional but it would take longer to remove what was attached than to continue.

'Finish,' Aeschelus commanded, assuming a neutral pose once more.

The tech-priest clacked an affirmative and the servitor choreography recommenced.

It was a patience-straining eleven minutes before Aeschelus' left pauldron was placed upon its reactive shoulder mounting, the Chapter symbol upon it freshly repainted, completing the process. The tech-priest extended a mechanical digit, its tip a flickering valve-stylus that sprayed a last mist of holy lubricant into the actuators just before the curved armour plate settled into place.

A serf in the red-and-blue garb of the armourium offered up the captain's helmet, which he took in his right hand, raising his left to touch the device embossed upon his chest plastron. Closing his eyes, Aeschelus offered up some words to the spirit of his armour and the Master of Mankind that had guided its crafting.

'My armour shields the body, but my resolve shields the soul. By the will of He on Terra have I been made whole. For His glory shall I fight. For His victory shall I strive. For His power I shall lay down my life.'

He nodded his thanks to the tech-priest, dipping two fingers of his gauntleted hand into the proffered golden goblet. Its viscous contents leaving a thread as he pulled his hand back, he touched the oil to his forehead, making a rough circle and then marking the cardinal points.

'To the priests of Mars I give thanks, and to the Machine-God that guides their artifice.'

It took all of his willpower to complete the ritual, marking the inside of his helm with the same unguent, a symbolic link between his soul and the spirit of the armour. He longed to hurry to the Navigators' pilaster to see what crisis had befallen them but waited in silence while the tech-priest burbled its own benedictions, commending the armour to its eternal master. It would not be wise to offend either his attendant or the warplate.

With a hum the systems fully activated, flooding Aeschelus with a sense of power. Flesh and armour became one.

The ritual complete, he did not linger but headed for the conveyor as swiftly as possible. While he ascended to the gate of the Navigator's tower he prepared himself for whatever setback had occurred. It was possible that his armouring would be in vain, the ship unable to complete the journey to Casparill. It would not be the first time the storms had cut off all passage.

He did not believe in the tales of the Cursed Fleet, the moniker that now dogged Fleet Quintus, but it was with some pessimism that he arrived at the gateway to the Navigators' quarters.

* * *

A quartet of household guards in golden helms and scarlet dress coats escorted Aeschelus into the Sanctum Navis, flanking the captain as he stepped through the broad double-doors into a well-appointed living area. His eye was immediately drawn to three figures, two standing over a third lying on a couch near the centre of the room. More red-clad attendants waited nearby, one with an ornate pitcher and cup, another with a silk handkerchief with which he dabbed at the mouth of the supine Navigator.

All three had their third eyes hidden behind metal bands, as they always did in the presence of servants or outsiders. To do otherwise was to threaten madness to any that looked upon their warp-orbs.

Kosa turned towards Aeschelus, straightening. She looked even more gaunt than normal, the fingers of one hand fluttering like a butterfly at the high collar that she wore tight about her throat. The other dismissed the guards with a wave.

Aeschelus had expected perhaps screams or moans from the afflicted Navigator, but she seemed entirely comatose as the captain looked past the orderlies at the figure on the couch. She was dressed in a tight-fitting tunic which had been opened at the front to reveal a bright yellow shirt within, her hands lying by her sides as though dead. He could see the slight rise and fall of the chest and hear the heartbeat, painfully slow it seemed. Not dead, but not altogether alive either.

Kosa moved away, indicating with an inclined head that Aeschelus should join her in an adjoining chamber. The captain loitered for a moment longer, entranced by the stare of the catatonic Navigator. Violet eyes gazed at some point beyond the lavish scrollwork of the ceiling, looking at something only she could see.

A cough from Kosa drew his attention back to the chief Navigator, who waited at the door to the next room. Ducking through, Aeschelus found himself in a more austere chamber set with a table and chairs, a small cabinet to one side. He realised it was where the attendants on duty would wait while not needed by their lord and ladies. The door swung closed behind them as Aeschelus squeezed the bulk of his armour between the furniture and wall, his head almost touching the ceiling.

'Why have we dropped out of warp space?' the captain asked. 'Did something attack your companion?'

'No, it was nothing like that,' Kosa replied, sitting down on one of the straight-backed chairs. She put her hands on the bare wooden table and spent several seconds examining her fingernails in some detail before continuing, without looking at the Space Marine. 'Dosellua has lost the sight in her third eye. Blinded, she activated the emergency translate before succumbing to the condition in which you now see her. There has been no breach of the Geller field.'

Aeschelus tapped a finger on the back of a chair as he thought. 'Nothing passed through the sanctuary of the Geller field, but your companion has somehow been struck blind. How is that possible?'

'I think her reaction is an artefact of her subconscious mind. Something she witnessed was so overwhelming that her brain decided to shut out all sight of it.'

'Something in the warp storm?'

'The opposite, captain.' The Navigator raised her gaze to the Space Marine's. 'The warp has been calming by the hour. As we travel towards Casparill it seems as though the worst eddies and currents have been… quelled.'

A knock on the door heralded the arrival of the other Navigator, Qurius. He was a lot younger than Kosa and Dosellua, and eyed Aeschelus as one might watch a seemingly docile predator. He flicked a brief look at Kosa before speaking.

'Dosellua is waking, Novius Primus. She is asking for you.'

Heading back into the main room, they found Dosellua sitting up, waving away a gaggle of concerned serfs. She struggled to her feet, swaying on uncertain legs.

'We must go back,' she said, voice cracking. She took a tottering step, hands out in front of her as though to grab something for balance. 'The way ahead is blocked.'

'The storm was abating, cousin,' said Qurius, hurrying forward to take Dosellua's arm. She flinched at his touch, though she must have sensed him approaching. 'Has it returned?'

'There is nothing.' Her gaze slid off her cousin and back to Aeschelus, the skin behind her brow-band furrowing. 'Captain?'

'What did you see?' he demanded. 'What did you see in the warp?'

'Nothing, captain,' she gasped. Her hand moved to her brow as though to remove the protective band. Qurius grabbed her wrist, preventing her from revealing the devastating power of her third eye.

'You are not yourself, cousin,' said the youngest Navigator. 'You have had quite an ordeal.'

'I saw nothing!' snapped Dosellua, shoving Qurius away. She snatched off her headband. 'Nothing!'

Aeschelus averted his gaze, knowing well that to look upon the third eye of a Navigator was to invite insanity, even for a Space Marine. 'By the Emperor, what are you doing?' he demanded, shielding his eyes.

'It is safe, captain.' There was an edge to Kosa's tone. Horror.

Aeschelus peered through his fingers, unable to fully abandon the sense of security his hand gave him despite Kosa's assurance. Yet when his gaze fell upon the forehead of Dosellua he saw only a blackened orb, dull and lifeless.

'How did this happen to you?' he asked, hand dropping to his side. 'What power inflicted this upon your third eye?'

'Nothing,' Dosellua said again, growing angry. 'There was nothing. No peaks, no troughs, no currents, no eddies. The warp disappeared into utter stillness. There was nothing to refract the Light of Terra, to disperse its power, and for a moment I looked upon the full might of the Astronomican.'

'I have never heard of such a thing,' said Kosa, moving alongside her, taking her arm to guide her back to the couch. 'Are you sure you were not blinded first and then saw nothing?'

'Which am I to be, a liar or a fool? Of course I saw what I saw. Or didn't see!' Dosellua got up again, fending off Kosa's attempts to comfort her. She could not stand still, filled with agitation. 'Just before we broke realspace I saw with the last of my othervision. There is nothing ahead.'

'So why can't we continue?' asked Aeschelus. 'If there is no storm we should make swift progress.'

'I fear we will make no progress, captain. The warp is dead and we shall be too.'

'Rest, cousin, I will speak with the captain,' said Kosa, entrusting her to the care of Qurius again. With a flick of the eyes, Kosa directed Aeschelus to the main doors.

'What is it, Navigator?' the captain asked when they had both exited, the stricken Navigator and her cousin left behind the closed portal.

'I do not know why Dosellua has reacted so badly, but she may have a good point. If we are in a warp lull we may not be able to continue. Using only the impeller motion of the Geller field, it would take us deeper into the becalmed stretch and we may be months from catching a current to take us clear. If at all.'

'It is possible to use the movement of the translation itself to create some momentum within the warp.'

'A slingshot jump?' Kosa pursed her lips in thought. 'It is possible. More likely a series. Once we lose headway we would have to drop back into realspace, recharge the warp engines and then slingshot again. It could take a dozen jumps to get across the lull.'

'Do you think I would countenance abandoning our mission, Navigator?'

Kosa looked Aeschelus in the eye and then sighed.

'No, of course not, captain.' She took in a breath. 'I expect you want to continue without delay?'

'Your expectations are correct.'

'Then I shall conduct the jump myself.' The Navigator looked unenthusiastic at the prospect. 'We still have the correct heading for Casparill. It should take perhaps ninety minutes to recalibrate for a slingshot translation.'

'Do it.'

Aeschelus turned away without waiting for any further confirmation. He would get *Ithraca's Vengeance* to its destination if it took a hundred jumps. There would be no more failures, no more retreats.

CHAPTER SIX

Sitting on his throne at the heart of his tomb fleet reminded Simut of the power at his command. The display wall was broken into sections, each showing the sensory collective from a different ship, in turn made up of its own companion-flotilla, accumulated through the flock of assault craft each had ejected from its interior. There was a fractal beauty to the image, akin to the startling mosaics that he vaguely recalled, or perhaps imagined, had once adorned his palaces, which seemed to show a hundred varied pictures as one crossed them on foot, but whose whole beautiful genius could only be truly observed from upon high. At a whim, the overlord could pick a view to expand, one moment looking through the sensors of a harvester vessel on the extreme left of the fleet, the next becoming one with a Scythe-class fighter patrolling around the central tomb ships. He was, to all intents, omniscient and omnipotent.

Yet it was not for him to flex every muscle of this composite beast. Ancient protocols that had been created at the height of necrontyr rule dictated the actions of his underlings. His was the will that impelled the fleet into the new system, but at the lowest levels it was a programmed instinct that set them into motion for war. He could impose his will if needed; King Szarekh had provided him with the necessary god-codes. That was not his role, though, any more than the pyramidion's job was to hold up the foundations of the pyramid. No, he was the gleaming summit that was elevated by the ranks below, the crown that gave everything beneath its purpose. Those lower levels existed only to lift him to the peak.

There was some enjoyment in experiencing the swooping flight of the crescent-hull attack craft as they streamed en masse towards the outer defences of the stellar system. Even the most basic observation revealed the presence of more humans here. The plumes of star-fuel that came from their engines were as distinctive as the stench of the swampfolk they had encountered at the outset of the expedition. And like those primordial savages, the humans would also be enslaved or destroyed.

The new resonator carrier had not yet arrived in the system, held back by Simut so as to avoid any invitation to the enemy. After the ridiculous oversight of his minions with the enemy citadel defences in the last system, Simut was not going to entrust them with the blackstone obelisk until the route to the surface of the target world was definitively secured. In its absence the overnull effect was much reduced, but it did not matter to Simut's plans. The humans were outmatched in every regard; it was a simple matter of time before their defences were eliminated or circumnavigated.

'Phetos, begin the assault,' he commanded the royal warden standing ready at the foot of the dais. Simut flung out a hand as though standing at the forefront of his host. 'Unleash the might of my army. Full attack!'

Messenger beams flared back and forth across the fleet, ascending and descending along protocol-hierarchies, activating time-honoured responses. The fastest ships accelerated into an outer picket line, forming a mobile attack force that would respond as enemy ships manoeuvred. Their task would be to frustrate any attempt to form solid battle lines, pinning down isolated vessels while the slower harvesters moved into range with overwhelming weaponry. Should they be threatened by any significant counter-attack, like skirmishers of old they would simply fade back into the main fleet and shelter behind the longer ranged weapons of the capital ships.

The humans were terribly four-dimensional in their thinking. Being wholly reliant on the neversea for their interstellar transport, their defensive structures had been placed into orbital spheres coordinated with the arrival of astromantically traversing craft. The drives of the necron warships suffered no such restrictions and had dropped out of cross-system flight at an angle unanticipated by the architect of the ring of human stations. Still gathering speed, three human flotillas converged now from defensive platforms in the orbits of the outer planets, scrambling to intercept the enemy that had, to their eyes, miraculously appeared at the system's edge.

Simut had learned during his first system assault that it was unwise to decelerate too far into the target system if it was defended. An unwelcome attack against his fleet from outer system ships while in orbit had forced him to delay the placement of the resonator. Now he was more circumspect, eliminating the void threat before taking up station to move the resonator into position. Even with their inertia-dampeners, there was a limit to how quickly the necron ships could traverse the stellar distances within the system, and the human vessels would certainly take some time before bringing the arriving fleet to battle.

Fearing boredom as the opening moves took place across the outer system, Simut slipped into a temporal weave, detaching his consciousness from the external passage of time. His artificial synapses firing at an almost infinitely small fraction of their normal speed, it seemed to Simut as though the universe accelerated. Moons sped about their planets with cosmic haste and asteroid rings spun wildly through the heavens. The target world had completed a hundredth of its stellar orbit in what would have been a handful of heartbeats, were he still to have such a crude organ sustaining his existence. Enemy squadrons formed while his fleet broke into four waves to meet the oncoming foe.

Disengaging the weave, Simut felt a mental jolt, so that for an impossible moment it seemed as though the entire universe stood still. It seemed the very same sensation that had come to him at the moment of biotransference, when his consciousness had been transposed into its artificial body. All of creation had held its breath for that instant.

The feeling passed as soon as it occurred but for a little while longer the passage of the ships across the void seemed tediously slow. Simut was tempted to accelerate his perception again but decided against it – there was a risk he would miss the battle entirely if he shunted into the temporal weave with the enemy so relatively close.

Instead he amused himself by moving his awareness from one ship to another, often to look at the majestic lines of his own tomb ship from without. The base of the ship was a massive crescent along the horizontal plane, its tines forming a twin prow. At the greatest width of the curve was set a sarcophagus-like superstructure upon which was raised the command pyramid, gleaming gold in the light of the star; a stepped ziggurat that had been bodily lifted from Simut's place of internment for the Eversleep, now given wings to fly the void like a hunting falcon. Within this structure was the corpus of the army, from the royal warden and lychguard down to the lowliest canoptek scarab. The wing of the ship contained numerous weapons capable of obliterating other vessels, along with particle effect systems that could eliminate surface targets from high orbit.

Like his artificial body, the ship was at the pinnacle of necron engineering, as befitted a ruler of the highest calibre.

As he admired this extension of his will, a flurry of data signals drew his attention to the approach of the first enemy flotilla. It numbered as many ships as his fleet, but far smaller in average mass. Scanners detected no astromantic readings at all. The poor, stunted things could not even escape the gravity of their birth-system! It occurred to Simut that perhaps these humans were not part of the star-spanning dominion he had previously encountered, but some regressive offshoot that had been abandoned to fend for itself like the runt of a livestock litter.

Using the sensory banks of the closest ships, Simut realised the error of this assessment. The incoming craft were blunt-nosed, brick-like vessels that looked more akin to castles in the void than starships. The double-headed eagle that was the symbol of their fractured empire adorned a keep-like superstructure. Their flanks bristled with weapon turrets, including powerful light-based weapons that sprang into life as soon as his Jackal-class scout ships were barely within range. The beams of red and blue flared across the void with little effect, the crude tracking systems of the human vessel barely able to keep up with the swift manoeuvres of the Jackals.

The scout trio banked hard around a scattering of asteroids, using the stellar debris as cover while they came around the sides of their less mobile opponents. Jets flaring to stall their momentum, the human ships did their best to aim their weapons as they turned, coughing rockets and explosive shells at the speeding crescent-shaped necron vessels, the clouds of their detonation creating a sea of fire in the wake of the arcing craft.

Inertialess engines biting deep into the subsphere, the Jackal squadron turned sharply, bringing their lightning arcs to bear on the closest foe. Their manoeuvre caused ripples of distorted space-time that washed over the rest of the fleet. Stored stellar energy speared out as three crackling beams enveloped a void-castle like a spreading net of electricity, coruscating over a sudden glow of energy-shunting fields. Power relays deep within the target overloaded, hurling pieces of hull out into the vacuum as they exploded.

The Jackals swooped away in perfect formation as a larger enemy ship powered up behind the monitor ships, a spray of torpedoes burning from its eagle-beaked prow. The necron fleet was forced to part to allow the blazing missiles to pass harmlessly through them, Simut's tomb ship among the half of the fleet forced to move further in-system.

'Lord of the Stars, Eagle of Victory, I have a communication from Plasmancer Ah-hotep,' announced Phetos from the lowest step. 'She has analysed the enemy attack and wishes to propose a response.'

'Inform the plasmancer that her advice is not needed,' Simut replied, watching as the battle escalated in a bloom of detonations and the crossfire of lasers and lightning flares. 'Our imminent victory is well in hand.'

'As you command, my overlord.'

It took no intervention from Simut to steer the fleet in its manoeuvres against the increasing enemy numbers. Strategic minds that had advised the greatest kings had laid down the appropriate actions in ages past, down to specific squadron formations and attack patterns. Clouds of smaller craft streamed from the carrier vessels to intercept a fresh wave of torpedoes while the scout vessels of the necron fleet broke away, creating distance that allowed them to circle in behind the onrushing foe.

'Plasmancer Ah-hotep respectfully requests an audience with your majesty, my lord,' Phetos reported, interrupting Simut's appreciation of the symmetry of war as it appeared in the main display. 'She believes that the enemy are trying to delay us in preparation for some further attack.'

'She is in error, my royal warden.' Simut's will scrolled the display across the fleet, moving through different scan arrays and sensory detection systems. 'There are no hidden enemies within three orbits.'

'She believes the preparations are on the target world, my lord,' said

Phetos. 'I cannot give her argument fully. Perhaps she should deliver it in person?'

'No. I have had enough of her interference.'

'As you will it, my lord.'

Irritated at the intrusion, Simut barely acknowledged the ongoing state of the battle. His enjoyment spoilt by the plasmancer's attempts to usurp his control, he allowed the fleet to continue its attacks as protocol required, spending his time trying to come up with a way he could persuade his cousin to remove her from the fleet.

Periodically he received protocol-led requests for engagement permissions, which he responded to without unnecessary consideration. There was no need to personally intervene as far as he could tell. Several of his vessels had suffered damage but the enemy were retreating, leaving behind nearly half of their attack fleet. Pursuit declarations sung back and forth across the signal net and he allowed them all, sending the fastest ships to harry the defeated foe back to their bases.

The battle had taken a little longer than anticipated but at no point had Simut's tomb ship been under threat, which was always his highest priority. Without him the fleet was worthless. He was about to order the summons for the resonator-ship to begin its approach when he remembered Ah-hotep's attempts at communication. Now that he could spare a thought, there might be something of note in her theories that would warn against commitment just yet.

'Phetos, have Ah-hotep convene with me at her earliest convenience,' he said, returning to his throne. The displays fell black, their contents no longer of interest now that the peak of conflict had passed until the next fleet was encountered.

'As you command, Lord of the Stars.'

The rendition plate buzzed into life almost immediately, revealing the plasmancer hovering like a wraith in the monochrome light.

'Lord Simut,' she began, inclining downwards in a sketch of a bow. 'We must press onwards with all speed.'

'You will recall that undue haste cost us in earlier meetings with the enemy,' Simut replied. 'We cannot have the enemy at our backs.'

'Nor can we have them sending for aid. Our astromantic detectors sense a build-up around the target world. I believe that they are preparing to despatch interstellar craft to seek aid from neighbouring systems.'

'Any enemy will arrive too late to help them,' Simut replied. 'The overnull will be in effect before these lumbering fools can return with reinforcements.'

'The overnull effect is only spread by our proximity, my lord,' interjected Phetos. 'At present it does not encompass the target world. With each system we claim, the greater the risk of enemy arrival before we are finished with our task.'

'I see.' Simut leaned forward, instinctively stroking his chin in thought. 'I see clearly that both of you lack the patience for true leadership. You would have us risk counter-attack from the foe at our step to allay distant phantoms conjured out of your fear.'

'Total system domination is not the optimal goal in every system,' said Ah-hotep. 'If we can swiftly deploy the resonator, the overnull will thwart all resistance as well as guarding against arrival through the neversea.'

Simut did not dignify her outburst with a response but instead waited patiently for the plasmancer to correct her oversight.

'My lord,' she added, realising the rebuke within his silence.

'I will consider your petition,' Simut replied.

He raised a hand and the tomb ship cut off the communications relay, scattering the plasmancer's image to falling static. The overlord turned his attention to the royal warden. Feeling his disappointment, Phetos bent to one knee, gaze averted.

'I exist to serve, my lord.'

'You do,' Simut replied, leaning back in the throne. 'Remember that.'

CHAPTER SEVEN

There was a point at which the extraordinary became ordinary. Praxa-medes was not sure when the *Ithraca's Vengeance* had passed that point with regard to the slingshot jumps. Likely it was at some time between the eighth and tenth, he decided, as he watched the main display chronometer count down to the next translation.

In his studies, he had read that during one period of Terran war the sea-going ships had been powered by the wind, catching its strength in massive sails. Though this allowed ancient Terrans to harness this nat-ural, inexhaustible energy it also left them prey to the vagaries of the weather. When such a vessel was becalmed, a ship's commander might order that boats be put out, attached to the ship with long rope, and rowed by the crew. It was a slow, back-breaking ordeal for those involved, and its purpose would be to bring the ship to a place where the wind might again be caught and the ship able to proceed under the power of its sails once more.

Instead of sailors bent to the oars, the *Ithraca's Vengeance* relied upon angular physical momentum at the instant its warp drive was engaged. Requiring precise timing to ensure the maximum amount of inertia was sustained and carried into the warp, the slingshot manoeuvre taxed not only the two remaining functioning Navigators but also the calculations of the tech-priests and the discipline of the command crew. In order to preserve the motion as long as possible the Geller fields that captured a bubble of reality around the ship could not be engaged until the last moment. Any delay beyond this point would mean exposing the ship to the raw warp. Premature activation would bleed off the momentum attained and shorten the distance of the jump.

It was a similar story when trying to get back into realspace. If the plasma engines fired whilst inside the Geller effect, the recursive nature of the reality bubble might redirect the plasma flow back onto the ship, or the *Ithraca's Vengeance* could rip its way out of its own protective capsule. However, some relative motion was required to give traction through the translational space between the warp and real-space. Usually this was provided by the action of the warp itself, the currents that the Navigators used to approximate spatial motion whilst traversing a dimension in which neither time nor space really existed. Without the motion-equivalent of the warp the only movement that could be used was the diminishing inertia of the ship itself. Even though the warp was almost wholly flattened, there was just enough granularity of it remaining to act like friction on the passage of the cruiser's Geller field. The effect was unpredictable and the time to translate back into realspace was as much a matter of instinct and experience for Kosa and her cousin as it was a calculable phenomenon. If the return to realspace was too late, they would bounce off the Impossibility Boundary – as the tech-priests had called it – and slowly drift to a halt in warp space, stranded until such time as the currents returned. On the other hand, even shortening a jump by a couple of light-weeks added to the overall number of jumps they would have to make before reaching tractable warp space again. Praxamedes disliked guesswork but had stopped trying to understand all of the intricacies of the physical meeting the metaphysical, and like the captain, now relied upon naked trust of the tech-priests and Navigators.

If they got their calculations wrong, there was nothing the Space Marines could do to resolve the errors.

Watching the chronometer approach the Zero Instant, the lieutenant wished he had not dwelt on their predicament so long. The sling-shot jumps lost their veneer of mundanity when he thought properly about what they were doing. The risks they faced with each jump were not the kind that were mitigated by practice. Repetition simply increased the chance of an oversight or mistiming.

He cleared his throat and announced the one-minute mark to Zero Instant.

'Warp engines ready.'

'Preparing diversion to Navigator control.'

'Geller field is nominal.'

Other acknowledgements echoed back across the strategium. Captain Aeschelus stood at the command throne, fists clenched at his sides, watching the star-filled display as though the empty void might betray some secret of what was to come. Or perhaps it was pure frustration that clenched the captain's jaw. The star centred in the read-outs was Casparill, their destination. After twelve jumps they had covered nearly three-quarters of the distance.

Four more jumps. Perhaps five.

Nemetus waited at the warp engine controls while Praxamedes oversaw the Geller field. This was the kind of patient, diligent work that the other lieutenant did not embrace. Praxamedes had taken some time to explain to his fellow officer that there was only the smallest margin of error for the sequence of events that had to happen during each translation. Holding off for just a bit more time, or urging the tech-priests to get a little more power out of the reactors, or following an instinct to make a tiny course correction were all forbidden. Nemetus had protested his innocence of any such thoughts and thankfully had so far been true to his promise not to improvise any part of the process.

'Thirty seconds,' declared Praxamedes.

'Redirect core power to warp engines,' announced the captain.

'Redirecting,' confirmed Nemetus.

The throb of the ship changed almost imperceptibly.

Aeschelus waited until the twenty-five-second mark.

'Bring engine output down to seventy-five per cent. Make headway full.'

The navigational officers did as commanded, eliciting another change in the tone of the ship's background noise.

'Transferring warp engine control to navigational pilaster,' declared Nemetus. 'All systems nominal.'

Praxamedes drew in a breath, a little longer than normal, just as he had done before each previous jump. He didn't want to change a single thing about the routine, and stood in exactly the same spot, every crew member assigned to the same positions. He started speaking as the chronometer flickered down to twenty seconds.

'Geller field generators on line. Ready to engage.'

'All decks secured for warp translation,' confirmed Shipmaster Oloris. 'Void shields inactive. Navigational shields inactive.'

As he spoke the main videolith blanked, turning to a slate-grey slab on the wall. All across the *Ithraca's Vengeance* warp shutters clanked across any external ports, while visual feeds were disabled. Any energy output that might interfere with the Geller field or warp drive was curtailed, dulling sensors and deadening manoeuvring thrusters. A moment of fragility before translation.

'Activate Geller fields,' commanded Aeschelus, giving a nod to Praxamedes.

The lieutenant did not need to relay the order; his attendants knew what to do. Controls whined into life at their touch. The augur banks fell dark as the Geller field activated, psychically charged waves pulsing from the generator located deep within the ship. Its effect was slight while in realspace, a momentary tension, like a tightening in the throat before a cough. Blind, the *Ithraca's Vengeance* ploughed on across the void in its own self-contained reality.

'Warp drop in five seconds,' Nemetus called out, hand hovering over the activation switches. He flicked the priming lever, eyes fixed on the small countdown display set within the controls. 'Three... Two... One...'

He flicked the final signal switch. In the heart of the engine decks, the tech-priests flooded the warp drive with power from the plasma reactors. Like the Geller field, it was not so much a physical process as a psychic one, the technologies barely understood by those on board, even the Navigators. Fronds of energy leapt out from the cruiser, tearing at the fabric of reality. Realspace parted with a kaleidoscope of colours, strange rainbow flashes that Praxamedes could feel rather than see, even though he was inside the shuttered confines of the strategium. A few murmurs broke the stillness. For even the most disciplined crew it was impossible to completely eradicate all sense of unease or discomfort.

Like a serpent shedding an old skin, the strike cruiser sloughed away the last remnants of space-time and plunged through the opening rift into warp space. The laws of nature gave way to unfettered emotion given substance, the physical falling away to the psychic. Protected only by the pocket of sanctuary sanity it dragged with it, the *Ithraca's Vengeance* crashed into a realm of nightmare and madness.

'Warp translation complete,' a servitor announced dully from beside Praxamedes, its mind-scrubbed brain incapable of appreciating the import or drama of the moment.

The intervox chimed as an announcement came through from Kosa in the Navigator's tower, thrust up from the dorsal decks into the warp like a lightning conductor in a storm.

'*I have con–*' the Navigator began, before her words were cut short by a shout of panic. Warning sigils flared across the warp engine controls in front of Praxamedes and the servitors started barking in unison with dry voices.

'Negative warp traction. Negative warp traction. Negative warp traction.'

Non-vocal alarms accompanied the warnings, blaring out across the vox-net until Praxamedes silenced them with a depressed button.

'Cease,' he told the servitors.

'Kosa!' barked Aeschelus, striding across to the warp engine controls. The displays bathed the attendants and servitors in red light. 'Kosa, make your report!'

Other than the alerts from the console there was no sense of what was happening. Praxamedes could only approximate the situation from the readings, which were changing too rapidly to individually follow.

'We're sliding, captain,' the lieutenant announced, fingers moving across the runepad to bring up a read-out of the last few seconds of data. 'Fast.'

'*Captain, the warp effect…*' Kosa's voice trailed off, replaced by half-heard muttering before the Navigator continued. '*It is impossible! There is no warp here.*'

'Nonsense,' growled the captain. 'What do you mean, Navigator?'

'*We are beyond the Impossibility Boundary but I cannot see the Astronomican,*' whispered Kosa, her voice taut with awe. '*The warp is flattened. Not even a mirror. Like vacuum. Empty.*'

'Rotational momentum detected. We are spinning, captain,' said Praxamedes.

'Geller field still nominal, brothers,' said Nemetus, leaving his position to join them. 'In fact, it is operating at one hundred and forty per cent efficiency.'

'How's that possible?' said Praxamedes. 'How can it be generating negative reality?'

'No warp pressure,' suggested Aeschelus, stepping back. He glanced around the strategium, but it was only the warp engine display that was not showing green across the banks. 'If Kosa is right, there is nothing to act against the Geller field, so it is still expanding.'

'Reduce energy input to Geller field by forty per cent,' Nemetus told the officers at the controls. They passed the order to the tech-priests in the bowels of the ship, glancing at each other in amazement as the readings continued to climb. 'Keep dropping it to maintain current coverage.'

'Captain, we are moving at speed without any means of changing course,' Kosa told them hurriedly over the voxmitter. 'We are also drifting slightly off-heading, as far as I can ascertain. If we do not translate back to realspace soon we will be dozens of light years away from our intended destination.'

'Understood, Navigator. You have permission to translate back to realspace.' Aeschelus flexed his fingers, obviously frustrated, but Praxamedes could see there was no alternative and was glad to see the captain being prudent.

'You do not understand, captain,' replied Kosa, voice trembling. 'I was not asking permission. We are moving through the warp while simultaneously lacking any traction to use to break back into realspace. I have attempted to translate twice since we dropped into warp space with no success! We are trapped!'

There were times when one simply had to accept that events play out as they will without any way of changing their course. Ah-hotep had resigned herself to this reality on a frequent basis since her assignment to Simut's fleet. She could not divine whether his total ambivalence to her advice was simply pride, distrust of her as a plasmancer or that he genuinely believed he was above such concerns and knew better.

The systems of her tomb ship were enthralled to the overlord's command protocols, greatly hampering anything she might attempt to cut off the humans' ability to use their astromantic capabilities. As a plasmancer she was keenly aware of the delicate cosmic flow of energy through the whole star system, from the raging radioactive fire of the star to the bio-fields of the thousands of humans inhabiting the target world and its far-flung outposts. She could not directly detect the presence of astromantic energy, but she knew enough from her studies of blackstone and the capture of human astromancers that there was always a residual physical effect to the presence of neversea energy. A shadow on reality, cast by unnatural powers.

So it was that she could sense the humans gathering together their astromantically potent forces on the major satellite orbiting their world. Its energy signature betrayed it as an object of artifice, a large space station hung above a sparsely populated planet. Even from several orbits' distance the gathering of personnel capable of interacting with the neversea was distinct.

The citadel of their previous battle would seem a small obstacle in comparison to a fully populated and defended artificial moon. As much as Ah-hotep wanted to see Simut humbled by failure, his utter humiliation had to occur in such a way that she was not implicated nor besmirched in its occurrence. Even more importantly, she considered it an unacceptable risk to require resurrection via the benevolence of Simut; it was likely he would stall the process to remove her from command, if not using the opportunity to erase her consciousness completely.

With her eternal presence uncertain, Ah-hotep's physical wellbeing was paramount.

All of which meant that when her ship detected a significant drop in radiating energy from the surface of the populated moon she knew it was a concentrated signal for help. The only way was to edge her vessel closer, using it to draw forward some of Simut's escort ships so that the overnull effect extended further into the system. The small adjustment, about half an orbit, was well within the parameters allowed by the protocols overlaid onto her command matrix.

Sometime after beginning the manoeuvre, she felt the presence of Phetos wishing to make itself known. She allowed the royal warden access to the hierolith.

'Greetings, Archimedion,' she said as the image of Phetos resolved above the projector plate, sparkling gold. 'I expect the overlord has despatched you to tell me to return to my appointed position?'

'The Great Hawk of the Void has not yet commented on your disposition, plasmancer,' the royal warden replied. 'I noticed the discrepancy and demand explanation in his name.'

'Demand? You take on too much authority, Phetos. I do not answer to you, even if you speak from under the shadow of Overlord Simut.'

'The fleet is splitting, Ah-hotep,' the warden continued with conciliatory pulses from his cortical field. 'There are human ships within a quarter orbit that may see this and choose to engage while we are divided.'

'Those ships are our least concern. Join your field to mine and see what I see, Phetos.' Ah-hotep extended a cortical invite to the royal warden, opening up a tiny window in her ship's sensor systems. She felt a moment of friction as Phetos accepted the connection. 'It is the will of the Silent King that we proceed without alerting our enemies to the nature of our work. The overnull experiment is in a subtle and vulnerable phase. Any aggressive counteraction by the humans or others could set back the whole project.'

'I see ships fleeing, nothing more,' said Phetos.

'Fleeing to the edge of their astromantic capability. They will break into the neversea if we allow it.'

'And you think you can catch them?'

'No, of course not. But we can use the overnull fringe to disrupt their attempts to break from the physical universe. If you could persuade the overlord to bring in the resonator now it would extend my efforts considerably.'

A sensation of detachment followed when Phetos withdrew his cortical matrix. The royal warden remained silent, giving away nothing of his thoughts.

'Very well,' he said after some time. 'The overlord has been persuaded that the path is clear to the target world. The resonator will be arriving shortly. I have not told him of your involvement, but continue to move forward as you planned.'

'My gratitude, Archimedion. You serve your lords and ladies well.'

'It is my duty, nothing more,' said Phetos as his image wavered and then disappeared.

Encouraged, Ah-hotep accelerated further, drawing out several more ships to create an outcrop of the fleet pointing directly towards the target planet. Her energy sensors spiked hard, surging across every wavelength and vibrational capacity, heralding the arrival of the blackstone resonator.

The carrier ships decelerated into the system two-thirds of an orbit behind the main fleet, subspherical waves preceding it into the inner system. The overnull grew immediately even though the resonator was not yet fully active, flooding outwards from the Szarekh dynasty ships like ancient beacon fires spreading across a wilderness. Not long after its arrival, Ah-hotep felt a backwash pushing against the overnull effect. She scoured the star system with her longest-ranged arrays, seeking the disturbance. One ship was almost at the boundary point between the gravitational pull of the star and the wastes of the outer system, where it could safely engage its engines.

She reacted immediately, tapping into emergency routines to briefly usurp the command protocols, allowing her ship and those nearby to leap forward, covering nearly a quarter of an orbit in a matter of moments. The overnull flowed with them, spearing out towards the escaping vessel like the waves of an incoming tide flowing up a beach.

'Plasmancer, what are you doing?' Simut broadcast directly, a voice-thought that slammed into her consciousness via her ship's own communications network, as though she shouted at herself. Her override had not been hidden and now the overlord had reacted. Ah-hotep could feel renewed command protocols clawing at the guidance and propulsion systems of her ship, as though prising her fingers one by one from the controls.

She needed just an instant longer. The human ship was building up astromantic power at an exponential rate, ready to breach reality.

Ah-hotep flooded her systems with a purging wave of cortical power, unleashing her own personal store of power to overload the matrix. Arcs of green flared around the command chamber, earthing onto her vaporators, crackling along her limbs.

In the last moments before blindness, her sensors picked up the swell of the overnull connecting with the astromantic ripples of the departing vessel. The power of the blackstone met the pulse of the warp engine. For just an instant the plasmancer felt a cataclysmic release of energy and then everything went dark, her ship left dead in the void.

CHAPTER EIGHT

The tinny echo of Kosa's words rang in Aeschelus' ears louder than any bellowed warning.

We are trapped.

It was impossible. They had been making headway, tortuously slow, but jump by jump they had been getting closer to their destination. Through persistence and expertise, the Ultramarines had improvised and overcome. Theory had been put into practice.

There were sobs from some of the deck crew.

'Quiet there,' the captain chastised, his sharp words swallowed by the tension that now hung over the strategium. 'Silence on deck.'

His gaze first moved to Nemetus at the Geller field controls.

'No incursions, brother-captain,' the lieutenant told him.

Next, he turned an inquiring look to Praxamedes. The only response was a shake of the head, reluctant but as foreboding as the single tolling of a bell.

Aeschelus swallowed and took a breath, knowing that he needed to say something. This was a moment that would define his leadership, such as it remained. His next commands would decide the fates of nearly two thousand Space Marines and serfs. What would he tell them? Not to be afraid? They were Ultramarines, human and post-human – they needed no speeches on bravery. To have hope? Hope fixed nothing. Hope was empty in the face of inaction.

So what were they to do?

He delayed, waiting for some further update from Kosa. Aeschelus was loath to ask for more details of their predicament. The summary and all that it implied was damning enough.

We are trapped.

Three words that would drive lesser captains mad with grief. Three words that every warp-faring soul dreaded to hear. Too many were the tales of ships lost adrift in the void. Everybody had heard a story or read a report. Worse still were the accounts of those that returned, ships denuded of their inhabitants or filled with the corpses of crew driven insane enough to slay one another and themselves. The physical support systems could keep them alive for some time but eventually food would run out. What then? The *Ithraca's Vengeance* was overstocked but also over-manned, expected to survive alone for years on extended duty if needed. That made the situation seem even worse. Their ability to persist in a state of uselessness only made their entrapment all the harsher.

The strategium doors growled open, breaking the tense silence.

A black-armoured figure entered. Judiciar Admonius. His head was bare, expression grim as he took in the scene, eyes scanning the crew until they fell upon Aeschelus. To arrive so soon after the announcement, Admonius must have been swift to journey to the strategium. Aeschelus knew why the Judiciar was there – to ensure that there was no laxity in leadership or courage at this pivotal time. The captain met the Judiciar's gaze with all the equanimity he could muster. This was still his ship, and although Admonius could claim moral rank, in practical terms he was seconded to Aeschelus' company and under his command.

'Your timing is impeccable, Brother-Judiciar,' said Aeschelus, deciding it was better to initiate conversation. His words rang hollow but he tried to keep any evidence of his woes out of his voice. 'This is a troubling situation and we must be vigilant among the crew.'

'Brother-Chaplain Exelloria is seeing to the mood of the ranks,' the Judiciar replied quietly. His stern gaze swept the strategium once more. 'I am here to ensure that setback does not become disaster.'

'Your strength is always an inspiration, brother,' said Aeschelus, returning to his command throne.

The strategium was quiet and dull without most of the systems operational. Still the warp engine displays cast a ruddy aura across a portion of the deck and crew. The Judiciar's presence had broken the immobility of thought that had chained him in the moments following Kosa's announcement. Now that he could give his mind free run again he started to turn his attention to the details of the ship's predicament.

'Navigator, can you confirm that we are unable to make any course adjustments at all?'

'*Like a stone cast across the void, captain.*' Kosa's voice was close to breaking. There was a depth of resignation to her tone that conveyed the emptiness of what she could see in the stillness of the warp.

'That is not so poor a fate as being caught upon a storm, surely?' said Nemetus. 'Eventually we will come upon some turbulence or current that will give us the means to break free.'

'*I do not share your optimism, lieutenant,*' Kosa replied, the intervox crackling as she sighed. '*We are not a stone skidded across an iced lake to reach the far side. The warp has no up and down, left and right as you understand these directions. We drift in all directions at once, sliding further and further from the Impossibility Boundary. More akin to being caught within a glass sphere, sliding around the interior until we detach from the surface, travelling without movement. Inexorably we are being drawn down to the base, deeper into the warp. The longer we remain, the greater the slope against us.*'

One of the attendants at the navigational relays, close to the voxmitter where Kosa's voice emanated, gave a choked cry and started to weep, bowing his head to the metal of the console.

'Leave,' snapped Admonius, striding across to the demoralised officer. 'Take yourself to the prow Reclusiam and think on your weaknesses until you are fit to attend your duties without distraction.'

The deck officer offered no argument as he fled to the doors, trembling with emotion.

'Any others, stand down now,' Aeschelus told the rest of the crew, keeping his voice level. 'We must be fully effective to exploit any opportunity that occurs. Your immediate duty is to be no hindrance.'

Three others turned from their consoles and followed, eyes gleaming with suppressed tears, their movements stilted with fear. Aeschelus saw worry in the eyes of more, but not so much that they were hampered by it. The noise of the doors closing broke the uneasy quiet, jarring Aeschelus back into action.

'Vibrations,' he said aloud, giving voice to the thought the moment it occurred to him.

'Pardon, brother-captain?' said Nemetus.

'Vibrations.' Aeschelus slapped his gauntleted hand against the arm of the command throne, the plasteel resonating from the blow. 'Navigator, do we still have angular momentum carried from realspace?'

There was a pause of several seconds before Kosa replied.

'As far as I can tell, the potential and kinetic energy is still caught within the Geller bubble. Yes. I would say that we do. But we have no way of using it inside warp space.'

Aeschelus ignored the Navigator's assessment and continued with his train of thought.

'And we are in the othersea? There is warp-stuff surrounding us, it is simply not moving.'

'It is more complex than that, captain. You can't think of the warp as a substa–'

'Are we in the warp or not?' snapped Aeschelus.

'We are,' said the Navigator.

'What would happen if Astropath Fedualis transmitted a message?'

'Nothing. Like the Astronomican, his thoughts move with the flow of the warp.'

'Nothing at all? His message just disappears?'

'Not disappears… Dissipates would be a more accurate description.' The Navigator let out a wordless, contemplative noise. *'Any effect on the warp would be so localised it would not help.'*

'Not enough to create traction for a translation?' asked Praxamedes, catching on to Aeschelus' idea.

'No,' the Navigator replied bluntly. *'There would be a faint rippling effect, but that would be absorbed by the dispersing Geller field as we dropped back to realspace. We would rebound from the Impossibility Boundary.'*

Aeschelus started to move around the strategium, flexing his muscles in the hope that it would help in flexing his brain matter. He was sure he was on to something, but could not isolate the concept.

'Rather than translate, could we use that effect as propulsion?' suggested Nemetus.

'Not for long,' answered Kosa, her tone miserable. '*I am not sure Fedualis would be able to sustain a transmission state for any useful period. It would be like shouting at full volume without pause for breath. And where would we go? Without the power to translate, we are still prevented from returning to realspace.*'

'Captain, I have Astropath Fedualis requesting access to the strategium,' announced the deck officer attending to the portal controls. 'He wishes to speak to you.'

'Let him in,' replied Aeschelus. It was highly irregular for non-Chapter personnel to approach the bridge. Navigators, tech-priests and other Adeptus Terra functionaries kept to their own quarters.

The doors were in battle setting for the warp jump, so it took nearly a minute for the locks to grind open and the hydraulic rams to withdraw once more. When the doors parted they revealed the slight, robed figure of the astropath leaning heavily against the wall. He staggered into the command bridge, his breaths coming in stuttering gasps. Blind eyes roved the strategium until they fell upon Aeschelus.

'Captain...' The words were a feat of effort judging by the twisted expression of the astropath's face. 'Captain, I warned you! I told you it would be folly to travel to Casparill.'

'You have no business here, Fedualis,' growled Admonius, intercepting the astropath with an outstretched hand. 'Return to your chamber and await instructions.'

'You cannot hear it,' wheezed Fedualis, pushing helplessly against the Judiciar's immovable arm. 'The silence. The silence swallows everything!'

'Remove yourself from this chamber, or be removed,' growled Admonius, taking Fedualis' robe in his grip.

'Wait!' Praxamedes moved towards the pair. 'Fedualis, tell us about the silence.'

'He is losing his mind,' said Admonius. 'Weakness is spreading all across the ship.'

Aeschelus did not know whether to take this last remark as simple commentary or a more pointed warning.

'Fedualis, what can you tell us about the silence?' Praxamedes asked again, ignoring the Chaplain-in-Waiting's remonstration. Admonius flashed a look at Aeschelus, perhaps thinking the captain would rebuke his subordinate. He did no such thing, but instead nodded to Praxamedes to continue. The Judiciar's frown deepened.

'Did it start when we jumped?' asked Praxamedes.

'No.' The astropath turned his dead eyes on the lieutenant. 'No, it came just before. It woke me from a dream. A dream of death!'

Fedualis became frantic, trying to pull himself from the grasp of Admonius, lunging towards Aeschelus.

'I had forgotten! How had I forgotten? Death. Death, but not the end of life. Annihilation, sweeping aside everything in its path. Total obliteration, stretching across the galaxy. Ending. Everything is ending!'

A wordless moan echoed from the intervox, across which Kosa had apparently been hearing the exchange,

'*That matches what we saw,*' groaned the Navigator, sounding like she was on the verge of breaking down. '*Nothing. Nothingness every...*'

A noise like scuffling broke the feed, followed by urgent whispering. A scrape of metal and a gasp came quickly after.

'Captain, it is a miracle!' gasped Kosa. '*A miracle! I can see something. A pulsing, a movement.*'

'I hear screams!' wailed Fedualis, tearing his robe as he wrenched himself from the fingers of Admonius. He stumbled towards Praxamedes, almost flailing into his arms. He seemed half-terrified and half-elated. 'Death! Screams of death!'

The astropath started laughing manically. Behind him, Admonius raised a fist to club him into insensitivity but Aeschelus spoke out before the blow fell.

'No, we need him conscious!' He thrust a finger at Nemetus. 'Attend the warp engines.'

The lieutenant moved across the strategium while Aeschelus steadied himself, trying to ignore the hysterical outbursts from the astropath.

'*Too far,*' said Kosa, her voice drifting away from the vox pickup, becoming fainter. '*We are moving past it. A hole–*'

'*Sorry, captain. Kosa is not herself,*' Qurius, the youngest Navigator's voice cut across. '*This nothingness, it saps the soul. She has exposed herself too long.*'

'I feel it too,' groaned Fedualis, pushing himself away from Praxamedes. He appeared cogent for the time being. 'Our souls are not reflected back from the warp! What is it, to live without our animus, our spirit, the light of the Emperor within us? It is the edge of the abyss, neither life nor death but the state of betweenness.'

'He's gibbering,' said Nemetus, but Aeschelus did not think so.

'Navigator Qurius, would an astropathic pulse push us towards the opening?'

'I am not sure I have the skill to ride such a subtle wave, captain,' he replied. *'But it is worth trying. I think the flash that Kosa saw was a warp drive breaching.'*

'A ship breaking into this nothingness? Is that possible?' said Aeschelus.

'No, I do not think so, captain. It was very sharp. A detonation I would guess, opening a hole that we can use to break into realspace. The breach will collapse soon.'

'I can do it,' said Fedualis, straightening his torn robe. He looked sheepish and glanced nervously at Admonius. 'I am myself again, Judiciar. I can do it.'

'From here?' said Praxamedes.

'As good a place as any, lieutenant.'

'Do it,' Aeschelus said sharply. He balled his fists, helpless in the face of these immaterial obstacles. He loathed having to put the fate of the ship in the hands – or minds – of these psykers, but there seemed no other option.

All eyes turned to the astropath as he steadied himself, standing a little apart from Praxamedes and Admonius. The two Space Marines were tense, their postures instantly recognisable to the captain, ready to strike. Golden light flickered across the dead gaze of Fedualis, seeming to bring movement to the orbless sockets. His lips started to move, silent at first, his voice becoming a murmur. Aeschelus recognised the same kind of identification stream-syllables the astropath used before formal broadcasts, not only sending this detail to any would-be receiver but using the act itself as a focusing mantra. Several times he repeated the nonsense words, voice growing in strength.

'Navigator, can you see anything happening?' Aeschelus kept his voice quiet, the vox capable of picking up even the softest tones. It seemed an intrusion on the astropath to speak louder. 'Can you see any effect?'

'Nothing yet, captain,' Qurius replied. There followed a bump and some whispered cursing.

'I see it, captain,' said Kosa, her voice husky. *'The tiniest ripples of thought. It is not enough.'*

Admonius leaned in closer to Fedualis. 'Think harder, astropath.'

It seemed such a ludicrous thing to say, Aeschelus almost laughed. A strange detachment afflicted him as he watched the unfolding scene, as though he was starting to float away, like fighting in a zero-gravity encounter without anything to mag-lock onto. Stray thoughts from training, mundane moments of his life crowded into his mind, distracting and yet comforting. The captain shook his head, trying to focus.

Fedualis was standing as stiff as a boarding pike, trembling slightly inside his dark green robe and hood, the glow of his false eyes bright and mesmerising. There was a beat to the emanation, a rhythm to their aura that synchronised with Aeschelus' pulse. He found himself again trying to remain present, to keep his thoughts honed to the unfolding event. Slowly, as one wading through sucking mud, he came to the conclusion that he might be suffering the soul-draining effect the Navigators had described. He came to this point without conclusion, feeling nothing at the realisation of this fact.

'That is better,' announced Kosa, her voice suddenly stark across the intervox, startling Aeschelus. The only sensation he could liken it to was the half-waking feeling he had encountered when he had been using his catalapsean node to rest portions of his brain on extended combat duty. Like surfacing from a daydream, the strategium swum into view after a few seconds of vagueness.

The nimbus of Fedualis' energy was dimming and he struggled to pronounce the words of his mantra. Aeschelus shared the feeling of strength leaching away, the flicker of the golden light becoming a physical rendition of his own wavering attention. Fighting back a dizziness that should have been impossible to his enhanced physiology, he passed his gaze over the bridge crew. Most were standing slack-jawed and vacant. Only the Space Marines still moved with any purpose, and even they were sluggish in their actions.

'It. Is. Working.' Kosa's voice was forced. She laughed, short and sharp. 'We are moving…'

Praxamedes turned to the warp engine controls with stilted movements and Nemetus stepped away, returning slowly to his place at the Geller field console.

'Traction increasing,' Praxamedes managed to report, bending close to the screens as though he had trouble seeing them.

'Shock wave!'

The Navigator's shout was a clarion call, rousing the Ultramarines from their soporific state for a few seconds.

'*The catastrophic breach has sent out a pulse,*' Kosa explained hurriedly. She started crying, sobbing between exclamations. '*It will hit us. Send us away from the hole. Void-cursed! So close. So far.*'

'Can you move us through it?' Aeschelus asked, addressing the question to anyone that cared to answer. He checked on Fedualis. Sweat streamed down the astropath's wrinkled face, each bead a glistening drop of molten gold.

'Geller field absorbing most of the output,' said Praxamedes. 'Kosa was right.'

'*Incoming shock wave,*' warned Qurius. '*Hitting us now.*'

A sudden throbbing rumbled through the ship. The throb turned to a lifting surge, a swell that was felt inside the mind rather than by the body.

'*We're being carried away!*' wailed Kosa.

'No!' roared Aeschelus. It felt as though the *Ithraca's Vengeance* was pitching sideways, flung back across the warp, though his rational mind knew such a thing was entirely a construct of his imagination. Waves of psychic force lashed at the Geller field, sounding alarm chimes across the stations.

Inspiration struck as the captain watched amber and red lights spreading over the Geller field displays. He charged across the strategium, barging Nemetus aside when the lieutenant failed to clear the way. Without a second thought for the dazed lieutenant, Aeschelus opened the runepad cover on the emergency shutdown. He punched in the deactivation codes. Sirens wailed from prow to stern along the ship, warning of the Geller field collapse.

'Are you insane?' roared Admonius, stomping towards the captain.

'We can ride it!' exclaimed Praxamedes. 'Warp engine has traction, ready for translation.'

'*No!*' Qurius' injunction was a shriek. '*We will be sheared apart if we translate.*'

Before the captain could issue any further orders, he felt a coldness sweep through him. A whisper flowed across the strategium, bringing gasps and cries from the human crew and mutters of discontent from the Space Marines. Everything was swallowed by a deepening twilight.

The air fogged with purple and green and leering faces danced across the dead hololith screens.

'Warp intrusion,' shouted Admonius, his tempormortis flaring with pale light as he raised the ceremonial hourglass like a lantern. 'You have doomed us, you fool!'

Flitting shadowlights moved through the walls and terminals without hindrance, forming brief figures and bestial shapes. They spiralled around Fedualis, fanged maws wide, claws glinting with golden light. One ghost passed directly through Aeschelus, its mouth emerging from his chest, a twitching serpent tail lashing past his nose before it disappeared.

He felt terror.

Not his own; he was biologically incapable of such a depth of dread. Like hearing an echo rather than a spoken word, he felt panic and horror second-hand, catching its wake from the apparitions that flooded across the strategium. Infected by this malaise, some of the human crew screamed and wailed, falling to the floor or burying their faces in their hands.

Pure fear.

Not mortal fear. The dread of immortals. The collateral emotion of fleeing warp-entities. This was no attack, it was a stampede.

Given movement by the inflowing warp-stuff, Aeschelus' thoughts fired quickly again, the link between body and soul briefly restored. He understood in a moment that the stillness had becalmed the creatures of the warp every bit as much as the ship. Given sudden form and motion again, the Neverborn filth were fleeing for survival, trying to escape the zone of warp silence.

Admonius' blade hissed from its sheath, but before he could strike at the swarming apparitions, they were gone. There was a few seconds of release, before the stultifying pressure started to build again.

'Captain...' Kosa's voice was strained, barely audible among the cries and whimpers of the traumatised deck crew. 'Captain, the breach is closing.'

'Can you steer us?' Aeschelus demanded, moving towards Fedualis.

'Barely,' said Kosa.

'Push, by the Emperor's might. Push!' the captain exhorted the astropath, though whether his words could be heard he did not know.

Admonius stepped up beside Aeschelus, the waning light of the hourglass bathing both captain and astropath. Though it might have been the movement of shadows across his creased face, it seemed as though Fedualis twitched, as though taking in a deep breath.

'Almost at the breach boundary.' Each word from the Navigator was forced. 'Almost... No! We are slipping away!'

'Engaging warp drive now!' Nemetus' cry was unexpected, followed a second later by the blare of horns as he engaged the main warp drive. The whole vessel bucked, artificial gravity plates screeching beneath the feet of the crew as they tried to compensate for the sudden shift from warp space. Terminals exploded, showering sparks across the strategium, while secondary alarms hooted and wailed their warnings from a dozen different consoles and the servitors grumbled the woes of their slaved systems. Everything juddered, throwing loose items to the deck, toppling a couple of deck officers who had been attempting to cross to their consoles. Aeschelus' armour creaked and moaned as reality rushed in where only the warp had been.

Fedualis gave a cry and fell sideways, only the swift reaction of Aeschelus stopping him banging his head on the unforgiving deck. Crouching, he lowered the astropath, who had fallen into a coma, breathing shallow but steady.

'We're through!' Qurius' announcement was part sob and part cry of joy. 'We're through the breach! Praise the Lord of Light! Hail the Master of Terra!'

Aeschelus stood and surveyed the strategium. They were back in realspace but there were fires and sparking conduits to deal with, and he could feel the crushing weight of the soul dampening had returned. It took him several seconds to gather his wits.

'Praxamedes, damage control,' he finally ordered, coming to his senses. 'Nemetus. Find out where we are.'

CHAPTER NINE

'There will be no further insubordination.' Simut glared down at the stooping plasmancer. Lacking legs, she could not kneel as was expected; instead she inclined herself almost parallel to the floor of the command chamber. 'Be grateful that I will restore minimal protocols to your control.'

'Barely enough to function,' replied Ah-hotep, bitterness flooding from her cortical aura. Simut was surprised at her defiance. Did she really think her position so secure that she could openly flout his commands?

'But enough to function, plasmancer,' the overlord reminded her. 'You almost destroyed one of my ships with your foolish behaviour.'

'My ship, Simut.' Ah-hotep rose up. Simut could feel her energy matrix probing at the data network of the tomb ship, accessing its sensor hierarchy. 'Its systems are restoring. There was no danger.'

'A ship sworn to *my* service.'

'A temporary gift from the technomandrites.'

Mention of the enigmatic tech-brokers gave Simut a moment of concern. Was Ah-hotep's belligerence a deliberate plan or just a symptom of her alliance with the technomandrites? Doubts flickered through his proteon synapses.

'Why did you not trust me?' he asked, changing the subject. 'Why this attempted conspiracy with my royal warden?'

'There was no conspiracy, merely communication, my lord,' Phetos interjected. 'I would not have allowed anything to happen that harmed your body or threatened your position.'

'You judged poorly, but the blame lies with Ah-hotep for entreating your help.' Simut leaned forward, the metal of his arms resting on his knees. He could recall the memory of the posture, more than he could genuinely feel it. Everything about his manufactured body was like a misaligned lens, a fraction removed from true synchronicity. The passing of aeons had not been kind.

'The ship did not escape,' Ah-hotep protested. 'The end vindicates our decisions.'

'Vindication? You are vindicated only if I decide it is so! I am your lord and judge.' Simut accompanied his words with a chastising control pulse that sent the plasmancer spinning across the chamber, landing with a crash to skid across the floor. The hum of deactivating stasis tombs flooded the room followed by the matched tramp of feet as the lychguard advanced around the throne dais and surrounded the plasmancer, weapons at the ready.

'You think me an idiot,' snarled Simut. 'If you are right, perhaps I am stupid enough to destroy you and risk the ire of the technomandrites.'

Simut descended the steps, gleaming energy coiling about his skeletal form. The lychguard parted to allow him to stand over Ah-hotep.

'Am I stupid, Ah-hotep?' he asked quietly.

'No.'

'You forgot something.'

The plasmancer looked up at him, eyes flaring jade for a moment before dimming with subservience.

'No, *my lord*.'

Simut stood there for a while longer, making his superiority plain. When he tired of displaying his dominance he stepped back, conjuring a manipulative field to draw the plasmancer up from the floor, as one might extend a hand. He had made his point, it would be unseemly to gloat.

'We cannot brook any more delays,' Simut announced, returning to his throne. 'If we do not make back the time we lost in the last system the Silent King will be displeased. With both of us.'

'I agree, my lord.' Ah-hotep hesitantly drifted closer. 'It is why we could not risk any outside interference.'

Simut waved away her attempts at justification. 'There will be no conquest. I will annihilate the occupants of this star system without pause, and when they are all dead we shall erect the resonator unopposed.'

He felt reluctance from both the plasmancer and Phetos.

'There is a problem with my edict?'

'It would be safer to secure the resonator site and use its powers to subjugate the humans, than attempt to fight a full-scale war with them, Bountiful Font of the Dynasty's Wisdom, Marshal of the Skies,' said the royal warden. 'Drawn out conflict could prove costly.'

'Not as costly as wearing out the patience of my cousin,' Simut replied. 'The expenditure of resources will be worth the expediting of our goal.'

'What would you have me do?' asked Ah-hotep. 'My ship is still repairing itself, but I can–'

'Nothing,' Simut told her. 'I want nothing of you, plasmancer. Speed is the vital component of this plan. King Szarekh values the completion of the task to schedule more than the continued existence of the system inhabitants. Zozar and his skorpekhs will lead the first attack.'

'You would unleash the Destroyers first, my lord?' Ah-hotep's spinal tail whipped in agitation. 'I thought them a resource of last resort.'

'You thought wrongly.' Simut motioned to Phetos with a regal nod, accompanied by the databurst of the command protocols that would unlock the Destroyer-quarantined tombs. 'They are a weapon. One that I have been too reluctant to use, which has cost me standing in the eyes of the king. I have perhaps confused mercy with prudence and the project has been placed in jeopardy. A mistake I will not make again – for the humans or my servants.'

The jolt of forced translocation shuddered through Ah-hotep as she materialised on the twilit command deck of her ship. Simut's casual use of his matter transporters was possibly his least edifying trait. It was symptomatic of his entire outlook that he treated his fellow nobles as nothing more than chattel to be shunted around as he desired. The overlord seemed particularly prone to using it as a form of chastisement against the plasmancer, with full knowledge of how humiliating it was to be thrown across the void at will.

Systems were minimal but recovering after her desperate protocol override. As promised, Simut had restored canoptek services and the rudimentary command protocols. Other systems, including weapons and the stasis chamber activation core, had been triple-locked against cortical incursion. The overlord was taking no chances that Ah-hotep might access her own military potential.

The energy surveyors were her primary concern. She needed to know what was happening in the system and fleet. Ah-hotep had no doubt that the necrons would meet with swift success behind the onslaught of the Destroyers, but at what cost? Every time they were forced to resurrect a warrior, every canoptek contact and cryptothrall engagement risked the Destroyer malaise spreading into a new part of the system – a system to which her own protocols were now adjoined thanks to Simut's overbearing presence.

Drifting back and forth across her dimly lit mastaba, Ah-hotep directed the canoptek swarms and higher beings to focus their attention on the sensor suite.

It did not take long for the primary detectors to come back on line, augmenting her personal energy sensory field a thousand-fold. While secondary systems initialised, Ah-hotep turned her artificial eye on the residue of the astromantic detonation she had caused, curious to see what physical fallout had occurred.

A variety of physical debris remained, spiralling slowly away from the point of catastrophic failure. A spectrum of radioactive particles and energy waves formed beautiful patterns of electromagnetism and plasma, overlaying each other in synchronous circles. Ah-hotep wished she could drain those expanding clouds, her hunger breaking the moment of delight. Drawn by the desire to feed, she lingered awhile, imagining supping on negative particles and collapsing photon streams.

She was about to return to a more mundane scan of the target world – more importantly the circling moonbase, where she had detected so much astromantic activity – when a spark drew her attention.

At first she wondered if it was a remnant of the broken starship's drives or energy generator. Electrical fluctuations betrayed a working power system, which further scrutiny soon revealed to be a functioning reactor shield. It was still possible that this was some protected core that had somehow been ejected in the detonation, but that supposition disappeared the moment it changed course...

Something else. Another ship?

She reviewed the memory store and saw nothing to suggest that two vessels had been trying to escape. If the gleaming dot she traced across the voids was a ship, it must have come through almost at the instant the other starship had exploded.

Who were they? Unwitting victims of the offensive about to commence, or reinforcements brought by the cries of the humans before the overnull had silenced them?

For the time being the ship would be invisible against the vast backdrop of the system energy base and the distortion of the fleet's presence. It was only because Ah-hotep had been focused on that small segment of the void that she had noticed it at all.

Simut would not have seen it.

Which meant it was imperative that, for now at least, Ah-hotep kept the newcomer a secret.

CHAPTER TEN

The *Ithraca's Vengeance* crawled through the outer void with engines, augurs and life support systems running on minimal power to preserve the strained reactors. Armed with only the most basic information about their surroundings, Nemetus studied the charts and databanks in an effort to narrow down their location. Given the length of time they had spent in the warp, their trajectory uncontrolled, he barely knew where to begin.

Basic sensor sweeps picked up the local star and the main orbital bodies, but any more detailed information was restricted to just a few hundred thousand miles in the immediate vicinity. Several worlds within the ecozone were potential candidates for habitation, so on the basis that the inner system would be more densely populated than the outer orbits, Captain Aeschelus had set course in-system.

Without any other information, Nemetus decided that the best way to locate the system out of the several hundred identified by the cogitators was to make a manual observation of the local starfield. The servitors of the navigational banks would be able to retro-calculate the location of the *Ithraca's Vengeance* from the observable stars, like an ancient ship's master sailing the Aeneid Sea on Macragge but on a vaster scale. With this in mind, he took a dataslate with a videograph attached up to the main gallery on the prow decks, furthest from the polluting glare of the plasma engines.

The viewing gallery was a glassite dome about sixty feet high, situated above the strategium. The system star dominated the view ahead, the eagle-break prow of the cruiser pointed towards the growing circle of light. Above gave the best view of the starfield, dense clusters of distant suns spread across the inner spiral arm of the galaxy. Nemetus recognised none of them.

While he took notations and videolithic data the door hissed open and Praxamedes joined him. The other lieutenant also had a recording slate in hand.

'Checking that I am doing this correctly?' said Nemetus. The words came out with more venom than he had intended, stopping Praxamedes mid-stride.

'I thought you might like some help.' The other lieutenant lifted a hand towards the star-filled void. 'That's a lot of cataloguing to do.'

The humble offer made Nemetus feel even more guilty for his accusation. There was only one way Nemetus knew how to remedy the situation: head-on.

'Apologies, brother. You did not deserve my scorn. I cannot help but feel you think me inferior, but it is only the shame of my shortcomings making themselves known.'

'I have never known you to be anything other than a superb leader and a devout servant of the Emperor,' said Praxamedes, starting forward again. 'Even I would find this task onerous, but it is a vital one.'

'Thank you, brother. All assistance is welcome.'

They stood side by side scanning for several minutes before the silence had gone on too long and Nemetus could not help but break it.

'How are the repairs coming along?'

'Slowly. The main power network is badly damaged, hampering other efforts. The tech-priests are dedicating more time to rerouting the cabling and restoring reactor integrity. We're fortunate that none of the shielding broke when we force-translated back to realspace.'

Nemetus considered this for a few seconds.

'Was that a rebuke, brother?' Nemetus half-laughed, to hide the doubt in his question. 'I cannot tell any longer.'

'An observation. What prompted you to activate the warp drive?'

'It was purely instinctual. I was worried that we would lose the opportunity altogether. The captain had already brought down the Geller fields. I reasoned that we had one chance to escape.'

'Reasoned, or guessed?' Praxamedes asked the question lightly but Nemetus could feel the weight of it.

'There was no time for reason, brother,' he argued, remembering why he thought Praxamedes was constantly scrutinising him. 'Had I waited even another second we might never have broken through the barrier.'

'And if you were wrong? Not for a second had you considered the possibility that the forces unleashed would tear the cruiser apart.'

'The situation required action. If it had been you, would you have triggered the warp jump?'

'No,' confessed Praxamedes. He studied his slate for a few seconds. 'I would not have gambled all of our lives on a guess.'

'We were adrift in the warp. There was nothing to lose. It was no gamble.'

'I disagree. There may have been another opportunity. We might have engineered a more certain solution. Future possibilities that you rashly ignored.'

Nemetus lowered his dataslate to look at his battle-brother. Praxamedes kept his eye fixed on his readings, whether from diligence or to avoid his brother's gaze was not clear.

'None of us are feeling right,' said Nemetus. 'The whole company is tense. The serfs are confused, easily distracted. We cannot afford to have divisions between us.'

Praxamedes finally turned his eyes on Nemetus, sighing heavily. 'You want me to accept your mistakes without comment for the sake of morale?'

'I do not accept that I made a mistake,' Nemetus snapped. 'And I do not seek your judgement. We are all alive because of what I did. There was not going to be a second chance.'

He moved away, turning his back on Praxamedes. Since his arrival Nemetus had been aware of the differences between him and his brother-lieutenant but they had never seemed to affect their ability to fight together before. Now he wondered if Praxamedes really would be second-guessing every decision.

'It isn't judgement,' Praxamedes said, following him. 'I'm trying to understand how you think. You and the captain, you have this manner, this quickness about you that I can't replicate.'

'Why would you want to?' Nemetus turned, surprised by the confession. 'Why be something you are not?'

Praxamedes did not reply. He turned his stare back to the swathe of stars.

'You think it is holding you back from command?' guessed Nemetus. 'The captain keeps choosing me over you for battle command.'

'Not just the captain. I had a ship command but was then assigned to the captain as his second. Why was that? What did Battle Group Command not see in me?'

'I cannot speak for others, but I would rather follow Aeschelus with you as his second. He has a hunger that you temper. Can you imagine what trouble he and I would get into without your presence?'

Praxamedes did not seem amused by the thought, lost in his concerns.

'Did you hear me? You would make a… You are not listening to me, brother. Is it the warp effect dulling your thoughts?'

'Can you see that?' Praxamedes asked, lifting a finger to point out of the great arched window. 'That light.'

Nemetus looked, scanning quickly across the stars until he saw what Praxamedes was indicating. A bluish globe.

'Some kind of dust lensing?' suggested Nemetus, though his hearts started beating a little faster.

'After-warp mirage?' said Praxamedes, with equal lack of conviction.

Nemetus looked carefully, trying to see with his eyes, not his hopes.

'Too regular to be a star or other stellar phenomenon. It's a station,' said the lieutenant, hearts speeding. 'A star base of some kind. Outer system Mandeville defence, perhaps?'

Praxamedes shared a glance and the ghost of a smile. 'I guess we won't need these any more,' he said, lifting his dataslate.

'I will keep mine,' Nemetus replied. 'You should report this to the captain.'

'If it's an Imperial station, that would be almost a miracle.'

'Maybe those prayers of the Navigators did some good after all,' said Nemetus.

Praxamedes nodded and hurried away.

Nemetus turned his attention back to the window and wondered what new challenges were coming. There was no way it could be an Imperial facility. That would be far too convenient for a ship of Fleet Quintus.

Closing with the seemingly dormant space station, the *Ithraca's Vengeance* was a shadow of its former power. Only one bank of void shields was operational, and those only available if they ran on power diverted from the engine array. The ship could have top speed or energy shields, but not both. Similarly, augurs and long-range communications were both crippled by the crash-drop from warp space – translating from the unprotected warp to the crushing reality of realspace had overloaded nearly every sensor spine and vox-circuit. Reactor power was steadier than before, but only eighty per cent of normal operational capacity. Red-robed tech-priests were all over the strategium, the fragrance of their incense burners and holy lubricants almost blotting out the stale sweat and bodily fluid odour of monotask servitors and sleep-deprived armoury attendants.

Aeschelus was aware that he was not at full capabilities either. The flattening of the warp that had stranded the ship worked both ways, shielding realspace from much of the warp's interaction. The Navigators had tried to explain the interconnectivity of the two realms but Aeschelus had got lost in the analogies, unable to twist his thinking to the dimensionless properties of warp space whilst thinking about physical beings. The short, crude version was that the lack of texture in the warp had a similarly dulling effect on the minds of sentient creatures, including the crew.

The astropath, Fedualis, was unable to provide further help as he was still in the apothecarion, comatose but alive. Occasionally he would murmur nonsense, his physical condition more stable than his mental state.

The captain did not allow these factors to overwhelm his thinking. They were hurt but alive, and that was the most important thing. Just as a Space Marine was deadly even without his bolt rifle and Mark X armour, so the *Ithraca's Vengeance* and company were still capable of influential action.

What that action might be had so far eluded Aeschelus. The presence of the warp-dulling effect suggested that whatever had happened at Casparill had spread to this system, wherever they were. There was no way of knowing whether the invasion was ongoing, completed or about to start, or if the enemy were here at all. Coming upon the star base was a stroke of good fortune, but Aeschelus was wary of such a boon. Short-range vox had received nothing from the Space Marines' hails and the sensor banks were unable to determine anything but the barest data about the station – its reactors were on line. This suggested occupation by either friend or foe, but the lack of any other vessels in the vicinity made it impossible to know which.

If there were xenos or heretic powers at work in the system, the Ultramarines would do everything they could to combat the threat. Even if Aeschelus had not been determined to drag some benefit out of the disastrous warp jump, he had no choice but to confront the enemy. Kosa had been explicit in her diagnosis of the warp engines and the ongoing conditions of the neversea: the ship was as stuck in this star system as it had been in warp space. Even if the warp engines were repaired the lack of intangible traction through the Impossibility Boundary made exiting the system impossible while the enemy suppression – however it was achieved – remained in effect.

'Captain, the vox-receivers are operational again,' reported Shipmaster Oloris. 'We are receiving a general broadcast signal from in-system. No ciphers, just standard Imperial channels.'

'Which channels?' Aeschelus asked, pushing his way past two tech-priests to attend to the shipmaster at the communications hub in front of his command throne. The red-robed adepts withdrew with clicks and whirring, their gaggle of cyber-altered monotasks lumbering after them.

'All of the channels, captain,' said Oloris. 'Blanket transmission over available naval, military and even command channels.'

'No cipher? I do not like the sound of that. Could be a carrier signal for scrapcode or some xenos assault.'

'There is no way of isolating the signal, captain, not with our equipment in such poor state.' The shipmaster shrugged. 'I am not sure what more damage a rogue signal could do, anyway.'

Aeschelus considered the problem and erred on the side of risk. His need for intelligence on what was happening in the system outweighed the minimal threat of enemy vox-attack.

'One other thing, captain. We have managed to break down the star base's ident signal,' Oloris added. 'It is called Leshk Station. Imperial Navy channel.'

'Pass that to Lieutenant Nemetus. It might give him what he needs to identify the system from the records data we have aboard.'

Oloris nodded and withdrew from the console, leaving the controls free for Aeschelus. The captain looked at the broadcast data that scrolled across an identifier screen. The line of numerals and symbols was meaningless, just standard datascript. The only thing it told him was that the signal used an Imperial carrier wave. It repeated, indicating an automated broadcast of some kind. That was little reassurance. The most basic of subterfuges could be used to mask a xenos origin, or the transmitter might physically be in enemy hands.

With a deep breath, Aeschelus accepted the signal code, transferring the message to the voxmitter in the console itself. A woman's voice crackled from the speaker.

'This is Sister-Chatelain Aures speaking on behalf of Imperial Commander Kaleb Monfrottine Lowensten, ruler by appointment and divine right of the Imperial Territories of Orestes under the auspices of the Adepts of Terra and the Master of Mankind. On behalf of said territories, Commander Lowensten offers immediate and unconditional surrender. We are powerless against this assault, and to preserve against unnecessary casualties the Imperial Commander grants you free passage to his worlds but for the sovereign territory of the Orestes Orbital Palaces. These grounds are to remain inviolate. There will be no aggression towards your occupation of the system. All force will be deployed to defend the household of the Imperial commander.'

The message hissed and began a new loop. Aeschelus shut down the speaker with a growl, the contents of the transmission like acid on his nerves.

'Cowards.' He turned to find the shipmaster still on hand. 'Capitulation in the face of the enemy is a heresy against the Emperor.'

'Indeed, captain, a very grave crime. The signal is still broadcasting, so I would wager that either the Imperial commander is dead, or the enemy have not accepted the surrender.'

'If he is not dead, he will wish he was when we get to him,' said Aeschelus, returning to his command throne. 'Also, you can tell Nemetus that he need not spend any more time with star charts and records.

Orestes System. I saw it when we were calculating our last jump. About six light years short of Casparill. We were not too short of our target.'

'I have never heard of a Sister-Chatelain before, captain. She did not sound pleased with the message she was relating.'

'One of the Adepta Sororitas, from the Orders Famulous. They usually concern themselves with maintaining the bloodline purity of Imperial commanders and brokering inter-system pacts between ruling families and castes. A Sister-Chatelain is assigned to a world as advisor on such matters and other Ecclesiarchy issues; she has no command authority. I expect she likely thinks the same as I do – it is an affront to the Emperor to surrender without battle.'

'It seems the enemy have moved on from Casparill, my captain.'

Aeschelus nodded and sat down, drumming his fingers on the arm of the command throne. There was little enough new information from the broadcast. It said nothing of the overall state of the system other than that the Ultramarines could expect no assistance for the time being. If the enemy were still here, the *Ithraca's Vengeance* would have to face it alone.

The defence station grew larger in the main canopy, the light of the local star drawing a stark terminus across its docking gantries and defensive cannon turrets. From Praxamedes' direction of approach, it looked like an inverted, truncated cone at the hub of a dozen gantry-spars, its upper and lower surfaces dominated by large cannon arrays. There was nothing on the augurs to suggest that the weapons were powering up, nor any of the multitude of smaller batteries ideal for blasting the gunship out of the void. Even so, the silence grated, every second of unresolved tension weighing heavily.

He tried the gunship's vox again.

'Leshk Station, this is Lieutenant Praxamedes of the Ultramarines Chapter. We are receiving your ident-cast. Respond on any channel. Failure to respond will result in being treated as hostile territory. Do you receive?'

Nothing but static replied. He caught the eye of the pilot next to him.

'If they're not answering the cruiser's vox messages, I don't think they'll answer ours,' said the lieutenant. 'Be prepared for evasive manoeuvring.'

'I always am, brother-lieutenant,' replied the pilot.

Praxamedes activated the gunnery machine-spirits, slaving them to the pilot's controls before he rose from the seat to stand at the door through to the main compartment.

'Landing zone is hostile,' he told the twenty Space Marines within. 'We have no information about the Imperial servants on board, so check your target zones. Assess collateral casualties on an individual basis.'

'No docking tractors, brother-lieutenant,' announced the pilot, meaning that there was nobody operating the booms that jutted from the starbase's exterior. They would have to manually dock, matching course, angular speed and planar velocity.

'Go topside,' said Praxamedes, turning to point to the uppermost docking arm. 'We'll start there and work our way down the station. The command decks should be somewhere near the main embarkation cluster. Once we have that under our control, we'll be able to see what we're up against.'

They passed within range of the anti-boarding defences without any sign of activity aboard the station. Praxamedes still could not relax.

He had never experienced such tension before, despite nearly a decade of fighting for the Emperor. His first instinct was to dismiss his concerns as symptoms of the soul-deadening; factors that would be negligible in normal circumstances seemed far greater than before. But he could not apportion all of the blame to the strange warp situation. The kernel of his discomfort came from Captain Aeschelus, or more specifically the captain's decision to place Praxamedes in charge of this expedition. Aeschelus had told Praxamedes that the unknown nature of the coming encounter was better met by his more level-headed approach. The lieutenant could not help but think that it was some kind of test, though. How he performed now would influence the captain's opinion for every subsequent engagement.

Under guidance thrusters, the gunship turned, sliding sideways towards the end of the docking spar so that the front assault hatch would line up with the end of the gantry quay. A screen flickered to life at the co-pilot's position, showing a basic schematic of the base. There were thousands of blurry dots and lines denoting power systems and life signals.

'Augur feed from the *Ithraca's Vengeance*,' said Praxamedes, examining the display plate. 'Looks like a full staff. Either that or an oversized occupation force. From the working energy grid but lack of defensive fire we can assume that if the enemy are aboard they do not have full control over the weapons systems.'

'Target at fifty yards,' reported the pilot. 'Deploying mag-grapples.'

Two cables snaked across the divide, their tips glinting blue. Coming into contact with the gantry the electromagnetic pads activated with a flash, clamping tight to the structure. The gunship vibrated as powerful winches in its nose started to pull it closer.

'We are receiving doorlink feed from the station,' said the pilot. 'Remote opening enabled.'

'On your mark, brother.' The lieutenant moved into the transport compartment where his force of Intercessor squads waited with a trio of Aggressors in Gravis armour. He gestured for the Aggressors to join him, their heavier warplate ideally suited to the vanguard role he required.

Waiting by the assault ramp, Praxamedes turned on the external vid-feed and watched on a small screen as the gunship closed the distance to the spar's armoured portal. When they were about ten yards away, the pilot activated the docking systems and a ridged umbilical extended outward, its near end expanding to encompass the nose of the gunship. Illuminated by lights from the craft Praxamedes could see the main door still closed, the floor of the umbilical forming from hardened slats.

'Docking complete,' the pilot told them. 'Door controls synchronised. Awaiting your command to open.'

The lieutenant operated the assault ramp controls, sending it wheezing down into the interior of the umbilical. With the Aggressors flanking him, three squads of Intercessors behind, Praxamedes stepped down from the gunship. In his hands he held the bolt rifle that had been gifted to him by his former captain, Gheris. Its weight was almost non-existent in his hand, the chased silver Ultramarines symbols in its casing and the stylised eagle around the muzzle gleaming in the light of the gunship's lamps. It was a beautiful example of Artificer Maraus' best work.

He stopped a few yards from the doorway. Around him the Aggressors raised their flame gauntlets, pilot lights flickering blue.

'Open it,' Praxamedes ordered the pilot. The targeter feed in his helm showed a spot in the middle of the portal – chest height of any person beyond.

A light turned green in the wall beside the gate and a tone sounded.

With a juddering motion the door hinged inwards and upwards revealing the airlock chamber, devoid of occupants. Praxamedes moved
forward with long strides, gun level, while he read the environment
feed in his armour's read-outs. The umbilical seal was tight, air pressure nominal.

'Brother Horatus,' he said, pointing to the inner door controls.

The Aggressor took a few steps ahead while the others targeted the
inner door. Praxamedes adjusted his aim, picking a spot between two
of his battle-brothers.

A simple flip-switch activated the inner door, which wheezed into
life and swung away like the outer door. The Aggressors pounded forward into the room beyond, peeling left and right while Praxamedes
followed close after. The airlock resounded to the feet of the Intercessors a few yards behind the lieutenant.

The room was a typical docking bay chamber, with silvery spacesuits
hanging on the wall to the right, a row of lockers and boxes to the left.
Directly ahead was another door and above it a broad window that
revealed the control chamber. Three figures stood there – two women
and a man – dressed in Imperial Navy uniforms. Praxamedes saw immediately something was wrong. The Navy personnel barely moved, staring
down into the dock chamber with vacant gazes, swaying listlessly from
side to side. One of the women frowned slowly, head turning to follow the lieutenant as he moved towards the doorway.

'Company command, we are aboard Leshk Station,' he voxed back
to the *Ithraca's Vengeance*. 'There is evidence of the warp malaise affect-
ing the crew. More extreme than our own, perhaps due to duration of
exposure. Investigating.'

While the Intercessors dispersed to secure the immediate vicinity,
Praxamedes and the Aggressors ascended the steps beyond the door,
coming on the locked entrance to the control chamber. A single kick
shattered the door's hinges, sending it flying across the bare ferrocrete
floor within. Sluggishly, the dock crew turned towards the new arrivals,
a ghost of reaction passing across their faces, their jaws working slowly
as though trying to form words. The man tilted his head, face screw-
ing up in concentration.

'Emperor's Angels?' he muttered, taking a step forward. He stopped
and blinked stupidly.

'Lieutenant, we have civilians,' voxed Sergeant Villina from outside the docking chamber. *'Minimal response to our presence. No threat presented.'*

Other squad leaders echoed the report, confirming Praxamedes' suspicion.

'Company command, I don't think the enemy are on the station.' He considered the implications of the crew's sluggish behaviour. 'The soul-dampening effect is in full force. Whatever weapon the necrons used at Casparill is here, or has been.'

There was a pause of a few seconds before Captain Aeschelus replied.

'Be wary, lieutenant. If this effect has stretched from Casparill to this system, there is no way we can predict how powerful it might become or how continued exposure may take its toll.'

'Understood, company command. Moving on to the main control chamber with all speed.'

'Understood, assault command,' replied Captain Aeschelus. *'We will move in to provide support. I will come aboard when you have secured station control.'*

CHAPTER ELEVEN

Leshk Station had been an outer system transfer port, positioned close to the Mandeville point where warp-capable ships could arrive and depart with the least risk from the system's gravitational influence. Interstellar vessels would unload their passengers and cargo into the station rather than undertake the time-consuming inter-planetary journey to the habitable core worlds. System lighters and bulk carriers ferried between the port and Orestes III.

Neither warp craft nor system vessels were docked when Aeschelus took a gunship over to the main docks to rendezvous with the Space Marines aboard Leshk, but as the captain viewed the exterior of the station he could see no sign of damage.

A contingent of Intercessors waited for him inside the passenger terminal, a substation that ran parallel to the main docking arms, closer to the station's centre of mass but clear of the coming-and-going merchant craft. It was a small facility, capable of handling only a few hundred arriving and departing individuals. Most would have been naval transfers and replacements.

Dozens of people lingered around the terminal complex, shuffling without purpose from the hall to the adjoining chambers. The majority wore uniforms of one kind or another, a few in civilian clothes. They seemed capable of basic motor functions and the rudiments of previous behaviour – Aeschelus could see two children pulling open rations packs from a broken crate, messily crumbling the contents into mechanically working mouths, drool running down their chins.

He observed more of the same behaviour as he and his escort made their way through the station to the command hub. Coverall-clad workers stumbled around their machinery, fumbling at controls they had manned for most of their lives. Men and women with the badges of petty officers staggered from one post to the next, mumbling incoherently, struggling to find the words to cajole and admonish their lackadaisical charges.

Given the overall cleanliness of the station and the state of grooming of its inhabitants, the captain estimated that only a few days at most had passed since the soul-consuming effect had waylaid the Orestes System. Aboard the *Ithraca's Vengeance*, it was still possible for Space Marine-supervised work crews to continue to operate under close scrutiny, but here it seemed that pure routine was the only force that compelled the people to act at all.

It was a four hundred-yard walk to the rendezvous, and the passage of the Space Marines caused some reaction among the afflicted. Most acknowledged their presence with stares and half-hearted salutes, but a few dozen trailed mindlessly after the captain and his warriors.

Coming to the main gate of the control hub, he found a squad of Intercessors surrounded by scores of Imperial Navy crew and civilians. The Space Marines were doing their best to repel the crowd without violence, but here and there they were forced to thrust back against the constant press of humanity trying to get to the doors.

'Shift change was twenty minutes ago, brother-captain,' the sergeant leading the escort explained. 'The next crew and guard are trying to get to their posts, but there's no aggression.'

'Captain!' Praxamedes spotted Aeschelus as he ducked through the door into the command chamber. The lieutenant was looming over a red-robed figure no taller than his waist. 'Over here.'

Aeschelus made his way past half a dozen Space Marines working at various terminals, most of which seemed as dead as the vox-channels.

'This is Aesthetek Korsin, one of the tech-priests assigned to the station.'

The lieutenant gestured towards his diminutive companion. 'She has been moderately helpful. It appears that her intellectual capacity is less diminished than that of her more organic colleagues.'

The individual that looked up at Aeschelus was mostly copper and silver, without even the approximation of a face beneath the red hood. A grating voice blared from a grilled box hanging around the tech-priest's neck.

'Captain?' Even through the artificial modulation the voice was hesitant, distant. 'Captain?'

'Captain Aeschelus,' Praxamedes said, slowly and loudly. 'Our commander. Please show him to the vox controls.'

'Vox?' The tech-priest clicked and whirred for several seconds. 'Vox this way.'

'Augur readings from the station logs are inconclusive,' Praxamedes reported as they followed the tech-priest to the far end of the long, narrow control deck. 'There were some massive disruptions about forty-seven hours ago. Probable arrival of enemy craft, but no warp signature detected.'

'What is happening with the vox?'

'There's an incoming signal, brother-captain. Ciphered for command only. We haven't been able to locate a cogent station officer yet, but hopefully your command override codes should access the channel for us.'

'I see.' Aeschelus stopped as the tech-priest pointed with a mechanical claw towards a small panel of speakers and dials, a manual pick-up hanging from a coiled cable on the wall beside it.

The captain found the blinking rune indicating the channel connection and tapped his cipher code into the alphanumeric pad. The rune turned green, illuminating a slider at the top of the keypad. Aeschelus pushed the lever fully across and the speakers crackled into life at full volume. The noise was brutally loud, bouncing back from the metal terminals and ceiling. Aeschelus moved the slider down to halfway, dimming the sound of the vox-static. A few more seconds passed before a man's voice could be heard.

'*Leshk Station? Praise the Emperor! Did the* Invigorous *get away?*'

'Do you think the *Invigorous* was the ship that tried to translate?' said Praxamedes. 'The one whose warp engine detonation allowed us to jump?'

'Could be.' Aeschelus picked up the voice-transmitter and activated his external address. 'Identify yourself.'

'What? Who is this? You don't sound like Marco or Scrollig.'

'I am Captain Aeschelus of the Ultramarines vessel *Ithraca's Vengeance.* De facto commander of Leshk Station. Identify yourself.'

'Ultram... Here, in Orestes? All glory to the God-Emperor that our prayers were heard so swiftly.'

'Identify. Yourself.'

'My apologies, captain. This is Charnfel Gusser, hailing from Commander Lowensten's palace on Orestes Orbital.' The man spoke cogently enough, given the confusion regarding the change in circumstances. *'How...?'*

'What is your current status?'

'I don't know what you mean, captain. I am unhurt?'

'Orestes Orbital. Are you occupied? Under attack?'

'Not yet. Our fleets have been scattered or destroyed, but the enemy seem to be approaching from the opposite side of orbit, avoiding us. We've lost power to other orbital stations and facilities, and there's been broken reports of enemy boarding parties on some of the defence platforms.'

'What is the *Invigorous,* Master Gusser? Was that a ship?'

'An Imperial Navy light cruiser, captain. It happened to stop by the system on patrol. The Imperial commander ordered them to depart for help.'

'The ship did not survive warp translation.' Sounds of distress moaned over the vox. 'However, its warp engine detonation did enable our arrival. I need an immediate report, Master Gusser.'

'It's Baron Gusser, not that titles really mean anything any more. So many have died we're just filling in where we can, trying to keep things working.'

'I need to know what happened.'

'Nobody is sure, captain. Three days ago we started getting word that there was unrest on Orestes III – the planet we're orbiting. There's not a lot down there. It's an agri world. A few hundred thousand labourers and Adeptus Mechanicus personnel. I don't know why anyone would attack us.'

With the *Ithraca's Vengeance* still half-blind, it was vital to get as much intelligence as possible from the system inhabitants. Aeschelus needed to confirm that the apparition they had seen in the astropath's vision really was responsible.

If it was the necrons, it cast a new, terrible light on the crusade. Until now the traitors had been the focus of the lord primarch's wrath, but if the mysterious necrons were starting to cut off whole star systems, that would halt the progress of the battle groups more surely than any number of enemy fleets. It made sense that the xenos acted now, when the Imperium seemed to be at its weakest point, but they had miscalculated. With the lord primarch to lead them, the Emperor's servants were on the attack, not vulnerable. As soon as Roboute Guilliman learnt of this nascent threat he would take steps to extinguish it, and Aeschelus had the fortune to be at the forefront of that new battle.

'Who attacked? Are they still here? Describe the enemy to me.'

'Oh, they're here all right.' Gusser could be heard choking back a sob. 'It's awful, captain, absolutely awful. Everyone started losing focus. Just wandering off from their tasks, getting confused, not recognising people. There were fights breaking out, and several megatractors crashed because their drivers simply lost interest in what they were doing. We got word from the Navigators on the ships at the outer stations, Leshk and Konova. The warp was closing, they said. Closing? What did closing mean? The ship captains put out from dock without permission and jumped. The Invigorous remained, bless Commander Illyuin, may his soul find grace.'

'Focus, Gusser! Tell me, who is attacking?' Aeschelus was losing patience with the nobleman and was forced to wonder what had happened to the proper vox personnel and why Gusser had not succumbed to the warp effect.

'We don't know!' Gusser sobbed the reply, the vox-link crackling and breaking as something brushed against the pickup. 'They're not here yet but they've sent raiders down to the planet. Our weapons are useless. They're killing everything down there. Nobody can resist them.'

'We can,' Aeschelus assured the Orestean. He muted the pick-up and turned to Praxamedes and the tech-priest. 'I want every system on this station slaved to the Ithraca's Vengeance. We will use its vox and scanners while we can. We are going to find the enemy and we are going to attack them.'

'Yes, brother-captain.' The lieutenant raised his fist to his chest plastron in salute. 'As you command.' He moved away, speaking quickly with the red-robed Aesthetek.

Aeschelus activated the vox again.

'Baron Gusser, tell the Imperial commander that he is to cease all messages of surrender immediately. You are to resist the enemy in any way possible, with your lives if needed. The Ultramarines will capitulate to no enemy, no matter how exotic. Only with courage will you prevail.'

'*You're coming for us, captain?*' the baron whispered, barely daring to utter the words. '*Will you save us?*'

'First you must save yourselves if we are to be of assistance. Stand by for further transmissions on this channel.'

He killed the link with a snarl, finally venting his disgust at the weakness in the man. The depression effect of the warp-nullification was in full force but it seemed the inhabitants of Orestes Orbital had found some way to mitigate it. That could hold the key to victory, but in the meantime Aeschelus needed something more tangible to work with. The system's inhabitants were on the verge of defeat; he needed to give them something to focus on, a signal that not all was lost. As harbingers of the Indomitus Crusade it was not just the battle-brothers aboard the ship that were important, it was the message they had carried. A message that was being taken across the storm-sundered galaxy.

Remembering this, he switched on the vox again.

'Orestes Orbital, this is Captain Aeschelus. Know this and spread the word. The Emperor has not forgotten you.'

Ah-hotep watched with interest as the small blip of energy she recognised as the alien ship moved away from the orbiting construct in the outer system. She wished to know more about this sly intruder but dared not activate any of her more aggressive sensors in case she brought the newcomer to the attention of Simut. The overlord appeared to be wholly ignorant of the starship's arrival and was in orbit over the target world having deployed Zozar and his Destroyer legion to the surface.

Reviewing the relative positions of the necron fleet, the scattered remnants of the system defenders and the unidentified ship moving inbound at increasing speed, Ah-hotep calculated that her ship would be in the line of approach. However, if the attacker had any idea of what they were facing, it was a small course correction to take them past the necron main fleet to the resonator flotilla about half an orbit further out. Ah-hotep made some quick scans and projections, eliminated the intruder from her musings, and formed the image into a cortical broadcast.

'Overlord Simut, I have discovered a potential weakness in our fleet manoeuvres,' she sent to the other tomb ship. She expected Phetos to reply and was surprised when her cortical projection was seized by the other craft and pulled into the command-mastaba. Though her physical being remained aboard her own ship, Ah-hotep's senses reeled for a moment while they displaced to her hard light facsimile aboard the *Barge of the Stormhawk*. She dipped in acknowledgement of the overlord's rank, emanating waves of submission.

'Weakness?' hissed Simut. 'What is this weakness you speak of?'

'If your lordship would allow me a brief interface with your systems, I shall demonstrate.'

Simut considered the request for a short while, making her wait out of simple spitefulness. Eventually he acceded with a nod and extended cortical connections to the tomb ship's main arrays. Ah-hotep pollinated the matrix with the adjusted data from her own ship, bringing the image to life in the air in front of the overlord and his royal warden. Two lines quite clearly showed unobstructed routes around the fourth planet towards the incoming resonator, if the enemy ship commanders decided the blackstone artefact was a target.

'Their world is under direct attack. Do you really think the humans will see the value in attacking a distant, unidentified vessel?' said Phetos.

'I said potential weakness, my lord.' Ah-hotep directed her explanation to Simut, knowing that he was far more likely to be confused and doubtful than his lieutenant. 'It may be nothing, but the resonator is vital to our operation.'

'We cannot afford to lose it,' said Simut with a nod of agreement.

'As you have forbade my involvement in the main assault, I humbly volunteer my ship to withdraw to a point that would allow me to intercept any gathering attack on the resonator.' The image wavered, replaced by another projection that showed Ah-hotep's tomb ship and a sphere of influence that protected the vulnerable approach to the blackstone resonator and its carriers. 'It may be enough to dissuade any ultimately doomed but possibly disadvantageous offensive by the remaining human ships.'

'You assume your escorts will go with you?' said Phetos. 'Your absence weakens our fleet within the third orbit.'

'There is nothing to threaten us here, Phetos,' proclaimed Simut. 'Once we have secured dominance of the planet we will launch an attack on the orbital station that is resisting the overnull. This time we will ensure there are no anti-ship weapons on the surface or in orbit before we move the resonator into range. I approve your plan, plasmancer. Move your ship and flotilla to the position indicated and stand ready for further command.'

Ah-hotep lowered in deference again. 'I shall leave my scan routines for your study.'

As she delivered the datastream into the sensor banks of the *Barge of the Stormhawk*, Ah-hotep also included a miniscule protocol hidden among the standard data. It was a tiny wrinkle in the datastream, just enough to propagate a singular blind spot in the tomb ship's sensor arrays. A blind spot that corresponded with the alien ship's energy signature and its likely route of approach.

'Do my bidding and you will find yourself returned to favour, Ah-hotep,' Simut told her, raising a hand to dismiss her from the command chamber.

'I exist only to serve the Szarekh dynasty, my lord.'

She parted from the communications matrix, restoring consciousness to her physical body. She could feel the command protocols for her ship and accompanying vessels had altered, allowing her to break from orbit towards the fourth planet. She engaged the drives immediately and in the build-up of power used the moment to pulse an energy wave from her ship, a low-frequency radiative vibration that highlighted her heading and the positions of the rest of the fleet. It looked like a simple navigational check to the other ships, but Ah-hotep hoped it served another purpose.

An invitation, of sorts.

The prospect of direct action excited Nemetus and had lifted the mood aboard the *Ithraca's Vengeance*, though the swell of optimism was gradually quelled as they moved in-system, closer to the alien fleet circling Orestes III. Nemetus had been manning the sensor banks when they had picked up the fortuitous energy burst from the departing xenos battleship. Although the exact make-up of the blockading fleet was not known, the general dispositions were revealed by an energy ripple in the exiting ships' wakes. With this information the tech-priests had been able to plot a course that maximised the stellar coverage of the cruiser's approach, pushing the engines as far as they dared while the orbiting fleet was eclipsed by Orestes III, using only existing momentum to traverse into the inner system when the xenos had possible contact lines.

The revival of Astropath Fedualis was also another sign of improving fortunes. Although far from full health, Fedualis was able to assist the Navigators in surveying the warp-dampening effect to some extent, using their senses and short 'positional' broadcasts to measure the reflection rate of the effect. It was growing stronger the closer they came to the enemy fleet but was peculiar in its dispersal, contrary to the impression from warpside. Nemetus was not sure of the significance, but thankfully it was on this subject that Aeschelus summoned a brief council as the cruiser closed on the enemy ships in orbit.

'Update on the enemy, Prax,' the captain began once he, Nemetus, Praxamedes, Fedualis, Kosa and Oloris were gathered in the anterium.

'No movement in the orbital ships that suggests they are aware of our presence, or at least that they feel threatened by it. The system defence monitors have been assuming a new role, moving out-system. This has drawn the secondary flotilla further from the main fleet.'

'Perfect,' said Aeschelus. He glanced at Nemetus with a half-smile. 'Possibly *too* perfect? We cannot be fussy at present; our options are very limited. Kosa, what chance of translating to the warp?'

'Almost non-existent, captain,' the Navigator said ruefully. She steepled her fingers in front of her as she continued. 'Coverage within the graviometric field of the system is patchy, far less consistent than what we encountered in warp space. This may be the effect of the planetary bodies themselves, the incompleteness of the aliens' methods of dulling or simply an artefact of positioning.'

'What does that actually mean?' said Nemetus.

'It is reasonable to presume that the spread of this effect is not necessarily balanced nor geometric,' said Fedualis, turning his empty gaze on the lieutenant. 'Because of the direction we were heading, it is possible that we encountered a more complete portion of the deadened zone while the area we are now in is still, hmm, under construction. It certainly seems that the xenos ships are in part responsible for the extent of the effect.'

'So you still concur with our current objective?' said the captain.

'Indeed, captain,' Kosa said with a nod. 'If we can eliminate the enemy capital ship that should disrupt the negative effect, hopefully on a system-wide basis.'

'Then we will proceed with the plan as agreed,' said Aeschelus.

'I have a proposal, brother-captain,' said Nemetus, realising that this would be his last opportunity to put forward an idea. 'I will lead a force to the surface of Orestes III to combat the xenos attack already taking place.'

'Afraid you'll miss some action staying aboard with me?' Praxamedes gave a short laugh.

'We are not making best use of our resources, brother-captain,' Nemetus pressed on, flashing an irritated glance at his fellow lieutenant before returning his attention to the captain. 'If you insist on leading the boarding action personally–'

'I do.'

'Then we will still have a sizeable complement of the ship aboard. We do not have enough gunships to carry every Space Marine in a single wave. There is little they can do on the *Ithraca's Vengeance*, but on the surface we could make a difference.'

'So, you've thought this through, brother?' said Praxamedes. 'What do you hope to achieve on the surface?'

'Three things. Firstly, we must pass within orbital drop range to engage the enemy. Deploying to the surface will mask the onward intent of the ship to attack the enemy fleet. The drop attack may force the enemy into manoeuvring into a more vulnerable formation. Secondly, if the enemy wish to support ground forces, or attempt their removal, they must remain within orbit. This will hamper their ability to respond to the void attack. They are already caged by the presence of the orbital palaces on the far side of the planet.' Nemetus paused, not sure if he should bring up his example. He decided it was worth the possible censure. 'It is the same trick that was used against us by the traitor Despoiler battleship. Use the enemy forces as a tether.'

'You said three reasons, Nemetus,' the captain prompted.

Nemetus was not sure exactly how to phrase the next part. He decided to plunge ahead and just speak as plainly as possible.

'It is not wise to stake all of our forces in a single action, brother-captain. Should the attack on the capital ship fail, there is need to prosecute a lengthier war. Our presence will bolster the defence. We have seen that not only will our military potential act against the foe, our fortitude against the null-effect extends to those around us. The space station crew were able to respond more fully after some time in our presence. My force will catalyse a greater resistance and act as a focal point for counter-attacks.'

'A well-reasoned plan, brother,' said Praxamedes. 'I'm sorry for my humour.'

'The mockery has been earned by past behaviour, brother,' Nemetus conceded with a smile.

'Even if my attack is successful, we may not be in a position to retrieve you for some time,' said the captain. 'Once you deploy, you are on your own for the effective duration of the campaign.'

'I understand, brother-captain.' Nemetus lifted a fist to his chest. 'Do I have your approval to assemble the remaining squads into a strike force?'

'You do.'

'We'll be in drop range within the hour, brother,' said Praxamedes. 'The Emperor's strength goes with you.'

Nemetus departed as the rest continued to discuss the finer points of the ship-to-ship action. As he strode across the strategium to the secondary door, he voxed Chaplain Exelloria. Some spiritual support against the xenos would be welcome.

The stain of life was being cleansed from this world. Zozar welcomed every death not for itself but as a step towards the grandest of all goals – the eradication of all sentient life. Each individual existence was a miniscule part of the whole, but its elimination was final. There was no return from the oblivion of death. He was numbered amongst those that had tried to avoid that fate, but they had failed. This existence was not life nor death but a limbo of torment.

Such was his mission that the skorpekh lord wielded his slaved warriors with the same ruthlessness that he wielded his own weapons. His Destroyers were a single entity driven by the shared desire to kill, steered by his will. Bound together by that fate, Zozar was each and every one of them, even as they were him and also nothing.

The world was proving a troublesome hunting ground. In his haste to begin the slaughter, Simut had not been diligent in his preparations. The humans were scattered across the globe, and Zozar's force had been deployed with little thought as to how they would chase down their prey across four continents and three oceans. The skorpekh commander had dispersed his legion into hunting teams, a mix of skorpekhs, warriors and skimmer-Destroyers in each. They were given autonomy to find and slay anything they detected. Zozar used these scouting groups to locate the greatest concentrations of targets and then converged on them with overwhelming forces. Though he was not able to be present at every slaughter, he made his influence known through the cryptek network that bound his corrupted legion together. Physically, he might be on another continent, but in thought he was there, guiding through the protocols slaved to his demands.

Now his force had come to a marshalling settlement where goods were gathered for transport to orbit. It was largely automated, the great star elevators still rising and falling with empty cars, the crews that manned them distracted by the effect of the overnull. Its soul-crushing presence was weaker here, though. A few hundred armed humans had mustered an approximation of a defence at the outer walls of the facility, banded about some cult leader dressed in ornate robes and a tall hat, waving a staff tipped with a bird of prey device. The man's exhortations seemed little more than platitudes to Zozar as he had listened in to the ranting speech, but the humans were moved by it. More precisely, the motivating oratory seemed to dissipate the effects of the overnull in the vicinity of the speaker.

The development was interesting but nothing more.

Zozar split his local army into two forces. The first was the warrior phalanx. These he sent directly against the settlement, drawing the defenders to one side of the wall. The swifter Destroyers and skorpekhs he commanded to loop about the wall seeking a weak point to exploit.

As he made these distant manoeuvres, his physical form was engaged in a far more direct conflict. A group of humans had shut themselves in a storage building. They had blocked the entrances with large ground vehicles and manned the upper windows with crude but accurate bullet firers. Zozar had only his first tier of skorpekh elites with him – twenty tripodal warriors armed with a variety of long-range energy weapons and dimensional phase blades.

It was enough, he was sure.

He split his consciousness between the two fights, while a background loop monitored other developments across the world. As shots spat down from the muzzle flare of the defenders above him, a solid wall of concentrated light beams leapt out from the perimeter of the lifting facility. His phalanx began their relentless march, forty warriors in step, gauss rifles at the ready. The hum of anti-gravitic motors carried the Destroyers aloft while their skorpekh allies broke into awkward yet swift runs after them.

Zozar lifted his beam cannon towards the humans, targeting symbols appearing over each one as his weapon protocols noted their locations. He opened fire as he raced forward, snakes of lightning leaping from the weapon to turn each target into a dissipating cloud of particles. His skorpekh minions fired with him, unleashing a volley of bright green beams against the defenders. Some vaporised the humans, others missed their marks, punching neat holes through the stone-like building material. Bullets pattered off his form, a few of them leaving welts that disappeared as his living metal body rejuvenated itself. Magnifying his light sensors, Zozar spied several heavier weapons being set up on the roof – as yet out of range of his cannons. He broadcast an alert to the skorpekh guard but there was nothing to be done except be aware of their arcs of fire.

The phalanx was now in range of the wall at the lifting station. Emerald lightning crossed with pulses of red laser, turning the air into a kaleidoscope of energy. Here and there a warrior fell, overwhelmed by several synchronous hits, the living metal unable to reform fast enough to preserve vital systems. The casualties on the wall were far higher. Gauss lightning crept along the ramparts, leaving atomic scatter in its wake. Gun emplacements that roared with larger projectiles and rapid-firing light beams fell silent beneath the excoriating assault of multiple gauss blasts.

To his right, a missile coughed into motion, flaring down from the storage building roof. One of his skorpekhs was too slow to avoid the hit, taking the explosion of the missile in the torso. Appendages flew from the body, parted by the vehement chemical reaction. The skorpekh attempted to continue but its remaining two legs were ill-positioned for balance and it toppled sideways. Still filled with the need to kill, the skorpekh dragged itself forward with its remaining arm, its cortical field pulsing with hatred for the living.

With the others close around him, Zozar reached the shelter of one of the large ground transporters that had been parked across the entryways.

Adjusting his mass-profile, he started to scale the slab side of the tracked machine, still firing as he clambered past the driver's cab and onto a lower roof. His skorpekhs followed, copying their lord as they unleashed a new barrage of fire from their higher vantage point. More missiles and bullets swept down into them, thinning their numbers by two more, the mangled remains hurled from the transporter by the explosions.

Resistance was fiercer here than Zozar had been expecting. He suspected that one or more of the fiery orators was located within, bolstering the nerve of the defenders and intercepting the overnull field. He leapt at the wall, claws digging into the porous material to secure his vertical advance. Now directly below, his skorpekhs fanned out along the wall to either side to clear each other's fields of fire; the necrons were a far harder target for the men and women at the windows, and virtually hidden from the roof-dwellers.

The flanking force at the lifter station was almost in position. A secondary delivery gate was located at a right angle to the main attack, providing a perfect opportunity to break into the facility and attack the defenders from within. Zozar was about to order them forward when sensor feedback from the skorpekh node-leaders demanded closer attention.

Skorpekh Amehon-destruct: *Receiving input signalling from orbital craft.*

Skorpekh Photorion-decimate: *Enemy presence detected. Incoming craft have entered atmosphere.*

Skorpekh Amehon-slaughter: *Trajectory estimates place landing point at our location.*

Skorpekh cluster-thought: *Continue kill-sequence. The living must be exterminated.*

Reaching the lowest of the windows, Zozar focused his primary field on his immediate surroundings. His phase blade lopped the protruding hand and weapon from the nearest human, an instant before the skorpekh lord heaved his bulk into the interior, glass and wooden frame exploding around him. His momentum carried him forward, metal claws skidding on a tiled floor, the body of the human falling beneath his bulk. Defenders were turning their weapons on Zozar, but this left them defenceless against the other skorpekhs bursting into the broad hall from both sides, guns stripping their foes down to nothing, blades cutting with the precision of surgeons.

+KILL THEM ALL.+

Zozar stabbed a foot into the chest of a charging human, living metal sharper than any blade honed by hand or machine. The human stared in disbelief while lifeblood spurted from the wound, slipping without friction along the silvered sword-limb that transfixed her. Zozar slid his claw free and beheaded the human with a swipe of his phase blade, its edge a shimmer as it dimensionally shifted to ignore the hardened breastplate collar that protected his victim's neck. The head rolled sideways, her body hitting the floor at Zozar's feet.

The Destroyers had smashed through the secondary gate at the facility, the skorpekhs following behind, targeting enemy squads stationed at guard towers to either side. Impending energy signals from above grew sharper and sharper. Zozar took control of one of the Destroyers, spinning it around on a gravitic plume so that he could look up into the sky.

A cluster of fiery dots grew closer and closer.

A sudden impact on his rear thorax region forced Zozar to concentrate his cortical field back into his form. A condensed light weapon of some power had hit him, slashing away a portion of his main body. The molten remnants hissed and spat as a puddle on the floor, useless for reincorporation. Nevertheless, he sent a signal to the canoptek attendants and cryptothralls that had gathered outside to attend the damaged skorpekhs. While his fellow Destroyers rampaged across the machine-filled hall, Zozar turned his beam emitter on the heavy weapon gunner. A single blast turned both human and cannon into dissipating molecules.

A quick sensor sweep confirmed that the human resistance was broken. Energy readings showed a few clusters holding out, but most were dead or attempting to flee. He took off all shackle protocols and allowed his skorpekhs to pursue freely, their own urge to slaughter the only imperative they needed now.

Directing his consciousness to the lifting facility, the incoming orbital craft almost at impact point, Zozar felt less confident about ongoing developments.

CHAPTER TWELVE

Rather than altering the timeflow while Zozar cleared the world of enemies, Simut whiled away the time in a mixture of reminiscence and daydreaming. Whether through imagination or recollection, he pictured the great feast days when the king summoned his full court and the skies were lit with polychromatic displays that lasted a full rotation.

A much-welcomed distraction from the spread of the sun-blight that was crippling their people. Beyond the garland-hung walls, the city seethed with discontent, only kept in check by the brutal presence of Phetos and his wardens. Locked in the high towers the greatest minds laboured at a cure for the flesh-devouring malaise that was running rampant across all of the kingdoms.

For a privileged few, for just one turn of dawn to dawn, there was release from the misery, to give thanks for another orbit survived.

One day they would return to the flesh, freed from both the sun-curse and the soul-theft. Such celebrations as the king would hold in the future would make the year-day banquets seem like a peasant's spring feast. When he stood at the shoulder of King Szarekh, his stellar kingdom forged by his own hand, Simut would be a lord greater than any that–

'Lord of the Stars, Eagle of Victory, Sun of the Dynasty.' Phetos' platitudes were like a thunderburst over Simut's parade, ripping him back to the desolate reality of his tomb ship.

'Why must I incur these disruptions to my musing? Can I not contemplate the mysteries of the cosmos in peace?'

'Apologies, my lord, but you should monitor this exchange among the boundary patrol.'

'Very well, transfer it to my cortical feed.'

Barque, Star of Natarun-4: *Unknown vessel detected.*

Barque, Star of Natarun-1: *Qualify statement.*

Barque, Star of Natarun-4: *Unknown vessel detected on closing course.*

Barque, Star of Natarun-3: *Ridiculous. There is no– Where did that come from?*

Barque, Star of Natarun-1: *What are you addressing? Confirm from central scanning field; there is no unidentified vessel. Some kind of refractive glitch. Recalibrate sensors, you fools.*

Barque, Star of Natarun-3: *It is there, I can sense it. Plasmic signature, human design.*

Barque, Star of Natarun-4: *I detect it clearly. It appears unwelcoming.*

Alarmed, Simut thrashed through Phetos to interact directly with the barque squadron, shunting the royal warden's consciousness aside.

'Where?' he demanded, filtering the escorts' sensor data through the matrix of the tomb ship. 'What are you seeing?'

There was nothing. A glitch, as the squadron leader had surmised.

'Further reports of incoming enemy vessel, Lord of Hosts,' said Phetos, reasserting his presence on the matrix. 'Triangulating position from reports, but it is not showing up directly on our scan grid.'

'Impossible.' Simut withdrew from the link even as he recoiled on his throne. 'The humans do not possess that kind of technology.'

'Their technological progress is idiomatic and isolated, Heavenly Hawk. Perhaps this is a unique vessel, an experimental design?'

'Where is it now?' Simut demanded, ripping the data from Phetos to throw it onto the main display.

A large ship, almost as big as the tomb ship, had crossed the orbital threshold from the far side of the planet and was now closing at speed.

'Some aelderite sorcery, stolen by the humans or volunteered?' pondered the overlord as he recalibrated the sensor sweep to draw its data from the secondary craft of the fleet.

'A small astromantic presence detected, my authority, but nothing significant,' said the royal warden. 'I suggest arming all weapons.'

'See to it,' snapped Simut, who had more pressing matters to worry about. If there was an alliance between the humans and the ancient enemies of the necrons, that posed a far greater threat than one vessel.

'Escort fleet requires directives, Lord of the Eight Seals,' said Phetos. 'Other enemy system craft are closing. Shall they engage?'

'No. My ship is more than a match for this intruder. Let us not waste more craft than necessary. Have them withdraw and stand ready to counter-attack once we have mastered this brute.'

At the urging of the royal warden, the escorts peeled back from the approach of the onrushing enemy, circling around behind it once it was beyond weapons range.

'Its weapons are targeting us, my lord,' announced Phetos. 'Energy beams, focused plasma and a large bore chemical reaction cannon.'

'Is that all?'

The fusillade hit the tomb ship along the rightward outer curve, lashing laser and shell into the exposed structure. The main turret gun of the human ship opened fire, a single high-velocity round smashing into the wound opened by the initial attack. Simut winced as though wounded, though his cortical connection with the ship was purely one-way.

Repair protocols sprang into action. Living metal bubbled forth from broken decks while canoptek facilitators rushed to the scene of the damage.

'Open fire with all weapons arrays,' commanded the overlord, gesturing imperiously towards the blot of movement on the display. 'Wipe them from the stars.'

Energy relays sparked across the breadth of the tomb ship, gathering power for beam emitters and dimensional bursts. The green glow broke out along the surface of the vessel, coalescing through the apertures of the weapons systems to burst forth in sprays of emerald power and forks of cosmic lightning. The storm of disruptive energy struck the incoming vessel amidships, scattering like jade sparks from its defensive screens, tatters of energy crawling across the glowing purple banks of its shields. Astromantic power spiked in the aftermath.

'Targeting data compromised, my lord,' reported Phetos. 'No direct hit. Their astromantic fields absorbed the energy input. It seems that the shields are working to a higher efficiency within the overnull.'

Plunging through the dissipating glow, the enemy ship came on, directly for Simut.

The assault ramp of the drop pod pitched open, bringing a waft of air baked by retro-thrusters into the compartment. Nemetus was out of his harness, shield and pistol in hand, even as the ramp hit the scorched ground. Boots clanging, he led the Intercessor squad out onto the surface of Orestes III. They were not the first to make planetfall. That honour had fallen to the outrider squad, whose specially modified pod had deposited their combat bikes half a mile away, beyond the other necron force. Even now they were circling around the spatial elevator station to assess the situation at the main defence.

Half a dozen more drop pods slammed down around the disembarking Ultramarines, each depositing a squad of fresh warriors into the overgrown grass surrounding the facility. Small brush fires spread from the last burst of thruster jets, wisps of smoke joining the heat haze of orbital descent.

'The enemy are pressing the attack, brother-lieutenant,' said the Intercessor with the long-range auspex, Brother Gaihalius. 'No response to our landing yet.'

'An error that we will make them pay dearly for,' voxed Brother Exelloria. The Chaplain approached in the company of the Aggressors, their flamers replaced with rapid-firing boltstorm gauntlets for longer range. The bulky Gravis armour of their leader, Brother Velecht, was further enlarged by a fragstorm grenade launcher mounted on his shoulders.

Within ten seconds, the strike force had assembled on Nemetus and was heading for the broken ruin of the secondary gates. Calls for aid from the facility occupants had drawn attention to their plight, and Aeschelus had agreed with Nemetus that keeping one of the orbital elevators operational was a strategic objective in its own right. That it was one of only a handful of relatively defensible positions on the whole planet made it an obvious choice for the drop assault.

'We will be swift retribution,' called Exelloria as the Space Marines sprinted towards the opening in the wall, weapons scanning the ramparts for any sign of the foe. They did not slow as they reached the disintegrated ruin of metal that had been the secondary gate but pressed inside at speed. The ground within had been sealed with ferrocrete, a stretch of about a hundred yards between the outer wall and the main buildings from which the immense sky elevators rose and fell. Gaihalius led them along a heat signature trail towards the closest terminal building. Other than a discarded lasgun a few yards from the gate there was no sign of the defenders, but muffled shouts and sporadic bursts of las-fire could be heard over the more continuous war-din from the other side of the compound.

Coming upon a row of tenders, their flat backs still piled with containers ready for orbital transport, Nemetus signalled a halt. The squads broke left and right into a perimeter defence without any need for the command, their bolt rifles and assault weapons at the ready. Nemetus could see that parts of the haulers were missing. Some had neatly scooped out arcs and almost complete spheres taken from chassis and engine blocks, while others were missing whole panels or tracks.

There was still no sign of blood, though discarded power packs still orange-warm in Nemetus' thermal gaze testified to an extended and recent defence of the position.

'Some kind of phase field or disintegration beams,' Nemetus told his command. 'Our armour may not provide much defence against such weapons. Be on your guard.'

They advanced in squads, covering each other while they crossed the rest of the outer transport park. A mesh wire fence provided a secondary barrier line but it had been ripped apart, the links cut through with weapons that left a perfect, shining end on every severed wire.

'Incoming!' Gaihalius' shout preceded a whine of motors by just a second, as a trio of skimming constructs whirred around the corner of the nearest building's roof.

Each was a centauroid skeleton, but instead of legs their bodies were carried on two lines of spherical anti-gravitic emitters that gleamed with jade energy, as did the eye lenses that turned towards the Space Marines. Twin-barrelled cannons crackled into life, but the Ultramarines were the swifter to fire, a hail of bolts screaming up into the air to meet the incoming xenos. Rounds exploded across them, plucking at the metal of their bodies, sending one of the alien constructs spinning groundwards. The others shrugged off the storm of projectiles and returned fire.

Emerald beams sliced down, converging on Sekora in the lead assault squad. Nemetus looked on in disbelief as the Ultramarine was enveloped by coruscating green energy, stripping down through his armour, into the skin and the black carapace beneath, finally melting away his organs and skeleton. In the space of a second, he had been turned from a fully armoured warrior, one of the Emperor's finest, to a greasy vapour drifting on the breeze.

'Destroy the unholy abominations!' roared Exelloria, charging towards the xenos. 'Spare this world the curse of the xenos. Bring forth your anger as you raise your weapons. Let your hatred guide your aim more surely than any targeter. Give no thought to the techno-sorcery of our foes. Your will is greater than any abhorrent conjuration!'

The necron that had been grounded was starting to recover, pushing itself upright from where it had fallen.

'Those that defy the will of the Throne shall not endure! The just punishment for the Emperor's enmity is death! Death!'

The Chaplain's bolt rifle spat fiery rounds into the alien, joined by a sudden flurry of grenades from Brother Velecht. Into the plume of detonations, the Aggressors unleashed a tempest of rapid-fired bolt-rounds, shredding the alien where it lay.

'Concentrate fire,' ordered Nemetus, aiming his plasma pistol at the incoming skimmers. He squeezed the trigger and a ball of pulsing blue energy hit its mark dead centre. The power of a miniature star exploded through the xenos, a fountain of blue fire erupting amid a welter of molten droplets. Bolt-rounds sliced at its tumbling corpse and the third flying warrior.

'More of them, on the ground,' warned Gaihalius. The Intercessor turned, auspex in one hand, bolt rifle coughing rounds in the other, aiming towards the mangled doors of the closest terminal building. The aliens that emerged were akin to the flying creatures but stalked forward on a trio of slender legs, their clawed tips tearing at the ground.

Fresh blasts of jade energy leapt out from the walkers' weapons, slicing neat cuts through Brothers Kallius and Demeter; the former lost his leg, the latter was bisected from crotch to shoulder by the dancing beams. The other Intercessors responded with disciplined volleys of fire, laying down a continuous hail of bolts between them. The aliens were staggered but not slain by the fusillade, pressing forward into the storm of fire rather than retreating.

Nemetus pounded forward, snapping off another shot from his plasma pistol as he closed, his suit telling him that Exelloria converged from the right. One of the necrons went down, its crippled body seeming to evaporate, consumed by jade light from within.

'The bodies are disappearing!' Brother Velecht exclaimed, referring to the skimmer-creatures.

The remaining necrons charged to meet the oncoming Space Marines. A silver-edged blade that faded in and out of sight lashed down towards Nemetus, who raised his shield at the last moment. He felt the impact jarring his arm, but the flare of power from the storm shield kept the xenos blade at bay. He responded in kind, sweeping up with his power sword, its tip finding metallic flesh between the two forelegs of his target. A cry from Exelloria nearly distracted Nemetus but he kept moving. He dodged past the next phasing blade swing to drag his weapon along the torso of his foe, severing it completely about the waist.

Like the others it turned to nothing as it fell, a crackle of emerald power consuming its parts before they hit the ground.

'Show no relent!' roared Exelloria.

Turning, Nemetus saw Exelloria surrounded by a quartet of Intercessors, their bolt rifles driving back a tripodal foe with incessant fire. The Chaplain was down on one knee. A short distance away was his hand, clutching his crozius arcanum, neatly severed just below the elbow. Blood seeped from the wounded limb, drying on the black of the Chaplain's armour, staining his blue loincloth.

'Brothers! Coordinated fire.' Nemetus fired another blast of plasma into the aliens. 'Suppress and destroy!'

The last xenos succumbed to the weight of fire, its shifting, regenerating metal flesh unable to cope with the number of hits tearing chunks from it. With what seemed like a snarled threat the alien disappeared in a crackle of power, leaving a ripple of energy on the ground in its wake.

Quiet reigned after the brief violence, but there was no time for relief or celebration. Sustained gunfire still sounded from the other side of the compound. Nemetus sought out Gaihalius.

'Any other readings, brother?'

'Multiple life signals, some strong, others weak. Xenos signatures detected across the north-east sector. Intermingled.'

'Sergeant Vayoz,' Nemetus voxed the squad leader of the outriders. 'Status report.'

When it activated the vox reply carried the growl of the outrider's combat bike.

'*The enemy have breached the main wall, brother-lieutenant. Massed infantry, unsupported at present. Defenders falling back. If they give up too much ground, they'll be overrun. We are moving in to support.*'

'Understood. We will rendezvous as quickly as we can.'

The Primaris Marines had started a sweep of the surrounding area but Nemetus called them back with a regroup command. The lieutenant checked the telemetry. Three warriors missing, disintegrated by the xenos beams. Exelloria was on his feet again, his crozius retrieved from his severed hand.

'Righteous justice shall be mine,' snarled the Chaplain. 'Lead the way, brother.'

CHAPTER THIRTEEN

Having examined his ship's data storage for any intelligence on the enemy, Aeschelus had found little more than scattered hearsay. The necrons, a recent threat that seemed to have come from nowhere and yet were now being encountered all across the Imperium, left little evidence of their presence in victory or defeat. They registered no warp presence and their bodies were artificial constructs, yet the psykana adepts maintained that they were somehow alive rather than a remnant of some Abominable Intelligence from the Dark Age of Technology. Their standard weaponry was terrifying, able to strip targets at a molecular level, while their self-repair abilities made them as tough as a Space Marine to disable.

Even less was known about their starships, but simply on size alone, it was clear the Space Marine cruiser was no match for this one in an extended duel. A lightning hit-and-run attack to disable a vital system seemed the most obvious tactic, especially given the crew's recent experience in such operations.

The captain was surprised by how easy it was to goad the enemy into a boarding position, as though they were ignorant of the threat. Not only had the aliens not responded to the presence of the *Ithraca's Vengeance* until it had opened fire, they became so prepossessed by the strike cruiser that they had made no effort to engage the gunships as they sped across the void.

'Assault force, final approach,' he announced as the lead gunship, his craft, swung towards the blister-edged crack in the side of the capital ship's hull. Repair mechanisms were underway, sealing the strange metal carapace as though healing a wound, but there was still a gap some fifty yards wide left by the combined bombardment cannon and gun deck strikes.

Movement sensors detected worker-creatures labouring at the break, easily swept away by heavy bolter and rocket fire from the incoming gunships. Able to set down in unison, the captain's assault party advanced swiftly from the breach, heading towards the blocky dorsal superstructure that the captain had assumed to be engines and control systems.

The first encounter of the boarding party was with small service creatures, not much bigger than an outstretched hand. Bolts and combat knives made short work of them, but as the Space Marines advanced, the enemy swelled in number, scuttling across the floor, walls and ceilings in waves. Around them, insect-like constructs and fractured wraith-creatures attended to one another. Still-functioning necron automata ignored the intruders in their midst in favour of returning to their repairs, even when targeted by the advancing Space Marines.

'Assault command, scan readings from the Ithraca's Vengeance; only penetrate to your current position,' warned Praxamedes, still aboard the Space Marine vessel and moving rapidly out of range. The plan was to withdraw the gunships into the planetary atmosphere rather than force the cruiser to remain under fire for evacuation duties. 'No enemy detected at your location.'

'No enemy?' Aeschelus looked around. In the flash of his suit lamps, he counted at least half a dozen scarab-constructs just within a few yards, their sparking mandibles working at sheared bulkheads. 'We are surrounded.'

'Then we are blind to them, brother-captain,' confessed Praxamedes. 'It is not that the xenos creatures are invisible on the auspex, it is just that they register exactly the same as their ship.'

Aeschelus checked his auto-senses and then called to the closest auspex-bearer, Brother Opheus. 'What are you picking up, brother?' he asked the Intercessor.

Opheus spent several seconds adjusting the bulky scanning device, panning one way and then the other.

'Only motion tracking seems effective, captain.'

'We're moving out of tactical vox range, assault command,' warned Praxamedes. The signal was beginning to break up. *'Do you need us to return for extraction?'*

Aeschelus gave it only a few seconds' thought.

'Negative, ship command. Continue with your orders.'

'Understood. Ship command out.'

That was it. They either pressed on or returned to the gunships.

His decision was forced by sudden bursts of fire and cried warnings from the lead squad. At just the same moment, the repair constructs around Aeschelus ceased their ministrations to the ship and turned towards the Space Marines, evidently receiving orders to respond to the invaders.

'Open fire, all targets of opportunity!' he snapped.

Despite their size, the beetle-like aliens packed a surprising short-range burst of energy capable of punching through power armour. In the sudden attack, Aeschelus lost three of his party – overwhelmed by clinging insectoid foes, their ceramite punctured by strobing detonations of jade energy. The flare of various grades of bolt weapons illuminated the interior of the alien ship, flashing bright from polished silver and exposed veins of crystal circuitry.

Aeschelus could not risk being drawn into a protracted fight; they had to push on towards their as-yet-unidentified objective.

'Incursors, lead the way,' he commanded. 'Judiciar, reinforce the Intercessor assault squad. Everybody else, breakout procedures.'

The Space Marines moved with renewed purpose, focusing their blades and bolts on the enemies standing between them and further ingress into the enemy ship. The Incursors scoured ahead, their enhanced armour systems a little better at picking up enemy signals before they attacked.

They carried the bodies with them, determined that no brother would be left aboard the xenos vessel, whether alive or dead. Taking the increased resistance as a sign that they were heading in the right direction, Aeschelus led the force onwards along a single front. He dared not split away any squads, the augurs unable to penetrate the ship's layout beyond a dozen yards.

Admonius fought ahead of Aeschelus in customary silence. There seemed to be an urgency about the Judiciar that carried the rest of them forward, as though he might singlehandedly carve a path to the target by sweeps of his greatsword. Aeschelus wondered if the Judiciar was trying even harder than normal to showcase his zeal or if it was simply a case of violent release after the mounting stress and frustrations of the warp-lull.

The tunnels – the semi-circular passages seemed more like tunnels burrowed through the metallic substance than corridors built out of walls and bulkheads – ran at peculiar angles to each other, converging from above and below as well as left and right. This arrangement suited the insectoid creatures far more than the Space Marines, who were forced to clamber up steep inclines and drop down shafts where their smaller, agile foes simply ran from floor to wall to ceiling without effort.

They ran into a new foe about three hundred yards from the entry point – the rangefinders were having difficulty getting an exact fix through the alien material of the ship.

'*Something larger coming up from below,*' warned Dorium, leader of the foremost Incursor squad.

'Something?' growled Aeschelus. 'Specifics, brother-sergeant. Direction, speed, threat.'

'*Large-scale movement, brother-captain,*' replied the Incursor. '*Could be several enemies or one larger construct; I cannot determine the details yet.*'

'*Coming up from a passage at a right angle to the level of our advance,*' added Lato from the other squad. '*Triangulation efforts hampered by the xenos material.*'

'Hold hard position until we arrive.'

Aeschelus hurried forward through the darkness, signalling to the Judiciar and a squad of Bladeguard Veterans to come with him. These warriors were among those first despatched by the lord primarch; Primaris Marines like Praxamedes who had been in the first torchbearer fleets and now returned with experience and skills to match many of the far older Space Marines.

In the glare of their suit lamps, the Space Marines saw the floor a few yards ahead opening, iris-like, to leave a hole three yards across. Aeschelus stopped and readied his shield, a great cruciform plate almost as tall as he was, forged in the foundries of Macragge itself. Purity seals and ancient oaths of moment were affixed to its edge, and upon its boss were mounted the bones of its first owner, Captain Heraphus of the Fourth Company. Aeschelus had been presented with it on embarking the *Ithraca's Vengeance*, a joint symbol of his authority, the protection of the Chapter and the traditions he was to uphold. With it had come a mantra of the forty-one captains that had borne it before him, from the middle of the thirty-sixth millennium to that day.

Emerald light heralded the arrival of the enemy, glowing from eye-plates and flickering bulbs that protruded from their spines. Like giant arthropods, the creatures did not walk but emerged from the tunnel on glimmering banks of anti-gravitic power, spine-like tails swaying as they rose up into the larger corridor. Not one creature but five, following the lead alien like a serpent follows its head, seeming a single foe that suddenly became a handful. Green beams flared and the Blade-guard pushed to the attack, raised shields deflecting the probing rays. Moving with them, Aeschelus felt the weight of the shield not as a physical thing – his physiology and armour more than compensated for its mass – but a mental burden. Never had an award been given with so much expectation attached. A reminder from heroes past that nothing less was required of him in the future.

Bolt-fire from ahead announced that the Incursors were under attack too, the flash of their weapons throwing large shadows along the passage, of something floating and arachnid-like. More of the scarabs burst out of smaller entry ports, lashing at feet and legs, grappling at the Space Marines' greaves as they tried to charge the apparitions before them. Aeschelus was forced to stop and kick away two of the creatures, shots from the Intercessors behind him blowing them apart as they skittered back to their feet. With the bolt detonations of their companions shrieking from the deck around them, the Bladeguard, captain and Judiciar plunged into the new arrivals, the gleaming blue of their powered blades shimmering into the jade gleam of their foes.

'Onwards!' Aeschelus told his battle-brothers. 'Every heartbeat of delay cedes the momentum to our foes! Give every instant your greatest effort, for anything less will see opportunity relinquished.'

Long claws lashed at Aeschelus, trying to rip his shield from his grip. A faceless head on a serpentine neck craned over its top. Slender beams flickered over his helm's face as the creature scanned him. He drove his forehead into it, hard ceramite cracking the questing appendage even as his sword rose up and sheared off two of the forelimbs clutching his shield.

'*Brother-captain, we have found some kind of energy source.*' Incursor Sergeant Lato's report came with gasps of effort and to a backdrop of bolt-round detonations. '*Clusters of cabling and glowing orbs.*'

'On our way, hold position,' Aeschelus answered, turning aside another flailing limb with the flat of his blade before plunging the tip into the ribcage-like torso of his attacker. He almost stumbled, his boot finding no purchase as it came down onto a scarab trying to blast at the sole of his foot. He crashed sideways into one of the Bladeguard, who righted him with a shove whilst fending off another necron construct with his shield.

'Cut a path for the Hellblasters,' the captain called to his battle-brothers, pivoting his shield and hurling himself forward like a ram, slamming a xenos wraith into the wall. Judiciar Admonius swung his executioner relic blade at the trapped creature, the edge of his sword gleaming with a flash of power as it struck. Behind them, the Bladeguard drove forward and then parted, pinning the enemy between them.

A hail of plasma bolts followed from the Hellblasters, turning the necron apparitions to scattered fragments, molten metal spraying against the forcefields of the veterans' shields. Another volley followed a few seconds later, pulping the last twitching remnants of the xenos, scattering the scarabs that had started to clamber over the bodies to repair them.

The intensity of fire from the Incursors ahead drew Aeschelus on until the passage brought them out at the bottom of a large spherical chamber, bisected by a waist-high wall clustered with glowing green spheres. Strange, angular hieroglyphs marked the ribbing of vaults overhead, which gleamed with their own light. Dozens of cables snaked in all directions, pulsing with the flow of energy.

The Incursors held the other four entrances, firing almost without end at gangling, floating shapes beyond.

'Good find,' Aeschelus told Lato, banging the sergeant on the backpack with the pommel of his sword. He switched the vox to company address. 'Holding positions. Intercessors and Hellblasters to the fore. Bladeguard as mobile reserve. Bring up the charges.'

While the squads arranged themselves, a small coterie of tech-priests entered, flanked by an escort of dull-faced gun-servitors. The contingent brought four large chests with them, each a seismo-melta detonator capable of ripping open a starship's armoured heart.

'How many do you wish to use, captain?' asked the senior tech-priest, its face consisting of overlapping metal scales punctured by two expression-less lenses for eyes.

'*Captain, detecting a surge in ambient temperature and energy readings off the scale.*' Sergeant Dorium had taken his Intercessors further out to provide a mobile perimeter. '*Some kind of mass activation. Hundreds of readings about two hundred yards above our position.*'

'Acknowledged,' replied Aeschelus. 'Fall back to support position and report any movement.'

It seemed likely that the enemy would respond with unmatchable force very soon. That was always the nature of the hit-and-run attack: get aboard, locate a vital target to destroy and then get out. The speed and surprise of the attack was rapidly dwindling. Even if the counter-assault did not quickly wipe out the Space Marines it would tie them down in combat, meaning Aeschelus would have to detonate with his force aboard, or fight his way out before he did so, risking discovery and the deactivation of the anti-ship charges.

'All of them,' Aeschelus told the tech-priests.

If he was not going to get off this ship, nothing else would either.

'Vermin!' Simut's anger resounded across the tomb ship command chamber as a metallic screech and shrieked out into the void as a pulse of electromagnetic rage. Having donned his panoply of battle, he now stalked back and forth across the mastaba, directing cortical field glares at his lychguard and Phetos. 'What are they doing? I can feel them grub-bing about in the tomb-levels like parasites in my gut!'

'They have gathered around the third vestibule of the cortifexal array, Sunlit Lord of the Gold Sands,' said the royal warden. 'Invasion cascade protocols are activating. Vaults have been woken to stop any further advance.'

'What is taking so long?' Simut's phase blade crackled with energy discharge, the halberd-like weapon shimmering with his anger. He wanted to strike out, to take Phetos' ignorant head from his body. Obviously that would have no permanent effect on his lieutenant but the chastisement would be remembered. However, if he did so, Simut would have to monitor the enemy and the response himself, sullying his cortical field in direct intercourse with the lower ranks. 'Where is my legion, Phetos?'

'The enemy numbered less than a hundred individuals. A small threat that the canoptek servitude constructs should have thwarted. Analysis shows that these intruders are not normal humans – they wear armour and their bodies have been physically upgraded. I personally ascended the defence protocols with the data, but response times have been slowed by the damage inflicted by their vessel.'

'Yes, where is that accursed ship? Must I fight this battle blinded and with one arm? By the Stones of Areki, Phetos, I swear that if you fail me like this again I shall wipe you from existence!'

Under the warden's urging, the sensor display rotated around the tomb ship, focusing on the flare of plasma trail from the enemy starship's engines. Simut sneered. Such crude physics, the ancient and laborious shackle of relative cause-and-effect of acceleration and deceleration.

'When King Szarekh's matrix is fully operational and the neversea is stilled forever, these petty races will be stuck in their star systems, ripe for enslavement.'

'Detecting energy build-up in the array vestibule, Lord of the Scarlet Dawn,' said Phetos.

Simut ignored him and watched the human vessel powering out of orbit. The escorts had scattered at its approach, unable to fully manoeuvre whilst caught in the gravitic friction of orbit and incapable of matching the raw firepower of its numerous weapons. But having launched its attack craft, which now patrolled around the lower regions of the *Barge of the Stormhawk*, it seemed as though it had abandoned the warriors left aboard the tomb ship. Did the humans really think a few dozen soldiers, no matter how well armed and physically augmented, could take over a tomb ship of the First Rank? The *Barge of the Stormhawk* would expunge them soon enough, leaving nothing of their presence.

'The enemy are moving again, my lord.'

Indeed, they were. Retracing their steps. A quick flickerscan confirmed Simut's suspicion that the assault boats were returning to the point where they had deposited the attack party.

'They are escaping, you fool! Do not let them get away!'

'Canoptek countermeasures are slaved to the damage control systems, Light of the Thousand Lanterns, as you ordered. It requires your personal override protocol, Voice of Heavenly Grace.'

Mentally grimacing, Simut extended his cortical field into the lower levels, bypassing several layers of ancient programming to access the core motivator channels of the canoptek servitors. Like dredging through muck, he pushed aside tier maintenance and resurrection imperatives, retracing protocol pathways into attack mode. Pulling back in disgust from their shared cortical framework, Simut felt them swarming together, bound upon their new mission by his singular will.

While he watched the tide of scarabs, plasmacytes, reanimators and other construct-spawn swelling through the passageways around the human interlopers, he flashed a burst of communication to Plasmancer Ah-hotep.

'Intercept their ship before it reaches the matrix resonator,' he snarled. 'Destroy it!'

'What ship, my lord?' the plasmancer's reply pulsed back a few moments later.

'The warship, you cretinous commoner! The one that attacked my ship and spat its degenerate boarders into my vaults.'

'My lord, it seems the same cloaking effect that masked our sensors is hampering the sensors of the plasmancer's vessel,' suggested Phetos.

'That would seem so,' said Ah-hotep. 'I shall move to protect the resonator but I cannot see any enemy as yet.'

Before he could form a suitable rebuke, Simut realised that one of the human attack craft had settled on the surface of his ship and was embarking its living cargo. The canoptek broods poured up through external vents and access filters, but strafing gunfire from the other assault boats was cutting deadly swathes through them, accompanied by fire from the human fighters themselves. They seemed fully capable of operating in the void, their armour sealed against the vacuum.

A full warrior phalanx was ascending as quickly as possible from the vault levels, but Simut could see that they would be too late to catch up with the swift exit of the attackers. Fearing what he would discover, he focused his internal scanners on the vestibule where they had tarried for a while. There were four distinct heat signatures, building slowly. Urged by his master, Phetos delved into the menial-cortex and repurposed a handful of nearby canoptek scarabs to investigate. The boxes left by the humans emanated distinctive radioactive and chemical traces.

'Explosives, Crescent of the Night,' the royal warden concluded. 'Powerful enough to destroy the array.'

'That was their purpose?' Simut watched the last of the assault craft powering away with its reclaimed warriors. He ordered his escorts closer, to burn them from the void, but the enemy attack craft sped planetwards, diving down towards the atmosphere where the barques could not pursue.

They would find no sanctuary there.

'Launch the reaper fleet. Scour the skies of their pollution.'

As the order thrummed along the cortical matrix the third vestibule of the cortifexal array exploded.

The detonation was accompanied by a focused blast of radiation that bore a hole up through the fabric of the tomb ship, cutting through a dozen levels to burst out into the void. Thus channelled, the explosive shockwave from the blast erupted upwards, melting and shattering everything in its path, breaking a crack two-thirds of the length of the tomb ship's wing. The dimensional grips keeping the tomb ship in place stuttered and then failed.

Simut howled in disbelief as the gravitic forces of the world below took hold of the crippled vessel, dragging at its mass, pulling it down towards a destructive embrace.

'All systems critical, my lord,' said Phetos, quite unnecessarily. 'Orbit rapidly diminishing.'

'Plasmancer!' Simut roared across the signal waves, the burst accompanied by a huge swell of control protocol. 'Come to me! Forget the resonator, I need you here!'

Any objection crushed by the command from Simut, Ah-hotep did not even have the opportunity to respond. Her ship banked away from its current course and accelerated back towards the planet.

His forces thwarted at the lifting facility, Zozar vented his unfulfilled destiny of carnage at the expense of the humans around the storage buildings. They scattered like vermin from the exterminator, finding nooks and holes to hide themselves while the Destroyers picked over the buildings like carrion eaters on a corpse. Stalking from hall to hall, alert for the slightest tremor of heartbeat or breath, senses honed to the temperature of human life, Zozar led the hunt. Such was his frustration, the Destroyer lord eschewed his beam cannons for a more personal killing method – his phase blade. Parting hated mortality from its physical shell with a sweep of his sword brought a sense of focus that was lacking when he merely disintegrated from afar.

The eradication of the storehouse defenders was simply the beginning. The blue-armoured warriors that had come to the aid of the lifting station defenders had broken the attack of the Destroyer cult warriors, but it would not be long before the casualties were resurrected. Even now their animus was being restored to new bodies in orbit. The remaining warriors were now instructed to keep the enemy occupied until reinforcements arrived. When he was done with his latest hunt, Zozar would demand that Simut gather the Destroyer forces again and translocate them to the position of the interlopers. They would be annihilated like all other life, but Zozar would take a modicum of satisfaction that a more earned retribution had been enacted.

None would thwart his destiny.

As he slashed apart another victim, the skorpekh lord felt a disturbance in the cortical matrix strong enough to distract him from the slaughter. A massive disruptive wave passed along his communications field and into his awareness. He briefly glimpsed his tomb vault ablaze, wracked with arcs of escaping power. A looped inflection command confirmed that the restoration tomb was not responding, and neither were hundreds of others.

He felt one of his warriors perish to the detonating ammunition of the armoured warriors and its presence flickered into nothing.

No recall, no reanimation. Finality.

It was a sensation Zozar had not experienced for an untold age, in slumber and then in unlife. Mortality. An ending to everything.

Was this what he had craved all along?

No! The Destroyer did not fight to be destroyed! Death before other life had been exterminated was failure. He was the bringer of ruin and after his elimination who would continue the great work?

Magnified visual inspection via one of his subordinate constructs showed the tomb ship aflame in the upper atmosphere, on the verge of total structural collapse. His resurrection protocols were aligned to Simut's matrix, and now that node had been severed.

With a roar, Zozar realised that he was trapped here with his cohort. Until new protocols were established there would be no translocation and his forces would dwindle. The battle had changed.

Now it was no longer about righteous extermination. Zozar was in a fight for life or death.

'Lieutenant, the enemy are breaking away.' Shipmaster Oloris grinned as he relayed the news, the first sign of humour he had shown in weeks. 'I think the plan worked.'

Praxamedes looked to Lerok at the patched-up augur station. Half the screens were blank and two servitor ports were empty, the corpses of their previous occupants removed by the tech-priests.

'Energy surge in Orestes III's atmosphere, lieutenant. Could be a ship entering.'

Next to feel his gaze was Officer Geltas at the vox-terminal. He nodded, one hand clamped to his headpiece.

'Getting confirmation that the gunships extracted the boarding force, lieutenant.' The officer smiled and nodded. 'Yes, all attack craft were safely away from the target before it pitched into the gravity well. They are traversing the upper atmosphere to avoid attack.'

'And now their secondary fleet has scattered,' Praxamedes said with some satisfaction. He had expected a fight against the second capital ship, but it had used its extraordinary engines to power away, and was still accelerating as it looped above the orbital plane to come back towards the doomed necron vessel, almost too fast for the scanners to follow. Its mission was unclear – there was no chance it would be able to launch rescue boats in time, and the captain's attack flotilla was safely inside the atmospheric envelope of Orestes III. Given the speed of the xenos' strategic collapse, Praxamedes was momentarily at a loss regarding what to do next.

'Lieutenant, detecting some kind of bulk hauler vessel crossing the orbit line of the fourth planet,' announced Lerok.

The officer passed the detection screen to the main display where Praxamedes could study it. The enemy ship's purpose remained unclear.

The battleship-class vessel might have been heading for the orbital palaces or to support the ground attack but had it been a significant threat it surely would have been deployed in the main attack. There were also half a dozen escort-sized ships in the immediate vicinity, which if allowed to gather might pose some problems for the strike cruiser.

'Sound general pursuit, gunnery crews to fire at targets of opportunity.' He used the datapad on the command throne to highlight three enemy ships that were manoeuvring together, trying to interpose themselves between the *Ithraca's Vengeance* and the departing capital ship. 'These ones should provide good target practice.'

Leaving tails of plasma fire, the *Ithraca's Vengeance* powered onward, leaving the necron bulk hauler unmolested.

There was nothing Ah-hotep could do while the emergency protocols of Simut controlled everything aboard the *Sun of Endings*. The portion of energy not coursing through the inertialess engines was powering up the tomb vaults and translocational grid for total evacuation. Even if she bent her entire mind to the effort, the ship would not respond to her will – the slave-codes prevented it. Secondary signals speared out to the escort fleet, commanding them to protect the speeding tomb ship at any cost. Even the barques escorting the blackstone node responded, curving away from their charge to intercept the lumbering human vessel.

Like a silvery comet, the tomb ship arced across the system plane, plunging down towards the gravity well of the third planet. Sensor readings showed the *Barge of the Stormhawk* was entering the upper atmosphere. In his desire to be saved, Simut transmitted an all-conditions code, unlocking every single vault interface aboard the *Sun of Endings*. Stasis chambers powered down in sequence, releasing more and more energy to the engines and translocator.

Paralysed in body, Ah-hotep watched in anticipation as the overlord's tomb ship fell further and further into the world's gravitic pull. Fronds of escaping power lashed through the atmosphere, sculpting towering storm clouds from the vapour, their innards lit with an emerald haze. Desperate translocator beams flickered voidward, like grasping hands seeking any purchase on a cliff face as the climber plummeted to their doom.

Ah-hotep did not know what would become of her afterwards, but willed the overlord's death with every particle of her artificial brain. She longed to reach out with her plasmantic field to siphon just the tiniest portion of energy from the ship's systems, but even that was beyond her in this imprisoning thrall-state.

A transfer signal flashed across the sensor arrays, redirecting into the tomb vault complex. The ship shook as massive generators force-activated, coming to full life in an instant. Self-preservation protocols collapsed under the onslaught of Simut's demands, shutting down the inertialess filter that sheathed the *Sun of Endings*. Vibrations rattled through its massive decks and a spear of energy leapt across the distance to the beleaguered *Barge of the Stormhawk*, bending down into the gravity well itself. At the moment of connection, matter became energy, leaping away from the tomb ship as friction-heat consumed the lower ziggurat of its command structure. Datasignals flared, slamming through the cortical matrix like a ram at a fortress gate, rapidly spreading out into every single translocation system.

With a brutal dimensional shunt that threw the *Sun of Endings* off course by the sudden increase in mass, Simut and his cohort translocated aboard. Canoptek systems burst with overloaded power as the incoming phalanxes breached vault capacity. The command-mastaba glowed with a haze that reformed into the stooping figure of Simut. His arrival cut off the enslavement protocol but even as Ah-hotep realised she was free to move, Phetos and the lychguard materialised around the overlord, an instant barrier.

Without the inertialess drive's grip to slow it, the tomb ship sped on, racing past orbital distance of the third planet and onward towards the local star, taking it far from the rest of the fleet and the enemy. Though Simut had assumed command, Ah-hotep retained a modicum of control from the oldest protocols. She gently raised the inertialess dimensional slip and decelerated.

Her presence touched upon the input phase of Phetos.

'A close escape,' said Ah-hotep.

'Fortuitous that your ship had not departed to guard the blackstone node any earlier,' replied the royal warden. Ah-hotep sought any sign of accusation in Phetos' mode or bearing but found nothing.

'Fortune favours the worthy,' she replied, slipping away from his cortical field.

Restoration loops cycled into life, preventing further energy bleed like the coagulation of a mortal creature's wound. Tendrils of Simut's command presence infiltrated the immediate vicinity, taking over what had been controlled from afar.

'I. Live.' The overlord straightened, his cortical field dimmed by the exertion, his physical light just a faint aura in the gloom of the command chamber. 'I. Rule.'

Ah-hotep released a scan program into the vaults, registering a twenty per cent increase in mass.

Only twenty per cent.

Discounting the Destroyers deployed to the surface, Simut had lost nearly three-quarters of his personal army in the destruction of his tomb ship, and until resurrection channels were reestablished Zozar was stranded on the planet. Simut's protocols had invigorated the *Sun of Endings'* vault circuits, activating Ah-hotep's force. She suppressed any display of delight at this discovery. For the moment, the overlord was still in charge, her constructs enthralled to Szarekh dynasty command codes.

For the moment.

PART III

'Into gloom the ships did stray,
When adventure took its high cost.
Constant dooms upon them prey,
'til many a brave soul was lost.
So light a flame and send a prayer,
For the souls of the Cursed Fleet.'

– 'The Lament of Quintus',
an Imperial Navy shanty.

CHAPTER ONE

The surge of energy Aeschelus had gained from combat still coursed through him, fuelling anger that had been stirred several days earlier when he had listened to the surrender broadcast. In one act, he and his warriors had dealt a greater blow to the enemy than all of the efforts of the Oresteans. The only reason he could think of to explain such a deficiency of effort was a lack of leadership and will – either through incompetence or deliberate intent.

'Captain, I can see by your demeanour what you intend, and I beg you to think again.'

Fedualis was forced to run to keep pace with Aeschelus' long, determined strides. The astropath seemed like a tattered green rag among pillars of cobalt as he slipped between the Bladeguard escort formed up behind their captain. The cruiser's broad corridor resounded to the crash of boots in unison, almost drowning out the human's words.

'We need allies, captain.'

'We have allies,' Aeschelus replied, glancing down at Fedualis with a scowl. 'Whoever replaces Lowensten as leader will be keen to help us, I am sure.'

'You cannot execute an Imperial commander, you do not have the authority!'

Aeschelus stopped. Behind him the honour guard halted, boots slamming on the deck in unison as they came to attention, swords held across shields as a salute. They were just a few yards short of the docking port attached to one of the orbital palaces' starship spurs, and beyond that was doubtless a reception delegation of greater or lesser size and pomp, and perhaps even the Imperial commander himself.

'I have not only the authority, and the right, I have a duty, astropath,' Aeschelus barked. 'The Imperial commander tried to consort with the enemy. I was created for this purpose. This whole crusade was launched to purge the Imperium of heretics.'

'Not a heretic, just a man trying to protect his people, captain,' begged Fedualis, laying a hand on the armoured forearm of the Primaris Marine. 'You are no inquisitor, to be the judge of an Imperial commander. Have his forces fired upon us? Has he declared his enmity to the Emperor? No. He made a broadcast to an unknown enemy, trying to protect his world.'

'He surrendered, to protect himself.' Aeschelus started forward again. Praxamedes awaited him at the doorway, which grumbled open at his arrival to reveal a brightly lit airlock that gave way to a docking arm descending slightly from the sealed join. The captain looked at his second-in-command. 'Prax, you are the sensible one. Am I allowed to shoot the Imperial commander?'

'I don't think there's anyone here that would stop you, if that's what you mean, brother-captain,' replied the lieutenant. 'I can't say I'm familiar with any legalities involved.'

'See?' Aeschelus glared at Fedualis. 'If Prax approves, I must be in the right.'

'Lieutenant...' The astropath turned his wheedling on Praxamedes. 'See sense. Why alienate the Oresteans? We need their safe harbour and the alliance of their troops.'

'Why are you so concerned with what happens to this Imperial commander?' asked Praxamedes.

'Good question,' grunted Aeschelus as he crossed the airlock and onto the station territory. The entry bridge swayed slightly under his weight, and sagged a little as the honour guard marched onto it.

'I am afraid, captain, lieutenant,' said Fedualis, looking defiantly at each in turn. 'Scared. Just like the people you are about to meet. We are not engineered to be immune to these terrors. We react. I am scared of the necrons and I am very scared of the nullification of the warp that they have engineered. We are stranded here, captain. The Oresteans probably know this better than we do. I do not know if the necrons care for allies, but if they do then perhaps their ambassadors would find more fertile ground for the seeds of their words if we arrive and try to take over.'

'I am not taking over,' said Aeschelus, dismayed by the thought. 'I am no bureaucrat.'

'And how does it appear, if a Space Marine captain comes into a system, executes the Imperial commander and makes demands for soldiers and arms? Is that not a coup? Are not the Adeptus Astartes expressly forbidden such authority and ambitions except on their recruitment worlds?'

Aeschelus was about to snap back a retort but after a moment's thought had to concede that the astropath might have a valid point. The Indomitus Crusade was about reconnecting the Imperium to the Emperor. He had been warned that he might encounter former Imperial societies that had fallen from the grace of the Emperor or been enslaved by alien ideals. Just as the lord primarch had striven during the golden age of the Great Crusade to bring peace and order, so his renewed endeavour was about the unification of humanity under the banner of Terra once more.

Doors buzzed open ahead, revealing two lines of red-jacketed troopers holding their lasguns to their chests. More red filled a hallway beyond.

A slender figure appeared from the ranks, dressed in a black habit edged with scarlet, her hood about her shoulders, a slender silver chain with the symbol of the Adepta Sororitas hanging across her forehead. She was middle-aged, hair greying at the temples, a slightly waxy appearance to her skin that suggested early use of anti-ageing tonics. There were callipers enclosing the digits of each hand, disappearing into the sleeves of her vestment.

'Sister-Chatelain Aures, I presume,' said the captain. 'Of the Orders Famulous.'

'Captain Aeschelus,' she replied with a bow. She pointed to the embroidered portcullis motif on her chest. 'The Order of the Gate.

You are of the Ultramarines Chapter. The gene-sons of the lord commander himself.'

'You are aware of the primarch's return?' Aeschelus was pleased. Such conversations were always difficult and he preferred to avoid unnecessary questions regarding Roboute Guilliman's apparent resurrection. 'You have been in contact since the storms broke the Imperium?'

'For several years, yes,' said Aures. She nodded towards Fedualis, who stood behind and to the side of the captain, fidgeting nervously. 'Your fellow astropaths will be waiting for you in their choir-hall, adept. You will be guided to them momentarily.'

'My thanks, Sister.'

'Where is the Imperial commander?' Aeschelus stepped forward and the Sister-Chatelain moved with him, maintaining an air of grace despite her rapid steps.

They passed between two lines of ten scarlet-clad soldiers, who fell in behind the Bladeguard. Ahead, two more squads of planetary troops formed up to lead the procession through a gilded arch. The walls of the gallery were lined with large portraits, several dozen in all. Aeschelus could see the familial resemblance between them. The floor was carpeted, strange underfoot after so many years of nothing but ship decks and battlefields to tread upon. It felt like sinking into mud. The walls were decorated with printed paper in ochre and green, the floral patterns intertwined with figurative iterations of the Imperial aquila. Evidently they had docked at some privileged station more accustomed to welcoming dignitaries and figures of rank from the Adeptus Terra.

'He is through here, captain,' the Sister replied, indicating the grand archway ahead. At its apex was a monogram shield held in the claws of a double-headed eagle, with the initials *KML*. Scrollwork beneath attested to the commander as Benefactor of Orestes, Chosen of Terra, Beloved of the Emperor.

Titles that spoke of ego, not service. Fedualis' argument that the Imperial commander had surrendered for his people seemed flat in the face of such evidence of selfishness.

Something in Aeschelus' expression must have warned Aures that his thoughts on the commander were not complimentary.

'I hope we do not have cause for regret for inviting you aboard our palaces.' Aures' words were a warning that the Oresteans would protect their leader.

Aeschelus said nothing and tried harder to keep any violent intent from his face and posture. If he was to act, it would be better not to broadcast the fact.

They soon came through the archway into a large audience chamber. The walls were hung with ornate drapes from a ceiling at least a hundred feet high. Banners from Orestes regiments that had been sent to distant wars hung in lines across the hall while clarion-cherubs flitted about the vaulted dome, sounding trumpets at the Space Marines' arrival. A group of several dozen lavishly dressed individuals gathered at the far end, while more guards were stationed to either side, several hundred in total.

Walking onto the hard marble, his boots ringing seemingly in time with the continued clarion call, Aeschelus reviewed the soldiers. They looked smart, but each showed heavy strain, dark rings around their bloodshot eyes. Trembling hands and quivering lips. Though they stood straight and proud they glanced at each other, or kept their eyes fixed on the floor rather than ahead. He saw a few whose lips were moving in whispers and, thanks to his augmented hearing, he could pick out the words of prayers – messages of thanks and calls for deliverance.

The crowd of nobles parted, revealing an older man, lines of supportive augmetics beneath the skin of his throat and laced into the backs of his hands. His hair was just a few wisps across a bionic-pierced scalp. He was dressed in a uniform of the Astra Militarum, a brocaded greatcoat of scarlet and gold, a filigree-hilted sword at his waist and a long-barrelled pistol on the other hip.

Many were the stories of self-interested governors that lived richly on the labours of their subjects. Corruption was rife and the captain had believed Lowensten a coward for issuing his surrender. The gaze that swept up to meet Aeschelus was not what he had expected. Grey eyes met his, unyielding even in the face of the giant warrior bearing down with one hand on the pommel of his power sword, and a massive shield hung on the other arm.

Further to Aeschelus' surprise, the Imperial commander stiffly lowered to one knee as the captain approached, bowing his head. A ripple of gasps and muttering coursed through the assembled nobles. One other remained close at hand, her black coat fastened with large golden buttons up to the chin, lacy white gloves bright against the dark skin of her hands. She walked with a cane topped with a small golden skull, her face hidden behind a veil that hung from two jewelled pins stuck through a small hillock of hair.

'Imperial Commander Kaleb Monfrottine Lowensten offers his profound gratitude for your arrival, Captain Aeschelus of the Ultramarines,' said the woman. 'Your arrival has reminded him of his own deficiency in duty and he is humbled by your example in bringing battle to the xenos without hesitation. He has erred and has sought penance from his Sister-Chatelain, but also offers himself up to the altar of your judgement.'

Aeschelus drew his sword, eliciting cries from some of the nobles, weeping from others. He looked around the hall. Many of the troopers were fixed on him, others looking away with shame or fear. He could see their officers, epaulettes and ceremonial swords picking them out among the scarlet. None seemed ready to intervene. They had been instructed to witness whatever came to pass.

It was an act of honour that he found difficult to reconcile with the furtive message he had listened to on Leshk Station.

'Stand.'

Hesitantly, gaze averted, the Imperial commander pushed himself upright.

'Look at me.'

Lowensten did so, swallowing hard, his jaw twitching. His eyes still carried a look of stoic strength.

'Do you believe you deserve death?'

The hard stare wavered.

'I… I would rather live, but I am resigned to my failures.'

'Why did you offer surrender to the enemies of the Emperor?'

'I was weak.' There was no equivocation in his tone or expression. The Imperial commander spoke as though he expected these words to be recorded as his last. 'We could not know what was happening. The Astronomican disappeared, the warp vanished. The will to live, the enemy sapped it from us hour by hour. Only here on the palaces did we keep some semblance of order. We could not protect a whole world. *I* could not. I feared that if they attacked us directly then all hope of resistance would be lost. Perhaps, just perhaps, we could divert their ire while we found a way to break the curse on our minds.'

'A ruse? It was a ruse?'

'I would lie if I said I did not consider it a capitulation. I was ready to surrender. But I did not intend to do so permanently if opportunity arose.'

The commander flinched when Aeschelus lifted his blade. It was a human response, nothing more. He owned his guilt plainly. Aeschelus could see strength there, and honour. Was it his duty to kill a man for a momentary lapse? Could he hold Lowensten to the same standard as an augmented officer of the Adeptus Astartes, to be unflinching in every circumstance? And though he was foremost a military officer, he was not ignorant of the political implications, regardless of what he had said to Fedualis. It was not his mission simply to slay the foe, but to restore the power of the Imperium.

He sheathed his blade and the hall was filled with sighs, whispers and relieved laughter.

Lowensten stood unmoving, face impassive. 'I thought you would do it,' he said quietly.

'I might still, if you disappoint me, Imperial commander.'

Lowensten nodded and signalled to his court to approach. Aeschelus turned to Praxamedes and gave him a nod. They had already discussed what preparations needed to be made. The Ultramarines had dealt a blow to the xenos scum but the foe was not yet defeated. They had to be driven from the system if the *Ithraca's Vengeance* was to make warp translation again. And any intelligence learnt here could be taken to Casparill and any other systems that were suffering the same fate. One battle was only the beginning of something much larger, but none of it would be possible if they faltered now.

Simut sat on the command throne of the *Sun of Endings* contemplating the events that had befallen his fleet. How had a single enemy ship sown such disarray? Which of his underlings had failed so miserably that the majestic *Barge of the Stormhawk* was now a splintered, blackened ruin upon the surface of a barbarian world? All protocols had been followed as decreed, yet the enemy had struck in such a way that every conceivable defence had been neutralised.

It all stemmed from the unknown shadowcloak that had prevented their early detection. Whatever technology they had employed was now defunct, however. The tomb ship's sensors could clearly pick up the enemy ship in close proximity to the artificial satellite. Other ships had gathered in orbit also, forming a blockade against the depleted necron forces.

The only point of optimism was the continued survival of the resonator. If the enemy had realised its value…

That they had not discerned its purpose was odd. Reviewing the aliens' actions pointed Simut to a single conclusion.

'Their whole attack was aimed at eliminating me,' he declared, drawing the attention of Phetos and Ah-hotep, who had been monitoring the renewed sensor data to formulate the next cascade to initiate. 'How did they identify me? You saw how they came directly for the *Barge of the Stormhawk*. This was an assassination attempt!'

'Impossible,' said Ah-hotep. 'Who would know that we are here?'

'A traitor,' snarled Simut, fists clenched. 'Not Phetos. He could no more betray me than tear off his own legs.'

'If you commanded it, I would make the attempt, Lord of the Golden Dunes.'

'A rival in one of the other dynasties?' suggested Ah-hotep. 'One of the Sautekh? Mephrit?'

'My cousin has kept his personal project secret. No others know of his ambition.'

'The experiment proceeds with success, Eagle of the Void. Another may have noticed the effect we are having on the neversea. A rival with power and influence might have discerned your involvement in some way, and is using the humans as proxies rather than revealing their hand.'

'An unlikely supposition, my lord,' said Ah-hotep, drifting closer. 'Yet the attack displayed remarkable knowledge of our protocols. Perhaps it–'

Before the plasmancer could finish, Simut felt a sudden encumbrance upon his cortical field. A powerful communications signal was incoming, and even before it arrived he could guess its source.

'You are dismissed,' he snarled, waving a hand. Translocators whipped the royal warden, lychguards and plasmancer to a secondary chamber several levels below. A pulsed imperative closed the doors, barring their exit until he was ready for them.

On the hierolith, a grainy image of Tholotep appeared, standing tall in full regalia. The manner of the transmission's arrival spoke volumes – a higher-powered insertion directly into the control matrix, not an underling's request for connection. Yet the appearance of the emissary was disappointing. Simut had thought such an authoritative transmission would come from the king himself, not a simple herald.

'Greetings, tongue of my cousin,' said Simut, rising slightly to incline his head. He sat down again. 'I am honoured by my cousin's regard.'

'There is no good regard, Simut,' barked the emissary. 'And cease this affectation of familial identity. King Szarekh is very disappointed. An alarming series of protocol breaches have been detected in your matrix. We cannot locate the *Barge of the Stormhawk* nor several of your attendant barques.'

'There have been complications in the seventh system of the Anarakh Veil. A brief resurgence of opposition that will soon be overcome.'

'The loss of your tomb ship is a complication? Pity you were not aboard it. The operation is at a critical juncture, gaining momentum across several systems. You were tasked with escorting resonators to blackstone-scarce worlds because it is a simple labour, quite within your capabilities. You need no expertise on alignment and construction, simply to guide the resonator to its appointed site and allow it to activate.'

'The barbarians are unsurprisingly resistant to the idea of being cowed,' said Simut. 'Did you not think there would be war?'

'Your excuses are futile. Only results have substance. What is your plan to regain control of the situation?'

'I will proceed with alacrity, escorting the resonator to the site and installing it as soon as possible. Its presence and activation will still any further combative elements the enemy can muster. They seem unaware of its role and so bringing it to the surface of the third world does not require much in the way of subterfuge.'

'Very well. This is your last chance, Simut. If you fail, if you take too long, the king will remove you from your office and banish you to the stasis coils.'

'*No.*'

The thought of an eternity in conscious limbo filled Simut with dread. Having woken from an aeons-long slumber to see the galaxy upended, he would not be rendered idle and impotent while the necrons reclaimed their glorious position of dominance.

'It shall be done. Tell my cousin he may have rivals in another dynasty. I have been the victim of an attempted assassination. Who knows what other plots are afoot?'

'Do not concern yourself with dynastic matters. When you have completed your task you may return to your place in court. Until then, be glad if I do not need to speak with you again.'

The image blinked away, leaving Simut alone in the darkness of the tomb ship. He could feel an insistent nagging from Ah-hotep, demanding to be released. Politer enquiries were made on behalf of Phetos. Remembering his promise to Tholotep, Simut opened the barrier wards and summoned his entourage back to the chamber. There was much to be done and not much time to accomplish it.

Ah-hotep despised hosting the overlord on her tomb ship even more than she had loathed being his puppet from afar. Just his raw presence at the centre of her personal matrix was an affront to all dignity, squatting in her command chamber like a parasitic worm eating at the guts of a king. His protocols polluted everything they came into contact with, as though incompetence was a virus. While the fleet gathered in strength around the resonator, ready to press on towards the third planet, Simut delved into her archives and vaults, raking over old encounters and activating her legion as though they were toys to play with. She was thankful to have had the foresight to wipe away every trace of the enemy vessel she had detected, so that it seemed her ship had been afflicted with the same blindness she had imposed on the *Barge of the Stormhawk*.

Unable to contain her frustration and revulsion, she excused herself on an errand into the depths and headed for the secret chamber isolated by the technomandrite protocols. To all cortical fields except her own, the room did not exist. The technomandrites had wrapped it up with dimensional wards that even she did not understand, its net of energies so finely described she could not follow the complexities. Only when physically stood at the boundary could she regard the chamber beyond.

Stepping inside, she knew it would not be long before Simut's impatience got the better of him and he looked for her. To all intents her persona was located in the adjoining vaults, a resonance on the energy streams that gave the impression she was working on a transference fault. If the overlord tried his trick of forced translocation… That would be a problem.

Ah-hotep activated the communications grid, considering her words. She held her feelings in check at first, remembering that her reports needed to be clear to have any function.

'An unexpected enemy has bolstered the defences of the system. Militarily they have achieved a victory beyond their numbers but it is their effect on morale and their ability to function adequately within the overnull that is of most interest. They are clearly humans of some sub-type, well-equipped and trained. There is something else about them. I have briefly seen their energy patterns and as well as possessing immense biological power their brain activity is heightened in a very particular way. I am sure the technomandrites have studied these creatures in more detail and perhaps will already be aware of this resistance. The greatest threat to the project is the way a relative few warriors of this sect can have a disproportionate effect on other humans. They are not astromancers in themselves but evidence similar properties with regard to the neversea and the effect of the overnull.'

She paused the broadcast to her distant masters, flitting a momentary inspection protocol from her data-facsimile whilst checking there had been no attempt at contact from the command-mastaba. Canoptek scarabs and reanimators busied themselves through the corridors, attending to the war-folk that had been released from the stasis tombs.

'I believe that Simut's incompetence will hamper the effort but not so much that the inevitable victory occurs. Szarekh is clearly growing short of patience and I fear that he will replace Simut with a more capable overlord soon. I know my purpose has been to observe and report to the technomandrites but I can sense the time is coming when I must act. It is not by a whim that they chose me for this task. Though it is in its foundational stages, the overnull project will soon prove its effectiveness. When that is achieved then the Silent King will press ahead with its rapid expansion, uncaring that its existence will come to light. By then it may be too late for the other dynasties to prevent him accomplishing his goals and stilling the neversea across his domains. When that is achieved he will focus his attention not only on the alien menaces but also his rivals within our great civilisation.

'I will stop him. Szarekh can never be allowed to attain the power he desires. As for Simut… Before the end, I will make sure his dreams are crushed and his legacy scattered to the cosmic winds. I will feed on his escaping essence! He will know despair before his end, and he will also know it is I that brings it! By the ancient rites of Sorek and Ashok, by the seven shadows of Cartha, I curse Simut and his line!'

Ah-hotep stopped, fearful that her anger-fuelled tirade might breach even the secure vault's silencing protocols. She felt better for the outburst, and armed with the righteousness of what was to come she quit the chamber and dismissed her cortical doppelganger. Now her state of mind was prepared. Every humiliation, every dismissive word, every forced translocation and arrogant summons would be answered. Flexing clawed hands, her spine-tail twitching as she made her way back to the control chamber, Ah-hotep no longer felt impatient for justice. Now she savoured the anticipation of revenge.

CHAPTER TWO

On his way back to the *Ithraca's Vengeance*, after concluding the council with Lowensten, Aeschelus was surprised to find Sister-Chatelain Aures waiting for him in the airlock vestibule.

'Captain, I need to speak with you,' the Adepta Sororitas official said quietly, directing a look at the red-coated soldiers that had followed the Ultramarines' honour guard back from the audience. 'Just a moment of your time, if you please.'

'Of course,' the captain replied. He turned to the Orestean planetary troopers. 'You are a credit to your world and you honour me with your guard. We are on the eve of fresh battle and I would not keep you from your preparations. You are dismissed.'

The platoon officer looked nonplussed for a few seconds and Aeschelus wondered if he was going to refuse the order.

'The honour is ours, Captain Aeschelus. To have the warriors of Ultramar at our side gives us all courage, even as this infernal curse of the xenos beats down upon us.'

'Remain strong and true to each other,' Aeschelus told them. 'A few more hours, maybe days, and we will know victory.'

Assurance seemed to work a wonder on their mood. Presenting their rifles in salute, the Oresteans departed with smiles and stiffer backs.

'Is that true, captain?' said Aures. 'You expect to destroy the necrons within days?'

'I would not lie,' said Aeschelus. He looked along the gallery, past the Imperial commander's ancestors, and saw that the honour guard had exited. 'Do you desire to come aboard?'

'No, that will not be necessary.' Aures produced a sapphire-blue data crystal from a pouch at her belt and offered it to the Space Marine. 'You cannot trust the Imperial commander. I did not agree with his decision to offer surrender but I am bound by my oaths to the Sisterhood to support his family and position. I think he may still be trying to broker with the aliens.'

'And this is proof?' said Praxamedes, stepping closer.

Aures darted him an accusing look before glancing at the other blue-armoured giants waiting nearby.

'Primaris Marines have very good hearing, Sister,' said Praxamedes. 'There's not a warrior present that did not hear what you said.'

Aures looked unsettled, surrounded by the bulky warriors.

'You can trust us all, Sister,' said Brother Garios, the leader of the Bladeguard squad. 'We are sworn to the command of our captain and if you trust him, you trust us.'

'Yes, of course,' said Aures, not sounding convinced.

Aeschelus motioned to Garios and the other Bladeguard. 'We must depart soon. I do not think I am in immediate peril, brother.'

'As you command, my brother-captain,' said Garios. He raised his blade, first in salute to the Sister and then to Aeschelus. The other Bladeguard did likewise as they each turned away and headed out through the airlock.

'This is not proof, not as would convince a tribunal, but it shows intent,' said Aures. Aeschelus held out his hand and she dropped the crystal into his armoured palm. It looked tiny against the blue of his gauntlet, a fragile thing to carry such weight of importance. 'These are recordings from the council chambers. Review them and see what you think.'

'We're about to embark on a joint military campaign with the forces of Orestes,' said Praxamedes. 'If you have concerns, we must hear them. You say we cannot trust the Imperial commander. What is he going to do?'

'I do not know, but I have been excluded from deliberations of the council since your arrival in orbit was detected. The court monitoring scribes have been dismissed as well. There exist no records of what has been discussed.'

'Suspicious, but not damning,' Praxamedes replied.

'I will look at this,' said Aeschelus. 'Thank you for bringing it to me. I assume there is some risk should your suspicions prove correct. You may have sanctuary on my vessel if you require it.'

'An offer I may accept at another time, but for now my place is with the court of Orestes, for better or worse. Perhaps the Imperial commander will take me into his confidences again and I can dissuade him from any folly.'

'Perhaps,' said Aeschelus, closing his fist around the crystal. He lifted it to his plastron and bowed his head. 'By the Emperor's Grace, Sister. I bid you fair fortunes.'

She returned his thanks with a nod of her own before hurrying back along the gallery.

Aeschelus did not wait to see her through the other doorway, but turned back to his ship, Praxamedes at his side.

'A serious business,' said the lieutenant. 'What do you make of it?'

'Trouble, either way,' said Aeschelus as they strode up the docking gantry and onto the strike cruiser. It felt good to have the deck beneath his feet again. 'Set course for upper orbit. I want a report from Nemetus regarding the situation on the surface. And prepare the anterium. We will review this data there.'

Nemetus hewed his blade through another beetle-like construct and kicked its twitching remains from the top of the berm that had been erected around the Orestes lifter facility. Its metallic carcass disappeared into the ether with an emerald glimmer just like all the rest.

He sighed. Two days of sporadic fighting, pushing out patrols and counter-offensives to protect the Oresteans while they improved their defences. More than forty-eight hours of bolter-fire and bladework and there was not a single alien body, limb or blood spatter to show for the honourable labour.

The lack of physical evidence made the whole experience unreal, coupled with the oppressive surge of the anti-soul effect with each enemy offensive. Nemetus had not realised before how much satisfaction there was to be gained from seeing the enemy dead heaped upon the field of victory. To see their tanks burning, their soldiers cut down, was an account of the punishment meted out for defiance of the Emperor.

He was not a bloodthirsty warrior, but he did enjoy his calling. He remembered nothing of his life before he had been chosen to become a Primaris Space Marine, but he could assume that he had been no stranger to violence.

The Chapters of the Adeptus Astartes did not recruit pacifists.

Bright stars in the firmament of battle.

This was not a battle for glory, but the presence of the Ultramarines was certainly an inspiration to the Oresteans. Wherever the warriors of Roboute Guilliman passed, hearts were lifted and spines stiffened. Without them, Nemetus was sure that all resistance on the surface would have crumbled, giving the necrons free rein to assault the orbital station with full force.

With the outer perimeter dyke now completed, the Oresteans had put down shovels and trenching tools and taken up their lasguns and shotguns again. Despite the bolstering presence of the Space Marines, their contribution was muted. The all-encompassing sense of hopelessness had disappeared; a less potent feeling of its return heralded each enemy attack.

Nemetus could feel the despair growing again. He saw it in the sagging shoulders of the troopers from the facility, and in their shuffled step as they moved to firing positions in response to the bugles of their officer corps.

Their eyes told the story most clearly. Not the resigned detachment Nemetus had seen in the gaze of soldiers of enduring service, but a detached disinterest. On the positive side, the cessation of feeling eliminated natural fear. But it did so at the expense of thought and passion, and hour by hour the lieutenant not only saw but felt the creeping doom coming back.

The roar of bike engines drew his attention to the return of Sergeant Vayoz and his outriders. They drew up a short distance from the seven-foot-high berm, the weapons of their mounts turned outwards.

'Numbers are building to the north and the south-east, brother-lieutenant.' Vayoz pointed with his bolt pistol as he spoke. 'We intercepted a fair number, but at least a company-strength formation at each. Warrior constructs, gravitic skimmers and those three-legged bastards. Support creatures too. A few thousand altogether, I would say.'

'It seems they have learned the virtue of patience,' said Nemetus. 'No more piecemeal attacks. Gathering for a concerted assault.'

'We can cover one or the other, brother, but not both,' said Vayoz. 'The northern contingent seems bigger.'

The lieutenant considered his position, and asked himself what Praxamedes would do in the same situation. Whether intended or not, Nemetus was now responsible for the defence of the planet. A wrong choice – an ill-considered moment of rashness – threatened utter defeat. The thought troubled him more than any news about the massing enemy.

'No, there is not much else we can do to prepare even if we have advance warning of the attack. We are ready. Resume patrol route alpha and pick off any stragglers you come across. They have been scattered and listless since we destroyed their command ship. There are bound to be more isolated pockets of enemies out there.'

'So why are they getting organised now, lieutenant?'

It was a question to which Nemetus had no answer to give.

'Praise the lord primarch,' he said instead. 'For Guilliman and the Emperor!'

'For Guilliman and the Emperor!' the outriders chorused before leaving in plumes of smoke and dust.

Nemetus activated his armour's vox-booster, hoping the *Ithraca's Vengeance* was in orbit above. They had been shuttling soldiers and supplies along with a few remaining system craft, using the lifter facility to bring the troopers down to the surface. Several thousand had bolstered the defence in the last six hours.

'Ship command, this is surface command. The enemy are delaying their approach and forming up for a more coordinated massed attack. Request disruptive bombardment.'

After a few seconds the vox hissed in response. Praxamedes' voice came through slightly muffled.

'This is ship command. Surface bombardment is not possible at this time. We are detecting multiple incoming void signals, approaching at speed. Off-loading last of our embarked troops so that we can manoeuvre and respond.'

'The necron fleet is coming back?'

'They'll be on us within the hour, brother. Expect a concurrent assault on the surface.'

'We are ready,' said Nemetus. 'What is the captain's plan?'

'To protect orbital approach and keep your position secure. The necrons seem more focused on the planet than the orbital palaces for some reason. If we can keep them from landing more troops, you should be able to hold off what has already been deployed.'

'I have a feeling that they are going to be harder to kill once the fleet comes back,' said Nemetus.

'Is your sword arm tired, brother?'

Nemetus laughed. 'No, but it would not hurt if you came down here and used yours a little, brother.'

'The captain has stated he will command any counter-attack force. I'll be wielding the cruiser again.' Nemetus heard a long sigh.

'You are a great commander, brother, and the captain knows it.'

'We have far greater concerns than my lack of recent field experience. I trust you will hold the facility and not get distracted.'

'Ancient Magnatus came down with the Bladeguard in the last orbital lifter carriage. The captain has sent me the company standard as a reminder of my duty to this place. Not that I needed it.'

'Of course not. The Emperor protects, brother. And we are the Emperor's will. I shall see you again when the battle is done.'

'The Emperor's grace follows you, brother.'

Nemetus killed the vox connection and looked out from the berm. Would the enemy attack first from the north or the south-east, or both together? Did it matter?

He disliked waiting for the enemy; it spoke of inaction and surrendering the initiative. But he had sworn to defend the lifting site. On the other hand, Nemetus reasoned, an aggressive defence was still a defence.

He opened a vox to the pilot of the gunship that had brought down Ancient Magnatus. After all, he was not a patient commander.

CHAPTER THREE

The humans were obliging in their ignorance. While Simut's fleet regrouped, they had wasted any chance of escaping by shuffling their ships around in orbit over the third planet. The course of the orbital installation that had proved problematic had brought it almost directly over the battle about to unfold on the ground. While the barbarians probably thought themselves safer under the protection of the huge artificial satellite, it simply presented Simut with a single target. He was not one to overcomplicate plans and so the fleet set forth at highest speed to confront the enemy while they were concentrated.

He noticed that Ah-hotep had spent a considerable amount of time in the resurrection vaults of late and now her cortical field was virtually cocooned within the *Sun of Endings'* sensor banks.

'What do you see, plasmancer?' he demanded, tugging at her communications matrix. 'What energising sight takes your eye from the battle?'

The hovering entity drifted closer to the command throne, eyes flickering with annoyance.

'I dance to the background radiation of the universe, my lord, and sway to the rhythms of the stars.' She bowed, as well as she could, and stretched a hand towards the photoglyphic plates. They burst into bright light, flooding the mastaba with a shifting, golden hue.

'It is beautiful,' Simut admitted. 'But hardly appropriate to be so distracted even as we close in on my final victory.'

'A marred beauty, my Lord of Hosts,' said Phetos, gesturing towards the display. The golden expanse shrank away, centring on an area mottled with black dots.

'What is it?' Simut leaned closer out of physical habit, one he had not lost over aeons of stasis. His proximity to the data made no difference to its clarity but it felt like it should. 'What am I seeing?'

'A faint ripple in space-time, my lord,' explained Ah-hotep. 'The echowave of dimensional shift engines.'

'Necron ships,' said Simut. 'Where?'

'Heading in-system,' the plasmancer replied. The data reorganised to show the incoming craft already at the outer system, moving fast. Dozens of signals blotted out the natural flow of the universe's energy.

'It must be Tholotep,' Phetos said, turning to his master. 'He leads a fleet to replace us, Lord of the Silver Mountain.'

'Treachery,' snarled Simut. 'Suddenly it all becomes clear, like the sunrise breaking over the Nathor Hills.'

He had no recollection of Nathor, having seen the beautiful range only in broken archive data, but the overlord fancied he had to have been born in such an auspicious location.

'It is Tholotep that has been working against us! He has manoeuvred us into a trap with the humans, setting a task he thinks we will fail.'

'To what benefit, Mighty Overlord of the Six Hills?'

'To rid himself of a powerful rival within the dynasty,' Ah-hotep answered quickly. She moved even closer, voice barely a whisper, her cortical stream a trickle of data. 'He is nothing but a glorified administrator, overlord. He desires the credit of success earned by others.'

'He has always tried to undermine me,' Simut replied. He looked at the size of the fleet and marvelled at it. If only his cousin had gifted Simut with half of that resource he would have swept away all before him. 'We must place the resonator before he arrives! He cannot take credit for an act already complete, and his duplicity will be revealed to King Szarekh.'

'And the humans, Majestic Ruler of the Void-Seas?' Phetos returned the main data-display to the target planet.

'Placing the resonator will silence them. The plan does not change.'

'Yes, my lord,' said Ah-hotep. 'With your permission I will continue to monitor the energy streams to glean more data and perhaps confirm the presence of Tholotep in the new fleet.'

Simut granted permission with a nod and a dismissing wave. He returned his attention to the humans, formulating his plan. It would not matter what losses were incurred in the installation of the pylon. Once the planet was under his dominion he would be within his birthright to take Tholotep's fleet for the continued success of the expedition. Its arrival was timely, and the overlord wondered if his cousin had perhaps seen something of Tholotep's plotting and despatched him to Simut for just that purpose. This recalcitrant barbarian system would not stand in the way of Simut's rise to greatness.

Her body was dust. Less than dust. Her particles returned to the great cycle of the cosmos, her soul set free from the woes of mortal concern. Yet Zozar was trapped in this realm of life, and while life persisted he could not know peace. It had been hard to find her among the newly created ranks of the necrons. The mass transference had seemed an impossibility when Szarekh had first conceived of it, but the lies of the sungods had settled deep in the king's heart and he would not be swayed. Zozar had seen how fragile life could be under the unforgiving, dying sun of their world and had been numbered among the first volunteers to lend his scientific intellect to the cause. How vain they had all been, and how naive in their vanity.

He flexed beweaponed extremities and looked at the fortifications raised up before his army. A prison.

His army?

He had been an engineer, and creator of dams and lifting machines and bridges. When had he learnt of war?

Zozar had become a hunter at first, desperate to be reunited with his wife and children. He had never found the young ones – lost somewhere in the innumerable, mindless phalanxes of warriors that had speared the expansion of the dynasties across the stars; resurrected so many times they had been processed out of existence. It was probably better that they remembered nothing of playing in the gardens and climbing the north side of the pyramid. Better that they were soulless, dreamless tools of war than know what they had become, like Zozar.

His wife he had found after seven days. She was one of the ones that had fared worst, her connection to life, her soul-strength so powerful that the transference had driven her insane. She had the artificial body of a queen but her thoughts were locked outside of it, wandering in the bright orchards of her mind, staring at softly lapping seas on golden sands only she could feel – yet knowing the agony of loss, her brightness dimmed, a sun behind the cloud of what had happened.

He had known then that he could not live with the burden of what he had done, what he had helped take place. So many millions of souls destroyed, replaced with facsimiles of life. Looking at her, seeing the puppetry of her body wrought in silver and gold, Zozar had joined her in madness. He had broken her form and smothered her resurrection field, the misery of it stripping away any last vestiges of honour or compassion. He tried to kill himself but awoke again in a freshly forged body, reincarnated in an exact replica.

Zozar had known then that it was only by eradicating all sentient life, by filling the neversea with the souls of all mortal things, would he finally be delivered from his living prison.

Every being that opposed him was an obstacle to be overcome in that greater goal. The humans that lined the earth ramparts and the walls beyond were doomed. They would die eventually, their bodies mouldering to nothing, consumed by the cosmos. But they might procreate, spawning new life to curse the galaxy with its presence. They defended future generations of taint. They had to be eradicated for the greater plan; it was not enough for nature to take its course.

With Zozar came lines of warriors, flights of skimmer Destroyers and his stalking skorpekhs. Many had resisted his command to assemble, their need to annihilate all life stronger than the command protocols that bound them to their Destroyer-liege. Some were separated by oceans, others embattled against other foes. Yet within a turning of the world he had brought together several thousand of his death-dealing kin and bound them to his single will.

He could not remember exactly why the station had to fall. It mattered nothing – the eradication of life was the only purpose he needed.

The first bullets and stabs of energy lanced out from the outer defences as his ad hoc cohort streamed across the crop fields, wading through waist-high cereals, emerald eyes fixed on the hated living. Around their feet scuttled a carpet of plasmacytes, a wave of canoptek organisms dedicated to keeping the rest of the matrix free of the Destroyer creed, which had the added effect of making them amazing reconstruction devices for broken skorpekhs and Destroyers. Where an explosion or condensed light beam was powerful enough to break open the body of one of Zozar's followers, the plasmacytes swelled in number, regurgitating stored Destroyer energy to bring their subjects back to artificial life.

The lead squads opened fire – a glitter of gauss energy that sprang up towards the defenders dug in at the top of their raised defence. Emerald beams dragged back and forth across the lines, vaporising every living cell they touched, cracking against crude barricades of crates and upturned storage bins. Haulers and smaller vehicles had been dragged into place to create more obstacles, but to the anti-gravitic engines of the Destroyers they were no hindrance. Rising above the advancing lines of the warriors, the Destroyers darted forwards, heavier gauss cannons stabbing down at the humans sheltering behind their improvised casemates.

Though they took casualties, increasing as the range shortened, Zozar impelled his legion forward without recourse to evasion or cover. Their bodies and canoptek resurrection were the surest defence against the enemy weapons, and speed of attack would eventually lessen the threat they faced.

The exchange of small arms intensified dramatically as the necrons reached open ground where scorched dirt and crop stubble, along with fuel particulates remaining in the air, identified a strategy of burning the ground cover. Bullets and energy beams came in a near-constant flow from along the rampart. On the walls beyond, heavier weapons hissed, roared and snarled into life, tracer ammunition and pulses of plasma flashing out towards the skimming Destroyers. More warriors fell, their torso cases broken open, limbs detached, heads pummelled by repeated hits. Emerald gauss beams flashed back into the storm, turning defenders to nothing in moments, opening holes in the line, lessening the incoming fire.

Zozar cared nothing for the fallen of either side. Battle was a means to an end, not some accomplishment in its own right. And as blunt as his attack seemed, it was part of a greater plan. Another force was approaching at an angle to his, smaller but speedier. With the enemy diverting their strength against the all-out assault, they would be helpless against the secondary attack.

It was only when he came within range of the enemy fire himself that Zozar noticed something strange. He could detect nothing of the chemically propelled mass-reactive warheads that had shattered so many Destroyers in the preceding attacks. He paused in his advance to probe forward with trans-spectral sensors, seeking the tell-tale blue armour and heat plumes of the enhanced humans.

He detected none.

Had they abandoned their lesser companions? Were they hiding in the facility, manning the most defensible walls while their more numerous chaff-vassals took the brunt of the first assault?

It did not matter. Their absence simply allowed even swifter progress to be made. At current projections, Zozar's forces would be through the outer defences and coming upon the walls even before the secondary assault arrived. He opened fire with his disintegrators, lashing beams of jade energy through a trio of human marksmen who had positioned themselves atop the cab of an abandoned freight-mover.

+ANNIHILATE EVERYTHING.+

The fate of the star system and its inhabitants had been sealed. Whether by Simut or Tholotep, or both, Ah-hotep knew the humans would be eradicated and the resonator positioned to extend the Contra-Empyric Matrix. That would bring Szarekh's plans closer to completion. If it was indeed Tholotep that brought the replacement fleet, his arrival indicated that the system had grown in importance, whether due to location or timing. There was little window of opportunity left to disrupt operations and Ah-hotep was running out of options.

She kept the bulk of her plasmantic protocols scanning broader, longer-ranged frequencies and emissions, but turned a small portion of her power to bear on the target world, and specifically the craft orbiting it. Looking at the placement of the enemy ships, she had to conclude they were set to defend the orbital station. Their cordon was ill-placed to prevent the *Sun of Endings* and the resonator carriers smashing through into orbit, ready for the descent. There was a chain of defensive satellites that had been overrun during the first attack, their systems overloaded and their crews rendered ineffective. If they were active, Simut would have to be less precipitous in his approach, which gave the humans more time to realise that destroying the resonator was their only chance of victory.

With Simut's protocols still streaming through every circuit, there was nowhere Ah-hotep could function without some scrutiny. She had exploited Simut's lack of diligence several times but sooner or later he would come across something amiss in her actions. She had one last chance to disrupt the overlord's plans.

Her discovery of the incoming fleet gave her reason to travel to the vault depths once more – to secure the protocols against aggressive action by Tholotep.

'My lord, if Tholotep has corrupted his loyalty protocols, it is likely he may do the same to our cohorts,' she told the overlord.

'Is that possible?' Simut pulsed emerald fronds of agitation. 'Could he take my warriors from me?'

'Not if we combine our protocols together, my lord. Mine are not Szarekh dynasty in origin.'

'Dual command?' Suspicion entered the overlord's tone.

'My will shall always be subservient to yours, Lord of the Legion.'

Simut's eyes gleamed brighter and accompanying tendrils of cortical intrusion pried at Ah-hotep's connection, seeking any sign of uncertainty. The plasmancer held her ground, fighting the urge to recoil from the shameful invasion of her cortical aura.

Eventually, after a time long enough to convince Ah-hotep that Simut's rummaging was more about domination than any real attempt to uncover treachery, the overlord withdrew. His eyes dimmed and he turned away, disinterested.

'Very well, you have my blessing.'

Ah-hotep needed no further excuse and translocated directly to the vaults, barely throwing up her field-doppelganger before slipping into the secret technomandrite chamber. She activated the communications array, thinking to broadcast the latest developments and perhaps somehow direct the humans to the importance of the resonator carriers. To her surprise, she discovered a communication on one of the human frequencies. It seemed very localised, almost as though aimed at the necron ships.

She hesitated. She knew nothing of human carrier waves, but thought it unlikely they possessed the kind of power needed to breach the protocols of a fully operational tomb ship. Her reluctance stemmed from the thought that the human signal might somehow propagate and betray the presence of the technomandrite-shielded room.

Judging it better to act than not, she traced the broadcast signal and relayed it through the tomb ship's tactical arrays, bypassing Simut's higher-level strategic protocols.

'*...suffered casualties in this conflict but further struggle-loss is unnecessary. We are sophisticated, reasoning species that can come to understand each other without warfare. There must be mutual land on which we can meet and terms to which we are both in agreement. We implore you to consider better outcomes for your people and ours.*' There was a short break and the transmission resumed, a looped message pleading for negotiation.

Ah-hotep activated a short-range, repeated scanner burst. Its emittance clouded any chance of the human signal being detected by any of the other nearby ships. The arrogance of the humans to presume they might parley with the necrons was astounding. Simut would disregard it as he had their prior transmissions, but he was no longer in total control and needing a swift victory. Ah-hotep was not sure what might yet be made of this development, but she was certain she could think of something inventive.

CHAPTER FOUR

Aeschelus reviewed the orbital data and then nodded his approval to the deck officer that had presented the dataslate. The officer saluted and returned to the augur terminals, where Praxamedes was still working with one of the tech-priests to bring the longest-ranged sensors back to full potential.

'I can feel the easing of the burden,' the captain said to his second.

'The prospect of decisive action, brother-captain?'

'No, more than that.' Aeschelus flexed his shoulders, his armour accentuating the motion with whining actuators. 'It must be the proximity of the orbital palaces and their contingent of astropaths. I feel we have been offered an opportunity – that its passage has brought all of the elements together, so that we can benefit from the shielding effect that kept its inhabitants saner than those below.'

'The coincidence of the palace's orbit over the lifting station Nemetus is defending is fortuitous, but it's a passing boon. And we don't know how fully we can trust our allies. You haven't reviewed the crystal that Sister Aures gave you.'

'It seemed the least priority when so much else had to be done. But join me now, and we shall see what perturbed the Sister-Chatelain.'

The two of them moved to the anterium, where Praxamedes activated the data reader. A small hololith crackled into animation atop the terminal, showing a wedge-shaped slice of a meeting hall. A long table ran down its length, the far end truncated by the extent of the holo-recorder's arc. At the near end sat Imperial Commander Lowensten. Aeschelus recognised the veiled noble from his meeting with the governor, and several of the other men and women sat to either side. There was a lot of talking over each other while Lowensten sat back, arms folded, his expression dour.

Praxamedes accelerated the playback, the voices speeding up along with the actions of the figures below. He returned it to normal speed a few seconds later when Lowensten's voice could be heard, his hand slamming down onto the table in unison.

'Enough! I called this council for advice and you give me arguments. Baron Cordaer, it is clear these are not some passing raiders but a significant invasion fleet. They are systematically destroying the outer defences.'

'We cannot hold them back,' said a young, uniformed man, his hair swept back by a silver band, a be-ringed hand catching the light as he waved upward towards the distant stars. Aeschelus presumed it was Baron Cordaer. 'Their weapons are too powerful. Perhaps if the *Invigorous* was to intervene?'

'One naval ship won't swing this battle. We need to send for help.' This came from an elderly lady with an attendant at her shoulder, who was feeding some kind of elixir into a catheter at her temple.

'The Imperium is in upheaval. The warp-storms are everywhere.' Lowensten sighed and sat back. 'Who would come in time?'

'Then we must buy ourselves time, commander,' said a short, broad-shouldered man in grey robes. A ranking Administratum envoy or liaison? 'The Imperium will respond. It falls to us to survive long enough to benefit from that response.'

'Surrender?' said the older woman, almost choking on the word.

'Negotiation,' said Baron Cordaer. 'If we can agree a ceasefire it gives us time to defend the orbital palaces.'

'Or evacuate,' said a woman out of the view of the recorder.

'We have nothing to bargain with,' said the Imperial commander, wiping a hand across his face. His fatigue was obvious. 'What do we offer them that they cannot take?'

'An easy victory, perhaps?' said the administrator. 'Our greatest defences are on the orbital palaces. Our exports are expendable. Let them take what they want without dispute. Crops will grow again. People still have babies to replenish the population.'

'What of this soul-draining effect the astropaths report?' said a grey-bearded councillor almost lost at the periphery of the recording. 'Would we have our minds dulled?'

'The palaces are proving more resistant,' said the older woman. 'Better to act while we can. If we resist we shall be slain, from which there is no return. If we are to succumb to this deadening, we shall not know of our misery, it seems. And if help arrives we might yet be delivered from it.'

'A season lost seems a small price to pay,' reasoned Lowensten, looking at his advisors. 'Our strength lies in this chamber, in these palaces. If we can preserve that, Orestes has not truly fallen.'

'We need to be of single purpose,' said the older woman. 'I am in favour. Who else?'

A chorus of affirmatives rung around the table. Aeschelus noticed a couple of the nobles remained silent, but none voiced objection. Perhaps they were too minor in standing to be counted.

'Then we are agreed; we shall do everything we can to preserve the existence of the orbital palaces, even if that means we must sacrifice our holdings below.'

The hololith projection shimmered and then stopped, fixed as Lowensten was rising to his feet.

'They voted for this misery?' Praxamedes seemed offended by the thought. Aeschelus was disappointed but not surprised.

'I can see why Sister Aures might have her regrets, but I see nothing here that condemns the Oresteans any more than their original transmission.'

'The surrender seems more premeditated than I imagined,' admitted Praxamedes. 'A strategic choice rather than a desperate necessity.'

'I would not venture to assume how the minds of these bureaucrats work, Prax. That might have been what passes for desperation among the higher class here.'

'I would caution wariness, all the same, brother-captain.' Praxamedes removed the crystal and the projection disappeared. 'It appears that Lowensten is quite happy to make an alliance of convenience.'

'The xenos scum would have no interest in surrender or negotiation now. What is to be earned by it?'

'You heard the Imperial commander. He offered unconditional surrender because he had nothing to bargain. Our arrival has shifted the balance of power. Now he has us to offer. I think that if events move against us, captain, that pragmatism will be turned on us as quickly as it was turned on their subjects.'

'In which case we must make sure we retain the upper hand.' Aeschelus stepped across the anterium to activate the tactical display. The positions of friendly assets were clearly marked in the hololith with blue runes. The necrons were moving at such speed it was hard to track them, an approximation of their incoming course sketched in red trajectories across the orbital plane. 'The plan is sound. Nemetus holds the ground. You will command the *Ithraca's Vengeance* to threaten another boarding action. I am sure these soulless xenos will think twice before letting the cruiser get that close again. I will reinforce the personnel on the orbital palaces. Whatever the source of the warp effect, the psykers there are best at holding it back. The enemy must be coming for them to complete the total dominance of the world. Between the location's defences and every ship we have, we should be able to destroy their last capital ship. That will relieve the pressure, just as it did when the first one crashed.'

'It is a sound strategy, based on what we know.'

'You have doubts?'

'Not in the plan, brother-captain, but in our knowledge. We don't know enough about these false beings to fully estimate their objectives and strategy.' Praxamedes pointed an armoured finger into the swirl of red light. 'There is a large non-combatant vessel. We first detected it when the necron fleet was scattered but assumed it was a second echelon supply ship. I'm not so sure now. They've moved it to the centre of the fleet.'

'A weapon, you think?'

'I really don't know. It can't be anything tactical, it would have been deployed in the initial attack. We know that necrons teleport their dead from the battlefield and can also teleport directly into battle; perhaps this support ship is some kind of function of that?'

'I will bear that in mind as events unfold,' said Aeschelus, shutting down the display. 'Too many variables, but we must fight with what we have against what we can see. The xenos would have us chase guess-work instead of working to solid military theory.'

'Yes, brother-captain.' The lieutenant banged his fist to his chest in salute.

They returned to the strategium together, where Aeschelus formally passed command of the ship to his second. He took one last look around the command bridge, aware that he might not see it again.

'I will do my utmost to return the ship to you in good condition, brother-captain.' So impassive was Praxamedes' expression that Aesche-lus could not tell if he was being sincere or deadpan.

'You had better,' he replied in similar spirit.

With that he departed, heading to the launch bays and the squads already waiting for him aboard the gunships. He checked the chrono-meter. The necrons would be upon them within the hour.

CHAPTER FIVE

Flanked by the Bladeguard and Judiciar Admonius, Nemetus leapt the last few yards from the ramp of the gunship into the heart of the necron advance. In the midst of the Space Marines rose the relic standard of the company, held aloft by Ancient Magnatus. Affixed to gilded wings were the bones of Calistes Orkbane, a favoured captain who had thwarted the orks of Sylphis nearly five thousand years earlier. Preserved in regal stasis, now his remains looked out on the hated xenos once more, an inspiration to every battle-brother that beheld them. Nemetus felt heartened by the relic's presence, reminded that all great deeds echoed long into the future.

Like a blue-clad thunderbolt, the Ultramarines spear tip smashed into the marching warriors, power swords cutting through living metal, shields blazing as skeletal fists and gauss rays struck back. Behind them the gunship landed, spilling squads of Intercessors, their bolt rifles ablaze as they formed into a firing line, striding purposefully towards the necrons.

The gunship lifted off and circled, its heavier weapons cutting down larger constructs as they closed with the Bladeguard, lascannons streaking down to slash through floating centauroids, missiles turning stalking tripodal creatures into scattered shards and limbs. Emerald lightning lashed back at it, leaving bright weals of exposed ceramite across its armour but unable to penetrate the thick plates.

At the rear of the enemy the outriders attacked, their bike-mounted bolt rifles roaring before they slewed away, escaping the venom of the xenos' return fire. Again and again they struck, whittling away at the rearmost foes, causing others to turn and confront them, lessening the pressure on the knot of veterans fighting in the centre.

Blocked to the south-east by a canal half a mile wide, the necron cohort had little room to manoeuvre. Set upon barely minutes after marching clear of a massive expanse of orchard-covered hillside, they had been advancing in a narrow, vulnerable column formation. No scouts had preceded them, so certain had they been of the Space Marines' desire to remain in static defence. Miles of freshly sown furrows separated them from the lifting station, devoid of any road that would have speeded their advance, the uneven ground treacherous beneath metallic feet.

The terrain provided no cover, so Nemetus had speared into the greater part of the enemy host. The necrons were less suited to close combat than a firefight. In the press of melee, they could not bring their devastating beam weapons to bear and their artificial bodies were no defence against the molecular-disruptive fields of the Ultramarines' power weapons. Reanimating scarabs crawled over the decapitated and dismembered remains as Nemetus and his companions pressed on, but these fell prey to the incoming Intercessors, whose volleys of bolt-fire were as precise and regular as a chronometer. The creatures that tried to resurrect the fallen necrons became the targets, blown apart by the incessant fusillade of mass-reactive warheads.

As a force, the necrons were slow to react, and half of them had fallen before they started to bring the much greater weight of their numbers to bear. More and more beams sprang up towards the gunship, forcing it higher. Skimming constructs abandoned their attempt to down the flying vehicle and turned their cannons on the Intercessors, the redirected flurry of beams cutting gaps in the line where Space Marines were stripped apart at the molecular level. Though still surrounded, Nemetus felt the closeness of the fighting breaking as the necrons withdrew from the Ultramarines' advance, attempting to give themselves room to manoeuvre and fire.

'The shock of assault is wearing thin, brother,' warned Ancient Magnatus.

'Another sixty seconds,' replied Nemetus, keenly aware not only of the changing battlescape but also of the other xenos force pressing its attack at the lifting facility. There was no point blunting the flanking army only to allow the main attack to gain the walls in the Space Marines' absence. 'We have to break their strength.'

'They have no will to break, brother-lieutenant,' said Brother Garios of the Bladeguard. 'I do not think we can fell each and every one.'

As though the words were a challenge, Admonius broke from the group, his raised greatsword trailing an azure gleam. Against the war cries and crackle of xenos weaponry his silence was stark, broken only by the thunderous sound of his blade of office crashing down onto the silvered skull of a necron. The alien burst apart, falling at the Judiciar's feet. A hand feebly clawed at his leg as his charge continued, his powered weapon splitting open the chest of another xenos opponent.

'As always, the Chaplains lead where we follow,' said Nemetus, breaking into a run, shield held against the sudden flash of beams that sprang towards him.

The downdraft of thrusters washed over the Space Marines as the gunship made one more pass, hull-mounted assault bolters and wing-tip rocket pods tearing a ragged furrow through the assembling necrons. Turning sharply, its plasma jets incinerating a dozen more foes, the gunship plunged groundward ahead of the Ultramarines. From its ramp, a squad of three Eradicators opened fire, their melta rifles vaporising the nearby xenos.

'Form guard!' bellowed Garios, lifting his blade as he turned to face the Intercessors following behind. To the left a renewed din of bolter rifles and engines announced the coincidental attack run from the outriders. The Bladeguard split, pushing outwards into the necrons trying to pull back from the gunship's position, while into the gap pressed the Intercessors, firing to either side before they broke into a sprint over the last few yards.

The whole formation collapsed back to the gunship a few seconds later. The Intercessors firing over their heads, Nemetus and his companions fell back to the side hatches. Ascending the boarding steps, Nemetus looked out. The battlefield was littered with broken silver, a swathe of destruction nearly a hundred yards wide. Reconstruction swarms were milling about through the living metal debris, overwhelmed by the task at hand. A quick transponder survey showed that he had lost six warriors in the attack. Six battle-brothers that would serve the Chapter no longer. He felt an odd chill at the thought, glancing to his side at the relic bones of Captain Calistes. Of the battle-brothers that had given their lives to Orestes, nothing remained. There was no blue among the silver to recover and honour.

'In our memories our lost brothers are honoured!' he declared. 'In our remembrances their glory is interred!'

Green beams sliced towards him, breaking his line of thought. Jets screeching into full life, the gunship raced upwards, the battlefield dropping away in a matter of seconds, alien weapon-lightning dissipating beneath it. Nemetus looked north to see the outriders breaking away, a streak of blue leaving wide furrows in the tilled soil. His view turned with the gunship and he leaned out from the boarding steps, just able to see the lifter cars ahead, the tip of the main building visible above the horizon.

The harder battle was about to begin.

Though he had no direct cortical link with Zozar – it was far too much of a risk that the Destroyer taint would spread to him – Simut could still monitor from afar the progress of the skorpekh lord. The overlord was aware that an attempted flanking attack had been forestalled by the enemy, but Zozar himself had almost breached the barbarians' defences.

With Tholotep rushing to steal his crown, Simut had no time for flourished manoeuvres or other subtlety. He needed to win; to place the resonator and activate the overnull. And he needed to do it as quickly as possible, which meant pushing the resonator carriers into harm's way. That required the enemy to be overwhelmed by more pressing concerns.

'Translocate the legion!' he announced, striding down from the throne to address Phetos and Ah-hotep. 'Full attack!'

'Where shall the legion attack, Light of the Stars?'

Simut regarded his royal warden with a mixture of confusion and disdain. 'The enemy, of course. Attack the enemy!'

The overlord felt a flicker of exchange between Phetos and the plasmancer.

'Might I suggest deploying the bulk of the cohorts to annihilate resistance on the surface, and a smaller strike force to occupy the orbital station?' said Ah-hotep.

'Yes, that is my will.'

'Which attack do you wish to lead, Sunderer of the Fourth Wall?'

'Lead...?'

Simut felt his enclosing panoply, the phase blade in two of his hands. It felt right that he should be at the head of the army as they gained his victory.

But the memory of his hasty departure from the *Barge of the Stormhawk* was still sharp. He was not confident of his full integration to the resurrection systems of the *Sun of Endings*, nor of its survival if it was attacked again. Even if he was waylaid and resurrected, his absence provided an opportunity for Tholotep to seize his command. The protocols the rogue emissary had wielded when communicating with Simut – stolen authority of the king – might well be turned to the vault matrix itself.

'The expedition still requires my strategic guidance,' he told his underlings. 'As much as I would glory in the role of battlefield general, the good of the mission requires that I remain in an objective position.'

'Then shall I guide the army upon the station?' suggested the plasmancer.

'You seem eager at the prospect. Why so keen, Ah-hotep?'

'The power, my lord. I will drain them to a husk if I can. I have not fed for too long.'

'I see.' The plasmancer's addiction made her so easy to control. 'Very well.'

Exercising his will, Simut crackled with energy, which leapt from his body into the waiting circuitry of the command-mastaba. Signals flowed through the requisitioned tomb ship, cascading through protocol streams and translocation nodules. Beside him, Phetos guided the signals, branching out the commands into the deepest vaults.

With a burst of power that plunged the whole vessel into darkness, the vaults activated, hurling the datastreams of the legion towards the distant world.

'For the glory of Simut and Szarekh!' the overlord commanded his warriors. 'For the future of all civilisation!'

A call from the gunship pilot brought Nemetus through the troop compartment to the control deck. Ahead the wall of the lifter station came into view, as did the host of silver and bronze that assailed it. The emerald gleam of necron weapons lit the crumbling defences, the bright flare of lasguns and muzzle flash diminishing even as Nemetus watched. Skimming constructs swept over the defences, targeting the Imperial forces as they fell back from the wall in their hundreds. Nemetus could see more scarlet-uniformed troopers moving from reserve to bolster the gaps in the line, waylaid by beetle-like attackers that crawled through every crack and swarmed over the breaches.

'Without us, their resolve has failed.' Magnatus spoke from behind the lieutenant. 'We trusted too much to the hearts of normal soldiers.'

'They can be rallied,' Nemetus insisted. 'We are not too late.'

His assurances sounded empty but he could not give up.

The gunship fired off its remaining missiles and rockets into the sprawl of unliving constructs that were tearing at the wall and clambering over its felled sections. While blossoms of deadly fire erupted below, the pilot braked sharply and turned the craft's dive into a curving descent to the compound. At the ramps and hatches, the Primaris Marines loosed what fire they could over the heads of the remaining defenders.

'Sectors three, four and eight, rapid reinforcement!' snapped Nemetus, directing his Intercessors as the gunship hovered at the same height as the wall's rampart. Leaping the gap, the Space Marines broke into squads, some pushing directly into the firing line, others dispersing to vulnerable points to the left. The Eradicators followed, heading right, turning their powerful melta weapons against the heavier skimmers roving to and fro overhead.

Nemetus stepped into the troop compartment as Magnatus, Garios and the other Bladeguard fell in beside each other, the Ancient and his standard at the centre of a cerulean shieldwall.

'Wait, brothers,' called the lieutenant, mindful of the broader objective. He imagined Praxamedes poring over the schematics of the facility he had transmitted from orbit, creating crossfires and pinch points in mobile defence. Nemetus spied Admonius ahead of them on the ramp. 'You too, Judiciar. The situation is dire but we cannot just throw ourselves into the fight without thought. We can still attack as well as defend, and perhaps bring time for our allies to restore themselves to order.'

He signalled the pilot to lift the gunship so he could survey the battle. Moving to one of the flank hatches, Nemetus took position on the step, looking down at the thrust of animated metal skeletons below. If the Ultramarines dropped in behind them, they might cause enough destruction to bring the ire of the aliens against them, before extracting rapidly by air.

Even as he conceived of the plan, the air around the station shimmered. At first he thought it some strange wind, but within seconds a miasma of flowing jade waves fell like a green aurora. As the cloud touched, shapes appeared in the gleaming mist. Floating, bunker-like war machines larger than tanks appeared, and from gleaming portals in their hulls marched forth more skeletal warriors. Hundreds of them.

And not only warriors. Great constructs larger than men stalked among the silvered cohort, with whip-like arms and cannons that immediately let fly with blinding jade bolts, while around them multi-limbed metal creatures slithered and stalked. More scarabs flitted around in swarms, their flexing mandibles letting out bursts of bright green sparks. Shadows passed over the trampled crops and the lieutenant looked up to see crescent-shaped fighter craft dipping down through the pale skies. Long, barge-like engines extruded from the lightning-wreathed fog, blasting away at the walls themselves with bursts of scintillating energy; others of similar design carried forward squads of skeletal warriors hanging from rib-like dorsal structures.

Perhaps victory was not as close as he had thought.

Zozar enjoyed a rare moment of satisfaction when a large portion of the curtain wall collapsed inwards, spilling more than a hundred foes to their deaths amid the rubble. His Destroyers surged into this breach, blades and gauss weapons slashing and flaying everything in their path. The Destroyer lord paused upon the broken stones as a massive amount of power thrummed through the cortical matrix. Around him warriors and skorpekh froze for an instant, paralysed by the projection of an immense war protocol.

Massed translocation beams slipped down to the surface. Zozar turned, sensing the congregating particles of hundreds of necrons in the colours of the Szarekh lords. A quintet of monoliths arrived first, establishing the transference field across a large swathe of the outer defences. From their portals a cohort of warriors marched silently at the centre, flanked by a myriad of canoptek servitors, from scarab clouds to plasmacytes and gangling reanimators. Doomsday arks and annihilation barges drifted out of the dimensional stream, attended to by more canoptek functionaries. Overhead, he felt the cortical cries of Doom Scythes and Night Scythes, pitching groundward at high speed from swirling jade sub-dimensional portals in the upper skies.

With them came the full force of the overnull. Even though Simut had not yet placed the resonator, the soul-deadening effect was extended by his minions' presence. Like a chilling wind it passed over Zozar. The effect on the defenders was almost immediate. Those trying to hold the breach were struck numb, their actions sluggish, their fire rapidly diminished.

The end was near. Zozar could feel it.

Long ago he had passed beyond elation, beyond the revelry of victory, but he sped forwards with renewed anticipation for the slaughter to come. He leapt up the broken masonry with long strides, fuelled by the thought of drawing one step closer to fulfilling his mission of galactic oblivion.

Though it was her translocators that carried her across the void, Ah-hotep still recoiled at the presence of Simut's protocols driving the dimensional shift, as if his hand was upon her, propelling her across the stars. The translocator beam targeted the centre of the station's mass, avoiding the obvious energy spike of a circle of reactors at its heart. Materialising into corporeal form once more, thoughts compressed back into her cortical field, Ah-hotep flexed her arrays, lapping at her environs with tendrils of sensitive green energy. Dozens more warriors and her personal guard of twenty Immortals arrived an instant later.

They were somewhere in the upper portion of the immense hemispherical station. The chamber had a low ceiling, unlit by conventional light, the pipes and cabling running through it emitting low levels of heat and electromagnetic resonance.

Most importantly, she read no bio-forms in their immediate vicinity; nothing bigger than vermin, she corrected herself as her sensors picked up various warm-blooded creatures and a sizeable number and variety of arthropods in the walls and under the floor. With no immediate threat, she was free to strengthen her energy tendrils, latching onto the nearby wiring. Electricity coursed back to her body, arcing down into the bulbous accumulators arrayed along her spine, lighting them with a pale green as she gathered more and more energy. The taste of it was like nothing she had ever experienced as a living being. It was physical nourishment and cosmic attainment in one.

She drew deeper, gaining confidence, reaching out further and further along the veins of the station, supping more and more of its lifeblood. Coruscating waves broke across her limbs and sparks glittered in her eyes. Deeper still she sought, her consciousness dividing and dividing, becoming one with the energy, seeking the source of the power, drawn along its modulating waves like a creature returning on instinct to its spawning grounds.

As she infiltrated the power network, she picked up other discharges. Bio-electrical impulses from passing humans; she felt their hearts beating, their brains firing in cumbersome flashes, the thrum of power through muscle as they walked. Sound waves were everywhere, vibrating the whole station from bow to stern, clattering engines and humming terminals, and voices – thousands of voices from every direction, setting the artificial world a-tremble. She honed her thoughts, listening in to scatters of conversation, the barbaric yaps of the humans filling her with a sense of omniscience.

Ah-hotep became data as she entered the internal digital matrix, flashing as static across flickering screens, spiking in read-outs and clattering from typesetting devices. The code used by the humans was idiosyncratic, crude on some levels yet impenetrable on others. She let its flow take her across the systems until she found what she was looking for.

The reactors.

While her data-self started disassembling the protocols of the control system, her electrical tendrils probed at the magnetic barriers shielding the power of captured stars. Even through the containment fields she could feel the throbbing power. It reminded her of the tesseract vaults that imprisoned the power of the C'tan shards and she wondered if one day she might get to drain a star god of its energy.

While she deciphered primitive equations, an idle data-thrall touched upon something else: barricades of locks and ciphers enclosing some morsel within. A simple flex of her cortical influence decoded the mechanism's identifiers and a frisson of joy pulsed through the plasmancer's being.

'Weapons control.'

CHAPTER SIX

Alarms blazed across the orbital palaces' command centre, accompanied by flows of vermillion across data screens and the rapid mumbling of servitors. The Imperial commander's staff reacted slowly to the alert as red lights flashed beneath the domed ceiling, their thoughts suppressed by the renewed necron soul-dampening.

At the heart of affairs stood Aeschelus and a number of the Imperial commander's senior advisors. Almost half as tall again and twice as broad as his companions, the captain knew he looked more like an animate statue than a living warrior.

'How exactly are we under attack?' Aeschelus demanded of the two figures in front of him.

One was General-Duke Hosul of the Orestes Household Guard: the grey-bearded man from the council meeting he had watched. The other was Magos Ortonov-Six, a barely humanoid confluence of articulated mechanical limbs, opaque bell jars and a red robe, topped by a large cowl that hid anything resembling a head or face. It was the ruling tech-priest that answered first, the words oddly sing-song in their cadence.

'Xenos incursion. Energetic influence. Data corruption and manipulation. All expenditure necessary to repulse intrusion has been deployed.

Massive dimensional weave detected on planetary surface. Energy foot-fall exponentially high.'

The captain understood barely a word of the explanation but knew enough that it was not positive. He turned to the ranking officer of the Orestean militia, answerable only to the Imperial commander. The man received a sheaf of autoprints from a mute functionary and reviewed them with a deepening frown.

'Aided by the tech-priests, we have isolated the source of incursion to a demi-level somewhere in the dead sectors between the main sensor suite conduits and the artificial atmospheric regulators.' He looked up, eyes widening slowly. 'The xenos are aboard the palaces, captain! My troops have engaged them but you've seen the kinds of weapons they possess, the indestructible nature of the beasts' bodies.'

'Nothing is indestructible,' growled Aeschelus. He shifted the weight of his shield and drew his sword. 'My warriors will prove that shortly.'

He caught the eye of Lowensten, standing to one side with a small crowd of chattering attendants. The Imperial commander's face was almost white, the blood drained from his features. He looked as dead as their enemies. He held up a hand and his functionaries ceased their overlapping protests and demands.

'A massive force has also been teleported to the battle below.' Lowensten's voice was a croak, the words stuttered.

'The necrons are not yet in orbit...' argued an officer in the uniform of the Imperial Navy, standing close to the sensor monitoring station.

The look Lowensten gave Aeschelus carried similar disbelief, accentuated by no small amount of absolute horror. The captain was aware that the oppressiveness of the soul-deadening had returned, and it seemed to be having a profound effect on the ruler of Orestes.

'A remarkable display of transubstantive technology,' remarked Ortonov-Six. 'Our scanners show that the ship in question is still approaching, but it has a much diminished energy wave.'

'They've exhausted themselves with such a long-range teleport?' suggested Aeschelus.

'Only temporarily, our projections suggest. They are regaining power, every second, every minute.'

Aeschelus tried to separate conflicting streams of thought. The battle on the surface. The incoming fleet. The powered-down flagship. The invasion of the palaces and accompanying attack on the control network.

Priorities. Priorities.

'Captain!' blurted Ortonov-Six from within the shadows of the voluminous hood. 'Reactor fluctuations. Xenos activity accelerated. Increasing scanning potential. Augur range has tripled.'

'Our sensors have been improved?' muttered Lowensten.

'New sensory vertex, detected anomalies. Early analysis suggests a second wave of xenos – a fleet heading inward, at high velocity.'

'We have already seen what the xenos ships can do at speed and range.' Aeschelus noticed the near-panic on the faces of various uniformed attendants and the sudden hastening of the tech-priests in the command module. There were a lot of red runes on the augur displays. 'How many?'

'Estimate only. Excess of twenty vessels. At least five capital class.'

Aeschelus was lost for words. They were barely holding against the forces from two capital ships, one of them already destroyed.

'Estimated time until they arrive at the threshold of attack used by the other capital ship?' he asked, subdued by the prospect.

'Two hundred and eight minutes.'

Roughly three and a half hours to defeat the enemy already on the planet and within the orbital palaces, and then to confront a vastly superior foe newly arrived to the war. Aeschelus turned from the others, trying to hide his dismay. He had no fear of death. The changes made to his body put him beyond mortal concern. But irrelevant to his life expectancy, there was no gene-enhancement or psychodoctrination that could shield him fully from the prospect of imminent, unavoidable and total failure.

His eyes fell upon the skull-faced helm of Chaplain Exelloria.

'Be strong, brother,' growled the Chaplain, stepping closer. 'This is beyond you.'

The captain recoiled, confused by the seemingly contradictory statements. He knew the situation was hopeless but had not expected to hear such harsh testimony from his spiritual aide.

'I will do what I can,' he managed to say.

The Chaplain regarded him for a moment and then shook his head. 'I was unclear, brother. I mean that the situation is beyond us all. It is greater than you, this force, the Orestes System. We have encountered something unprecedented. Even the lord primarch had not conceived of such an event at the outset of the Indomitus Crusade. Against such adversity we will strive to kill as many foes as possible but that will not be enough to bring victory. I recall the great words of the lord primarch: "The galaxy is the dominion of man, bought and paid for a billion times over with the blood of its sons. It is ours. Were the xenos ten times more mighty, it would still be ours. For never do warriors live nor die in vain."'

The Chaplain's stark assessment brought a different train of thought, freeing Aeschelus from the fog of the soul-deadening. He laid a hand on the Chaplain's shoulder and his thoughts cleared further, making him realise just how despondent he had become. Whether it was due to a renewed sense of purpose or the physical proximity of the stoic Chaplain was impossible to know.

'You are right, we cannot save Orestes. We must change the parameters of victory to incorporate these latest developments. Our lives only have value in the cause of success, so we shall chart a course to victory that can be achieved.'

The Chaplain lifted a truncated arm, its end cauterised, sealed with a long-bladed ceramite cap. 'I am heartened to know that we can still fight with purpose and glory.'

'Purpose, yes.' Aeschelus sighed. 'I think we may be short on glory, but that is no longer a matter of concern.'

He broke away from Exelloria and found the Imperial commander deep in discussion with the magos and general-duke, concerning the evacuation of the orbital palaces.

'What cowardice is this?' Aeschelus demanded.

'Not cowardice,' replied Hosul. 'Expediency. We have more chance of surviving on the surface.'

'That was not your assessment when the necrons first attacked,' said the captain. 'It is flawed logic now. The palaces are still a sizeable defence in their own right. You will not abandon them.'

'Captain, you are not in command,' replied Hosul, flinching as Aeschelus turned an unforgiving stare on him. He wilted under the silent glare of reproach but made one last attempt at defending himself, voice barely a whisper. 'The further from the enemy, the lesser the effect of this terrible mind-numbing.'

'We are all dead,' Aeschelus told them bluntly. 'There is nowhere to run, nowhere to hide. None of your ships or astrotelepathy escaped the system. My brothers and I are here by the grace of the Emperor and desperation. Nobody is coming to save us.'

Lowensten swallowed hard, lips trembling. Aeschelus could not believe how easily he had been deceived by the pretence of self-sacrifice offered in the audience hall. He was of a mind to do now what he should have done then and his sword arm lifted.

'Please, give me a chance,' said the Imperial commander. There was strain in every feature as though a war waged inside him. Teeth gritted, blinking repeatedly, Lowensten met the captain's harsh stare for a few seconds, pleading with a look. But it was a different kind of fear. A self-loathing flashed across Lowensten's face, as though he knew his weakness but could not control it.

The captain remembered how much more vulnerable to the necron soul-dampening the unaugmented humans were. The bolstering effect of the Space Marines was no longer enough to keep it at bay. Something was making it stronger.

Something, perhaps, that could be destroyed...

With an effort, Ah-hotep stopped herself from draining the artificial stars chained into the hearts of the humans' reactors. For a moment that lasted an eternity, she basked in the plasma cores, knowing what it must have felt like to be a star god. Their secrets were hers now, ripped from the minds of the C'tan by the artifices of the techno-mandrites, their knowledge seized in part-payment for the horror they had unleashed upon the necron people. She drank deep of the reacting particles, every tiny fusion bringing fresh vigour to her aeons-old circuits.

But Ah-hotep was not here to feed; she had a far better purpose.

Tearing herself back from the brink of gorging, she surveyed her surrounds. Her small force was positioned at every approach to her hiding place, holding ground easily against the lacklustre attacks of the station crew. She could feel the thrum of powered armour suits closing in from the nearby levels, though, and knew her minions would soon face a greater test. She did not have long.

Roving through her data tendrils, she could tell by the increased activity that the humans had benefited from her aura invigorating their sensory banks. Data-manipulators loitered at the boundary of weapons control until the very instant she needed them. Panicked by the approach of Tholotep's flotilla, the humans started arming the station's cannon batteries and torpedo launchers. Riding their access codes, the plasmancer passed into the barred systems, spreading from battery to battery, launcher to launcher. She carried on, recombining with her carrier waves to spring forth from the orbiting station to the ring of other satellites positioned about the world. Twelvefold she increased, taking over gunnery controls whose human attendants were listless beneath the onslaught of the resonator's advancing overnull field.

As she infiltrated every aspect of their defence systems, Ah-hotep scoured the sensor readings, tracking the incoming ships of Simut. To her dismay, the overlord had positioned himself beyond orbit, out of weapons range. Rather than support the attacks of his legion on the ground he watched from afar.

Simut's cowardice was so far thwarting her plans. She needed to do more. As explosive projectiles engaged the first of her Immortals, she brought down anti-decompression bulkheads, slamming them onto one of the attackers, sealing herself and her protectors into the cluster of chambers. Almost immediately she sensed the activation of localised, high-powered radiation cutters.

The quiet of the strategium aboard the *Ithraca's Vengeance* was broken by an announcement from the communications officer. Praxamedes had been revising his plan of attack against the enemy capital ship, ready to issue the final orders to the remaining Orestean ships coming to attendance.

'Incoming vox from the orbital palaces, lieutenant!'

Praxamedes saw immediately that the command-channel broadcast carried Captain Aeschelus' cipher codes.

'Activate reception.' He waited for the static of connection to clear. 'This is Lieutenant Praxamedes, ship command.'

He heard more crackles as another recipient came on line.

'*Nemetus here.*' His words were tense, every syllable strained. '*Heavily engaged.*'

'*Just fight and listen, Nemetus,*' said the captain. There was a change in his tone, a fluidity Praxamedes had not heard for many months. Confidence, he realised. '*We have a new plan. A second necron fleet has arrived and we cannot prevent them making planetfall. Our objective can no longer be the defence of Orestes.*'

'*Disheartening,*' grunted Nemetus.

'*There is still a goal we can strive for. The threat posed by the necrons is something unseen by the authorities of the Throne. For nine years, we have laboured greatly against heretics and secessionists, but never thought that the warp itself might be turned against us in a way even more devastating than the Cicatrix Maledictum. The Indomitus Crusade advances into a danger they do not expect and will not detect until it is too late. We need to get word back to the lord primarch. This soul-drain is far greater than one system, or even two systems. Only the might of the battle group – perhaps the whole crusade – will be enough to thwart the necrons' ambition.*'

'But such forces must be in place *before* the necrons arrive, ahead of the warp effect,' said Praxamedes. 'As we have discovered, reinforcing a system once attacked is all but impossible. Reclaiming one is probably beyond question.'

'*Exactly. The Imperium must be prepared for the necrons' expansion. The only good that can come of what has occurred here is that warning. We must break the* Ithraca's Vengeance *out of Orestes and back to Imperial space, even if it costs us everything else in the system.*'

'Lieutenant, we have an Orestean shuttle requesting docking security clearance,' announced one of the vox-officers.

'*The passengers are from me,*' said the captain, overhearing the exchange.

'Permission granted,' Praxamedes told the vox-operator. He returned his thoughts to the mission. 'We have to get as far from the necrons as possible if we are to have any chance of breaking through to warp space. I don't think we can do it.'

'*Not all of the necrons. I have confirmed with Fedualis that the soul-drain effect has a focal point. That rear-echelon ship? It is a weapon, but not like anything we were expecting.*'

'Destroy the ship, escape the system,' said Praxamedes. 'Simple.'

'*Not so simple. The* Ithraca's Vengeance *is the only warp-capable ship in the system. We cannot risk the warp engines being damaged in the attack. The system defence ships are not powerful enough to take out the necron fleet. They*' *will provide a screen and distraction for you to break out of orbit. Your ship has to get as far away as needed and translate.'*

Listening to Aeschelus and Praxamedes, it was almost impossible to cling on to any thought of victory, but Nemetus tried his best to assess his position objectively. Even as he listened, he fought, cutting down small knots of necron warriors with efficient bladework, keeping the next defence line intact for the time being.

Even so, the fight for the lifting station was not so much a battle as a slaughter. The expanse between the outer wall and the terminal buildings was a killing ground. Bands of silver-limbed monstrosities hunted down scattered troopers, the air crackling with emerald energy. Crescent-hulled fighters swooped from above, beams of jade energy scouring the outer reaches for those that had fled further afield. Afflicted by a resurgence of the soul-deadening, the militia troopers barely protected themselves, easy prey for the necron attackers striding through the breaches in the outer wall.

The lieutenant had drawn back the bulk of the defence to the terminal buildings, forming a corps of his Space Marines to counter-strike the swiftest enemy breakthroughs. Bolstered by their presence, nearby Oresteans formed a stiffer defence, but they were weakening with every passing minute, slowly succumbing to the mounting mental pressure Nemetus could feel grinding his thoughts into dust. The lacklustre retreat in many places was overwhelmed by the approaching aliens, and it was hard to see how any of them, Ultramarines included, would survive more than thirty minutes.

He decided to keep that to himself; there was no point complaining about a situation that could not be changed.

'What about down here? What is our objective?'

There was a long pause before Aeschelus replied.

'Fight well and die with glory, brother,' said the captain.

So that was how it was going to be. Nemetus was almost pleased that he could resign himself to this fate. No gambits, no last-ditch efforts to thwart the odds. Just a last stand, killing as many enemies as possible. There was a simplicity that appealed.

'Of course, you will not be there,' Aeschelus continued. *'This is my command and I will lead it.'*

'No, captain, that will not be necessary,' said Nemetus. 'You need to take the ship.'

'I concur, brother-captain. I will reinforce Nemetus' position.'

'I am already on my way to the surface,' the captain said, amused at the assertion. *'The first time both of my lieutenants agree on something and I have to overrule you.'*

'No, captain!' Praxamedes sounded distraught.

'I will brook no more insubordination, Prax.'

'Then I must exchange commands with Lieutenant Nemetus. We can all agree that his aptitudes are far more suited to this sort of daring escapade.'

'You want me to run away instead of fighting for a glorious death?' laughed Nemetus. 'I do not think so!'

'And we are back to the debates,' sighed Aeschelus.

'I am serious, brother-captain,' Praxamedes continued. *'I will bring down the shuttle that just docked. Lieutenant Nemetus can ride the orbital elevator.'*

'I need a clear head in charge, Praxamedes.'

'I feel I should resent that remark,' said Nemetus, 'but I cannot find an argument against it. Listen, brother. The captain is right. If you manage to get out of here, you need to get back to the Imperium-controlled sectors. I would likely get distracted. Run into orks or heretics and start a fight.'

'That is a good point,' said Aeschelus. *'Also, you are already aboard, Prax, and time is our biggest enemy. The orbital palaces have been engaged by a necron force. We are bringing down as many troops as possible to the surface to make our stand there.'*

'I welcome such fine company,' said Nemetus.

'It is only a matter of time until the xenos fleet closes in for the kill or the station's weapons are enslaved to the xenos intrusion and open fire. You need to break away now. Your arrivals are Chaplain Exelloria, Fedualis and the palaces' astropathic choir. Perhaps they will help break through the Impossibility Boundary.'

'I understand, captain. Once we are through to warp space we won't be able to communicate. I won't be able to tell you if we are successful.'

'I know you will do it, Prax. If someone can find a way, you can. I am entrusting the most important mission we have ever undertaken to you. This is your command.'

'Go with the Emperor's grace,' said Nemetus. 'And remember to mention my name to the lord primarch if you should happen to see him.'

'Your deaths shall not be in vain,' replied Praxamedes. *'This is ship command. Orders acknowledged. For the Emperor!'*

'For the Emperor,' they echoed.

The vox snarled into dead static and then fell silent.

Nemetus looked up and could see one of the immense lifter carriages descending a few thousand yards up. Not so much reinforcements as more meat into the grinder, but they would be cut to pieces if the station was overrun before they arrived.

The larger necron force was at the outer wall, slightly behind the first assault wave. His gaze was drawn by a crash of glass and shriek of ripping metal. Scanning the formations of xenos, he found that most of them were channelling through the main gateway of the terminal building. His best troops were stationed there – Eradicators and the Bladeguard, led by Judiciar Admonius. It was a bad tactic by the enemy, condensing the host onto a front that was too narrow for effective attack. When his gaze settled on a larger figure close to the forefront of the assault, a tripodal warrior with several arms surrounded by more three-legged constructs, he realised he was looking at a necron commander.

Time was its own victory. Perhaps there was still one more gambit, after all.

The moment of Simut's victory was so close he would have been able to smell it, had he not divested himself of such mortal senses in an age long past. Even so, his cortical field crackled visibly with excitement as he felt his troops constricting the humans like a great serpent. The serpent king? That was perhaps a worthy title for one that had crushed the resistance from the system. Simut slid it into the title registry of his subordinates for future use.

Ah-hotep had broadcast that she was in complete control of the human space station and was ready to unleash its power at his command. Zozar's Destroyers and the Szarekh cohort on the surface were in the process of eradicating the humans and their superior allies. The overlord was not sure whether the fighting would be over before the resonator arrived. If not, its placement upon the surface would seal the overnull and smother any remaining embers of defiance.

'Lord of the Silver Hosts, one human vessel is attempting to escape,' warned Phetos. The display magnified to a view of the accursed alien vessel that had assaulted the *Barge of the Stormhawk*. Hatred welled up within Simut.

'Destroy it! Turn it to ash on the cosmic winds!'

'You wish to take the *Sun of Endings*, Lord of the Starsea?'

'What? No! Send attack barques after it. Their presence will extend the overnull to prevent its break into the othersea. Three should be sufficient.'

'As you will it, Sunlord of the Upper Hills.'

Simut felt the fleet shifting when a depleted squadron of attack ships broke away from the flotilla guarding the resonator carriers as they moved closer into orbit. They curved out of the gravity trap and accelerated after the departing human cruiser.

The humans had cut through the outer bulkheads and were on the verge of destroying the door to the chamber into which Ah-hotep had withdrawn, surrounded by half a dozen surviving Immortals. Heavy gauss rifles at the ready, they guarded her silently while she let her sense free across the streams of energy that criss-crossed the station and connected it to the universe beyond.

Her plan was unravelling. The resonator was almost in position to begin its final descent. The enhanced humans were fleeing out-system, pursued by a squadron of barques. On the surface the scattered cortical flashes from Zozar betrayed imminent extermination of the defenders. Despite his serial incompetence and Ah-hotep's subtle influence, Simut was about to achieve his victory.

More drastic action was required. .

She weaved together a temporally locked data-packet and set it free through the humans' calculating systems. With this task complete, Ah-hotep reached out her cortical field to connect with the translocator beacons aboard the *Sun of Endings*. Gaining connection, she locked onto the signal with her bodyguard and remotely activated the beam-transport.

How refreshing to translocate by her own will! It felt more like floating than falling, and she arrived alert and ready aboard the command-mastaba of her tomb ship. Her Immortals materialised around her.

'Ah-hotep, why have you returned?' Simut demanded, rising from the command throne.

She ignored him, plunging her cortical field into the control systems of the tomb ship. Aided by powerful single-use technomandrite protocol-rites, she punched through the overlord's security routines and activated the drive of the *Sun of Endings*. She set the engines to accelerate, directly towards the planet. Simultaneously Ah-hotep unleashed an energy blast, scorching the circuitry of the vault controls, leaving them vulnerable to another technomandrite-coded incursion that released her phalanx from the Szarekh protocols.

'Kill the plasmancer!' bellowed Simut, even as his cortical field rushed back into the tomb ship systems to stop her.

Phetos pounced, blade swinging towards the plasmancer. An Immortal intercepted the attack, gauss rifle hewn in half by its glittering edge, but deflecting the blow to the side. Simut's lychguard came to life with blazing green eyes, shields and guns raised.

'No!' Ah-hotep released the power siphoned from the miniature stars of the reactors, unleashing a lightning storm across the mastaba that hurled three lychguard to the wall and staggered the others. Streaming forward into the breach, she headed for Simut, her weapons and claws leaving trails of emerald sparks.

The overlord raised his glaive, armour gleaming as defensive circuitry activated. Phetos shouted a challenge from behind but Ah-hotep ignored him, rushing through the shadows with blade held aloft to confront Simut. His phase blade met hers with an explosion of interdimensional energy as both tried to slice through subspaces and pass each other. Feedback power detonated, throwing the two opponents apart. Detecting the surge in a lychguard's beam cannon, Ah-hotep flexed and swooped, the green ray slashing into the ceiling where she had hovered a moment before.

Pushed to one knee by the dimensional blast, Simut straightened.

Phetos' blade caught Ah-hotep in the tailspine, severing an energyglobe from her back. The container burst with fronds of power, enveloping them both in a powerful but brief whirlwind of green. The royal warden recovered fractionally quicker and opened fire, just before Ah-hotep released a burst of pure kinetic power. Phetos' beam carved through the living metal of her arm, sending the limb and her phase blade clattering to the floor even as he was smashed through his lychguard like an artillery shell, to crumple in a broken heap at the foot of the cracked display wall.

Protocols of command thrummed through the tomb ship, purging the technomandrite incursion. Obedience demands slashed at Ah-hotep's cortical field, paralysing her, while her presence in the *Sun of Endings* recognised the down-shift in the engine drives, bringing them to a stop. Behind her, the plasmancer's Immortals fell still, their loyalty to her once again overridden by immutable Szarekh protocols.

'Pathetic,' sneered Simut, approaching with his blade levelled towards her chest. 'I do not know which is more insulting – your treachery or your underestimation of my power. You have failed. Your attempt to hurl us into the world has been thwarted by my will.'

Ah-hotep said nothing, locked within binding coils of manifested cortical energy. An energy she could not absorb.

'I will not have you atomised yet. I will have your datacore disassembled and your cortical field stripped to find out who is trying to kill me.'

'*I* am trying to kill you, you preening mollusc!' Though Ah-hotep's will was great, the bonds of paralysis laid on her by the loyalty protocols stopped even the smallest spark escaping from her trembling, outstretched fingertips.

'You?' Simut shook his head and turned away with a dismissive wave. 'You are not important enough.'

'Look at me!' screeched the plasmancer. 'Look into the face of the person that will encompass your doom. Look into my eyes and I will look into yours as the long aeons come to an end and your miserable existence is obliterated. Know that it is I, Pharozin-Consort Aat Muphekta Ah-hotep Khia! I am your executioner.'

'Muphekta?' Simut turned back, eyes blazing with shock. 'The Muphekta dynasty were eradicated after the long sleep. By my word they were wiped out.'

'Not all of them,' laughed Ah-hotep.

Aboard the human starbase, the delayed data-packet unfurled into the control systems, locking its weapon systems to the tomb ship, now within range. An instant later came the order to open fire.

Praxamedes watched on the main viewer as the orbital palaces and their accompanying weapons platforms unleashed their full fury on the necron ship in one blaze of coordinated destruction. Laser lances sprang out, slicing at the sweep of the outer wings, while rapid-firing plasma batteries pumped volatile blasts across the void. The volley of blue stars slammed into the damaged structure, punching deep into its silvery hull. Torpedoes sped across the vacuum, splintering into hundreds of smaller warheads while mass drivers super-accelerated solid rounds that pierced through the breaking ship, moments before the torpedo missiles detonated, engulfing the capital ship with swirling atomic clouds and wreathing electromagnetic storms that tore its skin away in scattering spirals.

From the firestorm, the remains of the ship emerged, breaking into thousands of shards, its superstructure burning with ghostly jade energy, forks of lightning churning from its shattered body.

'Necron escorts are still in pursuit, lieutenant commander,' Lerok told him.

'What are your orders, lieutenant commander?' asked Shipmaster Oloris.

Praxamedes turned to the group of green-robed men and women clustered to the side of the strategium – Fedualis and the astropaths from the station. With them was the Chaplain, Exelloria. Captain Aeschelus had posited that the reclusiarch's spiritual strength was as powerful as the psychic might of the astrotelepaths. Praxamedes was unconvinced, but it was good to have another Space Marine aboard the *Ithraca's Vengeance*. The only others were a few comatose warriors in the apothecarion – ones that had lost limbs and organs to glancing necron beam hits.

'No, not yet,' said Fedualis, face strained. 'The warp-nullification still reaches us.'

'Keep going,' the lieutenant told Oloris. 'All power to the engines and shields.'

'The enemy are closing, lieutenant commander,' said Oloris. 'You want us to shut down gunnery?'

'*All* power, Mister Oloris,' said Praxamedes. 'We're not fighting our way out of this one.'

CHAPTER SEVEN

The lifter container had several external vid-links, directed upwards and to the surface. Monitoring the feeds, Aeschelus saw the sudden new star in the darkening sky that heralded the end of the necron capital ship. It did not matter what madness or idiocy had possessed the necron commander to come within range, perhaps thinking the orbital palaces were out of commission. The result was all that counted. The read-outs told him that his force of several dozen Space Marines would be on the ground in a matter of minutes, but his future was a secondary concern now.

'Ship command, what is your status?' he voxed. The container-elevators had dedicated channels to the ground and orbital terminals, but the station tech-adepts had overridden them and increased their power so that he could remain in contact with the *Ithraca's Vengeance* for several hundred thousand more miles.

'*Still no warp traction, brother-captain,*' Praxamedes replied. '*We are trying to get out-system but are being pursued. If we turn on our attackers, I think we might lose our opportunity.*'

'I see,' the captain replied, heart sinking. It had been a long shot, and perhaps just a hope-dream rather than a plan. 'Keep going as best you can. I trust you to make the right decision, brother.'

Adjusting the channel, he responded to a signal from the orbital palaces. He recognised the voice of the Imperial commander himself answering.

'Captain Aeschelus, this will be our last conversation.'

Lowensten's words automatically brought to mind the warnings of Sister Aures. Aeschelus had left the Imperial commander aboard the palaces, but suddenly doubted the wisdom of that decision.

'What do you mean, Imperial commander?' he growled. 'What are you planning?'

'I received a notice from the aliens shortly prior to the destruction of the enemy capital ship. It confirms that the bulk carrier vessel we have been ignoring is the key to their attack. There is no ship in orbit or weapon on the ground that can defeat it. I–'

'Your betrayal will not go unpunished, no matter what you think, Lowensten,' snapped Aeschelus. 'In this life or in the abyss, vengeance will find you.'

'An accusation I have perhaps earned, captain, but you interrupted me before I could explain my actions.'

'There is no excuse for heresy.'

'I am no heretic. I might one day be remembered as a martyr. I have been inspired by your sacrifice. We have evacuated all but essential station personnel and are at this moment disengaging the gravitic stabilisers.'

'Why would you do that? The stabilisers keep you in controlled orbit.'

The vox crackled with distorted laughter.

'I know well what they do; they have literally sustained my family for many generations! They also keep the palaces on their fixed course around this world. The necron weaponship is out of range. We must break free from the ages-old orbit chosen by my ancestors. We will bring the station's batteries to bear upon the structure and destroy it.'

'Without the stabilisers, orbit will decay. Your palaces have no atmospheric entry integrity.'

'I know, captain. This is my penance, our penance, for showing weakness. Nobody will remember it, of course, but I go to my death knowing I have done what I can to atone to the Emperor for my weaknesses and sins. Goodbye, Captain Aeschelus of the Ultramarines. I, Imperial Commander Kaleb Monfrottine Lowensten, abdicate and dissolve all authority for the Orestes System and of this moment place it in trust of the Ultramarines Chapter

of the Adeptus Astartes, until by such convenience of the Adeptus Terra a worthy successor may be installed. These are my final and irreversible commands. For the Emperor, captain.'

'For the Emperor,' Aeschelus replied, but the vox had gone dead before he finished.

The battle took a turn for the bizarre. Nemetus watched in disbelief as the necrons at the wall froze in place momentarily, some of them toppling over mid-stride, others falling down slopes or sliding over the broken masonry, bumping and tumbling on their way down. The keening of wind on wingtips heralded the arrival of the attack craft, plunging out of the sky. A few had been passing low and crashed into the terminal buildings and walls, slamming into the surrounding compound like mass driver shells, their detonations hurling aside troopers and necrons. Through the breaches the light from the gleaming transporter-engines flickered and died, the fortress-like machines listing sideways, settling to the ground or tipping like felled trees. Floating warrior-carriers crashed into the walls, spilling puppet-like silver skeletons across the ferrocrete, while stalking monstrosities teetered dangerously as they clambered over bulk transporters and shattered wall sections.

The disarray lasted for several seconds before the army resumed its advance in a far more fractured fashion. Several squads broke away to march towards the rear while many of the skeletal assailants walked directly into the remaining pockets of defenders, heedless of the storm of bullets and lasbolts crashing down into them, their own weapons firing sporadically.

But not the enemy at the gatehouses. Though everything behind them inexplicably stuttered, the tripodal necron commander and its immediate entourage crashed through the gates and into the terminal building, beams and blades filling the hall with a fluctuating jade light. The Bladeguard were there to meet them as Eradicator melta rifles turned onrushing tripodal constructs into puddles of quivering slag. Troopers fired from both sides, positioned at gantries where once merchants had haggled for cargo loads. Las-beams by the score pelted the necron force, red slashes that ricocheted from polished metal skins.

'Judiciar, with me,' shouted Nemetus, heading for the necron that towered over even the Primaris Marines. 'Brothers, clear a path!'

The Bladeguard bashed and hacked at the stamping machine-things, creating an opening for the lieutenant and the Judiciar. Side by side they hurled themselves at the giant creature, power sword and greatsword trying to sweep its legs from under it. A glittering blade swung down, crashing against Nemetus' shield, nearly knocking him from his feet. He stumbled back, the shield falling from his arm, bisected by the impossible sword. Wordless, Admonius swung his weapon up, crashing its snarling edge into the underside of the monster's torso. Sparks exploded, showering across the black armour of the Judiciar, leaving a deep welt in the artificial flesh of his foe.

Tossing aside the remnants of his storm shield, Nemetus took up his sword two-handed and leapt back to the attack. Behind him he felt other necrons closing in, clattering and screeching blows against the shields of the Bladeguard. He could not assume that the greater army would remain in disarray forever; the time to strike was now.

Bright stars in the firmament of battle.

To light the way for others. To be the beacon of hope.

A claw-limb rose, slashing out to rip his pauldron from his right shoulder, spinning him sideways. He almost fell into the barrels of another xenos' cannon, cutting it in half with a sweep of his sword even as its deadly green glow swelled in brightness. Following up his sweep, he smashed his elbow into the necron construct, sending it stumbling backwards on its three legs. Garios was upon it in the next heartbeat, his blade cleaving it in half, the pieces scattered to the floor.

Amazed, Nemetus watched the pieces slowly spinning to a stop. They had not phased out.

'They die!' he roared, coming at the xenos leader from behind. He lashed his blade at a leg, hacking deep into the joint at the hip. A green-edged weapon swung back towards him, forcing him to retreat a step. Shifting its weight, the necron stumbled. Its cannon thrummed into life and moments later erupted with a fluctuating beam of emerald power.

The blast struck Admonius.

Taken aback, the lieutenant watched the black armoured body fall, the head and a semicircle of the torso neatly removed.

'Avenge our brother!' Nemetus bellowed, kicking hard at the alien's damaged limb, fending off another crackling blade attack to drive his remaining pauldron into the leg.

Letting go of his sword with one hand, he wrapped his arm about the shining metal, feeling a strange resistance to his grip. He dropped and rolled, twisting the leg from its joint as he did so. Nemetus crashed to the floor as the necron commander sprawled backwards, blade and cannon impotently flailing to retain balance, tripping over the supine lieutenant to slam into the hard floor.

Like the true-scarabs that the canoptek constructs had been modelled upon, the enhanced human warriors descended upon Zozar's collapsed body. Rather than burrowing at dead flesh with mandibles, they hewed at the living metal of his form with rapacious blows of gleaming blades. The skorpekh lord tried to rise, hardening his cortical shield against their assault, arms assisting his remaining two legs in the attempt.

It was impossible to defend against every attack. A blow hammered at the back of Zozar's head, splitting it to the neck. With growing detachment, he watched part of his skull drop down his torso and clang to the floor.

The greater cortical network was awash with convulsive signals. There were no protocols, no automated translocation programs to remove heavily damaged vessels from the battle. His retrieval broadcast went unanswered, drifting out into the empty void of space.

He was utterly alone.

Zozar closed off his sensors, cocooning himself against the continued blows raining down upon the outer shell of his being. It was a body; one he had modified continually in his quest for efficient lethality. It mattered even less now that it would not be replaced. Death was imminent.

Death.

The cessation of life. His mission had been to serve death, an uncompromising killer in pursuit of an orderly universe without the anarchy of sentience.

He had no regrets. It was too late for that.

Power supply was almost diminished, expended trying to repair wounds that could not be healed, warding off blades out of instinct, removed from any conscious desire to remain alive. His cortical field retreated to the core nexus, a particle-cluster in the heart of the engine he had created for killing.

In absence of all other stimuli, a singular image imposed itself upon the last vestiges of awareness. A face, beautiful, lit by the red sun of Zozar's world. It was rife with lesions and scabs, balding and radiation-burnt, but it was still smiling.

She was gone and his rage had tried to extinguish all life to mask the pain. He had not succeeded and in the last instant of cogitation Zozar admitted his failure.

Yes, life was persistent.

Aeschelus and a cluster of his warriors watched the real time vid-feed from the palaces as the massive installation powered out of its ordained orbit. Heat and light flared from the lower levels as they skimmed the outer atmosphere. Ahead, the necron bulk hauler hung like a black obelisk against the distant stars, the jade engine-gleam of its transports shining across bizarrely faceted sides.

The palaces' guns opened fire, streaming plasma and shells into the alien vessel. Amid the fury of the Imperial commander's fusillade the glow of atmospheric entry grew bright. Fronds of white and yellow passed across the vid-feed, briefly eclipsing the blue of plasma bolts and dark red of high explosive detonations.

'In the Emperor's name, they shall be remembered,' Aeschelus intoned solemnly, watching as a green crack of light spread along the length of the alien obelisk. Secondary fractures snaked outwards as the palaces continued their bombardment.

The view was almost lost as the flare of atmospheric friction grew brighter and brighter, but in the final few seconds before the feed died, Aeschelus saw the mysterious alien edifice split, a shard larger than a starship falling away from its side, the break blazing with emerald sparks.

The screen turned to static even as Aeschelus felt a lifting of the burden that had weighed upon his thoughts for many days. He heard a laugh from one of the Primaris Marines behind him, for no particular reason yet infectious all the same. Aeschelus turned and smiled at his battle-brothers, giving release to the relief he felt.

He thought of the massive enemy fleet still coming towards the planet but met the recollection without fear. In the other direction, the *Ithraca's Vengeance* had passed out of range, accelerating towards the periphery.

'May the Emperor speed you onwards, Prax,' he whispered. 'By our deaths we honour the Lord on the Throne, but by your life you protect His servants.'

* * *

There was no way to outrun the xenos scum, Praxamedes concluded with reluctance. Admitting that they were not going to turn back meant he faced a decision. He had hoped when the sensors had picked up the destruction of the necron heavy hauling ship that the escorts would be afflicted in some way. They had not. With single-minded persistence they continued to close on the *Ithraca's Vengeance* despite running the strike cruiser's engines at one hundred and twenty per cent capacity. Very soon the plasma drives would explode under the pressure.

He viewed the system charts, looking for inspiration, wishing he could have some lateral leap of thinking like Aeschelus or Nemetus. Something like using a gravity well to accelerate, or a way to slow down the necron attackers.

A sudden blurting from the navigational servitors drew his eye. Officer Kaloses translated their distress.

'Lieutenant commander, we have a spatial obstruction four thousand miles ahead.'

It was a stretch of asteroids; hundreds of thousands of ice and rock chunks ranging from dust to behemoths larger than the strike cruiser. With the augurs running on minimal power, they had not been seen further out.

'Suggest course change to heading oh-forty-two, declination seven, lieutenant commander,' said Oloris. 'We will need to reduce speed for thruster manoeuvring.'

Praxamedes said nothing and turned to the display controls. He brought up the local charts again and superimposed the augur readings, such as they were. The asteroid field was a big one, tens of thousands of cubic miles. The theory of void warfare held that smaller craft like the pursuing escorts were better at navigating such phenomena. The *Ithraca's Vengeance* would have to slow to give the helms officer any chance of avoiding the largest asteroids with enough time to steer round them.

He thought back to what Nemetus had said about his decision to activate the warp drive.

'There was no time for reason, brother. Had I waited even another second we might never have broken through the barrier.'

'The situation required action.'

'We were adrift in the warp. There was nothing to lose. There was no gamble.'

271

'Lieutenant commander?' prompted Oloris.

They were two thousand miles from the edge of the field.

'Power engines to nominal,' Praxamedes commanded helm control. 'Navigational fields active. Power to gunnery.'

The deck officers relayed his commands, working quickly at their terminals, their affirmatives sounding back in the following half a minute. Quiet descended – only the faint murmur of servitors, clack of telemetric gauges and clicking metriculators could be heard. It was broken by Shipmaster Oloris.

'Helm orders, lieutenant commander?'

'Ahead steady,' Praxamedes replied calmly.

He saw disbelief in Oloris' eyes. 'Ahead steady?' It was a rare loss of discipline from the veteran, one that earned him a barked reprimand from Exelloria.

'Attend to your orders, shipmaster, or recuse yourself from your role.' The Chaplain stomped across the strategium while Oloris saluted and passed the order to helm. Exelloria continued on the vox-link, unheard by the deck crew and astropaths. *'It seems that we are plunging straight into a volatile celestial phenomenon with enemy contacts at our starboard quarter. Is that your intent, brother?'*

'The marshes of Cothyria, Brother-Chaplain,' replied Praxamedes. He switched to vocal address so that the others could hear again. 'I recall the lord primarch's actions in the marshes of Cothyria, as related in the *Book of Macragge.*'

'I think this is poor timing for a history lesson, lieutenant,' rasped one of the astropaths.

'In the days before he took up the rulership of Macragge, Roboute Guilliman led a patrol along the Cothyr ridge, at the border with rival Illyria,' Praxamedes continued, paying the interruption no heed. He watched the asteroids getting closer. Navigational warnings flickered amber across the main display. 'He was following an Illyrian raiding column that had crossed over and razed several settlements. The lord primarch was only meant to locate them but as a heavy rain fell, he stumbled upon the Illyrians in the downpour.'

'Entering navigational obstacle,' reported the navigation officer.

Alarms sounded briefly, accompanied by warning red runes. There was muttering from several directions and disquieted gasps.

'Silence!' bellowed Exelloria. 'Attend to your tasks! *I hope you are right, brother,*' he continued across the command channel.

Praxamedes switched the view to the vid-link from the prow, a real-time feed of the debris ahead. Red flares and streaks showed where the low-power navigational shields shunted aside the smaller asteroids. He felt a moment of release. It was too late to change course or power down. The instant of commitment had passed, but this time he had acted.

'The Illyrians were a five-hundred-strong cavalry company, far out-matching even the lord primarch,' he continued, turning to face the crew. 'As their camp roused at the intruders, revered Guilliman realised he could not outrun them, nor outfight them.'

Many of the crew were looking at the display, not him. Some shared worried glances, others were whispering among themselves. A glance at Exelloria showed that the Chaplain had also become fixed on the main display, the crew's transgressions overlooked. Praxamedes strode across to the gunnery terminals and made some adjustments, powering down most of the portside batteries to bolster the energy distribution to the starboard side and dorsal cannon.

'Rather than trying to retreat back towards Macragge Civitas, he headed further *into* Illyrian territory. He knew that the foothills quickly gave way to a river delta marsh, much swelled by the recent rains.'

The main screen was almost full scarlet as the cruiser continued to bull its way through the chunks of rock and ice, the crackle of the fields now audible within the strategium, accompanied by the occasional clang and crunch of smaller pieces hitting the hull.

'The Illyrians pressed on after him, confident of overwhelming the much fewer enemy, ignorant of the super-warrior that led them. But it was not the lord primarch's physique and skill that won that day but his intellect. The Illyrians' horses were soon bogged down by the marsh, the riders stranded, and from out of the rain the lord primarch counter-attacked. No more mobile than their foes, out of their element, the Illyrians were butchered. Only a third of them survived to flee back to their treacherous king.'

'He changed the battlefield to one that equalised both sides,' said Exelloria, finally turning from the large screen.

'He gave up some of his advantage to negate an even bigger advantage of the enemy.' Praxamedes lifted a hand to the gunnery officer. 'Pay attention, all of you. Prepare for split fire. Helm. Ready for new heading, hard turn to starboard.'

The lieutenant watched the necron ships slowing as they approached the asteroids. He thought about the rest of the account of Cothyria marsh. The part he had chosen to keep to himself. The Illyrians had been defeated, but Guilliman also lost half his patrol in the battle. The lord primarch admitted in his reflections that had the enemy dismounted before pursuing, his plan would have failed.

Like the young primarch and Nemetus, Praxamedes had come to a point where he had nothing to lose. Preservation of future opportunity was no longer a reasonable objective.

They either escaped or they did not. There would be no second chances.

Barque, Star of Natarun-4: *Slowing. Enemy has entered celestial debris.*

Barque, Star of Natarun-1: *Slowing. Enemy has made a mistake.*

Barque, Star of Natarun-4: *Desperation.*

Barque, Star of Natarun-3: *Slowing. Detecting high-density obstacle field.*

Barque, Star of Natarun-4: *Enemy course unchanged. Enemy sustaining damage from impacts.*

Barque, Star of Natarun-1: *Enemy is stupid. Partial acceleration. Close range for weapons fire.*

Barque, Star of Natarun-3: *Enemy is clearing path for us. Targeting weapons at engines.*

Barque, Star of Natarun-4: *Targeting weapons at engines.*

Barque, Star of Natarun-1: *Energy pulse – enemy flank thrusters activating.*

Barque, Star of Natarun-3: *Enemy taking more damage, turning into debris field.*

Barque, Star of Natarun-4: *Weapons have range. Target locked.*

Barque, Star of Natarun-1: *Enemy arresting speed, incoming targeting lock.*

Barque, Star of Natarun-4: *Enemy weapons signature increasing.*

Barque, Star of Natarun-1: *Enemy turn accelerating rapidly. Massed weapons coming to bear.*

Barque, Star of Natarun-3: *Enemy is preparing to open fire. We are compromised.*

Barque, Star of Natarun-1: *Disloyalty will not be tolerated! Formation protocols active. Pursuit command protocol override.*

Barque, Star of Natarun-3: *Evasive manoeuvres required.*

Barque, Star of Natarun-4: *Evasive manoeuvres required.*

Barque, Star of Natarun-1: *Evasive manoeuvres required.*

Barque, Star of Natarun-3: *Insufficient clear space. Evasion compromised.*

Barque, Star of Natarun-4: *Target lock. Cannot manoeuvre to evade.*

Barque, Star of Natarun-1: *Break formation.*

Barque, Star of Natarun-3: *Insufficient room to bre– Target firing.*

Barque, Star of Natarun-1: *Aversion protocols inactive. Pursuit command active.*

Barque, Star of Natarun-4: *Energy weapons dischar–*

Barque, Star of Natarun-1: *Barque 4 lost. Incomin–*

Barque, Star of Natarun-3: *Protocol direction to engage. Opening fire. Target–*

Fire-dampening fog filled the strategium, forcing the deck officers to don their rebreather masks and anti-flare goggles. Still encased in their armour, Praxamedes and Exelloria herded the astropaths into the sanctuary of the anterium, their charges choking and spluttering until the door sealed behind them.

'Warp engines on line,' Praxamedes commanded, activating the console within the secondary chamber. 'To my terminal. Activate Geller fields.'

'*Affirmative, lieutenant commander,*' Oloris replied over the intervox.

'Now?' coughed Fedualis.

'We are in an asteroid field!' moaned one of his order from the station.

'Navigator, are you ready for translation?' Praxamedes asked, ignoring the complaints. He turned his attention to the green-clad psykers. 'I need you to broadcast now. Together. We cannot risk the soul-dampening returning. This is our chance.'

Fedualis silenced any more objections with a raised hand.

'Together, brethren and sistren,' he said, holding out his hands. With varying degrees of reluctance, the astropaths joined in a circle, regarding each other with empty eyes. Praxamedes' armour reported a several-degrees drop in the chamber temperature. Moisture from the astropaths' laboured breaths and the anti-fire gas condensed on the terminal plasteel.

'*Ready. Awaiting the command, lieutenant,*' Kosa told him from the dorsal pilaster.

'Helm control to Navigator's tower,' Praxamedes ordered. The routine settled him, allowing him to push aside the massive stakes at play and the distinct possibility that they would all die within the next few minutes. That was beyond his control.

The air around the astropaths was getting colder still, puffs of vapour forming briefly. He saw their lips moving, silently voicing words together, the regular transmit-identifiers that preceded all broadcasts. Fedualis was shaking, as were two of the others. Frost started forming on their eyelashes.

'Now, lieutenant,' croaked Fedualis, barely heard.

Praxamedes wished he had something poignant to say, some brief exhortation to mark the moment. He voiced the only thought that came to him.

'For the Emperor and the primarch! Courage and honour!'

He touched the runes that activated the warp drive. A few seconds later, reality disappeared.

EPILOGUE

The night sky bore witness to the fiery demise of the orbital palaces. True to his pledge, the Imperial commander and his closest advisors had remained on the station during its destruction, their luxurious homes becoming a martyr's pyre.

The last of the other inhabitants disembarked from a newly arrived orbital elevator carriage. Orestean officers guided the non-combatants to the central buildings while Nemetus issued a stream of orders to the arriving troopers and specialists. Many were having difficulty focusing, the necron soul-dampening having grown stronger again as the second alien fleet approached. The high spirits Aeschelus had enjoyed after the demise of the obelisk had passed.

Scanning the crowd, the captain saw the distinctive robes of a Sister-Chatelain among them. He eased his way through the throng, people parting before him as water breaks before a ship's prow, until he came upon Sister Aures.

'You did not follow your appointed master into death?' He turned so that the Sister could precede him out of the press of people along the path he had forged.

'It is not my place to choose martyrdom, and I did nothing worthy of the penance.'

'The xenos fleet is less than twelve thousand miles from their teleportation range. They will be upon us in minutes. Your survival is short-lived.'

'And yet duty demands I am here,' said Aures. 'As are you, Captain Aeschelus of the Ultramarines. Why did you not leave on your ship?'

'Every second of delay to the departure put the escape at risk.'

'Do you truly believe Lieutenant Praxamedes managed to break warp?'

'I have no idea, Sister,' Aeschelus admitted. 'They could be dead, or adrift in the becalmed wilderness of the warp, lost forever. We will not know before we die.'

They came away from the bulk of the crowd. Pieces of necron were scattered all about. A crashed assault craft burned with emerald fire just a few yards away, its remains buried yards-deep into the curtain wall. Some pieces were stirring – severed limbs twitching with renewed life, cracked skulls with flickering jade gazes.

'Their unlife returns with the arrival of new lords,' said the Sister, kicking at a creeping hand. 'Even their destruction is stolen from us.'

Aeschelus said nothing. This was not the ending he would have crafted for himself. Was this punishment for his pride? It helped nobody to be drawn along such lines of thought. He had done as he thought right at every turn. The arrival of the second necron fleet did not diminish the achievement of the first's destruction. Had the Ultramarines not come to Orestes, the system would have been overrun without incident. Perhaps, in some way, the xenos plot would be thwarted by his intervention and the warning he entrusted to the *Ithraca's Vengeance* was speeding back to the Indomitus Crusade and the lord primarch.

But he also resolved himself to the idea that this was it; an end without meaning beyond himself. That was enough.

He would die here, alone and unremembered.

As the first emerald mist clouded the sky and a squadron of crescent-ships appeared, Aeschelus drew his blade. He recalled another piece of Imperial wisdom, though he did not know who had first voiced it.

'Duty is its own reward.'

ABOUT THE AUTHOR

Gav Thorpe is the author of the Horus Heresy novels *The First Wall*, *Deliverance Lost*, *Angels of Caliban* and *Corax*, as well as the novella *The Lion*, which formed part of the *New York Times* bestselling collection *The Primarchs*, and several audio dramas. He has written many novels for Warhammer 40,000, including *Ashes of Prospero*, *Imperator: Wrath of the Omnissiah* and the Rise of the Ynnari novels *Ghost Warrior* and *Wild Rider*. He also wrote the *Path of the Eldar* and *Legacy of Caliban* trilogies, and two volumes in The Beast Arises series. For Warhammer, Gav has penned the End Times novel *The Curse of Khaine*, the Warhammer Chronicles omnibus *The Sundering*, and recently wrote the Age of Sigmar novel *The Red Feast*. In 2017, Gav won the David Gemmell Legend Award for his Age of Sigmar novel *Warbeast*. He lives and works in Nottingham.

YOUR
NEXT READ

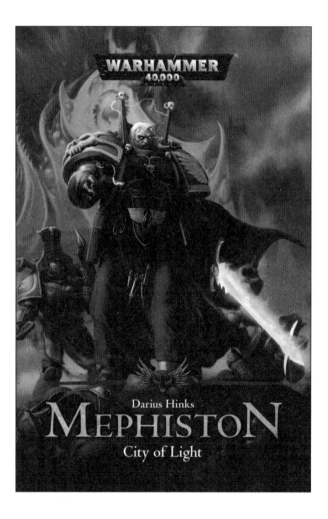

MEPHISTON: CITY OF LIGHT
by Darius Hinks

Deep in Imperium Nihilus, Blood Angels Chief Librarian Mephiston and his comrades are drawn into battle with a cabal of Thousand Sons sorcerers – with worlds at stake and hidden truths threatening to overwhelm him, this is Mephiston's darkest hour…

An extract from
Mephiston: City of Light
by Darius Hinks

Blood thralls gathered along the Ceremonial Way, dwarfed by statue-filled recesses and crumbling sarcophagi. Hidden emitters droned a requiem and serfs emerged from reliquaries and scriptoria, their voices raised in memory of a fallen lord. Ivory masks gleamed under crimson robes and as the procession moved slowly towards them, the thralls cast handfuls of earth across the flagstones, soil from the foothills of the Cruor Mountains, ballast for the fallen, binding the dead to Baal.

Beyond the lines of thralls, battle-brothers of the Blood Angels Second Company had gathered. They were arrayed beneath a towering sepulchre topped by a marble statue of their primarch, the Angel Sanguinius, his body twisted as he drove a spear into a writhing serpent. The Blood Angels were resplendent in full battle-plate, carrying newly stitched banners and freshly painted honour markings. A procession was approaching them down the Ceremonial Way and as they waited to greet it, candlelight flickered over their crimson armour, catching on the mouth grilles of their helmets and lending them a daemonic aspect.

At the head of the procession was Commander Dante, Regent of Imperium Nihilus and Chapter Master of the Blood Angels. An ancient among ancients, he tore the darkness like a flame, his armour a blaze of golden ceramite. His mask was a likeness of Sanguinius and as he strode from the shadows there was no sign of the trials that had recently befallen his Chapter. Dante looked like a figure from legend, clutching a weapon forged in the ashes of the Horus Heresy – the Axe Mortalis, its blade glimmering with inner fire.

At his side marched a figure no less imperious but far grimmer. Mephiston, the Chief Librarian of the Blood Angels, wore armour that was sculpted and lacquered to resemble a flayed corpse, painted deep crimson and polished to such a sheen that it looked slick. Like Dante, Mephiston approached the shrine with his chin raised and his eyes fixed on the middle distance, but where the Chapter Master looked noble in his flawless mask, Mephiston's face was cold and defiant, as though daring the congregation to look his way. His hair trailed behind him, so fair it was almost white and his features were a sharp caricature of the usual Blood Angels countenance. He bore all the hallmarks – imposing, inhumanly perfect features built on a grander scale than those of a mortal man – but his unblinking eyes were dark with secrets. It was as though, in him, the dream of Sanguinius had become a nightmare. He carried his ancient force blade, Vitarus, and his armour trailed plush, blood-red robes that whipped up dust as they hissed over the flagstones.

Behind the Chapter Master and his Chief Librarian flew a robed servitor, no bigger than an infant, with narrow, wrought iron limbs and an ivory mask like those worn by the blood thralls. The servitor was borne on frail, mechanical wings and it was carrying a salver – a huge disc of polished brass, covered in intricate runes and diagrams.

Behind the servitor marched two more Librarians, clad in the blue of their order, their heads framed by tall, cable-lined collars that harnessed their psychic power. Archaic markings on their battleplate marked them as members of Mephiston's inner circle, the Quorum Empyrric. The first of them was clearly ancient, even by the long-lived standards of the Blood Angels. His armour was so crowded with battle honours that he looked almost as gilded as his Chapter Master. His tightly cropped hair and beard were silver-grey and his eyes were like sapphires, gleaming mementos of long years gazing into the warp. His name was Gaius Rhacelus and he paid no heed to the crowds casting soil beneath his boots, keeping his gaze locked on his master and friend, Mephiston.

Beside Rhacelus marched a younger-looking Librarian, Lucius Antros. Antros' face would have been a more archetypal vision of the Chapter's angelic beauty were it not for the mass of scar tissue that covered one whole side of it. He had a mop of blond hair that shimmered in the torchlight and like Rhacelus his stare was locked on the Chief Librarian.

Behind these statuesque warriors marched one final Blood Angel, a battle-brother named Albinus. Like the others, his armour was draped in medals and gilded insignia, but he also carried several unique relics that denoted him as a high-ranking Sanguinary Priest. There was an intricately engraved chalice fixed to his belt, and attached to his left vambrace was a narthecium: a brutal-looking collection of chain-blades and drills that Albinus used to save his fallen brothers when he could, and to harvest their valuable gene-seed when he could not. The assembled blood thralls glanced at Albinus with almost as much awe as Dante and Mephiston. During the recent attacks on Baal, it was Albinus who had been tasked with protecting the Chapter's gene-seed off-world. It was a unique honour and there were rumours that Albinus might one day ascend to the role of Sanguinary High Priest and become the Keeper of the Red Grail. Like Dante, Albinus was not a regular visitor to the cloisters of the Librarium. It was a sign of how significant the occasion was that such luminaries had set aside their duties to march at Mephiston's side.

The procession halted at the foot of the sepulchre and exchanged salutes with the officers in charge of the honour guard. The clatter of armour roused Mephiston from his reverie and he realised how far his mind had wandered from Baal. He forced himself to focus. His auguries had indicated that this would be a significant event. There would be a surprise of some kind, before the rite was complete.

He followed Dante beneath a grand arch and into the domed sepulchre, where a body was laid out in state: a Blood Angel, divested of his armour but unmistakably more than human, his exaggerated musculature visible under a red and gold shroud.

Albinus approached the body first, confirming that the Blood Angel's gene-seed had been removed and preserved for the posterity of the Chapter. It was a formality. Codicier Peloris died months ago and the surgery had been performed moments after death, while the progenoid gland was still warm. Albinus moved the shroud slightly and an acrid, chemical smell filled the vault. He pretended to examine the cold flesh and muttered an oath. Then he replaced the shroud and stepped back, nodding to Dante.

As Dante approached the body, the singing blared louder through the speakers outside and the blood thralls dropped to their knees, clasping their hands in prayer. Dante took a book from a thrall and flicked through the pages until his hand settled on a suitable passage. He cleared his throat and was about speak when he paused and turned to Mephiston.

'Chief Librarian,' he said, his voice echoing strangely through the sepulchre. 'You knew Codicier Peloris better than anyone. Will you remember him?'

Mephiston was staring intently at the shrouded corpse, still lost in thought. He looked up in surprise at Dante's words. 'My lord?'

Dante held out the book. 'This will be the last of these ceremonies. And it is now many months since Peloris and the others died. It is time that you marked their passing, Mephiston.'

Mephiston searched the Chapter Master's face for a sign of duplicity, but he knew that was not Dante's way. Incredibly, despite everything that had taken place during their recent campaigns, he wanted *him* to read the prayer. He hesitated a moment longer, then nodded and took the book.

'We grieve in vain,' he read, his voice flat and quiet. As Mephiston spoke, the thralls fell silent, surprised by this turn of events. Peloris' final days were spent fighting xenos scum and warp-born horrors. But it was not xenos that had killed Peloris. Nor was it daemonic hosts. It was Mephiston. When the moment came, when the Chapter had most needed him, the Chief Librarian had failed to harness his powers. On a ship called the *Dominance*, Mephiston had unleashed a fury that had been building in him for centuries. This corpse was the result.

The next words would not come. Mephiston could see them on the page, illuminated by blood thralls in his own scriptoria. Could he carry the burden he had chosen? After the events on the *Dominance*, the tech-priests of Mars had given him a new chance at redemption – a second rebirth. Everyone believed the process a resounding success. Only Mephiston understood what it meant. Only he understood the sacrifice he had made to return. Was he strong enough? Could he really be the shadow on the Chapter's face? Could he be the darkness in their soul?

Dante watched him closely.

Mephiston closed the book and handed it back to him. Concern flickered in Dante's eyes but before he could speak, Mephiston placed his hand on Peloris' shroud and said: 'We grieve in vain, for those that die. The Angel's blade, they fortify.'

For the next ten minutes Mephiston recited the Song of Passing from memory, with no need of the leather-bound hymnal. There were few books in his Librarius he had not read and his memory was faultless. He held Dante's gaze as he spoke but he could feel the others watching him, waiting to see if he would falter. With each line his voice grew stronger, more confident, until by the final lines of the prayer it was ringing back down the processional route, quickening the hearts of all who would doubt him.

BLACK LIBRARY

Including Limited and Special Editions

Multiple formats available

MP3 AUDIOBOOKS | BOOKS | EBOOKS